NIGHT SHADOWS:
QUEER HORROR

T0126156

Visit us at www.boldstrokesbooks.com

NIGHT SHADOWS: QUEER HORROR

edited by

Greg Herren & J. M. Redmann

A Division of Bold Strokes Books

2012

NIGHT SHADOWS: QUEER HORROR
© 2012 By Bold Strokes Books. All Rights Reserved.

ISBN 13: 978-1-60282-751-6

This Trade Paperback Original Is Published By
Bold Strokes Books, Inc.
P.O. Box 249
Valley Falls, NY 12185

First Edition: October 2012

Credits
Editors: Greg Herren, J. M. Redmann, and Stacia Seaman
Production Design: Stacia Seaman
Cover Design by Sheri (graphicartist2020@hotmail.com)

This is for all of our coworkers at the NO/AIDS Task Force

Contents

A QUESTION OF GENRE

So, we'd just turned in our companion volumes of gay and lesbian noir (*Men/Women of the Mean Streets*) and were congratulating ourselves with a couple of Cosmos (or three...four...maybe six or seven; don't judge us!) and wondered what, if anything, we could do for a follow-up. This led to a rather sloppy discussion about genre, which eventually led to the decision that should our publisher want us to do a follow-up, we'd tackle horror.

Genre is the bastard stepchild of literature, always looked down upon by the highbrows in their ivory towers. They generally say the word sneeringly, with their lip curled in distaste, like they are scraping something off the bottom of their shoe. "Oh, you write *mysteries,*" we've heard, and other genre writers can attest to the disdain with which those who prefer serious lit-ra-CHOOR treat those who pollute the world with our lowbrow works; sometimes something they stepped in gets more respect.

But as a best-selling mystery author once said, to much applause from the audience, "It's either genre, or it's just boring."

Probably the biggest complaint (or accusation) the Academy throws at genre fiction is it's *formulaic,* which really makes little or no sense. Who would read a mystery where the case wasn't solved at the end? Who wants to read a romance where the couple doesn't resolve everything at the end? For that matter, isn't a jury trial *formulaic?* Isn't a pregnancy? A wedding?

The Great Gatsby, after all, is nothing more than a murder mystery told in reverse—the crime happens at the end instead of at the beginning. The book is arguably about Gatsby's murder, and all the pieces that fall into place before he is shot and his dead body falls into the swimming pool. *Sanctuary* by William Faulkner is a crime novel at its heart; it's a crime that drives the narrative; so is *Crime and Punishment,* and *Les Miserables,* and…you get the picture.

But why horror? Why would two writers primarily known for their mystery novels dabble in the world of horror?

Horror and mystery are a lot closer than most people would think.

The problem with classifying literature into labels is that there are always books that don't really fit snugly into the box the shelf stocker at the local Barnes & Noble wants them placed inside; the mystery genre encompasses everything from police procedurals to private eyes to amateur sleuths to spy thrillers to noir, so there are always sub-genres inside of the genres themselves. And even those sub-genres can be divided into further sub-genres; private eyes can be divided into soft-boiled (Agatha Christie's Hercule Poirot, or Ellery Queen) and hard-boiled (Mickey Spillane's Mike Hammer, Raymond Chandler's Philip Marlowe, Ross Macdonald's Lew Archer, Sara Paretsky's V. I. Warshawski).

Likewise, when most people think of *horror,* they think of werewolves and vampires and zombies; they think of Stephen King and Peter Straub and Poppy Z. Brite. But horror isn't just supernatural creatures, nor does writing about supernatural characters make the author's work horror (Charlaine Harris, who writes the Sookie Stackhouse novels the HBO series *True Blood* is based on, considers herself a mystery writer, not a horror writer). Daphne du Maurier, best known for the novel *Rebecca* and primarily considered a writer of romantic suspense (a subgenre of mystery that also includes writers like Mary Stewart and Phyllis A. Whitney), wrote some extraordinarily macabre short stories that are some of the creepiest and scariest short stories ever published (she wrote "Don't Look Now," "The Apple Tree," "Kiss Me Again, Stranger," "The Blue Lenses," and "The Birds"—which the famous Alfred Hitchcock film was based on). Patricia Highsmith, best known for *The Talented Mr. Ripley* novels (without which there could be no *Dexter*) and delightfully noir classics like *Strangers on a Train,* also dabbled in horror with her short fiction. Edgar Allen Poe is claimed by both genres; in modern times so are Michael Koryta (*The Ridge, So Cold the River*) and Dean Koontz; Stephen King was named a Grand Master by the Mystery Writers of America. Peter Straub has also on occasion blurred the line between the two genres.

So, what is the link between the two? It's very simple, actually.

Mystery and horror are both about death, and violent death at that.

Few characters ever die of natural causes in a mystery or a horror novel. Death drives both genres, and it is this interest in exploring the causes of death, its nature, and how we as humans cope with death that is the underlying similarity between the two genres.

Both genres are also driven by suspense, and the best writers in either field know how to build tension, to create page-turners that keep their readers up till all hours of the night reading, unable to stop until they know how it all comes out in the end.

This literary struggle between life and death, darkness and light has an especial resonance with queers. Gays, lesbians, bisexuals, and the transgendered, as members of both a repressed and a suppressed community pushed to the margins by the mainstream, can understand and identify with the themes that mark these works—for both genres also focus on the marginalized and the outsiders, those who live in the shadows on the very edge of the mainstream world. Horror writers have recognized kindred spirits in the queer community and have often included queers in their works honestly. Karl Wagner was writing short fiction with lesbian and transgendered characters in the '70s and the '80s, and doing it in a non-judgmental way; their sexuality was just another character trait, and thus they came across as realistic and three-dimensional. Poppy Z. Brite's work was including queer characters in the early 1990s, and Brite's brilliance influenced an entire new generation of horror writers. Stephen King's *It* included a terrible hate crime in its shifting point of view opening, switching back and forth between the present and the past. The list of horror writers who've included queer characters in their work over the years is too long to recount here—so it's a little surprising to realize that queer horror—horror work by queers about queers for queers—is far behind the mystery genre in this respect. Sarah Dreher, of course, included supernatural elements—everything from ghosts to time travel—in her Stoner McTavish mystery series, and Greg Herren's Scotty Bradley mysteries has also dabbled a bit in the supernatural (the main character is a psychic; *Jackson Square Jazz,* the second in the series, involved the main character communicating with a dead man), but for the most part the queer mystery genre has developed much more quickly than its horror counterpart.

But that has changed somewhat since the turn of the century. Michael Rowe edited the two superlative anthologies *Queer Fear* and *Queer Fear 2,* and just last year his brilliant novel *Enter, Night* was released. Vince Liaguno and Chad Helder won a Stoker Award for their queer anthology *Unspeakable Horror: From the Shadow of the*

Closet; Liaguno has also published an acclaimed novel, *The Literary Six,* while Helder has published *The Vampire Bridegroom,* an omnibus of his own horror poetry and short stories. Lee Thomas has published two extraordinary novels, *The Dust of Wonderland* and *The German,* as well as a brilliant body of work in short stories that any horror writer would envy. Noted journalist and anthologist Victoria A. Brownworth has also produced some extraordinary horror work; her collection *Day of the Dead and Other Stories* is a vastly underappreciated jewel. Rowe, Liaguno, Thomas, and Brownworth are included in the pages of this anthology.

Jewelle Gomez is an acclaimed poet and playwright whose fictional stories about the lesbian vampire Gilda (one included here) were collected as *The Gilda Stories* in the early '90s; highly acclaimed, the book is still in print some twenty years later.

Felice Picano, of course, is an icon in the world of gay letters who has displayed an amazing versatility in his work—ranging everywhere from the suspense thriller (*The Lure*) to literary fiction (*Like People in History*) to the supernatural (*Looking Glass Lives*). Including him in this collection was a no-brainer.

Carsen Taite and Lisa Girolami are primarily known as romance writers, yet their contributions are deliciously creepy—evidence of a dark side to their own creativity that we hope they will continue to explore.

Steve Berman is the author of *Vintage: A Ghost Story,* a wonderful horror novel for young adults, and is a master of the short story.

We are also pleased to include works by three up-and-coming writers you will be hearing a lot from in the future: Carol Rosenfeld, Jeffrey Ricker, and 'Nathan Burgoine.

Enough of this bloviating! Turn the page and enter the darkened world of the macabre…and enjoy your stay.

—Greg Herren
—J. M. Redmann
New Orleans, June 2012

THE HOLLOW IS FILLED WITH BEAUTIFUL MONSTERS
LEE THOMAS

His name was Zach, and he was nineteen years old when he left me for a man named Lincoln Schon, a man with whom I had an uncomfortable history. Straight from an Iowa suburb with his dirty blond hair and striking, perpetually adolescent features, Zach arrived in Manhattan to begin his freshman year at NYU. Though he dropped out of school after two months, he remained in the city, intent on experiencing what he considered real life. Using his simple charm and an approach to sex that was desert-like in that it was hot, completely open, and wildly expansive, he did well for himself. We dated for five months, and then he told me he was leaving. Not the city, mind you, just *me*. When I found out whom he'd left me for, my reaction was part fury, part amusement. The amusement lasted.

More than a year after he stuck me with the bill at Gascogne and earnestly hoped we would always be friends (the last in a lengthy succession of break-up clichés), Zach called while I was having a drink in an Upper West Side bar.

An unfamiliar number appeared on my phone screen, and I considered ignoring it. I'd erased Zach's contact information after the breakup, not out of anger or a dramatic act of closure, but simply because I assumed our days of talking on the phone, talking at all, were over. In matters of organization, I tended toward expediency. If a shirt didn't fit or no longer met my aesthetic needs, it got dropped off at the donation station; I didn't keep it around to burden my closet, hoping that one day I could squeeze back into it or I'd find its color once again pleasant. Relationships fell under this same broad umbrella of organization, except they were easier to come by in New York than closet space.

My first thought, upon hearing his garbled, disoriented voice, was that Zach had taken a bad pill or too many good ones. His speech slurred and he babbled, and of the few words I could understand, "beautiful," was the one he kept repeating, though in his impaired state, the word came out as "bootifuh." During our time together, I'd never seen him overindulge in chemical recreation, but he'd been riding shotgun with Lincoln Schon for more than a year, and that meant he was in a significantly faster lane than me. Keenly aware of my surroundings—a cocktail lounge with too few people for me to manage a conversation with any genuine anonymity—I slid off the bar stool and made my way to the restroom, closing the door behind me to muffle the ambient chatter.

"...buh-iss-bootifuh," said Zach.

I smiled at the stupid kid's intoxicated rambling and shook my head. "Zach, who are you calling?"

"Cawing *you.*"

"Who do you think this is?" I imagined he was trying to track down Lincoln and had poked the wrong name in his contact list. But he said, "Raw-ee," which was as close to my name as he could manage. "Okay, Zach. Why are you calling me?"

"Loss," he said. "I'n loss. You not home."

Had he said he was lost? And if he was lost, how did he know whether I was home or not?

"Where are you, Zach?"

The conversation went in circles for too long. Frustrated, I was about to hang up when he finally managed to explain himself through the lazy-jawed, inebriated gurgle that was his voice. He was in front of my apartment building. He wanted to see me, but the doorman had directed him to the curb because I wasn't home. I considered asking him what he wanted but figured it would take an hour to get any kind of coherent answer from him.

"Zach, I want you to walk back into the building and put the doorman on the phone. I'll tell him to let you wait in the lobby until I get there."

Though the bar wasn't far from my building, I hailed a cab and winced at the stench of incense in the car as I thought about Zach. Why had he tracked me down? What had he taken to get so thoroughly messed up, and why hadn't he called his partner, Lincoln, or just gone home to ride out his buzz? I felt nervous about seeing the kid, and I told myself twenty times during the brief ride that I should have cut him off and hung up and continued on with my evening.

Miklos, my doorman, met me outside and gave me an amused

smile as he held the lobby door open. I shook my head in a display of complete exasperation, and the burly Czech chuckled and bounced his eyebrows.

"That's enough," I told him as good-naturedly as I could manage.

Zach reclined on the brandy-colored leather sofa in the center of the lobby. He'd fallen asleep with one arm dangling, fingertips only a hairsbreadth from the floor. His hair was longer and currently disheveled, and he was dressed head to toe in Gucci, but otherwise he hadn't changed. I still found him strikingly beautiful—he was too boyish to be called handsome—but a thrum of syncopated annoyance tempered my longing. During our time together I'd been taken by Zach's youth, his energy. My ego had purred when we were seen in public, so many envious eyes. But after he left, I discovered the ache that followed was the by-product of rejection, not the sense that something important had been excised from my life. The rejection evaporated like a low puddle on a summer afternoon, and soon enough Zach was a memory, neither wholly pleasant nor worthy of hate.

Behind me, Miklos continued to chuckle.

At the sofa, I knelt down and said, "Zach." His eyes fluttered and then closed again. "Hey, Zach. Wake up. You can't stay here." Up close, I noted how deeply his clothes were wrinkled. Smudges of dirt ran up his pant leg and freckled the sleeves of his shirt. I also noticed his shirt was unbuttoned to the navel.

"Rawley," he muttered as if in a dream.

"Yeah, hey, Zach, you gotta wake up. I can't have you sleeping here. I've got neighbors."

"Mmm."

"What did you take, Zach? Do I need to call an ambulance? Should I call Lincoln?"

When I mentioned the name of his partner Zach's eyes flashed open, and he righted himself on the sofa while scanning the lobby with darting eyes. He scrubbed at his face with his palms, bringing a touch of blush to his tanned cheeks.

"What am I doing here?" he asked. The slur and stammer had left his voice. Confusion replaced the dazed expression.

"That's what I'm trying to find out."

"I'm thirsty," he said. "You got any water?"

Of course I had water, but that meant taking the kid up to my apartment, and who knew what quantity of shit that would bring into my life? I didn't know what he'd taken, but it had obviously fucked him up badly enough to consider my place a welcome harbor. Furthermore, I didn't know if it had truly worn off or if he was in the eye of a drug-binge hurricane.

"Maybe we should call Lincoln."

He fixed a warm and appealing smile on me. "Rawley, I just want a glass of water. I don't need Lincoln's permission for that, do I?"

"I don't know what you need Lincoln's permission for."

"That's not what I've heard."

"Really?" I said.

Apparently, Lincoln had decided to fill Zach in on our history. I wondered how much of the truth he'd used in his version of the events, and my guess was, he hadn't used much.

Lincoln was a Fifth Avenue dictator, a man of absolute confidence who managed every aspect of the world around him. A highly regarded and highly paid event manager, Lincoln planned celebrity weddings, post-award-show parties, corporate banquets, and fund-raising events for foundations that hadn't genuinely needed supplementary funding in decades. His small army of assistants, a glaring of brown-nosed twinks, obeyed his every whim, lapping up his disdain and abuse like cream. He exerted similar dominance in his personal life, and his friends knew better than to argue, question, or disappoint him. He destroyed with an expression. He executed by remark. Even before his real success, in the days when we had been dating, he'd been insufferable. After enduring a dreadful affair through the better part of a summer, I cut my ties with the man using a speech, which in memory was remarkably similar to the one Zach had used on me, though I'd issued my good-byes to Lincoln Schon at least a year before the dazed kid on the sofa had been born.

"Hey, Rawley," said Zach. "Can I get some water or what?"

"Sure."

In the elevator, he seemed to have come back to his full senses. I'd never seen anyone recover sobriety so quickly, and I began to wonder if the inebriate act had been a performance, though what Zach thought it might achieve was beyond me. Whatever the case, he spoke clearly, told me about a fight he'd had with Lincoln two nights back, explained that Lincoln treated him like a pet, a toy, a bit of ornamentation to be moved about decorously to suit his mood or the atmosphere of a room. It didn't come as news to me.

"I still don't understand what you're doing here."

"I think I wanted to see you."

Upstairs, in my apartment, I poured Zach a glass of water, which he guzzled down. Then he returned the glass for more and wiped rivulets from his chin with the back of his hand. After he finished his second glass of water, he tried to call his partner, but Lincoln wasn't answering the phone, likely employing a petty avoidance tactic. Zach caught his reflection in the living room mirror, sneered at the image waiting there, and asked to use the shower.

"You know where everything is," I told him.

As my ex made himself at home in my shower, I sat on the sofa and stared at the blank television screen, attempting to puzzle through what was happening. He *thought* he wanted to see me, but what did that mean? Did he honestly miss me? Had he stumbled in a stupor to my doorstep in the name of reconciliation? As the notion wriggled into my head, no hope or elation accompanied it. The only part of me that wanted him to stay was my cock, and I'd learned what an ignorant bastard it could be. Most likely, Zach was looking for drama, a familiar name he could flaunt in Lincoln's face to spark a jealous outburst before they forgave one another and fucked out the remnants of their anger.

One of my long-ago exes, a man named Aaron, used to say, "God likes to shake the plate," meaning that once a guy had his life neatly arranged—his carrots in one quadrant, his rice in another, meat nestled and tidy—something would invariably trip him up, knock his arm, do something to make a mess of the organized dish. At first, I'd thought it was a quaint notion. Then I came to realize God, however defined, had nothing to do with it, and neither did the other people crowding that man's life, for the most part. More times than not, a man tripped himself, shook his own plate consciously or not. In the past year, I'd managed to get my plate arranged. The carrots didn't touch the rice; the meat and gravy occupied a solitary region. If anything happened between Zach and me, if the plate shook and the menu blended and became distasteful, I'd have only myself to blame.

Wearing just a towel, Zach dropped into the chair beside the sofa and smiled at me. He'd combed his wet hair back, revealing his high brow, and dried himself haphazardly so that a trickle of water ran from the subtle cleft between his pectorals and down his taut stomach to pool at his navel.

Refusing to accommodate the ignorant bastard below my waist, I shifted my gaze to his face. "All set?" I asked.

"What else are you offering?"

"I don't remember offering anything."

The weary smile turned to a smirk and Zach leaned forward,

displacing the edges of the towel. I let myself peer into the shadow falling over his thighs and his balls and his cock, but then I regarded Zach earnestly and said, "You should go home."

"I'm starving," he said as if I hadn't spoken. He rubbed his stomach, massaging the drops of moisture into his skin. A soft sleepiness added a layer of sensuality to his expression.

"Plenty of restaurants between here and there," I told him.

"You really don't want me here?" he asked. His face melted into a practiced and wholly insincere pout, one of the less effective expressions from his immature collection. It looked ridiculous. Insulting.

"I really don't," I said.

Don't misunderstand—I wanted to fuck him. That was the clearest thought in my head. My skin was hot with it, and my arguments darted like tiny fish, impossible to grasp or keep hold of. But the desire nettled me because I knew I didn't want him, not really, not in any substantive way. I just wanted his skin and his spit and his eager pleas for more of whatever I chose to do to him. And I reasoned that if I did give in, he'd have what he wanted and he'd leave, take his conquest back to Lincoln, and the two of them could hash it out however they saw fit. Win-win situation. But through all of this I felt certain I was being played—though I didn't know exactly how—and it infuriated me, and my aggravation grew every moment he was there.

Silence took over the room for a time. I didn't know what to say, and apparently Zach had used up his allotted charm for the evening.

"I just keep thinking about P'town," he said. He slumped into the chair and his eyes closed. "Do you remember P'town?"

"Sure," I said.

I'd taken Zach to Provincetown to celebrate my forty-first birthday, something of a tradition for me. We stayed in a quiet bed-and-breakfast on Bradford Street. It was a wonderful house. I'd known the owners for years. My birthday fell during the off-season, so tourists weren't overrunning the place and crowding the sidewalks. A spring rain had drizzled over the city the entire trip, but the weather did nothing to intrude on our enjoyment. We spent most of the weekend smoking joints and fucking, occasionally going out for a good meal. Three weeks later, the son of a bitch dumped me.

"I've been thinking about that a lot," Zach said, eyes still closed. "Probably the best weekend of my life. It was amazing. You were amazing."

His voice had begun fading with the first sentence and was all but inaudible by the time he finished. Clearly, his revitalization had been short-lived. The kid was falling asleep in my chair.

"Hey, Zach. Hey, come on. You can't stay here."

"Why not?" he mumbled.

"Because you can't."

"Lincoln doesn't love me, not the way you did."

If his declaration was meant as a flattering revelation, it fell short. His lament was mercenary, but I couldn't have expected more from him. Zach was a child, still forming, still searching. He didn't know the terrain of life or what his place in that landscape would be. He wandered forest paths, many of them circular, heading the same direction time and again, hoping the familiar trail would resolve into a new vista. All the while, he burned what he needed to stay warm—the men who bought him drinks and told him how beautiful he was. I'd spent enough time as kindling, too many years warming others, becoming reduced to char and ash in the process. The look in Zach's sleepy eyes showed me he already had his lighter sparked, posed, ready to set a fresh blaze.

"Get dressed, Zach." I stood and walked to the edge of the room. "I'll take you downstairs and get you a cab. You need to go home and talk to Lincoln. Work this out."

He mumbled a vague protest, and I marched forward and slapped him across the back of the head. It wasn't hard, but it was enough to get his attention. Zach lurched out of the chair and gave me a wounded gaze, rubbed the back of his head as if I'd physically injured him. A dozen remarks, varying from cruel to rational to kind to apologetic, lit on the tip of my tongue, crackled like sparks, but I said nothing. I followed Zach down the hall and waited for him to dress, and then showed him to the door.

❖

I stopped dating after Zach left me for Lincoln Schon, promising myself a break from the drama and frustration. Friends occupied my evenings and weekends: dining out, catching plays or movies, visiting museums, doing what sounded interesting to me rather than trying to impress a romantic companion. As for sex, it was easy enough to find when I wanted it.

On the Saturday following Zach's unexpected visit, I was in bed with a closeted married guy named Rick who lived in Hoboken. He'd become something of a regular, but I usually only saw him on weekday evenings, when he managed to convince his wife he had to work late. Somehow he'd slipped away early Saturday afternoon, and since I had no plans for the day, I let him invite himself over. Conversation with Rick often proved easy enough, as I rarely had to participate. After the sex—*always* after—we would talk. Lying in bed, Rick would regale me with stories I'm certain he found fascinating. They were invariably about him or his wife or his kids, a dull and predictable family dynamic, surprising and exceptional to him alone. I endured his monologues because he was handsome, well built, hung, and generally speaking, uncomplicated. The sex was good and I could tune out his ramblings during the afterglow.

That afternoon, the day's dreariness—a storm that painted the world outside my windows gray and black—and the repetitive tapping of the rain had lulled us to sleep. It was a good, deep sleep, which made waking from it all the more startling.

My cell phone buzzed on the nightstand, rattling noisily atop a scattering of coins. Still groggy, I answered and a stone of unease crashed to my stomach when the caller said, "Rawley, this is Lincoln Schon."

"Lincoln," I said, knowing the call must certainly be about Zach. "How are you?"

"I'm not interested in niceties, Rawley. Just tell Zach to pick up his things tomorrow or they're going in the trash."

"What are you talking about? Zach isn't here."

"Oh this," Lincoln said. He sighed, sounding exasperated as if the conversation had been going on for hours. "If you want to play your melodramatic games, I suggest you play them with Zach. Personally, I have neither the interest nor the time for them."

"How long has he been gone?"

It had never occurred to me that Zach might have needed help that night. Like Lincoln, I'd assumed he was drawing me into some kind of game, and he may well have been, but the alternate and very real possibility was that he'd genuinely needed shelter or care, and he'd used promises of his body, the only currency he perceived as valuable, to that end. I had declined to negotiate, but others might not. A kid like that could draw a hundred different kinds of crazy; he'd be a target.

"Just give him the message, Rawley. I will not deal with this nonsense."

"Lincoln, I'm serious. I haven't seen him in days. He came here and I sent him home."

"Of course you did. What a charming and useful Boy Scout you are, but as I said I'm too busy to bother with charades just now. Zach wanted to make a statement, an infantile decree of independence. He did so, and now I've responded."

"He's...*not*...here! Did it ever occur to you he might be in trouble?"

"Please, Rawley, put away the dramatics. Boys like Zach *are* trouble, but they're never *in* trouble. If he's not scavenging off you, then he's found another trough in which to gorge himself. If you do see him, pass along my message."

The call ended and I dropped back in the bed. Staring at the ceiling, drifting on tides of annoyance and worry, I flinched when Rick's palm slid over my chest. I'd forgotten all about him.

"That didn't sound good," he said.

"It's not," I said. "But it's also not my problem."

I didn't want to talk about it, felt no compunction whatsoever to discuss Zach or his boyfriend with a closet case from Jersey. Instead I rolled over and wrapped my arms around him and lay my face against Rick's chest. When it became clear he wanted to talk, I turned the conversation toward him, and Rick was out of the chute. He told me about his ailing father and the work he and his wife needed to do on their apartment if they were going to sell and move to Morristown (which apparently was their plan) and he attempted to start a second round of sex by stroking my cock, but I had no passion for the act, so I pointed out the time and suggested he clean up and catch the PATH train home. Feeling lousy about my abruptness and the vague expression of hurt it had brought to Rick's face, I joined him in the shower and soaped him down, kissed him, fingered his ass until he got off.

Closing the door behind Rick, I experienced a sudden burden of loneliness. I didn't want Rick to stay, but I didn't want to be alone with so much day ahead and so much night to follow. Mostly, I didn't want to think about Lincoln or Zach. Already I wondered what might have happened to the kid. Who knew what he'd gotten himself messed up in. What kinds of drugs? What kinds of people? He may have had some experience under his belt, but he was still a kid, and his naïveté burned far brighter than his intellect. Had he even thought to put money aside or had he expected to move from one generous home to the next in a series of uncomplicated transitions? As I'd told Rick, Zach's whereabouts wasn't my problem, but concern for the kid haunted me all afternoon.

Fortunately, a pair of friends—a couple from Park Slope—called with an invitation for dinner and a movie. Normally I wouldn't have trekked to Brooklyn through such inclement weather, but I jumped at the possibility of distraction.

❖

Zach called two days later. Monday afternoon, and I was sitting in my office perusing a marketing budget that refused to add up. Grateful for a break from the columns of numbers, I answered quickly. His voice rolled through me like a trickle of ice water. Again, his words were slurred and made little sense, only this time, he sounded deathbed weak, as if calling from a hospice in his final moments.

I pictured him on a soiled mattress in a dingy room. Paint flaked from water-stained walls. A litter of drug paraphernalia covered the floor. I imagined him in an alley, surrounded by refuse, both inanimate and human. The images struck me hard, hard enough to shake the plate. Wholeheartedly, I believed Lincoln had been wrong: Kids like Zach were often in trouble; a belief in their own allure and invulnerability made them ripe for it.

My first question was "Where are you?" And I asked it a dozen times until it cut through his confusion enough for him to say, "Ow-side the lawyer offi'."

Then he said, "Iss cold."

"You're at a lawyer's office?"

"Ow-side. Iss cold."

"Zach, tell me the name of the lawyer."

"I'n thirssy."

"Zach, is there a name on the door? The outside of the building?" I reached for a pen and snatched a scrap of paper from the edge of my desk.

"Sigh."

"What?"

"Name on sigh."

Sign?

"What's the name?"

He said something that sounded like Bodum, but I couldn't be certain, so I asked him to carefully spell the name. Three minutes later, after a number of incomprehensible tangents and several utterances of the non-word "Bootifuh," I extracted the name Andrew Bogen. Keeping Zach on the line, I ran a Google search and discovered the offices of

Andrew Bogen were on Ninety-third Street just west of Broadway, only eight blocks from my apartment building. With the address folded and stuffed in my pocket, I raced through the office, passing coworkers who formed a gauntlet of concerned stares and hushed questions.

On the street, I considered the density of traffic, slowed further than usual by the rain, and chose to take the subway, hoping it would get me uptown in half the time. Waiting for the train, I kept Zach on the line, listening to his babble and trying to make sense of phrases like, "Povince, all-ays povince," and "The how iss fill wi' bootifuh monsess." I didn't care what he said as long as I maintained contact. When the train came, I climbed on and stood clutching the bar.

I should have known I would lose the call before the train rolled out of the station. The double beep signaling our disconnection hit me like a punch to the throat. I called him back again and again, but every attempt failed.

When the train doors opened at the Ninety-sixth Street station, I sprinted across the platform and up the stairs, which exited on Ninety-third. The icy mist locked around me before I reached sidewalk level. At the near corner I turned right, and raced down the block, stopping when I saw a sign, emblazoned with the word *Lawyer.* Beneath the ornately carved letters, Andrew Bogen's name had been etched in a more conservative font.

Zach was nowhere to be seen. In his state, he might have strayed anywhere, might have been buying a bottle of water from the bodega on the corner or from the CVS drugstore across the street, could have sought out my apartment building to amuse Miklos again. Or he might have returned to the source of his intoxication, disappearing into the building in search of another fix. I felt certain the law offices were nothing but a point of reference for him; no lawyer would take the chance of having a stoned kid meandering through the lobby or loitering on the walk. But the sign dominated the side of the building. To the right was the battered wooden door of a walk-up, and that seemed like a more likely destination, but I found it locked, and with no way of knowing where Zach was taking refuge—what floor, what apartment—I sensed with some tremendous alarm that my attempt to rescue the kid had ended in failure.

In my panic to find Zach, I completely forgot about the phone, and when this obvious and logical tack occurred to me, feelings of idiocy joined the revving anxiety in my chest. I tapped his number to make the call, and after a moment I heard the ring. But it wasn't the vibrato tone playing through the earpiece that I noticed, or at least, not just that; it was the sharp and clear ring of Zach's phone, coming from somewhere very nearby. I drew the phone away from my ear and began to search for the source of the sound. It guided me away from the doors of the apartment building and to the top of a concrete staircase that descended to the floor beneath the law offices.

Such sunken retail spaces were common throughout the city, usually the location of hair salons or herbal shops or laundries. I hadn't noticed the stairs in my haste, but the trill of Zach's phone guided me to them and down until I stood outside a door that had been left ajar. My call went to Zach's voicemail and I redialed his number. His ringtone chimed again. Before entering the place, I scanned the window and the door but found no indication of what manner of establishment operated behind it. Only the name *Holloway* painted on the window identified the space. But the paint had faded and was all but scratched away. The last two letters were little more than ghosts on the dark glass. A large *For Lease* sign lay on the concrete at the foot of the stairs. I toed open the door and peered inside the dreary shop front, which had been gutted down to the concrete and the plaster. Not so much as a display case remained. Phantom stains haunted the walls.

Zach's phone lay in the middle of the floor; its screen glowed. I retrieved the device, dropped it in my pocket, and then used the screen of my phone for light in the gloom. Graffiti ran over the stained walls— some of it written in ink, some of it scrawled through the dust. On the far wall, slogans and names had been jotted down, some so faded and covered in filth they proved illegible. Others appeared fresh as if written soon before my arrival: *Bobby Rocket, 2003*; *The Fabulous Freddy*; *I never want to leave*; followed by *Leaving is not an option, bitch. Tee hee*; *I love you Derek*, and *I'll wait 4EVR*. On opposite ends of the wall, I found two phrases that struck chords with me. The first read, *Why Lincoln???* Naturally, I thought of Lincoln Schon, and wondered if Zach had penned this question on the grimy wall—though the ink was so faded it appeared as if the words had been written years ago, not days. The second odd missive—*The hollow is filled with beautiful monsters*—clarified something Zach had said before I'd lost his call.

He'd said, "The how iss fill wi' bootifuh monsess." On the wall before me, written in what appeared to be candy apple lipstick, was the translation of that cryptic message. Turning back to the window, I noted the scratched and faded sign: Hollow——. That place, that gutted and filthy shop, was the hollow, or it once had been. As for the monsters, I began to sense that if I remained there long enough they might come to say hello.

For all I knew a makeshift crack house had been established in the back rooms of the abandoned retail space. Guards with knives or guns might stand just beyond the doorway to my left or through the archway at the far side of the room. I stepped away from the wall and peered through the dimly lit chamber at the two passages I'd considered, and there at the far end of the shop, staring at me from the shadows, stood a pale young man with sunken and vacant eyes. He was naked but there was nothing erotic about him. Skinny. Sickly. The shadows defining his ribs ran like bruises around his sternum, and his belly had seemingly collapsed. I turned the light of my phone to him, but he slid to the side, vanishing.

I knew the boy was not Zach; the height, the build, the hair color were completely wrong, and yet, he shared the same weakened and dazed constitution Zach had exhibited that night at my apartment. I followed him.

Next to the place where the boy had been standing was a passageway so narrow I had to turn to the side to step into it. With my back against one wall and another only inches from my face, I scooted along the alley. When my shoulder hit an obstruction, I used my phone's light to make sense of the space, only to find that I'd squeezed myself into the first corridor of a maze. The alleys were short, some no more than a few feet, and the construction offered no options in direction. The entire thing seemed to have been created as an obstacle rather than a real puzzle.

Left. Right. Forward. Left. Claustrophobia clenched my neck and chest as I squeezed through a particularly tight gap and had to suck in my chest and belly to proceed. The two walls sandwiched me uncomfortably, and the way ahead, visible in the glow of my phone screen, appeared narrower still, but longer than the other halls. Halfway along this path, the wall against which my chest was pressed ended, and I paused, taking deep breaths, expanding my chest as much as I could as if surfacing from a dangerously deep dive. Then dry fingers touched my neck, and a rasping sob blew foul breath over my face. My body responded by lurching back, but it had nowhere to go. The sob came again and I lifted the phone over my head to cast light on whoever faced me.

Standing in a niche of the corridor, like a corpse in a cheap coffin, was the pale, emaciated boy. A sorrowful grimace twisted his mouth, and frightened white eyes bulged from grim, dark sockets. My heart kicked in my chest. My hands shook.

"It'll be okay," I whispered.

"Wherss Pilip? I nee Pilip. He juss leff me."

Pity and disgust wove together behind my eyes. I wanted to help this ill young man, but I also wanted to be far from him. I repeated my assurance and then scuttled away from the chilling sight as quickly as I could manage.

After several more turns, which might have amounted to only a handful of seconds but felt interminably longer, my trembling body emerged into a chamber, and I saw Zach, and I saw all of the beautiful monsters.

Weak, piss-yellow light fell from an exposed, ancient bulb in the center of the chamber. Soft moans and gentle hisses of air punctuated the stillness of the room, which stank of fermenting sweat, human waste, and another foul odor I could only describe as diseased. Saint Andrew's crosses, six in all, had been lined up on either side of a central aisle, like a display at a national S&M competition. The heavy, black beams canted forward, supported by the walls and by brackets affixed to the concrete floor. On the far end of the room, a skeletal youth, wearing fouled and sagging white briefs, faced the corner, arms straight at his sides. Three of the crosses were in use, with young men draped over them, inclined on the crossbeams and facing the walls, spread-eagled. One kid was completely naked, his muscular back and ass appearing healthy and vital, particularly in contrast to the shrunken bodies of his peers; a Latino kid wore baggy jeans that barely managed to clutch the curve of his hips; and the other, Zach, wore black slacks, the same pants he'd worn the night he'd found his way to my apartment building. His intoxicated gaze was fixed in my direction, but I knew he wasn't seeing me, wasn't seeing anything in this miserable chamber. He swam in open-eyed dream, a blissful smile on his lips.

Standing at the feet of the occupied crosses were the monsters. These creatures—alien or demon—suggested the shape of slender men, with four appendages approximating the location of arms and legs, but that's where their resemblance to my species ended. Their hides were sleek and a color of yellow-gold, shimmering yet murky, like a rainbow shade reflected in motor oil and frayed like unevenly stacked cloth with folds and tails of ragged edges overlapping all along the form. Round silver eyes, circled by streaks of black and crimson, peered from high on the smooth, golden plane of their faces. Their heads, like nuns' habits, flared at the brow and long triangular flaps of skin draped down their backs. These flaps rippled and snapped, and from beneath them, silken tendrils of the same uncommon gold connected the creatures to the young men on the crosses, affixing high on the nape of the men's necks, just above the hairline.

The sobbing boy from the maze emerged behind me, and when his hands pushed against my back, ushering me out of his way, I yelped in fear and scurried to the corner. His sobbing done, he shuffled along the aisle and took his place on one of the unoccupied crosses, leaning against the beams and all but collapsing. He lifted his arms and slid his hands through two leather straps, and he waited, but only for a moment. One of the golden monsters appeared from a black nook in the wall and took its place behind the emaciated youth, and the triangular flap hanging from its head rippled as if caught in a gentle wind, and the thread-thin tendrils snaked out and across the distance separating the creature from the kid. The boy sighed, and a smile broke across his cracked lips. He closed his eyes, and he sighed again, and the monster sighed with him.

What I witnessed was some perverse symbiosis, though the exact nature of the exchange was indeterminable. The boys received an opiate from the monsters, this much was clear, but I hadn't a clue what the creatures extracted in exchange, and it didn't matter. The young men were dying, wasting away while consumed in euphoria. Eventually thirst or starvation would end their narcotic dreams.

With no understanding of these creatures or their capabilities, I was uncertain how to proceed. They had seen me enter the room. At some point since finding this chamber, each one of them had glanced in my direction, fixing me with their silver eyes, only to return to their tasks. They exhibited no aggression toward me, no interest at all. I might have just walked through them and murdered each in turn if I'd have had a weapon of any kind, but even if I'd had a weapon and sufficient knowledge of their anatomy to pursue a violent course, I was, initially, too frightened and dumbstruck to move.

Eventually I tried to use my phone but found no signal in the chamber. My motion again drew the attention of the golden creatures, and again they dismissed me after perfunctory glances.

Only when the monster at Zach's cross withdrew its filament connections and moved away did I summon the will to step deeper into the room. My heart kicked against my sternum, harder and faster with each step. The creatures again turned their eyes to me, watching my labored steps, and when I crept into the aisle between two of them, my head grew so light I thought I might topple over. Pausing and breathing deeply, I waited until Zach emitted a soft moan. The sound broke my paralysis, and I was able to continue toward him.

With Zach face-down, inclined away, I had to press against the wall for him to see me. I asked if he could hear me, asked if he was okay. Each question I posed earned a guttural, incomprehensible response. I repeated the questions several times. Then Zach recognized my voice, and he whispered, "Raw-ee?"

"I'm here. Can you move? Can you walk?"

"Happy," he muttered. "Povince is bootifuh. Thanks fo taking me."

Povince? "Do you mean Provincetown?"

His response was unexpectedly clear, though his eyes were unfocused and wore scrims of euphoric absence. "So happy. Never been so happy. They let me stay there, and they share my joy."

"What do you mean? Zach, what are you talking about?"

But he closed his eyes, exhausted, and began to breathe shallowly. I tried to wake him, speaking his name and gently slapping his cheek, but he was in a deep, inescapable sleep. I checked on the beautiful monsters, but none of them showed interest in my actions. They carried on with their tasks, drugging the young men for a purpose I didn't understand. I thought to carry Zach out of there, drag him through the narrow maze and into the street and back to my apartment, where I'd watch him and care for him and chain him down if necessary to keep him from ever returning to this place, but I didn't notice the creature emerging from its alcove, nor did I see it gliding in our direction. Wholly unaware of the monster, I struggled to remove Zach's hand from the leather strap holding it, and the monster took up its position behind me, and its filament-thin tendrils reached out and burrowed into my skin.

...And the scent of fresh cinnamon rolls woke me, and then the aroma of the ocean crept in with the sweetness. The bed was so comfortable, I didn't want to open my eyes, but he was walking down the hall, and he hummed lightly, and it was the Birthday Song he was humming, so I opened my eyes and remembered I was in Provincetown to celebrate my birthday, and the man passing from the hall into the bedroom and carrying the tray laden with a carafe of coffee and a plate full of fresh, gooey rolls, and a small vase with a single rose was the

most handsome man I'd ever met, and I loved him, and I had never been happier in my life.

❖

I woke on the street, dazed, standing on the sidewalk facing a sign that read *Lawyer.* The word made no sense to me. Where had it come from? How had I gotten from Provincetown to this hard, ugly place where the scent of the ocean could not permeate the stench of so many people and their garbage and their machines? A thorough depression enveloped me, and everything hurt. My head throbbed, as if I'd been struck by a hammer. Each muscle in my body had a particular misery it shared with the others in a chorus of crying nerve endings. Even the blood sluggishly oozing through my veins felt as if it carried shards of glass on its tide.

❖

The next time I woke, I was lying in a hospital bed. A television jutted from the wall before me. Daylight streamed through a window. I blinked, and it was night. I blinked again and the pale pink light of morning bathed the floor. The cycle started over again, and another day passed before I could open my eyes and make sense of the room, and the nurses, and the doctor.

They told me I had been admitted with a double concussion, a broken arm, a sprained ankle, and two cracked ribs. Further, they told me I was lucky. A secretary from a law office had stepped outside for a cigarette and found me sprawled at the bottom of a concrete staircase, bleeding from the head. That happened three days before the kindly polar bear of a doctor smiled down at me and said, "Gotta watch that first step. It's a doozy."

❖

When I felt capable of speaking clearly I called the police and reported suspicious, possibly drug related, activity at the supposedly vacant shop on Ninety-third Street. I never heard back, never saw a word about it in the paper. No exposé on the cavern of monsters. No word of an investigation. No mention of Zach.

I imagine he ended up in the river or perhaps hauled away to some distant burial ground where all of the once-pretty bodies were secreted and left to rot.

Throughout the early days of my recovery, pain medication pulped my thoughts and fueled both paranoia and nightmares. During that time I imagined returning to the hollow and setting fire to the place, blocking the doors so that flames devoured the monsters and purged their grotesque den. In more lucid moments I considered the businesses on the street level, the apartment buildings, and the young men below, enraptured and possibly incapacitated, and arson vanished as a solution. Alternate plans—equally violent and equally impossible—swam through my opiate imaginings and disintegrated when my thoughts cleared.

I even thought to confront Lincoln Schon with a paranoid supposition: that he and men like him used that place and those creatures to rid themselves of unwanted companions. Once they were no longer pleasing—too cloying, too brash, too independent, too old— the young men were sent away, directed to the hollow and blissfully euthanized. And I thought of the call he'd made, threatening to throw out Zach's belongings, and it could have been false, as a means to throw off suspicion should I or anyone else come to him with questions. But the only thing I could hope to gain from such a confrontation was confirmation of my suspicions, and likely an untimely end myself.

When I wasn't entertaining myself with myriad conspiracies and horrors, occasional moments of doubt punctuated my recovery. I thought how impossible, how ridiculous, that place and what I'd witnessed there were, but these were transient respites, instances of denial, far too brief.

One afternoon, a month after I was discovered at the bottom of the concrete staircase, I found myself drawn back to Ninety-third Street. Arm in a sling and my system clear of painkillers, I stood on the far corner and eyed the *Lawyer* sign across the intersection. A part of me ached to return to the hollow, and it had nothing to do with violence or bringing an end to the hateful place. I wanted the fantasy.

But fantasy is the wrong word, suggesting phantom memories with no more substance than dream. Visiting Provincetown through the creature's narcotic influence was tantamount to reliving the experience, not remembering it. The steam from the coffee warmed my upper lip; its smooth flavor excited my tongue. I felt the man with me—his mouth and his hands and his body—and every act possessed genuine intensity and physical authenticity. I could taste and smell and feel the details of my surroundings, including the absolute pleasure infusing every moment of that day.

And I wanted to relive the best day of my life, until the end of my life. The best day. Before so much serrated history. Before Zach.

In the hollow, attached to the beautiful monsters, we had both returned to Provincetown, and I had been Zach's companion. He hadn't been mine.

The day I experienced—the best day of my life—was my thirty-second birthday, which happened to fall only two days after a major promotion at the office and one month after I'd started dating a man named Aaron, a man I fell so completely in love with I denied the reality of his nature for nearly four years. The trip I'd arranged with Zach was meant to recreate a beautiful memory, meant to recall a happier time when I'd had a younger heart.

Day after day, I returned to the corner and struggled, and often enough I imagined it was only a matter of time before I descended those concrete stairs and returned to Provincetown and happiness: joy without suspicion; pleasure without fear. A few fucking moments of love.

By the time Zach and I had found one another, I'd fallen from romanticism and lived as a weary victim of nostalgia. The relationship we'd shared had done nothing to change that; it wasn't his fault. Not really. Each partner, each date, each trick, had left his mark on me. Lies and disappointments, arguments and indifference inflicted tiny wounds that, over time, amounted to severe and irreversible damage. Scraped. Gouged. Excavated. And the greater the hurt, the more men I invited in to sustain it. I was as guilty as I was innocent, inflicting the pain I'd endured, winning the games I'd once lost. But regardless of blame, whether deserved or not, life had left my heart hollow, and the hollow ached to be filled.

THE ZEALOUS ADVOCATE
CARSEN TAITE

I tugged my knife through the steak. Not a hint of red. I despise when waiters refuse to believe I want a bloody piece of meat. I tossed the knife onto the tabletop.

"Is something wrong?"

My beautiful date didn't have a clue how long I could rail about the things that had gone wrong the past week. The list was extensive and the overdone steak was the smallest of my worries, but at that very moment it was the only problem I could fix. And I would fix it. "Not to worry. I'll have this taken care of in a jiffy." I called out to the tuxedoed waiter as he attempted to ostrich his way past our table.

"Uh, yes, ma'am. What can I do for you?"

Ma'am. Hate the word. "When you asked me if I was sure I wanted my porterhouse rare, I said 'absolutely', isn't that true?"

He shuffled in place, but answered, "Yes, ma'am."

"And do you recall how you went on to describe that a rare steak would have a cool, red, bloody center?"

"Yes, ma'am, but—"

I held up a hand. "Please just answer the question, yes or no. And you recall that when you described the red and bloody center, I responded 'yes, that would be perfect.' Isn't that true?"

He hung his head. "Yes, ma'am."

I seized the knife and ripped through the wasted filet. "This isn't bloody and red, is it?"

"No, ma'am. It's well done."

I let his extra words go unchecked and shoved the plate to the edge of the table. "Please remove this offensive meal and bring me what I ordered. And, stop calling me ma'am."

He grabbed the plate and his head bobbed up and down. "Yes, ma—, I mean yes, right away."

Shelia leaned across the table, her large bosom heaving against her own plate. "You think you might have been a little hard on him?"

"I like what I like. Something wrong with that?" I licked my lips to signal she was on my list of likes. She shook her head, her blond waves lilting. "No, baby, nothing wrong with that. Is that how you are in the courtroom? All badass and in control?"

If she only knew. "Pretty much, but I have to say I do my best work outside of the courtroom." I risked a subtle glance at my wristwatch. I had some work to do later tonight, in fact.

"Maybe you could show me after dinner. I can play disruptive juror and you can put some order in my court."

From your lips, sweetheart. There was a time when I sought the company of women who weren't such, well, bimbos, but after a while I discovered the complete lack of curiosity and reflection was actually a bonus. I had too many places to be and people to see in my chosen work, and I couldn't afford to spend my time with ladies who had the wherewithal to notice my odd comings and goings.

Our waiter didn't waste any time serving my new meal, a feat made easy since the steak wasn't actually cooked. I sliced, effortlessly, through the raw meat and salivated at the trail of blood my knife left smeared across the plate.

I used to hate the smell of blood. Its heavy metallic odor clung to my skin, filled my nostrils, and colored all of my senses for hours after a particularly messy encounter. But not long after the first time, I began to appreciate how the odor reeked of victory. Reliving the sensation at mealtime was a symbol of how necessary it had become in my life. I ate every bite.

I waited until Shelia ordered dessert before I feigned an emergency call and made well-practiced excuses. I made idle promises about meeting her later for real dessert, but I couldn't guarantee it. I knew exactly what I had to do and how long it should take, but every case was different and I'd learned long ago not to assume the work would go as planned.

The alley was dark. No surprise there. I'd scouted this place and knew every crevice of the wretched strip of crumbling buildings. This part of town wasn't on anyone's radar. At least not now. In a week the place would be crawling with spectators, looking for clues, looking for news. My client didn't want to wait, but I'd warned him I couldn't guarantee results unless he followed my instructions to the letter. A few weeks in a cell was a fair trade for a lifetime of freedom.

I pushed open the large steel door and crept into the storeroom. As sure as I was no one was around, I didn't risk a flashlight until I stumbled into the bundle I'd left and made certain it was where I'd left it.

She was still unconscious. Close to death, but just far enough away to allow me the final maneuvers.

This one would be the last. I'd had to stalk this one for a week before I found the perfect moment. In court all day and in the streets all night, the work had taken its toll. When I first started taking these cases, I was young and I had the stamina to handle the work. Now the heavy lifting, the gruesome mess, the keen attention to detail—all left me aching, sore, and mentally drained for weeks after the act.

And the cleanup. I despised the cleanup. Removing all traces of my presence while ensuring every discoverable detail was perfect. Four years of college, three years of law school, and twenty years in practice and I still couldn't get away from cleaning up other people's messes.

The toil was worth it. My father, damn his soul, was likely tossing in his grave as I took my best revenge—being better at the law than his chosen heir, my older brother. Michael had chosen to give his talents away rather than take the reins of Daddy's thriving practice. While he defended the rights of humanity in some godforsaken land, I did real work. Grueling, but profitable. Very profitable.

Reminiscing wasn't part of my plan. I set aside reflection and drew the plastic bag, the string, and the MAC professional boning knife from my bag, while mentally chanting the details I'd memorized. Seven cuts now, seven after. I'd brought a book to read for the in-between time. She wouldn't wake up—I'd perfected that part of the process for the cases that demanded no signs of a struggle in the final moments. I liked those best. Less chance of leaving something of myself behind.

The ribbons of blood were almost pretty. I watched as the trickles flowed down her side, but when the trail ended, I wasted no time placing the bag over her head and tying the string tightly around her neck. Eerie how the plastic drew in and out around her features; the shallow breaths were the only sign of life left. I imagined I could get a few chapters in before it was time to cut again. I shined the light on the latest Grisham novel and drank in the sameness of his storytelling. Ritual is comforting.

❖

"I wondered if you were going to bother coming to work today."

I ignored Jeffrey's comments and walked directly to the coffee machine where I mixed a strong pot. I'd been super tired the last week. The kill, the waiting, both had taken their toll. I needed coffee and I didn't need to explain myself to anyone, especially not Jeffrey.

I'd inherited Jeffrey Talbot from my father. They'd graduated from law school together, gone into practice together immediately. *Talbot & Lassiter, Attorneys at Law.* "Uncle" Jeffrey had always been a part of my life, and not always a burden.

I'd just graduated from law school when Jeffrey lost it. His wife was kidnapped, raped, and murdered. The police focused on the usual suspect, the spouse, until another woman met the same fate, mere weeks later when Jeffrey had an alibi. Didn't matter. Even cleared of all suspicion, Jeffrey never recovered. He missed his wife, he missed his life. He continued to practice, but he was a shell, barely able to focus on his cases. Dear old Dad kept him on. They were like brothers, he said. Jeffrey would always have a place in his practice.

Dad was long gone, but Jeffrey lingered on. Michael and I had inherited Dad's half of the practice, but Michael took off to save the world, leaving me to run a business with a doddering old man who couldn't handle anything more challenging than a simple will or a speeding ticket. The inheritance came with a condition—Jeffrey would stay on. Even after I relocated, time and time again, he stuck with me. Easier for him to ride my coattails than to find a life of his own. I didn't need him, wished him gone, but not enough to do anything about it. When the moves didn't shake him, I gave in to having him around until he died or retired. Daily, I wished for one or the other.

"Have you seen my book, *The Associate*? I think I left it in the conference room, but it's not there now."

"No," I lied. In fact, I knew where his Grisham novel was. In my briefcase. I was certain I'd placed it there after I'd finished my work the night before. I'd sneak it back into the conference room when he wasn't around. His nasal voice interrupted my thoughts.

"A woman called for you. Dora"—he referred to the seventy-year-old spinster assistant who'd been with us since my dad had been alive—"said the woman was quite insistent that she speak with you today. I tried to find out what she wanted, but she wouldn't tell me anything." Jeffrey thrust a scrap of paper my way. "Here is her number."

Kylie Ward. Didn't know her. Could be anyone. I started to crush the bit of paper in my fist, but stopped. Women desperate for my attention have always been a weakness. I glanced across the room. Jeffrey watched my every move. He always had. Worthless in his own right, it was as if he longed to find weakness in me as well. Good luck with that, old man. I made a show of smoothing the crumpled paper and staring at the name and number. Then I flashed him a smile and went into my office and shut the door. Bastard probably only waited a few seconds before leaning in to listen.

I picked up the phone, punched the numbers, and waited through three rings.

"Detective Ward."

Detective. Interesting. Even with the extra information, the name didn't register as familiar. Guess she wasn't after my body. Probably assigned to a case I was working on.

"Michelle Lassiter. You called my office?"

"Thanks for calling me back. I'd like to meet with you. Are you in right now?"

Her voice was husky. Nice, but my guard was up, especially since I was in the middle of working a case. I'd be calling the police myself, but not yet. "May I ask what it's regarding?"

"Actually, I'd rather discuss it in person. It's an old case. You may not even remember. I'm just down the street, at Leon's. Maybe we could talk now?" She projected ease and urgency in the same breath, and alarm bells sounded in my head.

Leon's coffee shop was buzzing at all times of day. Now that I was in waiting mode, I didn't really have anything else to do. Better to deal with whatever this was in a crowd of strangers instead of sitting in my office with Jeffrey listening at the door. "I'll be there in ten minutes."

As I walked toward my office door, I remembered the book. Jeffrey could be such a nag when he wanted something. Best to put it back as soon as possible. I clicked through the combination lock on my briefcase and the lid sprang open. A few files, some pens, a stray paper clip or two. The book wasn't there and suddenly I knew exactly where it was. Damn. I didn't have time to deal with this detail before I met the detective. I considered calling her back, but curiosity trumped caution. I wanted to know what she had to say. I could retrieve the book after the meeting.

Jeffrey leaned back as I strode through the door, not even trying to hide his eavesdropping. I knew he was only jealous. He didn't understand why I took the gruesome cases I did, and then to win them? Well, that really set him on edge. When my father was alive, he never would have let me accept murder cases. Not appropriate for young women to become involved in matters of blood and gore. Better I work on sterile matters involving taxes, property, and setting up businesses. Like all young people, I became obsessed with the forbidden. He'd only been dead a month when I gave into temptation.

George Cartwright. Young, handsome, and incarcerated. His father, George Sr., had money to burn. The money wasn't the temptation. The challenge was what drew me in. George Jr. was a hard case. Police thought him a stone-cold killer, psychotic even. They were right, which meant I had to hone skills I hadn't known I had. I'd litigated plenty of cases, about who owned what and who should pay for what. Georgie's case called for special talents.

Jeffrey urged me to refer the case out. We knew plenty of prominent criminal defense attorneys who could handle the case. We did, but I wanted to be one of them. I could do this. As sure as I was that I could, I struggled for days with the law and the facts, neither of which was on my side.

Until one night I woke with an epiphany. I had to get George Jr. to tell me his story. Every little detail. If I could gain my client's trust, I could win.

It took quite a bit of cajoling. George Jr. was proud of his work, but averse to sharing. I primed his pride and goaded him into disclosure. Once he started talking, the details came pouring out. I memorized every one. He was guilty. In mind and deed. The law wasn't going to help either one of us, but once I had the facts, I was determined to make them work.

"Ms. Lassiter?"

I turned toward the voice. I'd let my thoughts distract me from my surroundings. Dangerous for someone in my profession. She stuck out a hand. "Detective Ward. Would you like to go inside or would you rather take a walk with me?"

She was tall, thin, but wiry. Handsome in a worn and weathered kind of way. Not my usual fare, but I was intrigued. "Let's take a walk."

We walked side by side for two blocks, making idle conversation. She was from Dallas. I'd started practice in Dallas. She worked homicide. I represented murderers. She declared it hot outside. I thought the weather only mild. As we strolled through the streets lined with shops and restaurants, I wondered if she felt as I did, that this was a bit like a first date. Both of us asking vague questions designed to size the other up, both on guard. I had the most to risk. Dallas was a remote time in my past, but the details would always be with me. I knew why she was here, and I quickly grew tired of pretending we were two acquaintances on a walk. I stopped and pivoted to face her. "I'm quite certain you didn't drive down from Dallas just to chat me up about the weather. What can I do for you, detective?"

"Sam Dalton."

The name caught me off guard. Sam had been number three, the last one. Before Sam, I'd gone ten years without using my special skill. By then I'd achieved an unparalleled level of success. I hadn't needed to resort to the methods I'd used with George Jr. and the second one, Tim or Tom, I didn't quite remember. But I'd sensed the economy was on a downturn and I didn't want to leave anything to chance. Sam's case had been the easiest. He hadn't been very inventive and the details of his handiwork were easy to imitate once I had the necessary information. The signature move, a custom-made purple scarf, didn't turn my stomach like some of my other clients' creepy maneuvers.

"I recall Mr. Dalton. That case wasn't in Dallas."

She ignored my last remark. "I'm sure you do remember him. Big win for you, wasn't it?"

"Not my biggest."

"Fair enough." A few beats passed before she spoke again. "You seem to have handled many similar cases. George Cartwright, Timothy Richards, Sam Dalton."

"It's been a while, but I don't recall anything similar about those cases. All of the allegations were very different—stabbing, gunshots, older women, teenage boys. Each was unique, complex."

She smiled and held up a hand to stop my discourse. "Yet you won each of those cases. Either won or got the charges dropped. *That* was the similarity I was talking about."

"Oh. I see." I knew this day would come. I'd planned for it as best I could. The only contingency I hadn't anticipated was that it would happen when I was in the middle of a case. I needed to wrest control of this situation. Quickly.

"Do you have a specific question you'd like to ask?"

"I suppose I'm curious about the secret to your success. All of these men were charged with murder following thorough investigations that seemed to clearly implicate them. Yet you managed to walk them all under the theory the real murderer was still at large. Care to explain how you achieved such extraordinary victories in the face of insurmountable odds?"

I fought the desire to puff up a bit. It was true, the odds had been insurmountable. But I was willing to take risks other lawyers weren't. I'd known my luck would run out someday. Could this really be the day? "I'm a zealous advocate. I took an oath and I take it seriously."

She waved a hand as if my declaration was a fly in need of swatting. "Zealous. That's a good word for it. I hear you have a new case. Aren't you representing Donald Gosling?"

I feigned a look of surprise at the abrupt change of subject. The only thing about this visit that surprised me was how long it had taken. "I have a lot of cases. Dallas news must be slow for you to want to follow the goings on down here. Have you solved all the crimes in Big D?"

She shook her head. "Nope. Still have a couple hanging on. No one's ever made another arrest in those three cases you worked, Cartwright, Richards, and Dalton. But I'm still looking."

She punctuated her comment with an intense stare, which I easily returned. Likely, she thought she'd caught me off guard, that after all these years I would have become careless. She didn't know me at all. I was ready for whatever justice she planned to mete out.

Almost. I had one more detail to attend to. I glanced at my watch. "As much as I've enjoyed this visit, I have things to do."

"I'm sure you have plenty to do." Her smile was sly. "Go ahead, attend to your business. I'll be around until I get what I came for."

She'd get what she came for. I had no doubt about that. Thankfully, the difficult tasks were behind me. I wouldn't be able to retrieve the book, but a plan began to form in my ever-active brain. First stop, the bank. A certain safe deposit box needed emptying.

❖

The next morning I shuddered at the sight of the greasy pizza box on my beautiful granite countertop. Not my idea of a decent meal at any time of day. I rang down to the front desk. "Gerald, Michelle Lassiter here. I have some trash in my apartment that can't wait until tomorrow. Do you think you could send someone up to take it out?" He promised I'd have relief in the next half hour. Plenty of time.

I tiptoed to the bedroom and glanced inside. Shelia, sprawled across the bed, snored with abandon. She'd earned her rest. In addition to being able to account for my whereabouts last night, she'd been the dessert I'd wanted, but hadn't had time for until now. I shut the door and returned to the offensive pizza she'd insisted she needed to sustain her for a night of passion.

She'd only eaten a couple of slices. The rest was mine. I may not eat the stuff, but I wouldn't let it go to waste. I donned a pair of latex gloves and carefully broke the cheap pay-as-you-go cell phone into tiny little pieces. I used scissors for the SIM card and slid all of the remnants under the now congealed cheese of Shelia's late-night binge. This particular evidence would soon be tangled with the detritus of my hundred neighbors, buried in the bottom of a commercial Dumpster. Shelia's hunger had managed to come in handy in more ways than one.

I left her a note, explaining I had to go to work very early to prepare for a case. Not entirely untrue. I wondered what Detective Handsome would think if she came by and found Shelia naked and sated, alone in my apartment. The mental image brought a smile to my face. I needed the levity. Today would be trying.

Briefcase in hand, I walked the few blocks to my downtown office. At seven a.m., the city was just starting to wake. The nature of my work meant I'd had to become a creature of both late nights and early mornings. Each case demanded a different schedule, and flexibility was the key to success.

Neither Jeffrey nor Dora was in. Just as I'd planned.

I opened my briefcase and studied the contents. I'd never indulged my desire to exhibit these trophies. Many attorneys keep souvenirs of their cases prominently displayed on conference room walls or lining the shelves of their office. I'd resisted the temptation, instead keeping these special objects locked away in a box at the bank, but I took a moment now to relive the special memories associated with each piece.

The filigree pearl earrings were beautiful and I'd taken them the moment I laid eyes on them. The old woman had struggled hard to keep her jewelry and I'd gotten pretty bloody in the quest. I'd learned from that incident to wait until the end to claim my prizes from the others. I perused the rest of my bounty: the dainty gold butterfly necklace, the chunky garnet class ring, and the cloisonné ladybug pin—definitely the least valuable, but the one I revered the most since it would be my last.

The clock on my desk read 7:30 a.m. Time to finish up and settle in for the wait. I wrapped up my treasures and found the perfect place to tuck them away. Dora burst through the door at eight sharp, transferred the phone lines from the answering service, and brewed a pot of the weak decaf blend that Jeffrey adored. By then I was ready. I wondered how long it would take for the action to begin.

"Your detective came by yesterday afternoon."

I glanced up from my desk, feigning annoyance at Jeffrey's interruption. I wasn't actually doing any work. The waiting had me on edge, but for once his intrusion was welcome. "Is that so?"

"It is. She had a lot of questions about our caseload. She was under the mistaken impression you were in charge of the office. I made it clear that I'm the senior litigator at this firm."

I couldn't have scripted their interaction better. I played along. "Of course, Jeffrey, you are the backbone of this practice. I wouldn't be anything without you. I owe all my success to you. I don't thank you enough for all that you do for me."

He backed away, uncertain how to handle my uncharacteristic kindness. Out of the corner of my eye, I saw Dora twist slightly in her chair. Ever Jeffrey's champion, she raised an eyebrow at my rare praise and nodded her approval. Normally, this entire exchange, Jeffrey's self-aggrandizement, Dora's tacit defense of him, would have made me ill. But the exchange played perfectly into my plans. I had only to wait.

He left for lunch. He always did. Whisky and a steak at the Club. A daily indulgence I'd begrudgingly allowed him to expense for years. He hadn't been gone more than twenty minutes when my long wait ended. Detective Ward accompanied the team, but I knew she didn't have any authority here. She didn't need it—she'd brought a bevy of local police officers ready to find what she was looking for.

"Ms. Lassiter, we have a warrant to search these premises." The burly lead officer braced himself for resistance. Lawyers weren't big on cooperating. I pretended to read the document, and then shattered his expectations. "Looks like everything is in order. I'm certain you won't find what you're looking for," I lied. "Take your time, gentlemen." I stared at Kylie Ward, "And lady."

I sank into one of the chairs in the reception area. I wasn't required to stay, but I needed to at least act interested in this affront to my privacy. Besides, even though I knew how this would end, there was no substitute for the live event.

As the gloved officers began rummaging through Jeffrey's desk, I saw Dora make a move. Detective Ward held her back, but she spewed her protest. "That's Mr. Jeffrey's desk. I don't know what in the world you're looking for, but Mr. Jeffrey's the most honorable man I know." She pointed at me and I struggled not to react. "If it wasn't for Mr. Jeffrey, Michelle wouldn't be the successful lawyer she is today. He's sacrificed everything for her."

Beautiful. I wiped away a nonexistent tear. As if on cue, Jeffrey burst into the room. "Michelle, what in the world are all those police cars doing out front?" He followed my gaze across the room into his office and scurried over to confront the culprits. "What are you doing in my office?"

The burly one turned, his hands full, and jerked his chin at Ward. "It's him. You wanna do the honors?" She reached around her waist and within seconds she had Jeffrey locked into a pair of handcuffs. "You have the right to remain silent, but I guess you know that, right, Counselor?" She rattled off the rest and then handed him to a pair of uniformed officers who escorted the sputtering Jeffrey out the door. Dora shot me a look of disgust before she followed along behind.

Time for me to play my part. "Detective, would you like to explain what's going on?"

She took her time staring me down, but my indignant expression was firmly fixed in place. Finally, she spoke. "How about you explain what your law partner has been up to?"

"I have no idea what you're talking about."

"Did you ask him to kill those women, or was it his idea to help his best friend's daughter win a few high-profile murder cases?"

I assumed an expression of shock and sank back into the chair. While she tapped her foot, I ran through my mental checklist. The 911 call reporting the location of the dead girl had been made from the pre-paid cell phone, but they'd be able to triangulate the location of the call to this block. I'd made sure Jeffrey was working when I'd slipped away from naked Shelia, ostensibly to retrieve the pizza from the downstairs doorman. She slept so soundly in-between bouts of sex, she didn't notice I'd been gone longer than necessary. Long enough to slink a few blocks through the dark, stand outside the office, and make the call. When I'd returned and woken her, panting, Shelia assumed I was as hungry for her as she was for the pizza.

And the souvenirs, locked away in Jeffrey's desk. I'd hated to part with them. They represented my greatest successes, symbols of my willingness to do anything to win a case, but they were also the key to my freedom, and if you love something you're supposed to set it free. Or something to that effect.

But I had to admit, the thing that sealed the deal was the damn book I'd carelessly left at the scene. At least I'd worn gloves, so the only fingerprints on the tome were Jeffrey's. Funny, after all these years, my only mistake positioned me perfectly for success. Well, almost. An image of my current client, Donald Gosling, flashed through my mind.

My skills weren't enough to save us both. With Jeffrey the copycat exposed, Donald would go down for the murders he'd committed. I couldn't manage to summon much pity for the poor boy. And Jeffrey? Losing a case was a small price to pay for shedding that albatross. I could already see the headlines: LAWYER WILLING TO RISK ALL FOR DEAD PARTNER'S DAUGHTER. Or the more succinct MEDDLING MENTOR IS COPYCAT KILLER. I didn't care. I wouldn't be around to read the stories.

Detective Ward was still waiting for an answer. I gave her all the honesty I had. "I didn't have any idea what Jeffrey was up to. I'm as appalled as anyone to think he would commit murder so we could win a case."

She didn't believe me, but it didn't matter. She'd never prove I'd been involved. I excused myself to "reflect on this tragedy" and slipped out of the office.

I had kept one item from the safe deposit box. Time to gather the bundle of cash I'd squirreled away over the years and find a new place to live. Maybe I'd even start a new practice somewhere. Maybe Shelia would want to come along. We could talk about it on the road, maybe even stop somewhere nice for dinner. I longed for a blood-red hunk of steak. I doubted I'd ever get over the craving.

ROOM NINE
FELICE PICANO

T he hotel was prepossessing enough in that red-brick overstuffed Victorian manner. If, that is, one discounted its somewhat confined appearance sandwiched between a round-cornered, recently erected, multistory strip of shopfronts and an enormous concrete slab car park undergoing what seemed to be perpetual reconstruction.

He'd entered that latter labyrinth to leave off the hire car, secured inexpensively if incorrectly at the vast, impersonal Midlands airport where he'd alit from a cramped aisle seat in an economy aircraft after an eleven-hour-and-forty-minute flight.

The period since then had been distinguished by his attempts to follow printed-out Internet directions so irregular that a logician would conclude the country's road plan to be at best provisional: Street names, when actually posted, had a curious habit of altering without warning, from one corner to another. Numbering, naturally enough, observed the same Lewis Carroll process, retrogressing from, say, 398 to 12 with stunning amorality.

Still one more confounding element was the suddenness, extent, depth, and finally the interminability of a low-lying mist that set in and hovered between the rental vehicle's bonnet and the streetlighting's upper metal. That a cloudless, starry, black night rose all above those lights provided the further impression that he somehow was motoring through a particularly uninspired museum diorama, perhaps one titled "Mediocre British Manufacturing City of Certain Age and Decreptitude."

Nevertheless, once he was within the warmth and relative newness of the hotel's most external lobby, his three oversized pieces of luggage almost completely in hand by then, he paused.

The typical foyer gave almost immediately on the right to an atypically attenuated gallery of a bar, with uneven tiled floor and an unpolished timberland of painted-black spindly tables and chairs of the cheapest assortment. Opposing them was the by no means contemporary, utterly undistinguished, long-uncleaned, dark wood stand-up bar, its uppermost regions plastered about with blazing company adverts, all of it redolent of beer, whiskey, and wine.

The second he peered in, a fusillade of lascivious, mixed-gender laughter erupted from out of an unseen section of the public room, so he quickly withdrew, only to focus abruptly upon a figure seated nearby in a straight-back rattan chair, a figure so ubiquitous and unmoving that at first he'd deemed it part of the background.

An elderly fellow, Mid-Eastern, Parsi perhaps, given the ethnic-appearing hat shaped somewhat like a bottle cap, dust speckled of course, wrinkled by antiquity and immutable usage. Beneath what might be a very old and dingy gray lambswool coat, the stick-like teak-colored personage seemed to sport tiny mementoes of his unspecified homeland in the shabby edges of a once-bronze-toned, silver-thread-embroidered vest and an achromatic shirt and collar of exotic fabric, all indubitably hoary and begrimed. His narrow head was so sculptured and noble in that UNESCO poster mode, his face so grim and unmoving and unquestionably toothless, and the old thing was muttering something in such a low consistent voice, that he could not possibly be understood unless one moved directly beside what was certain to be his noxious exhalation.

So he turned instead to the hotel desk, such as it was, a timid affair, squashed into one end of the aforementioned bar and separated from it by only the merest of particle boards. An effulgent violet cloth notebook, like that an eight-year-old girl would use as a photo scrapbook, lay ajar as the hotel register.

He knew this, as it was immediately thrust toward him by an amber-skinned, all but kohl-eyed youth, effeminately pretty in a graphic novel way, wearing a matching if more metallic, purple *blouson*, who never once ceased speaking quietly—he presumed amorously—into a mobile phone held against one ear as the clerk juggled a melange of items.

In the light of the hung-high competing monitor screens above— one an unchanging perspective of the front steps, the other a television tuned to a silent talking heads information show—the young hotel-keep's skin and especially his improbably tinted (hennaed?) hair cast off glints of apple green, lilac, and mauve.

After a sufficient amount of time evading the letter thrust, rethrust, and repositioned for greatest effect upon the registration desk, the young *houri* on the mobile phone excused himself from his all-important caller to ask if he wanted to check in.

"The university booked for me," he responded. "It's paid for in advance."

Despite these facts, he still must show his passport as well as a "valid credit card," which he found slightly galling and undoubtedly an abuse. Funds were tight enough as it was: He didn't need to have to constantly monitor some bank company trying to clear off frivolous charges being made from this desk.

"Room thirteen. You enter past the bar," he was instructed, with a fluid wave in the general direction of where the laughter had squirted out at him before.

The key dropped in front of him, he all signed in, he still waited, as the unending barely audible mobile phone chatter went on. The heaviness of his bags had been obvious enough when he entered to require assistance. He waited until he had to actually interrupt the interminable conversation yet again: "Someone to help me up. The bags are so..."

Prettily unmotivated, the lad oozed from behind the desk and went directly for the smallest and lightest bag, which our friend, seeing his intent, quickly took up himself, forcing the youth to irritatedly lift another, heavier piece of the remaining two.

The lad pranced ahead through the bar, hips closely encased in boisterously bleached denims, swaying provocatively through the nearby doorway. Leading the way, he ignored the table of revelers— two middle-aged salesman with whiskey-wrinkled countenances, and an oddly unlined tart, once pretty and young, still dressed and coiffed in the style of Julie Christie in her high days of the Seventies.

He was guided through the quite long bar, where he was certain the trio were staring at him, ready to comment the second he was out of sight, through a doorway and up two sets of steps, down a stair. There a key attached to a plastic ring was flung into his hand, his third bag was released with a thud onto the wooden floor, and the young Middle Easterner was gone as entirely as though he'd never been there.

A struggle with the key ensued, while he remarked to himself how unseemly warm it was in the hallway. At the same time as the door finally opened to a small and dingy room, he turned to the nearby central heating grill and splayed his hand to test the temperature. Nonexistent, he discovered. Cool. Wherever the heat was coming from, and it was now almost chokingly warm in the narrow hallway, it wasn't from that grate.

A step into the room confirmed two unpleasant facts: The room was even more stifling than the corridor, and one reason might have been that whatever windows it possessed—two of them, single-paned, head high above the narrow single bed—opened not onto the street, but onto yet another hallway.

When he stepped out of the room a minute later to see exactly where they did open onto, he was surprised to walk directly into a wall. No ingress in that direction. And none in the other direction either, as that gave way to a stairway with tiny windowpanes.

He stood only a few seconds reflecting. He'd been hired for an indeterminate amount of time by the university. He hadn't expected grand accommodations. But this ghastly room, small, dingy, and worse, with no possible ventilation, was an abhorrence. He couldn't stay in it a single night, never mind weeks, possibly months, of nights.

Unwilling to drag his luggage back down again, he left them in the room, locked it, and went back down the stairs and past the bar—and the Dickensian-looking trio—to the front desk, where unsurpisingly the exotic youth was primping into a small mirror folded out onto the desk while still nattering into his mobile.

"That room won't do at all. It's hot in there. Too hot. And that room has no windows onto the street for ventilation. I'm certain you weren't told to put me into such poor accommodations."

The kohl-encircled eyes rose briefly from their adoring perusal of themselves, and the young hotel-keep turned to the back wall of the registration area where he himself could see dozens of hooks patterned onto a board of tiny squares—with only one single pink-plastic-ringed key hanging. The clerk lifted the key delicately—or was it distastefully?—off its hook and swung it mesmerically before his eyes. "Room nine is the only other room available."

He grasped at the key. "I'll take a look."

"You enter past the bar," the clerk said, indifferently returned to poring over the fold-up mirror in search of any overlooked fatal flaw.

Past the trio of loungers and bar again, up the two landings, past room thirteen, around another corner where a closed door stood two feet off the ground, locked, and completely unexplained, and from there on to another, one step down dropped, corridor and to a single door reading "9."

Even though the hallway had been stifling, the room itself was cool. Its single tiny mullioned window looked out onto an air shaft between the hotel and a blank concrete wall of the large car park where he'd earlier left the hired Vauxhall. The room was ridiculously tiny. Smaller than the not-very-large bathroom in his flat at home. There was barely room for a single cot of a bed, at the feet of which the window began, with one tiny space barely adequate to place his largest bag. Opposite that loomed a built-in closet, with it seemed enough shelves and hanger space to hold his meager wardrobe. Between that and the corridor door, nearly hidden, lurked a minuscule desk and chair.

One had to move the chair to open the closet. One had to close the closet door and move the chair to open the bathroom door. That too was tiny. A small, ugly, once dusky-pink painted room, its height greater than any other dimension, with a light brown tiled shower built in under an overhang, so it resembled nothing so much as a dark glass coffin, next to a sink barely large enough to place a sponge flat into, and opposite, a dullish pink toilet. But like the room itself, the bathroom was blissfully cool, even though windowless.

"It's small but it will do until something larger comes up," he told the uncaring desk clerk some five minutes later, after yet another trek around corridors and down stairs and again past the unsavory triumvirate at the bar, by now, he was sure, quite sick of seeing him. "At least it's cool, and opens to the outside."

"Room nine," the clerk said, altering his registration book, then turned unconcernedly back to the unending fascination of his complexion.

"But as I'm staying for a time, I'll need a larger room," he insisted, he was certain unlistened to and unheeded.

The old ethnic fellow was muttering more loudly as he passed, so he turned to see the old stick of a thing who was now almost vibrating with a kind of inner excitement.

"What is it, old-timer? What's got your motor going?" he asked, he thought kindly enough, taking notice when no one else about seemed to.

And listened to the fossil mutter words that he would later—from hearing them so daily—make out to be "Something not quite right, you know!"

"More than something," he would respond to the same uttered mantra daily in the weeks to come. "More than just some one thing is not quite right around here!"

❖

Called into Dr. Blethworthy's office, he sat, regarding the report he'd made, which faced away from him and toward the American Studies department head, standing, facing a window that gave onto one of the university's less insalubrious commons. His chief for the past three weeks, Edwin Blethworthy was a tall, well-built fellow, even a rather handsome fellow, despite his high color, who dressed himself and in general spoke and acted with the casual impudence of someone of equal rank in, say, Wisconsin or Nebraska. Upon them first meeting, Blethworthy had made some half-joking remark about the length, extent, and even the "substantial depths" of his own personal American experiences as a cultural exchange student, summer student, then assistant professor in "the States." All of it totaling, as far as he could make out, but a few years at most; yet more than sufficient to make Blethworthy rather a personage at the university here. One with powers and perquisites either he or one of his minions were always bringing forth whenever the merest suspicion of a hint of criticism was in the slightest danger of arising.

"Let us review," Blethworthy now spoke into the window panes he faced, "your task here, young sir, these past few weeks."

"My task, as I understood it, was to read the text being used for the final year of American Studies courses, and to compare it to a newer text covering the same material which it has been suggested might replace it."

"And then?" Blethworthy urged.

"And then to evaluate the one over the other based on various criteria...Isn't that precisely what I've done...here?" He lightly tapped the report on the desk. "I thought that's exactly what I'd done," he concluded.

Blethworthy covered his handsome face with one large, fluid hand, then spun around and seemingly in a single movement placed his body in his chair across the wide desk, where among other papers and books, the report in its pale blue plastic cover now glittered, a touch cruelly.

"What you've done, young sir," and here one of Blethworthy's large, masculine, yet somehow extremely elastic hands shot out and covered his own hands laid on the desktop in a light, slightly caressing grasp, "is...excellent! If...altogether...preliminary."

"How could it be...preliminary? I covered every chapter and..."

"Preliminary...since you could hardly be expected to do all that work, all that judging, all that reading, all that thinking, not to mention all that evaluation in a mere three weeks and one day."

"Yet I did," he protested.

"You did so...preliminarily," Blethworthy corrected, caressing his hand with such fervor that he became somewhat uncomfortable and wondered if he dared slip out of the grasp. "It's a three-fortnight task. At the least. Four fortnights makes more sense to me, before you could possibly have all the material in hand."

Eight weeks? Eight weeks on such a simple task? Blethworthy had to be kidding. He'd done it in three, three and a half weeks already at a half dozen universities already. Not these texts precisely, of course, but others awfully similar, since they were all awfully similar. He had evaluated American Studies courses in Reykjavik, in Mayaguez, in Riyadh, in Bangalore, in Darwin, even in Vancouver. The material was, one must face it, limited. The "takes" that textbook authors adapted were a mixture of the couth and un, of the trenchant and the bland, of the factual and the speculative. One, for example, might spend pages decrying the folly of "The Vietnam Adventure." Another barely mention it in the context of "The Counterculture Wars" or "The Sixties Rebellion."

No matter. He knew the material seldom varied, as the authors' attitudes toward the material by now could be filed away into a mere handful of approaches, all needing to be toned down, of course, made more generalized, to be worthy of conclusive text.

He'd been hired by the university here, by Blethworthy himself as it turned out, based on all that previous work, all those evaluations he'd done, all over the world. What was all this now, suddenly, about the work being preliminary?

"You wish me to take it back," he asked, and watched the blandly handsome features for a hint. They softened, the cool blue eyes gleamed, the upper cheek creased. "You wish me to take it back and spend five more weeks evaluating the material?" he asked, just to make certain that indeed was what Blethworthy required.

"To get it exactly right," Blethworthy agreed instantly. "You see, that's not so hard, is it? Not so hard to work at it a bit more. The salary, I dare remind you, is not 'by the job' as it is 'by the time spent,' you know...And that," after a brief respite, Blethworthy's hands had found his and were once more caressing them, "that couldn't possibly be construed, even by the most pessimistic, as a discouragement, now, could it?"

"No. No, of course not," he had to admit. That he needed the money badly was certain. That double the amount he'd signed on for would be late Brahms to his mother's ears back in the States, he knew for certain, almost managing to pay his brother's extensive medical bills for the period. "Except," he was forced to say, "well, except… there is one matter that is discouraging. Quite awfully so."

"My poor young sir," the blond-haired hands now all but did a dance atop his own, "what ever could that be?"

He winced having to say it, knowing it was far from the first time he had said it, right here, and into that blandly handsome face, "The accommodations! I'm afraid they remain unaltered from the first day I arrived here and…"

The big hands released their captives, the big body retreated, the handsome face closed against him, turning inward.

"Ah, but you already have heard how utterly out of my hands that situation is?" Blethworthy mewled.

"I have indeed. But it doesn't in the least solve the problem."

"The problem being a small space." Blethworthy had listened—at least once.

"A monk's cell is larger," he confirmed. "And considerably warmer."

"But this isn't 'the States,' you must know, with its endless prairies and deserts of space, nor its unstinting central heating!" Blethworthy repeated words he'd uttered at least twice before.

"The hotel has central heating," he argued. "The corridors are hellishly warm, day and night. It's my room alone that remains icily cold no matter the weather or the central heating." And before he could be stopped, "And even that monstrousness I can put up with. I have put up with, all these weeks. But the bathroom…the bathroom is… impossibly icy. And the shower. Well, it's simply unusable. There's some kind of film, not quite mold, not quite fungus, but—and it can't be scrubbed off. I've tried. Bought a local scouring product and scrubbed and scrubbed. To no avail. Once only have I showered in it, and the water began warm enough only to become quickly arctic. While the shower tiles were all but alive with some growth, who knows what exactly…! Never again. I swear it."

By now Blethworthy was staring closely at him.

"I'm not an expert, but," sniffing, "you aren't of particularly high odor, you know."

"Probably because I've been using other people's showers. Well, one other person. A young woman down the hall. It's not what you think!" he quickly corrected, as the blond-furred hands had crept forward onto the desk again, approaching his own. "We meet over breakfast downstairs most mornings. I was upset and I confessed my problem and she's never actually in the rooms when I use the shower, naturally, and I clean it down properly, afterward."

"And so you see, you've solved the prob—"

"Except that solution won't do any longer," he quickly interrupted. "As the young lady's been forced by circumstances I don't...well, anyway, she's been forced to leave the hotel. And no," he headed the dean off at the other path, "I've not yet met anyone else with whom I can share my problem or whom I've come to know well enough to possibly even ask—"

"Nonsense!" Blethworthy's hands now did sidle over and take his own in a loose, warm grasp, and for a second, he wondered if there was a shower bath here, behind the big office, one he could come use whenever he wanted. Until Blethworthy said, "I've just the place for you. It's mid-distance between here and your domicile. Always spick-and-span clean. Large, empty at certain hours, and with scads of blistering hot water and soap."

He waited for the other shoe to drop.

"My club! Or rather," Blethworthy corrected, "my former team's clubhouse." He suddenly stood and was at a cabinet tray, turned, and cast some keys upon a heavy metal ring onto the desktop midway between the unsatisfactory report and his lap.

He could make out two door keys and a thinner locker key attached to a metal tag carved to represent a soccer ball.

"In truth, I still belong." Blethworthy swaggered a bit. "They hung up jersey number fourteen for good, you understand. So I'll simply ring the grounds manager and tell them to expect you in my place. It's only busy around practice time and game time, of course. So most late mornings no one uses the place at all. You can stop, take as long as you wish in the large shower bath, and arrive here sparkling clean and lovely, as you always are."

He picked up the keys and admitted that they in fact did solve the problem, or at least the shower problem, if nothing else. So he said, yes, okay, he'd stay, he'd do more work, he'd reevaluate the manuscript yet again, and at greater length and depth, yes, he could even bear the cold little monk's cell for that longer period of time.

"That's a big fellow." Blethworthy raced to where he'd just stood up and grasped him in what he could clearly now feel was a former winning amateur athlete's grip around the middle, all but lifting him off the ground, and planting an official kiss on his cheek. "You're so needed! I just knew I could count on you doing the right thing!"

❖

Cregnell listened to him relating the gist if not the details of that meeting, strangely unmoved by it all, a few hours later. His interlocutor had one ear tilted away, as usual, aimed toward the corner aluminum food service bins where other scholastics tended to gather and murmur news and gossip that he couldn't make out but that he was sure Cregnell could pick up, given his extra-sensitive hearing.

"It's transparently clear, then!" Cregnell placed a slice of pineapple from the salad bar at the widest possible angle to his lips. "The Great Bleth intends for you to approve of the replacement text and discard the one in use."

"No, he doesn't."

"Of course he does! That's what he's telling you by making you redo it and paying you handsomely for your effort."

"But why would he want to do that? It's no better than the text already in use."

"No matter. He personally knows two of the four authors of the new volume. By getting their text approved, he washes their hands. Next time they find some way or someone to help wash his."

It was such a cynical statement that he simply sat there, unbelieving.

Cregnell jumped into the silence. "He's clearly got you seduced with his big blond head and footballer's body!"

"Men do not interest me in that manner," he said quietly, so as to not seem to protest too much. He strongly suspected they interested Cregnell in that, and in other manners too.

"Not to mention those big blond-haired hands. I believe he puts some kind of elixir on them to encourage that specific hair to grow. Possibly, he even tints it to blond it up more than would be natural." Cregnell seemed blasé enough about his outrageous statement.

"He's done nothing in the least to lead me to conclude that he wishes to seduce me."

"You certainly resemble enough that Irish tosh he went gaga over." Cregnell snapped up his pear triangles like a happy alligator. "The one who was here last season. What was his name? Agathorn?"

"That's a character from Tolkien. A deposed prince. I'm almost sure of it."

"A. G. A. Thorn. The Crowley specialist. The Great Bleth seduced the bejesus out of him."

"Excuse me if I don't fully credit your account of Dr. Blethworthy seducing younger men he works with. Has he ever made anything even resembling a pass at yourself?"

"He doesn't have to. He knows I'd fall to my knees at his feet, eyes closed, mouth a..."

"It's your fantasy entirely, then. It...is...not...reality."

"That's what Agathorn said to me at this very table. And look at him now!"

"How can I? He's not here at college."

"What did I tell you? Seduced and abandoned!" Cregnell assured him, holding up an index finger as though pointing out the moral.

"Isn't that Jocelyn Cardew?" he observed of one of the younger women who'd just entered the dining hall. He found her pretty and nice, and, hoping to end this profitless conversation, he zealously waved her over.

"It's not going to help," Cregnell said. "Being all la-di-da and making up to the girls like you do."

"I happen to like girls. I like them a great deal."

"Excessively, perhaps?" Cregnell suggested, blotting his lips with a napkin as though he'd just applied lip gloss.

"Not excessively!...Suf-fic-iently."

"Well, that's too bad, then, for them. And for you too. As," and here he whispered furiously, "Bleth's got you by the short hairs already."

"Miss Cardew!" He greeted her. "And is that Mamselle LaFoyant? Please join us! Won't you?"

❖

He'd been alone so completely in the weeks that had passed while here in the huge pale green tiled shower or steam room that he had to shake his ears free of possibly interfering water to realize he was actually hearing voices. Meaning someone else was here at the club besides himself. Just beyond the showers, undressing, he postulated, at the triple row of stand-up lockers. Not quite conversing, he thought, over the loud whoosh of his heavenly warm shower, so much as playing around, as young lads tended to do. So he ignored them. Especially when their voices took them around the tiled wall to another queue of showers which were suddenly turned on deafeningly, almost but again not totally drowning out their voices.

If the showers were heavenly hot, his hotel room, despite the change of seasons, remained glacial. No wonder he all but leapt to come here daily, sometimes twice daily, to warm up, to and from his study cubicle at the university.

Blethworthy had only stopped him once in the weeks since their talk, during a chance encounter at a local pub frequented by the staff, to confirm that "matters were working out as promised." They were so much so working out here at the club that he couldn't bring himself to remind his superior that his room still needed looking into.

Certainly his mother appreciated the protracted checks arriving back in Indiana. She'd even gotten Robert to shakily endorse a tasteful thank you card, doubtless one she'd herself picked out, as his brother, though nearly thirty now, tended to favor artwork emblematic with cuddly bears and large-eared elves.

Therefore he would make do, as he said he would. Eke out things, really, he reminded himself, since sending home such a large ratio of earnings allowed little for forays into public houses here, even for an occasional half pint, never mind restaurants or "cinema dates" with any of the younger women, including La Cardew and Mlle. LaFoyant, whom he now daily stopped and chatted up.

Still, matters could have been worse; coming to the club, he could use the toilets at leisure, avoiding his room's polar, daily cleaned yet somehow everlastingly loathsome lav—except for lightning-fast whizzes.

Right now spotless, warmed to the core once again, relaxed, he shut off his showerhead and grabbed for a bulkily soft club towel to wrap around his middle. Steam saturated the large chamber, and he exited onto the floor into yet more billows of it, groping his way back to the borrowed locker, until the mist seemed to abruptly clear, enough for him to stop and look and see...

Not five feet away in the other large shower, in which oddly there was almost no steam at all, but instead, quite clearly, two young men he'd never seen before, who had to be athletes given their musculature, rocking together front to back, wrestling perhaps, making peculiar grunts like horses or... He realized precisely what they were actually engaged in the very second that the larger and redder-haired fellow, who was clutched behind the other, turned, and without for an instant losing his stroke, noticed him watching; noticed and scowled.

Shamed to the roots of his hair as though it were he, not they, who'd been witnessed in full *flagrante*, he fled that face and those rocking bodies, fled to his locker, where he changed into his street clothes as quickly as humanly possible, flinging on clothing and footwear any old way, as though it burned his skin, not bothering to properly dry his hair, driving the metal door shut just as he heard their commingled voices rise to a unanimous, not quite human pitch, indicative of shared passion. He thrust the sopping towels onto the floor and raced out of the bottom-level rooms up and out into the clean seamlessness of a chill late morning.

He didn't stop rushing until he felt the hot burn of a stitch in his side. Then he stopped, gasped in pain, watched by strangers, gesturing them off—he was okay, okay.

Later that day, he almost related to his lunch companion, Cregnell again, what he'd witnessed in the club's changing room, then decided he'd actually derive greater amusement withholding it, since that was exactly the sort of drivel Cregnell craved to hear. Making that decision he ate on, feeling a certain superiority.

That sensation, alas, didn't last. Returning to his chamber that night, while standing on a street corner, he couldn't help but notice the entire side of a passing omnibus, as it waited for a traffic light, was plastered across its lower half with an advert for the local football team. And there, pictured flying into the bright yellow air behind a head-struck soccer ball, was the very fellow he'd seen cohabiting in the shower. "The Derrick's Going to Do You Right!" the ad read.

"Isn't that Derek Stransom the dreamiest ever," he heard behind him and turned to see two pretty coeds ogling the poster. Turning back to the bus, he was startled to think he saw Stransom's eyes following him as the vehicle took off.

In the days that ensued, he encountered The Derrick more often than he could ever desire. He'd been told that no one from the club used the showers during the morning, yet there were young men there all the time now, four mornings in a row. Unable to tell in all the steam who was who, and wanting to avoid the particular pair he'd stumbled upon, he withdrew from the field altogether. Until those around him made it clear that he needed to clean himself.

He decided to try going during lunch break, even though it meant a bit of a run to and fro. The club was blissfully unoccupied, and he indulged himself in both a shower and steaming. Only when he was all dressed again, exiting the still-fogged-up room, headed up the ramp, did three players descend toward him. Though he slid obliquely to one wall to let them pass, one was Derek Stransom, who recognized him, who threw out a long arm to grip his shoulder hard briefly, intoning darkly, "Got my eyes on you!" Making the other players turn toward him with scowls as he cowered against the wall. They moved on as one, and down at the locker room, he heard Derek say something he couldn't quite make out and heard them all laugh.

Derek was there again next lunchtime, alone this time, a towel wrapped low about his hips as he daintily shaved tiny areas on his face in the floor-to-ceiling mirror.

Before he could turn away, he'd been spotted.

"Don't go yet!" Stransom said in an almost inviting tone of voice. Without turning away from his perusal of his face, he added, "We've got a little talk, you and me."

"Who, me?" he asked.

"That's right. Club member, are you?"

"No. I'm using Professor Blethworthy's membership."

"That's all right, then." Stransom seemed conciliated.

He sidled over to the locker, opened it, and began to cautiously undress, ready to make a dash at any suggestion of trouble. He'd gotten down to his tunic when the player was suddenly before him, towel off his midriff and up around his shoulders. Derek stood erect, large, and it was bobbing up and down all on its own.

He fell back, consternated, against the locker, wishing he could fit into it entirely.

"Now, I know we're not going to ever say a word of what we oversaw."

The thing bobbed and grew as it bobbed. He couldn't stop looking at it, but dragged his eyes up to the menacing face, the huge arms and shoulders capable of so much harm.

"I don't actually know what you're talking about." He managed to stutter out what he hoped would be appeasing words.

"You're a damned liar. But that's all right. I just wanted to show you what you've got to look forward to," it bobbed and grew, bobbed and grew, "in case you change your mind. From me and from a half dozen of my closest mates. And that will just be the beginning, understand," he added, making a fist the size of his head by way of illustration.

He was able at last to look away, murmuring in the smallest voice, "Never. Not a word. Ever."

"That's the boy!" The rock fist dropped onto his shoulder in an abrupt, sinew-burning grip.

When at last the hand was gone and Stransom was walking away, his perfectly square buttocks pistoning up and down like a machine of annealed flesh, he mewled, "I needn't come here anymore! If that's what you wish. Not ever?"

Stransom either didn't hear or didn't wish, as the athlete vanished silently into the steam billows of the shower.

He quickly dressed again and dashed out. Periodically during the day at school he would find himself shaking all over. When Cregnell came upon him having a late cup of tea, he wondered how archly the Assistant Prof. would react to the threat of being beaten and gang-raped by a rugger team, but thought it prudent not to reveal an iota of his distress.

He did return to the club, slowly, every three days, each at differing times, so as to avoid detection, and each time found himself blissfully alone; except one time when there was a boys' team at the club, none over the age of ten.

So it was that slowly, he began to be less afraid of the rugby champion and his threat.

❖

Pauline LaFoyant had said yes. Or as much as had said yes, which was good enough for him. This evening in the garden at the Applewhite Arms American Studies department party they'd found themselves alone, wandering. She'd come closer, they'd kissed, he'd been enveloped in a lacework frisson and their kisses had deepened and continued. He'd "taken liberties" with her soft upper body until the two of them had nearly coalesced into one, with her at last pulling away for breath, which he had to admit, he was in need of too. With none of their compeers anywhere near, they'd once more coalesced for an even longer time, and when they'd been forced to break away by the arrival of others in the lantern-dimmed garden, he whispered, "I must see you again…alone." And she, thoughtfully, had responded, "Jocelyn won't be home tonight. You know where we live?"

Did he ever. But they mustn't be seen going there together, of course, she said. And Jocelyn might still be home a few minutes before she left, so he'd need to stand out on the street where Pauline would signal him with a window shade, and of course, he needed to make certain to bring with him "protection," didn't he? All tiny little travails, silly small obstacles, easily leapt over.

Which was why, however, he found himself racing up the entrance to his hotel at eleven thirty of a Saturday night, then stopping dead at the sheer population, noise, and depth of some kind of party being thrown at the hotel bar, a completely unprecedented thing, which seemed to even include the mumbling old Asiatic, on his stiff chair just inside the bar, who was decorated with the green and silver colors of whatever team or group it was celebrating.

He'd been threading with difficulty through the crowd, being forced to say hello, to "make nice" to this one and that, including the three grotesques who always sat at their table—now newly festooned in some team's colors—when he realized with a bump why he knew those colors so well. They were from Blethworthy's football club. A closer glimpse at the festivity-makers made it clear that one or more of them were team members.

"…off to Madrid! I tell you! A first for our boys! Then on to take those Juventus wogs and the World Cup itself!" Someone instructed him so he understood that the team he showered with had risen to the very top of their nationals and was headed out. Good for them, he felt, with a bit of shared pride, and even downed the dregs of a half pint an overcosmetized brunette offered him to toast them.

But he had other matters to attend to now. Pauline LaFoyant, to be precise. He was trying to remember where he'd hidden the condoms he'd packed so many months ago. He'd have to crack at least one out of its packet to see they were still lubricated. Maybe even give himself a fast sponge bath, highlighting areas soon to be exposed.

At last he got through the crush and onto the back stairway. More partygoers loitering there and on the first landing, he had to sidle around several, until he could get free to the next floor.

Just as he did, a hand shot out and grabbed his foot from below.

"Hey there!" He turned to a young face he didn't recall. "Aren't you him? That toff of Derek's?"

"Who? What?" Fear shot up the back of his head, as he pretended not to understand. Then he faked cheer. "Congratulations, fellows. You're the best! Knew you could take the nationals." He managed to shake off the hand by reaching down to shake it. "Sorry to leave. Nature calls."

He sprinted up the stairs, thinking is he following, is he following me? Stopping, to try to hear, above the renewed noise from downstairs as the door opened into the bar whether he could hear anyone following. Yes. No. Who knew? And now nature did call.

No revelers this high up or this far away from the bar. No one in the hallways. So he dashed to his door and struggled with the key. Inside, it was, as always, Baffin Island, and he threw off his jacket and kicked off his shoes on the icy floor and rushed into the lav with its Moons of Uranus frigidity, where he relieved himself and began to run what he hoped, dreamed, would be the merest speck of non-frozen water to bathe his face and genitals in—who knew what she'd think to touch, being French—and heavens be, he managed it, got water to come out of the H which if not really hot then at least was more than tepidly warm.

Of course it all got very damp and cold immediately after, given the milieu. Him more or less clean, he felt dankish. Must change his undershorts.

He was back in his room in the midst of that, humming to himself, when there was a rapping at the door.

No one had ever once in the months he'd been here rapped on the door. He looked through the peephole provided, but it was almost frosted over with age and wear: All he could make out was a rather distorted face. The rapping resumed with more force.

"I know you're in there." The sound came through clearly. And the voice now seemed familiar. He peered again through the frosted porthole, trying to see if was at all possible if—

"We know where you live now," the voice repeated, and even though it was somewhat slurred, he knew now it was indeed, and the porthole confirmed it distortedly, Derek Stransom.

"We know you're in there. Robbie saw you go in just now. Didn't you, Rob?"

Words of assent followed, joined by the sound of yet another, then another person. There were at least four of them. Maybe five.

"What do you want?" he began to ask. Just then a body slammed against the door. "What is it you want?" he repeated in a more strained voice. Another body slammed against the door, which took it poorly.

"What do we want?" was yelled into the crack between the door and the molding. "Don't you read the adverts all over town, you bad little toff? What do they read, boys?" There was an inarticulate shouting. Then "That's right! The Derrick's Going to Do You Right!—And his boyboys too!" This was illustrated with another slam against the door, then another.

Fear filled his head. He leapt to the bed to the window. It opened, barely enough for him to squeeze his body through. But there was no landing, not even a shelf for a foot. At least not for another forty feet down. And what he'd land on would be the concrete lip of a side roof of the car park. No.

Two more slams against the door shook the timbers of the room. He could see the door frame splitting. If there were five of them out there, drunk and enraged, they'd have the door down in a few minutes. Gathering up all of his strength, he managed to pry the bed away from the side wall and semi-wedge it against the door, which was now being slammed into so regularly and with such shouting and cheers from the other side that it would clearly go in a minute. He threw suitcases upon the bed against the door, just as a section of door frame ripped loose on one side and a shoulder smashed through the wood of the door.

"The Derrick's Going to Do You Right Good!" two of them shouted, and arms reached in, tossing the suitcases aside, ripping down the door to unwedge the bed.

He retreated into the frozen bathroom. Locked the door, had the sense to wedge one last piece of luggage under the door handle. But they'd gotten into the room now and were shouting, headed here, and this flimsy door was already under barrage.

There was no explanation for why he suddenly turned and opened the shower bath door, a door he'd not opened in months. In his mind the place had been so disgusting that he couldn't even think of it. There was no real reason why he opened it, except that in his extreme panic, it beckoned him, glowing cleanly, healthily, pink and wholesome for the very first time.

He peeked in, curious, as the assault continued on the bathroom door, which couldn't last even as long as the room door. They still chanted with glee: "The Derrick's Going to Do You Right Good! And We Are Too!" and he looked at himself in the shower glass's sea wave reflection, thin, wearing only one little under-brief, utterly set for the taking. As the party raged on, as the revels in the street outside continued for Their Boys, he would be assaulted, raped again and again, harder and harder, beaten and pummeled all the while, with no one to hear his screams, until there would be no life left in him. He didn't understand how this should come to be, only that it had. He had no choice.

He stepped into the shower bath and it wasn't gross and splotchy, loathsome and awful. Instead, it was rather sparkling. To block out the noise and chanting, the fearful sounds he could no longer hear, he reached up and turned on the faucet's H. And it came out warm. Not tepid. But warm. He held himself against one side of the shower, waiting for it to turn cold. But it didn't. It got warmer, and a steam even developed around his feet. That was when he thought, well, might as well, and removed his undershorts and stepped under the showerhead.

It was warm. Luxuriously warm. And the soap was soft, so he tossed his underwear out the shower door, and settled into the shower box, indulging himself in the first warm shower he'd ever had in the wretched little frozen rooms.

They must have crashed through the bathroom door just in the nick to have his shorts flung at them. Because they came at the shower stall enraged.

And the most curious thing happened. The shower seemed to simply seal up. It was like fresh warm putty rushing out of the walls and sealing off the door, from the sides, then top, then bottom of the door, as they pounded on it. It began doing cross stripes of sealer all across the door, on the frosted glass ceiling, each stall side, as their shadows dimmed the outside light, and he no longer felt in any away afraid that they would get in, but instead, safe, utterly safe. After a while they seemed to give up, to go away, and he showered until he was happy, and warm, if utterly exhausted, so he sank down slowly into the caressing waters of the shower bath, which received him tenderly and rocked him like a blanket-lined bassinet into the supplest, gentlest slumber he'd ever imagined. All safe now. Free from harm.

❖

Detective Sergeant Gryce hated this sort of thing. Hated the poorly or badly explained crime. The criminal not there. The victim plain as day and wrong, off, daft in some way as this one was, fetal, smiling, holding the curled-up face cloth to his face like a baby with a blankie, drowned in his own shower bath in mere inches of water, and who was to say how or why it even had collected there when it should have flowed out, while the football party went mad outside and downstairs, and room doors were torn off and luggage strewn about by perpetrators unknown. It wouldn't do. Looked bad in reports, Looked worse in his mind and memory. Hated it. Simply hated it.

"That police tape is up there for a reason!" he lectured the kohl-eyed Wog Ponce behind the desk. "You understand. Once we're done here, all that shower must be torn out and replaced. It won't do to have shower baths that can't drain properly. And when repaired it shall be inspected."

The dark-skinned Nancy pouted his understanding.

Detective Sergeant Gryce looked about one last time at this dump of a hotel and just then noticed the wizened old brown creature on his chair, vibrating like a mechanical top, trying to get his attention.

"Yes, old-timer!" Going up to him. "What is it you want to tell the police?"

He got nearer and heard the thin old voice pronounce, "There's something not quite right."

"Something not quite right?" Detective Sergeant Gryce asked. "Something not quite right about what?"

"Something not quite right about Room Nine," the voice barely whispered.

Detective Sergeant Gryce stood up. "Thanks, old fellow. I'll heed that advice. Jermell! Douad! Take over! I'm done with this scene!"

THE PRICE
J. M. REDMANN

The footsteps paused. They always did, a brutal tease as if this time he might open the door, might—but she could no longer imagine what was possible—offer her freedom? A moment when she didn't have to stare at the closed and locked door? Sunlight? The smell of rain?

He had promised her eternity. It was she who forgot to ask what he meant. A lost soul in a locked room. She had stopped counting the passing of time—it was the one thing she had too much of. When she thought about her life slipping away, the torn and moldy wallpaper seemed a blessing, the thin gray mattress a place to find rest. The room was small, one tiny window, too high and dirty to see out. It only allowed a wan light to mark the time between day and night. Three paces across and three back. She had lost count; miles traveled three steps at a time. Now the wallpaper—faded yellow roses with each thorn etched so finely they could almost make you bleed—was a curse; if she never saw it again, it would haunt her dreams.

The footsteps started again.

Then paused a second time.

She knew every groan and creak of this misbegotten, miserable place. The steps always continued down the hallway. This was the first time they had paused a second time.

They came back.

Stopped at her door.

Freedom or damnation. She would take the latter to be released from this tiny, shabby room. No, hell could not be worse.

The door opened.

The clothing he wore was different, but his face had not changed one line or wrinkle over the passing centuries, his half smile one of someone who ruled over many and was in turn ruled by many. They had talked briefly as he led her here, before the door was slammed closed. A slaver, one who understood keeping beings captive. There was no room for mercy save that which furthered his own ends. He knew not how he came here, except that it was after unloading his human cargo on a sun-bleached island—those who had survived—he took his customary tankard of rum, stumbled off the dock into the blood-warm water, a hand had grabbed him, asking if he wanted to live. When he said yes, he found himself here. He kept the keys to these rancid rooms. He was as trapped by his captives as they were by him.

"They have use for you," he said softly.

Finally! She wanted to exalt, but dared not give way to emotion.

"The years have passed; you must be willing to change with them," he continued.

"Yes, of course." Her voice cracked, timid from lack of use.

"If you succeed, you become...free."

As she had not asked what eternity meant, she did not ask what free meant. There would be a price to pay; nothing was ever truly free. But she would pay it willingly to escape the numbing, bitter purgatory she was in now.

"You will send the weak and the damned here. As long as there are enough to take your place, you will not return to this room."

"Yes, just tell me what I need to do." Her voice was stronger now, the beckoning taste of wine and green of spring calling to her.

"They want women. You must bring them women. You must touch them and bring them to their final ecstasy." His smile didn't change, but his eyes gleamed; he knew each word was a blow.

"I can't..." But those were not the words that would free her. "Why me? Why did they pick me for this mission?"

"Why do you think, Sister Mafalda?" A taunt.

"I did not live a sensual life. I was a woman of the cloth, chaste, a woman of..." A woman of God—but there were no gods here, no hope or salvation except this twisted offer.

"A zealous woman, indeed, serving your god. All too happy to do what needed to be done. Forcing novices to strip naked, throwing them into water chilled with snow when they disobeyed. Making them lick your shoes clean after you had traipsed through the stable. Clean your undergarments when your days came around."

"They had to learn discipline."

"Did you enjoy disciplining them?"

"No, it was my duty!" Her voice was loud in the tiny room.

"Perhaps it wasn't just your shoes they licked. Did they lick you clean at times? While you bled?"

"No! No! I was chaste!" Her face burned. He knew; he knew everything, every shame, every secret.

"Why did you send Sister Ysabel to the flames?"

"I did not. She was found guilty by the Tribunal of the Holy Office of the Inquisition."

"You gave them her name."

"Her father was a converso, still holding secretly to his Semitic ways. She was his price to prove that he had converted. She confessed to me her doubts of the true religion."

"Ah, and which one would that be? The one that conveniently confiscated all wealth and property from those accused of any crime?"

She remembered Sister Ysabel, crying her fears, her brother condemned as one who had not truly converted, her father arrested. Ysabel's head was against her chest, their hands clasped as the young woman sobbed against her, hot tears soaking through her habit, until her skin itself felt aflame.

They had been seen, the torrid thoughts she dared not think ascribed to her by others. Her only defense was to tell the truth. Ysabel had doubted a faith that would so readily take her family and believe them still Jewish on the word of an unknown accuser. She had, she claimed, allowed the transgression, the too-familiar touching only as a means to hear the young woman's confession.

"She did not die at the stake," she defended weakly.

"No, she died in prison, before she ever went to trial."

"God must have wanted her."

"Or the devil wanted to get rid of her."

That was her other curse, she could still see Ysabel, her delicate features, deep brown eyes, the yearning look in them. The yearning for her.

"But no matter," he continued. "She is now dust and you are here."

"And I have a chance for freedom."

"One you will do anything for?"

"Anything, yes." She did not ask what anything might mean as she followed him from the room.

❖

Kerrie Keller held the phone away from her ear as she checked her text messages. She had no reason to listen to the conversation, as she had heard it all before.

"But the damage wasn't from the water; it was the wind. How could the flood have blown my roof off?"

"The flood shifted your house and caused the roof to come off. The assessor told you that. I've told you that and no argument you can make will change that. We're not liable, we're not paying."

She had more important things to do than listen to him babble on endlessly about his lost home. He didn't have flood insurance. His house had been flooded. That was his problem, not hers.

She had heard the same story over and over again. "But I wasn't in a flood zone" only meant they were too stupid to realize that the entire city of New Orleans was a flood zone. "But we never flooded before." Ditto, and also too stupid to realize that insurance wasn't for what had happened before but for what might happen.

There was a good reason she lived on the Northshore, away from the quagmire of a city. She put up with the sacrifice of driving every day across the Causeway, twenty-four of the most boring miles on earth. Monday through Thursday, that is—she worked from home on Friday, coming into the city just often enough so her staff couldn't get away with anything like leaving early. She had come in once at 4:45, parked across the street and watched. The office door opened at 4:55 and they were all out by 5:05. That meant they were packing up and getting ready to leave when they should still have been working. This was her business; she had built it into what it was. True, she had inherited it from her father, but she had worked hard, edging out her worthless brother. He didn't seem to understand the whole point was to make a profit, not listen to people's sob stories and give them money because you felt sorry for them. Insurance was a business. They bought a product. If they wanted really good insurance, they had to pay for it. Most of them didn't.

Soon she was going to have to have secret cameras and keyboard monitors installed. She was the boss; she got to do what she wanted. They were the employees; they had to do what she wanted.

"I'm sorry, I've got another call," she told the distraught man on the line and hung up on him in mid-sentence. She didn't have another call; it was just an easy lie to tell.

Kerrie had a date. It was so hard to find suitable women, the ones who appreciated the finer things in life. So many lesbians seemed to have decided that the life of a selfless social worker was for them—student debt and working in homeless shelters. She couldn't imagine coming home to cuddle with someone smelling of sweat and cheap peanut butter sandwiches. Kerrie had spent two excruciating hours with one such creature. She was pretty enough, but her clothes were cheap and the smell of her day job lingered. Kerrie had claimed a migraine and ducked out on the date.

Her circle of friends was useless at turning up appropriate women, so Kerrie had turned to Internet dating. She had scheduled two tonight, one for a drink after work at 5:30 and another for dinner at 7:30. If the first one was a bore, she wasn't stuck alone on a Friday night. If the first one worked out, she'd skip out on the second. A tedious process, but as Kerrie had found out, you had to kiss a lot of frogs before you found a princess. So far it had been all frogs.

Her staff lingered, not wanting to leave before the boss. At ten after five she had to shoo them out. It wouldn't do to have her staff see her putting on lipstick and her good pearls.

She had selected the bar, of course. It was a nice uptown one, not a gay one in the French Quarter. She didn't like her women to be too dykey looking, and if her date wasn't comfortable here, it was not a good sign. Kerrie had hopes for this one, a lawyer. A tax lawyer. The last lawyer she had dated turned out to be a gay rights lawyer, making less than a social worker and dressing about as badly.

As planned, she got to the bar a little early. She quickly ordered a beer and paid for it up front, then found a small table near the door.

Also as planned, she spotted the woman first. The car she got out of was a Honda or Toyota, one of those small, sensible vehicles. Kerrie cared for them as much as she cared for sensible shoes. The woman was short and her picture had done a good job of hiding the extra weight she was carrying. Kerrie sat down her half-finished beer and slipped out the back door just as the woman was entering the front one.

Maybe next time I need to define what I mean by height/weight proportional, Kerrie fumed as she started her BMW. This woman was a good twenty pounds overweight and had probably never seen the inside of a gym since high school when it was required.

She had an hour and a half to kill before her dinner date.

❖

"That can't be your name," he said as he threw a stack of clothing at her. Her modesty meant nothing to him; she would have to change in front of him.

"Why?" She turned her back to hide what she could of her naked body. Then screamed when she saw a hag staring at her, an aged creature as close to death as one could be, hair white and wispy, the skull beneath the skin clearly visible, the flesh shrunk away. She moved her hand to her mouth and the hag mimicked her.

He laughed and she understood. "The years have passed, Sister Mafalda. The bloom of your youth has faded."

A mirror. She turned in horror from her visage. "Who am I?" Her voice a low moan.

"Nobody," he answered as if discussing the weather on a pleasant spring day. "A pawn in the game of others. You'll get a new shell, a new name, and do what they want you to do."

Or go back to the room. It was unsaid.

"What shall my name be?" she asked, carefully avoiding any glimpse in the mirror.

"Muffy, Maryann, Melva, Megan, Madison, Marigold. Anything that doesn't sound five centuries old."

"I only know the names of my time."

A cruel smile touched his lips. "Isabel."

"No!" She ripped off the tattered cloth covering her. He could have no carnal enjoyment of her withered flesh. "No. A new name, one of this time."

"Malda," he named her.

She did not protest.

"Now, you walk through the mirror; it will give you a new body—the illusion of one—to go with your new name."

Mafalda—Malda did as she was instructed, his cruel laugh following her as she approached her decayed image, the shrunken eyes burning into hers until she walked through them.

❖

Date number two had started on a more promising note. The woman wore an actual dress and had on makeup. But her slim legs were the high point of the evening. She worked as a secretary and was seeking a woman she could "pamper and take care of" quote/unquote. Kerrie's side of the equation was to shell out for everything, including the pampering. Kerrie got stuck paying the entire cost of the dinner, including an expensive bottle of wine. She considered taking the woman home and fucking her, just to get something out of the evening. But the woman was "staying with friends" so they would have had to go to Kerrie's place across the lake—or take a hotel room, which she would have had to pay for. In the end it wasn't worth it. Kerrie used her migraine excuse and left the woman at the restaurant. She could find her own way home.

❖

It sickened her, hunting for lost souls, as if some vile thing was growing in her with every one she found. She took the ones already close to death, insensate with drugs or alcohol as they huddled under a bridge. Only the thought of going back to the room with its faded wallpaper kept her going.

As she brought each one in, he shook his head in disappointment.

With her fourth victim, a scraggly homeless man, he grabbed her arm.

"This isn't what they're asking for," he hissed in her ear. "Are you still a virgin? I can change that, you know."

She shrank from him, but his grip was too strong. It was the clench of a desperate man; he, too, knew that as depraved as his role was, there were worse places in this hell. Kicking the homeless man into a slimy fissure, he dragged her down the hallway.

It will be quick, she told herself, compared to the endless eternity in the room. He would be on her for a few moments and it would be over. She had seen the endless stream of young servant girls, the younger daughters, all who had been sent to the convent to be out of sight, their tales of being grabbed in the kitchen or street, held down by men they could not fight. Some died in childbirth, but most had survived the rape.

But that was not his intent. He wanted her to bring in victims who were fresh and alive, not those on the edge of death. Ones who could still feel terror.

He brought her to an ornate door, tapped on it but waited for no reply before opening it.

"Your ladyship," he said into a room so dark she could see no one. "I've brought someone for you. You can have her for the entire night.

Teach her well." He grabbed at her clothes, ripping most of them off before shoving her into the darkness.

The door closed, leaving her in utter black.

Then in the far corner, a scratch of a match and its flame lit a candle.

Standing before her was one of the most beautiful women she'd ever seen. Tall, Nordic, perhaps. Hair of newly mown hay and eyes the color of sky in the early morning. The woman said nothing, walked toward her with the candle held high, staring at her.

Malda looked down at herself. She had been given the flesh of a young woman, herself as a young woman, breasts high and full, the soft swell of thigh to full hips, her eyes a deep brown, her hair a dense, wavy black. A woman who would be considered handsome in any age.

The Nordic woman stood before her. A finger brushed Malda's torn shirt away, then traced a path to her breast, stopping at the nipple. Malda started to pull away, but the woman pinched her nipple painfully, holding her in place.

"Don't," the woman said, "fight me."

Malda nodded. Was it a sin if she had no choice?

At her acquiescence, the woman let go of her breast, the hand suddenly snaking into her hair, dragging Malda into a harsh kiss. She again started to struggle, until she felt the flame of the candle close to her skin. She let the woman kiss her. Let the surprise and fear slide into enjoyment, a feeling she thought she'd never feel, hot, carnal flesh. Malda started to kiss back, to let her tongue and lips seek their own pleasure.

The woman broke off; with her hand still twined in Malda's hair, she pulled her to a bed. It was not the thin cruel mattress of her old room, but a thick, lush bed, pillows everywhere, a red velvet canopy above.

The woman pushed Malda onto the bed and was quickly atop her, kissing, caressing, letting her finally feel all the things she had dared not think of. Her body turned hot and languid, as if she was pinned to the bed by not only the woman's weight, but her own desires.

In a swooping stroke, the woman grabbed Malda's wrists, yanking them above her head, swiftly encasing them in cold metal.

"I will teach you everything two women can do with each other," the woman whispered in her ear. "Some you will like; some you won't.

I expect you to be a very good pupil. There is a high price to pay if you are not."

In this purgatory, Malda's screams went unheard. Or worse, enjoyed by those who could hear. Some were screams of pleasure, some of pain and agony, some both. The woman used her tongue between Malda's legs, bringing her to ecstasy. Then she used a false cock, shoving it inside her, a mix of pain and pleasure. Then behind her, first "in your cunt—learn to say the word—both men and women like to do this," the woman had instructed, then "in your ass, not everyone likes this, but you should know how it's done." Pain, intense pulsing as if something inside her was ripping. Then pleasure with the woman's fingers stroking Malda gently, again bringing her to ecstasy.

Finally the physical pleasure and pain blended into fatigue. The chains were taken off. The woman, too, seemed tired, willing to quietly rest next to Malda until they both succumbed to sleep.

When she woke, the room showed a faint tinge of light, as if the day was struggling weakly to get in, defeated by the dark curtains. The light was too dim to reveal much, not even the door out of the room. Malda next noticed the air, a heavy fetid smell as if it too was without light.

Malda was lying on her side, something—someone, curled behind her. The woman. An arm was around her waist, felt more than seen in the dim light. Maybe the woman was as much a prisoner as she was, her giving of pleasure a way to make up for the pain. Malda understood the night had changed her, seduced her into carnal pleasures that she had been taught to shun as evil. Carnal pleasures that she would have to engage in over and over again to survive. They didn't just want living bones, it had to be a game, a pursuit of wit and will.

The woman's arm tightened around her waist. Malda looked down, expecting to see pale smooth skin.

The decaying smell grew denser.

The arm pressed against her, a prison. It was more bone than human—no pale youthful skin, instead a hide weathered to dark leather, wrinkled and scarred, the arm pushing her down on her back.

The woman was again on top of her.

Malda screamed, terror this time. This foul creature had touched her, caressed every secret place, given her more physical pleasure than anyone had ever given her.

A creature of the grave, red eyes shrunk in a skull face, the waft of decay about her. Lips shriveled to rawhide strips, the teeth loose and green. Her skin was slack, sliding over the bones as if only a bag containing what used to be human.

Malda struggled, but the creature was swift and cunning, pinning her down, again binding her hands, the smell of decay gagging her.

"Let's review some of the things you learned last night," the creature said, her mouth a rictus grin that widened into a harsh laugh. She wrapped her claws into Malda's hair holding her still enough to force a kiss. She broke it off only as Malda started to retch.

She shoved another pillow under Malda's head, propping her up to watch as the monster kissed and fondled her. The lips and fingers were dirty sandpaper, the kisses leaving foul wet greasy splotches.

Malda panted through her mouth. She had thought that being forced by a man would be the worst thing that could happen. The wallpapered room now seemed a sanctuary. "Let me free and I'll bring the goddamned pope in," she muttered.

"Oh, we have plenty of those," the creature replied. "No, you'll have to do better." Her hands shoved Malda's thighs apart. "You liked this last night."

Malda felt the hot, rancid breath between her legs. The lizard tongue started to stroke her there.

"No, please, don't," she begged. But as the words left her, she understood that there was no mercy here. Asking for it only let them know your weakness.

The bony, decayed finger slid inside Malda. "Yes, you liked this a lot last night."

Malda jerked her hips, trying to pull away. But the creature held on, her skull head fastened between Malda's legs.

Malda gagged, starting to retch, but she had eaten little, so only a wet stream came out of her lips.

"You don't much like me as I really am, do you?" the creature said.

Malda knew not to reply.

"You're going to have to do better, you know. I won't stop until you feel the same pleasure you felt last night."

"I can't…"

"Oh, yes, you can. Or you can spend another eternity chained to this bed."

"No!" The word was out before Malda thought to be silent.

"Imagine your delightful Ysabel here instead of me. Picture her delicate tongue touching you as mine is now."

"No!" This time Malda meant to speak. She had betrayed Ysabel in life; she would not use her again.

"As you wish. It's been a long time since I've had company. I'll enjoy yours." The hag again started kissing Malda, her bony finger sliding in and out.

Malda shut her eyes, breathing through her mouth to keep the decayed stench out of her nostrils. She tried to imagine the woman of last night, the beautiful Nordic blonde, but the image always turned into the monster she really was. She tried an imaginary woman, but could only hold the image for a static moment, the false visage too amorphous for her to bring to life.

Her body was rebelling, the constant rub and touch making her swollen and wet, yet with no relief possible. Yet only relief would end this horror.

Brown eyes, a light olive skin, flawless and young. Her perfect smile, a small gap between her front teeth. The sound of her laughter, her voice, the way she walked, she knew them well.

"Forgive me, Ysabel," Malda breathed, so softly no ghost could hear.

They were in an olive garden, the early-morning sun warm against their skin. It was here, now, a future far from the convent. A time when touching each other was possible. They were alone. Touching, kissing. Giving each other pleasure. It was Ysabel's mouth on her, loving her as they had been forbidden those eons ago.

It was Ysabel who made her shudder and moan, gave her the final pleasure that racked through her body.

It was the woman-monster who cursed her and threw her out of the room, naked and covered in her sour sweat and guilt.

He was there, waiting for her, a sardonic smile on his face as if he knew what she'd done.

"I hope you've learned your lesson well," he said. He walked her back to the mirror, only throwing clothes at her at the last moment.

❖

Boring, boring, boring, Kerrie thought. Life was unfair; she was tired of hearing about it. The woman had been pretty enough, young enough, perhaps too young. She worried about things like social justice and poor people. Kerrie didn't even pretend to do anything other than look at her watch. Her date paused mid-sentence.

"I'm sorry, I feel a migraine coming on," the woman said, her tone making clear this wasn't true. She put twenty dollars on the table and left.

Kerrie was nonplussed, then angry. Women didn't leave her; she left them. She had a comfortable six-figure income and a luxurious house in an exclusive location, drove a new and expensive car, and looked a good ten years younger than her forty-two years. No one walked out on her.

Of course, the woman knew that Kerrie was about to do the same thing and was just enough of a bitch to do it first. She finished her drink, not wanting to appear as if anything unexpected had happened, and perused her date book. It wasn't a calendar, but a list of the women she dated. It wouldn't do to accidentally date someone she had already rejected. One more tonight, so all was not lost. In fact, the woman, by being so rude, had saved her the trouble of ditching her to make the next date. And her twenty dollars covered the cost of both their drinks. No tip, but the bar maid hadn't been that attentive.

This last one wasn't a real date, more a sex hook-up, or so Kerrie hoped. She was tired of her vibrator and watching girl/girl porn to get off. The ad had been simple: *In town on business. Looking for someone to have some fun with. Open to all kinds of fun.* A woman seeking other women. She claimed to be twenty-six, which probably meant she was thirty-two. No, Kerrie didn't list her real age, but she went to the gym three times a week, used expensive lotions every morning and evening, and had a spa day once a month.

The woman had suggested meeting in the hotel bar. It was on the edge of the French Quarter and parking was always a pain there. But the woman wasn't from here, probably didn't have a car, so Kerrie couldn't suggest one of the uptown bars she preferred.

"This had better be worth it," Kerrie muttered as she gave up finding street parking in a safe enough area and settled for paying to valet park at the hotel.

The bar was packed. Of course, it would be, a Saturday night full of conventions in town. *How the hell do I find someone I've never seen before in a place like this,* Kerrie thought. She valued discretion and wasn't about to go up to various strangers asking if they were…she had already blanked on the woman's name.

Just as she was retrieving her date book to look up the name, a voice said in her ear, "You must be Kerrie."

Kerrie turned to face one of the most beautiful women she'd ever seen, certainly the best-looking one in the bar. "Yes, I am. How good of you to find me," she said as she glanced down in her book for the name. "Megan." She was tall, ink black hair with startling blue eyes and dressed in designer clothes, including a leather jacket that clearly was not bought off the rack.

"It was easy, you're the most beautiful woman here," Megan said, a seductive smile playing on her face. "Thank you for agreeing to meet me."

"You have an accent," Kerrie said. "Where are you from?" It was slight; she spoke English perfectly. Kerrie could deal with that.

"Spain," the woman answered. "But I haven't lived there for a long time." She took Kerrie by the hand and led her to a back corner where two seats had opened up. She didn't sit, instead asked Kerrie for her drink order.

Kerrie was gratified to notice that the woman ordered top-shelf Scotch for both of them. Yes, this one was promising. She was already beginning to picture the woman naked when she returned with their drinks.

She was easy to speak to, nodding sympathetically when Kerrie talked about managing a business, adding, "Yes, money is a burden that few people realize. It must be tended to." She knew wines and liked to travel, could name fine restaurants in many cities. She was everything Kerrie was looking for in a woman. What was her name again? Kerrie quickly checked her date book when the woman went to get another round of drinks. Megan. She had even insisted on paying, claiming that Kerrie was nice enough to keep her company in this strange city, it was the least she could do.

As she had hoped, the evening ended with the woman taking Kerrie up to her room. Kerrie had had more to drink than usual, but the woman took the lead, with Kerrie naked by the time they made it to the bed. Then a night of passion that ended too early as the woman had to be up in time to take care of the business she had in town. Odd for a Sunday, Kerrie thought, but maybe international business didn't hew to American rules.

"Can I see you later?" the woman asked as she walked a groggy Kerrie to the elevator. Megan said she would change her plane, as she had planned to be gone this evening. Kerrie readily agreed. This was her dream woman.

Once they parted, Kerrie raced back to the Northshore. She had to shower and change her clothes. Not to mention a frenzy of house cleaning. She wanted to bring the woman back here, show off the fine things in her house. Everything had to be perfect for this perfect woman.

She didn't even bother looking for street parking, there was no time. The price of parking was a good deal to have this woman in her life. Kerrie was already fantacizing about a long-distance romance, passionate meetings in faraway places.

Megan was waiting for her, tall and beautiful in her expensive leather coat. Kerrie smiled at her smile. A lot of frogs to find one princess.

"Show me your city," Megan asked.

Kerrie knew she meant New Orleans and not the town where she lived.

They wandered through the French Quarter, past the antique stores and art galleries on Royal Street. The woman had amazing taste, almost the same as her own, Kerrie noted. Their shoulders touched, as lovers do.

Kerrie was in such a state of bliss that she didn't recognize the woman with the fake migraine from last night until she was in front of them. The woman looked past her, as if Kerrie didn't exist.

"How's your migraine?" Kerrie asked. She had little time for this woman, but she wasn't going to be ignored.

"Obviously all gone." The woman looked at her and then at Megan.

Of course she stared at Megan, she was a beautiful woman. But she stared a bit too long for Kerrie's liking, especially as Megan kept her eyes on the other woman.

"Glad to hear it," Kerrie said. "We've got to be going."

"Have a great time, Kerrie," the woman said.

"You, too…" What was her name? "Ingrid."

"Isabella. My name is Isabella."

❖

It couldn't be. Had her torrid imaginings of Ysabel conjured her spirit? Her face? The woman they walked by matched in every detail her memory of Ysabel. She wanted to run from this prattling woman with her chatter of the "finer things," all material, no soul in any of them. Run back to the woman and…and what? Ask if she had once been a nun in Spain all those centuries ago? If she had loved another of the sisters, who had returned her love with betrayal?

No, Malda told herself, it is my guilt seeing through my eyes, punishing me for conjuring her image to rid myself of the hag.

She had her task. This woman thought the world belonged to her and she would fight and yell and scream when those faded walls closed around her. That was what they wanted; that was what she would give them.

She pretended to listen, pretended to agree, pretended to think the woman beautiful. It would be over soon. They had dinner in one of the expensive restaurants. Malda paid, of course, still claimed to be grateful to Kerrie for the companionship and showing her around the city. One of the lessons Malda had learned on her long night was that touching—sex—didn't need love; it could be used for many purposes: punishment, control. A trap, like the one she was setting now.

After dinner they strolled along the riverfront. In the place between the streetlights, Malda kissed the woman. She couldn't request, had to wait to be invited, but a few ardent kisses might hurry things along.

"Would you like to come home with me?" Kerrie finally asked.

"I desire nothing more." Kerrie had described her home, quiet, secluded. Neighbors far enough away that they couldn't hear her cries for help.

After one final kiss, they retrieved Kerrie's car. It was a long drive. Malda couldn't understand living this far away from a jewel of a city like New Orleans, trading in its vibrant streets, mighty river for the sterile newness of the far side of the lake. To cover the time, Malda asked questions, pointless questions about favorite trips as if hinting they would travel together.

The vile thing felt like it was still growing in her. Her only solace was that it would keep the vile things outside her—the tiny room, the monster lover—away.

Malda was disappointed in the house, expecting some grand thing to rival the palaces she had glimpsed in Spain. Yes, it was large, six bedrooms, four and a half baths, but the walls would not hold through time, it would last at most a century, no span for history to take hold.

The niceties were observed. Kerrie poured them drinks, noting the expensive liquor.

Malda sipped slowly, letting Kerrie be well into her second drink before she finished her first. Unlike her tormentors, she didn't enjoy the struggle and had no desire to prolong this.

She didn't let Kerrie fix her another drink, instead kissing her, running her hands under Kerrie's shirt. Malda was sad to notice her body responding to the warm flesh of even a woman like this. That was another thing she had learned in the night—when holding someone in a warm embrace it is easy to steal their soul.

Malda feigned passion, hurrying because she wanted to get this done, not from ardor. If she could find lust with this woman, where would she not be corrupt? But she had to let this happen, had to do it to survive. Had to let this shell she was living in, feel everything her own body never had. She howled when the physical release coursed through her. Her scream was anger, pleasure, pain, guilt. And calculating enough to test that Kerrie's pleas would go unheard.

Finally, after several bouts, the woman fell into sleep. Malda could not. She was the hunter and had to be more cunning than her prey.

She waited a few scant hours, until the sun started to tinge the sky, then roughly grabbed Kerrie, holding her down.

"Um, honey, I'm glad you're interested, but I have to pee first," the sleepy woman mumbled.

"I'm not interested in sex," Malda said, her voice tight and cruel. She pinned Kerrie's wrists.

Kerrie's eyes flashed open. "What do you…look, I really need to pee. I'll ruin the bed if I don't."

"It's not a very nice bed. It needs to be ruined." Malda straddled Kerrie, pushing her groin against her abdomen.

"Stop that! This isn't funny."

"It's not meant to be funny." Malda started riding her, a hard bounce. She saw fear in Kerrie's eyes and felt ashamed at the growing carnal desire she felt from her groin pressed and rubbing against the woman. The fear didn't make it go away.

"Please, I'll do anything you want. Just don't hurt me," Kerrie begged.

"Or your bed," Malda said as she again pushed down.

"You don't need to do this. I'll give you money!" Kerrie screamed.

"I don't want money," Malda whispered in her ear. She yanked Kerrie's arms, pinning her wrists against her breasts with one hand. Malda slid down Kerrie's body until she was sitting on her thighs. She started to stroke and play with her with her free hand.

"Stop! Please stop!"

Malda ignored her screams. No one could hear them. She roughly put two, then three fingers inside Kerrie, shoving in and out. She felt Kerrie's muscles tighten, trying to hold back what her body needed. Yes, she was going to fight.

Malda barred her teeth, swooping down at Kerrie's breasts, as if to bite her nipple. She stopped just short. But the fear was enough. A wet stream spewed over her fingers. She kept thrusting until it stopped.

"Why?" Kerrie brayed. "Why did you make me mess up my bed?"

"Because you're so proud of it." Malda wiped her sticky fingers across Kerrie's face.

The woman sputtered and spat, shaking her head against the wetness.

Then asked, "Are you going to kill me?"

Malda answered, "No, something far worse." She yanked Kerrie off the bed and to the mirror.

This time Kerrie's scream was louder and more harrowing than the others. The mirror reflected Malda as she really was, a decayed hag, withered face, eyes so deep they were almost black holes.

"This one will do," he said as they emerged on the other side of the glass.

Kerrie jerked out of Malda's grasp.

"Who are you?" she demanded. "I know a lot of good lawyers, and if you don't let me go right now, you'll regret it."

"Regret is all we have here," he said. "Let me show you to your room."

Malda had a glimpse of the wallpaper, that horrid wallpaper, and then the door was shut on Kerrie's outraged yelling.

"You've done well," he said. "Now you must do better."

"So soon?"

"It's your freedom. Her ladyship is already missing your company. One night is not enough time to play with whips and fire as she desires."

Malda shuddered. "So I must get another one?"

"Yes, but not just anyone."

She felt the blow before it landed.

"The pretty girl you met on the street," he continued.

"I met many pretty girls."

"You know the one I mean." He shoved her back into the mirror.

Malda couldn't. She wouldn't. She found a hotel on the outskirts of town, made no attempt to seek Isabella out. A day. A week. Time passed. Maybe they forgot about her. Maybe she could...

"Malda!" Her name called as she shopped for groceries in the little run-down store near the hotel.

A beautiful woman. Tall, Nordic. "Malda," she called again, approaching, the same cruel smile Malda remembered.

Her smile widened as she said, "Oh, don't worry, I'm not here for you. No, I have a date with a pretty young woman tonight. I believe her name is Isabella."

"No, you stay away from her!"

"Why? You don't want her. If you did, you would have had her by now." She laughed, a laugh as cold as the deepest grave.

"No, she's done nothing to deserve this."

"No one does anything to deserve this. The worst murderer doesn't deserve this. It's evil and we're part of it."

Malda reached for the woman but she was gone. Isabella. Did it matter? It was only her guilt. It couldn't be the same Ysabel that she had known. A new, younger version of her? Their paths had crossed in time in Spain. Mafalda had named her to those in power. That was the past; it could not be undone and it could not come back into this world.

Malda hurried back to her small hotel room. The thoughts wouldn't leave her. Even if she wanted to, how could she save Isabella? She had no idea how to find her, let alone warn her.

Kerrie. That awful woman. She knew Isabella.

Malda hesitated at the mirror. Maybe they would leave her to her freedom if she didn't go back. But she saw that for the lie it was. The woman had easily found her. When they wanted her they would find her, too.

She stepped through the mirror.

"I thought you'd gone rogue on us," he said, waiting for her in the hallway as if he knew she would be here.

"Is that a possibility?"

He shrugged.

"You sent her to take Isabella," she accused.

"Her ladyship volunteered. They're getting impatient. I just do my job."

"The woman I brought, I need to talk to her. She'll know where Isabella is."

"Be my guest. She won't be happy to see you."

Malda hesitated. "If I go in the room, can I get back out?"

"That scares you? Being alone in the room with her for a very long time?"

"I like my freedom."

"Then I'll assume this time you'll do whatever you can to keep it. Go in. You can come back out."

Kerrie flew at Malda as the door opened. Malda flung her back across the room.

"Let me out!" Kerrie screamed. The time had not been kind to her. Her skin was coarse, her hair lank, madness oozing in.

Fighting would take too long, Malda reasoned. This woman was doomed. Another lie or two couldn't matter.

"I can do that if you help me."

"You can? How?"

"You must help me. I need to find the woman we spoke to that night in the French Quarter."

"Why? Why do you need to find her?"

Another lie. "So she can be here instead of you."

"I...I don't know her. We went out once."

But Malda could see the desperation in Kerrie's eyes. She would do anything to get out. "You must remember. How did you contact her to go on that date?"

"I wrote her number down. In my little book. But I don't have it," she said, despair rising in her voice.

"Tell me where it is and I can get it."

"I'm not sure..."

"You must remember; it's the only way you can get free."

"In my house, it'll be in the bag I had...that night," she slowly remembered. "It'll be in the hallway, either on the side table or hanging on the coat rack."

That was enough. "Good. Thank you," Malda just remembered to say.

"Wait! When do I get free?"

"Soon." The final lie. She closed the door behind her.

Malda again stepped through the mirror, this time going to the one in the bedroom where she'd captured Kerrie. The urine-soaked mattress reeked and fingerprint dust was everywhere, but the police had long gone.

Malda hurried down the stairs, relieved that the purse was

hanging on the coat rack as Kerrie had said. It was a date purse, not her usual purse, and had been overlooked by the police investigating her disappearance. It held only a small wallet with a little bit of money, some lipstick, a cheap cell phone. And the black book.

Malda flipped through it. Isabella. As if waiting for her all these centuries.

Then Malda hesitated. As she had not been able to stop the Inquisition, she could not stop this. She had no power then, she had none now. What was she supposed to do? Dial the number and ask if Isabella remembered a previous life? It had seemed for a moment she could be a better person, but as before it wasn't possible.

Below the name and phone number was an address. It had a line through it. Kerrie had obviously marked her off the list.

Again, a spark of hope. Malda could go there, maybe stop them. Maybe it was too late, but this time she had to try. Could she go from this mirror in the foyer to the mirror there, one she'd never seen? Malda was unsure of her powers.

She looked at the mirror, at the hag she was. What did it matter where she went? It was a chance, and this time she would use it. "Take me there."

A bedroom. Dark. The soft moans of a woman's pleasure. Malda wasn't sure where she was. Her destination? Or some cruel joke. The moans stopped. Someone was aware of her.

Then the scratch of a match and a candle flared. Two women. The tall, Nordic woman on top of Isabella, ravishing her.

"You!" the beautiful monster screamed. "You will not stop me, not now!"

"Who are you?" Isabella asked, her voice groggy with desire.

"A friend. This time a friend. You must not trust this woman, she will harm you."

Isabella was naked, a trickle of sweat between her breasts, the nipples taut and her face flushed. Malda stared at her, the vision she'd never seen, never allowed herself to conjure until the hag forced her to do so. *You should be that way for me,* Malda thought, her eyes feasting on the delicate flesh.

But her pause gave the monster the desperate opening she needed. She pounced on Malda, a strong arm around her neck, choking her hard. Malda's hands scrabbled against the forearm against her throat, but her position was weak and she could do little more than scratch at skin too decayed to notice such small insults.

As Malda struggled for breath, the monster grabbed Isabella by the hair, jerking her off the bed, dragging them both to the mirror.

Malda still struggled, but the mirror was too close, they were through it and outside the hated ornate door. She had Malda shoved against one door post and Isabella against the other, her hands on their necks, tightening.

The man was there. "Ah, good hunting, your ladyship," he said. "Two when I expected only one."

"I get them both?" The monster licked her lips.

"Welcome, dear Ysabel. United finally with Sister Mafalda," he said.

"Is this who you really are?" Isabella cried, kicking at the fiend, and watching in horror as she transformed into her true self. First the arms holding them turned to slack leather; the breasts sagged into empty, flaccid sacks. Malevolence burned from her shrunken eyes.

"No," the man said, "Sister Mafalda is the other one, your would-be rescuer."

"Mafalda...," Isabella said. "Please. Can it be you? I never stopped loving you, never believed you were the one to betray me." She stopped kicking, stopped struggling, her beseeching eyes on Malda.

Malda could not answer, could not admit her sin.

The monster tightened her hold. "I get them both?" she again demanded.

"Perhaps," the man said. "I'll let Sister Mafalda choose. You and your precious Ysabel can be together forever. You can watch as her ladyship places her fine honed instruments in the delicate parts of Isabella's tender body. You can listen to her screams of agony. Her only relief will be to listen to you as she screams in the same agony."

"No! I don't choose that."

"Then you have two other choices. Her ladyship can have you. Or she can have Ysabel."

"No! No, please no," Malda moaned. Hell for her or the hell of betrayal once again.

"Those are your choices," he said harshly. "Make it quickly."

"She can have me," Isabella said. "Take me. Save yourself."

Malda hesitated. The words echoed in her head, the same words Ysabel had used when they questioned the two sisters. Malda had taken her at her word and saved herself.

"Choose," he demanded.

Malda remembered the agony of the woman's blackened fingers

probing into her most secret places, the torture as orifices were forced open. The vileness growing in her as she took pleasure where none should be taken. One night had been a horror. She couldn't go back.

"I can't...I can't," she choked out.

"The choice is made," he said. "Your ladyship can have Ysabel. Sister Mafalda has betrayed her once again."

The hag grinned an evil smile. She dropped Malda, letting her gasp on the floor as she turned her attention to Ysabel, her desiccated mouth fastening on a soft breast, the green teeth greedily taking a nipple.

Ysabel's screams echoed down the hallway as the creature took her through the door. Even closed, the heavy wood didn't silence them completely.

Malda hung her head, shame and guilt new again. A second chance and she was no stronger this time. "Now," she said through the tears she was crying. "Now do I get my freedom?"

He looked at her as if only remembering she existed. "They say that if people sacrifice themselves, they gain their freedom. It's happened so rarely, I'm not sure if it's true or not. So few are willing to pay the price."

"No! No!" It was a long, keening wail, piercing enough to drown out Ysabel's scream.

He gave her a bare minute to howl her grief, before prodding her with his foot. "Come, they are waiting. You must feed them. Unless you'd like to join her ladyship or go to your old room with a new roommate."

Malda wiped the tears away. Everyone was weak. Everyone deserved this. She had lost the one soul she had wanted to save—none would get mercy now. Her grief hardened to fury. She had not been strong enough, but no one was. She would hunt them, trap them as she had been trapped and prove them even weaker than she was. She walked to the mirror without his prodding.

MATINEE
VINCE A. LIAGUNO

August

Adam flinched when the ax split Marcy's skull. He knew it was coming, knew the attractive brunette had violated the rules. Yet as many times as he had seen the ax rise and fall, knocking into the lone overhead light of the latrine as it fell, he still cowered slightly at the sight of Marcy slamming against the wall, her body sliding down its surface as the ax protruded incongruously from her head. Someone down in front of him let out a stifled burst of delighted repulsion.

Amateurs, he thought with contempt. *Some people just have no business.*

He squinted in the dark and could just make out the top of the head of the object of his disdain: a woman cuddled into the crook of the arm of a male companion. They were the worst kind—the ones with no real interest in the art itself, just in the prospect of portraying themselves as vulnerable to the opposite gender. They screamed for the sake of screaming. Adam hated bitches like that.

Farther ahead of them, it was raining now. Heavy torrents of precipitation battered the flimsy cabin with forceful pellets. Brenda was standing in the open doorway, peering out. She had heard something. A scream, maybe? But Adam knew these dumb bitches never trusted their own instincts. And it always got them killed. *Always.*

Brenda would meet her end right after the game of strip Monopoly—always a big no-no in situations like this. She was too sexually aggressive, flaunting herself in her bra and panties in front of Steve and Alice. Steve liked it, hoped he would get lucky. But Alice was uncomfortable and reluctant to go along with Brenda's provocative suggestion. That indecisiveness spoke to a higher morality and would serve her well later.

To Adam's left, the sound of snoring intermingled with the rain and giggles over the ramifications of landing on Baltic Avenue. He glanced to his left and spied a bald guy asleep in his seat, his chubby hands folded neatly atop his rotund belly. The fluttering sound coming from the man's open mouth was distracting. He hated such annoyances. How could any asshole sleep through a splatter film?

Adam reached into his jumbo box of Goobers. Pinching one between his forefinger and thumb, he lobbed it at the sleeping asshole. The confection hit its mark; the man roused and glanced around with the halfhearted realization that someone had thrown something at him. Despite the fact that there were only a handful of patrons in the movie theater on this hot August afternoon, the man's embarrassment quickly eclipsed his indignation and he settled back into his seat with a wary eye on alert for further candy-coated attacks.

Brenda was now backing toward a huge mounted bull's-eye in the rain. Stupid bitch left her cabin in a nightgown to go investigate a cry in the dark. Hadn't she ever watched a film like this before? At least she had brought a flashlight. She squinted into the stormy night, backing slowly toward her mark. How stupid could she be—traipsing around the archery range like that? She deserved to die. Adam only wished he could witness the arrow tips piercing her flesh, Indian head points tearing through the cheesecloth nightgown and drawing blood in copious squirts. Yeah, Cunningham had missed the boat on the kill; Savini would have rocked doing the effects for that one. At least he had the hindsight to have Brenda make an appearance later in the film.

Sleeping asshole was dozing again. This time Adam ignored him as poor Alice began discovering the bodies: Steve on a door…Marcy in the shower…Annie in the jeep. The final girl always found the bodies, and Adam knew from her screams why she passed her screen test. Adrienne had great lung capacity. Shame she never did more slashers. Adam heard once that she quit the film biz because her screams had invited a real-life stalker.

By the time Pamela Voorhees arrived to seemingly comfort poor, distraught Alice, sleeping asshole was blowing trombones and the stupid bitch down front had surrendered her tongue to her boyfriend. Adam remained glued to the screen, intermittently popping Goobers as Alice came to realize that Pamela wasn't her kindly rescuer after all. He felt his stomach muscles tighten in anticipation of the denouement, eyes widening as Alice swung the machete and Mrs. Voorhees lost her head in the most literal sense. His fingers opened and closed on his lap in slow-motion unison with Mrs. Voorhees as her headless torso took its last steps. He wondered if she could see her body still standing from where her eyes blinked in dumbfounded amazement from the ground. Adam wondered about the sensation of being headless. He thought it would sometimes be cool to take the weight of your head off—the load of crap he carried around in there.

That made him think of the guy he'd talked to on the chat line last night, the one who begged him to decapitate him. Adam stiffened in his pants when he recalled the man's urgency in wanting his head lopped off, the frantic need in his voice over the phone line. He had climaxed and hung up on the guy, severing his long-distance pleas for cranial relief. Maybe he'd call back tonight and try to find the guy again.

Maybe he'd get an address.

Adam's reverie was interrupted by a shriek from the stupid bitch. This time, the scream was pure, the kind that erupts spontaneously in response to an unexpected fright. Adam smiled to himself. Jason's surprise entrance during the otherwise tranquil final frames got them every time.

That Cunningham was a fucking genius—even if he'd missed the boat with Brenda.

October

Brittle leaves swirled at Adam's feet as he waited in line for the matinee. The autumn sun hung low in the sky, beginning its seasonally dictated premature descent behind the buildings across the street from where the small crowd had gathered. Goddamned Halloween had to fall on a Saturday, bringing out all the idiots who thought the idea of seeing Michael Myers on the big screen again would be a fun way to spend the holiday. He silently cursed the line of people with whom he stood outside the old Liberty Theater for the casually nostalgic ruminations that brought them there. He felt an illogical ownership over the matinee showing, his reward for being one of the diehards.

Adam indifferently glanced around, his eyes sweeping the moviegoers around him. They were like a herd of lapsed Catholics who only attended Mass on Christmas and Easter. Their pilgrimage here on the holiest of horror days was a sacrilege. Only the most faithful should be permitted entrance, not banal idiots in search of novelty.

He'd underestimated the crowd, expecting the usual handful of people who sought refuge inside the theater from the everyday things they were hiding from—nagging wives, abusive boyfriends, and alcoholic mothers. He thought of his own mother, a sagging stick figure of a woman who chain-smoked Benson & Hedges and drank herself into irrational rages. He had first started coming to the Liberty and its glorious matinees in his early teens to escape her wrath, the darkness of the theater cloaking him in anonymity and serving as an oasis in the desert storm of his childhood. As the crowd inched closer toward the ticket booth, Adam recalled the slasherfest that was his own early life, riddled with physical and mental brutality at the hands of an abusive mother. He remembered one particular incident in which his mother had flown into a rage over the refrigerator door being left open. She had thrown him to the floor and stormed off down the hallway toward his bedroom, returning moments later with the familiar box that stored his beloved comic books. He watched, horrified, as his mother picked each issue up and tore it slowly down the middle. With demented glee, she had methodically torn each *Justice League, Batman, X-Men,* and *Tales from the Crypt* in half, then quarters.

She would teach him to care about other people's things. She'd teach him to pay more attention to something other than his goddamned comics.

But with each rip, Elaine Mitchell, bitter and stewing in the putrid excretion of her own miserable life, sent her son's heart and spirit spiraling into an emotional paper shredder that day.

Adam came to understand the depths of human cruelty.

He had retreated into himself that day and into the comforting sanctuary of the Liberty. Buying a ticket for *The Bad News Bears Go to Japan,* Adam expertly ducked into *Halloween* when old man Carson had his back turned. Tears coursed down his cheeks that afternoon as Tommy Doyle presented a stack of contraband comics to his kindly babysitter Laurie and asked her to read them to him. How he had ached to jump into the celluloid images of the screen, to have Jamie Lee wrap her loving arms around him and comfort him the way she did ungrateful little Tommy Doyle. He pictured himself safe in the Doyle house carving pumpkins with Laurie and Lindsay Wallace while Michael Myers wrapped a telephone cord around his mother's throat in the house across the street.

The horror of *Halloween* became his safe haven.

"How many, please?" The voice pulled him from his daydream. Adam looked skeptically at the blond-haired kid behind the plate glass window, momentarily disoriented.

"Do you want a ticket or not, buddy?" The kid couldn't have been more than sixteen or seventeen, yet appeared oddly sophisticated in his formal usher garb. Two teenage girls behind Adam giggled at his hesitation, much to the pleasure of the kid behind the ticket window who gave them a conspiratorial wink.

"One, please," Adam finally said, pulling out a crumpled five-dollar bill from his jeans pocket and sliding it under the window. The kid was looking at him the way the bullies back in high school had looked at him, with unfettered contempt and anger for what they perceived as weakness. Adam hated the way the kid was looking at him, his expression obvious enough to further engage the little sluts behind him. They cooed and cackled like miniature harlots.

"That'll be four fifty, *sir,*" the kid said with mock formality. The sluts erupted in giggles. Adam looked at him as he slid him his change. His name badge read *Brad*.

As Adam turned away from the ticket booth, movie stub in hand, he heard one of the sluts say to the other, "I didn't realize the *actual* Michael Myers would be here today." The sound of the sluts' cackling and Brad's uncontained laughter followed him into the theater.

He was careful to choose a seat far away from the little sluts who followed him into the theater. They seemed to forget all about him in the space of seconds, moving on to more important topics of adolescent chitchat—such as which of this year's football players was the cutest. They were miniature Elaines-in-the-making, mean-spirited whores whose callous words cut deeply and then continued on, oblivious to the wide swath they had slashed in the emotional landscape behind them.

The lights finally dimmed amidst nervous giggles of excitement from the crowd, and the film started. From the initial strains of the piano-laden score, Adam felt a sheath of comfort creep over him, contentment coursing through him. No more tricks for Adam, only treats. For ninety minutes, he would finally be at home on the night he came home.

December

Adam hurried down Main Street toward the theater, flurries swirling around his head as both Bing Crosby's dreams of a white

Christmas and his dreams of a black Christmas were realized in Barnesville. His feet left large imprints in the freshly fallen snow on the sidewalk, his boots vilifying the purity of the holiday snowfall. The streets of the town were bare, save for the occasional car undoubtedly on its way through the woods to Grandma's house. Adam appreciated the preternatural silence of the afternoon, the way sound muffled as if the town lay beneath a heavy down comforter. His spirits were unseasonably high as he approached the Liberty.

Then he stopped.

Despite the snowflakes that dotted his eyeglasses and blurred his vision, Adam could see the unmistakable form of Brad behind the ticket window. The kid had gotten suckered into working the holiday shift at the Liberty by old man Carson's son—now the owner following his father's stroke several years ago. Adam felt his stomach churn at the recollection of their last encounter. Brad would be pissed that he wasn't home opening gifts with his idyllic suburban family, pissed that he wasn't home watching college football with his father, who beamed with pride for his own son's athletic accomplishments. Brad would be pissed—and Adam would be an easy target. He approached the window.

"One, please," he said, his voice cracking with apprehension. Adam braced himself for Brad's unadulterated contempt, but a welcome indifference greeted his request instead.

"That'll be four fifty," Brad said flatly. This lack of enthusiasm for preying upon an easy target like Adam momentarily unsettled him slightly. He slid a five-dollar bill under the window, and Brad pushed two quarters back at him with gloved fingers. "Enjoy the show," he said mechanically, barely glancing up before returning to the sports magazine on the counter in front of him. If he had remembered Adam from their Halloween encounter, he wasn't letting on now.

Adam took his ticket, resisting the momentary urge to wish Brad a Merry Christmas, fearful any expression of humanity would summon the kid's inner rage. He entered the theater and was hit by the concentrated smell of buttered popcorn. He viewed the candy counter, instantly spying an improbable mountain of mini-meteors of popped kernels spilling out of the popcorn case, their cragged surfaces glazed with greasy butter topping that looked slick and shiny under the warming light. Standing alone in the lobby, Adam wondered who would be eating all that popcorn.

"Hey there, Adam," a voice called from behind him. "What can

I get for you?" Louie Carson, eldest son of Alfred Carson and now proprietor of the Liberty, approached him from behind carrying a cardboard box filled with assorted candies to restock the display case.

"Hey, Mr. Carson," Adam returned. "Merry Christmas." Despite his penchant for splatter, Adam was a polite man, etiquette and manners having been beaten into him as a child—often with a wooden spoon at the dinner table or a quick backhand while standing on a neighbor's doorstep.

"Same to you, buddy," Carson said, smiling absently. Louie Carson was a kind man of almost fifty, with a retreating hairline and an extra jowl that gave him the appearance of a sea lion. He was one of those born-and-bred Barnesville boys who never quite made it past town lines, destined to a life of first-name familiarity with almost every store clerk and civil servant in their shared New England hamlet. Adam imagined that the deep lines branching out from the corners of his eyes were created by rivulets of tears cried year after year over his disappointment with life in this godforsaken hellhole. But if Carson was bitter over the lot in life he was cast to play, he never let on; he dutifully took over his father's business after his stroke, forsaking his own position as one of the town's more in-demand freelance carpenters to run the family movie theater.

The Liberty itself was something of an institution in Barnesville. Built in the early 1900's, the theater first rose to local prominence featuring raucous burlesque shows that brought patrons in by the dozens to the fledgling town. The Liberty found itself at the forefront of the burgeoning motion picture movement following an influx of Quakers to the area and the prohibition of anything deemed immoral. Townsfolk, and those on the outlying farmlands around Barnesville, made Saturday afternoons and evenings all about the delightful moving pictures flashing across the larger-than-life screen, creating entire evenings out around the novelty of this new entertainment medium. The arrival of talkies seemed to coincide with the town's booming textiles business. When the town's young men marched off to war in the '40s and '50s, the good people of Barnesville used the Liberty as an escape from the cruel reality that many of the young men would never return. In the '60s and '70s, the Liberty introduced color cinema to the town just as hippies and free-thinkers unleashed their own colorful way of life upon a nation entangled in a web of civil rights struggles and radical social change. The theater forged its way into the '80s riding the wave of low-budget horror flicks that caught on like wildfire, despite a growing threat from the cancerous malady known as the multiplex. And although the Liberty eventually succumbed to competition from nearby mega-cinemas (as well as a short-circuited popcorn machine that necessitated substantial remodeling following a fire in '89), it rebounded, finding a niche as a neighborhood bargain matinee, lovingly bringing back celluloid images from the golden years of cinema once it ceased showing first-run features.

For more than eighty years, the Liberty had stood sentry over a town that had lost track of its own history, as a beacon for those needing an escape...those needing a reprieve from the harshness of the world around them.

"What'll you have today, Adam?" Carson asked, setting the box down with a thump behind the counter. "Your usual?" He reached for the Goobers.

"Nah. Today is special...being Christmas and all. I think I'll go for a large popcorn," Adam replied. Despite being in his late thirties, his voice was almost childlike.

"Popcorn it is, then." Carson grabbed a monstrous bucket from a stack next to the soda dispenser and scooped several large shovels into it until it threatened to overflow the rim. He handed the bucket across the counter to Adam, who was fishing in his pockets.

"Popcorn's on the house," Carson said, holding up his hand. Adam looked at him, confused. "You keep me in business, Adam. Been coming to the Liberty since I can remember. And I can always count on you showing up for one of these damn slasher flicks." He chuckled.

"Thanks, Mr. Carson," Adam said, taking the bucket and avoiding the man's eyes. Gestures of kindness were so foreign to him that he lacked the capacity to accept them with any degree of grace.

"Enjoy the show," Carson called after him as he headed toward the theater doors.

Adam found the theater to be exactly as he enjoyed it—empty. Christmas was good for one thing—keeping people at home and away from his matinee. His mother used to say that only Jews and Chinese people went to the movies on Christmas because they hated Christ. Adam wasn't sure if it was the snow or a love for the Christian savior that kept people out of the theater today, but he was happy nonetheless for their absence.

He settled into a row almost dead center in the theater and hunched down into the seat just as the film sprang to life on the screen. The Liberty's no-frills bargain matinee came with no previews, no clever little animated jingles instructing you where to throw out your trash or how to escape in the event of a fire. No, a matinee at the Liberty was a bare bones moviegoing experience. *The way it should be,* Adam thought.

Adam shoved a handful of popcorn into his mouth as the peaceful image of the Pi Kappa Sig sorority house came into view against a snowy night backdrop while an unseen angelic chorus sang "Silent Night." Soon, Billy was looking in the windows as the hapless sorority babes inside went about their yuletide merriment unaware of the psychotic doings about to befall them. Somewhere between Billy's climb up the trellis and the first obscene phone call, Adam sensed movement behind him and heard the heavy thud of someone plopping into a seat. He hated people who were late for movies. Why even show the fuck up? He strained his eyes to the far left, careful not to turn his head lest the latecomer should think he gave a rat's ass.

As if in answer to his silent curiosity, a voice spoke behind him.

"How old is this fucking movie?" Brad said loudly, in disregard of movie theater etiquette.

Adam swallowed hard. Why did this asshole have to ruin the holiday matinee he had been looking forward to for weeks? "1974," he answered curtly.

"Me and my girlfriend went to see the remake a few days ago over in Spring Hill. Movie rocked," Brad said from behind him, his mouth full of something.

"Original's better," Adam shot back warily. "A classic."

"Even see the new one?"

"No."

"So how could you know this one's better?"

"Because remakes suck," Adam said forcefully. Brad continued to chew behind him. There was sudden movement behind him, and Adam braced for the sting of Brad's hand against the back of his head in response to his snappy retort. But then he realized that Brad was heaving himself over the row. He landed with a heavy plunk in the seat next to him.

"You really dig this old shit, huh?" Brad asked from beside him. He popped a handful of M&M's into his mouth.

"The classic slashers rule," Adam replied, eyes facing forward as he watched Margot Kidder grab the telephone from a fellow sorority sister and give Billy a verbal lashing on the other end. Billy would get her back good for that later, with the glass unicorn.

"But the new stuff is so much better, dude," Brad said. "Better special effects and shit."

"The new movies are just copycats of the old stuff. Half the crap in these new WB-populated PG-13 rip-offs is watered-down versions of the classics. *Black Christmas,* on the other hand, is the most underrated slasher film in history."

"How so?" Despite Adam's unease at playing Ebert & Roeper in the darkened theater with Brad, the kid seemed genuinely interested in hearing his theories. Against the advice of the little voice inside his head that told him never to trust, he relaxed a bit in his seat.

"Well," Adam began, "even though this movie predated it by five years, *When A Stranger Calls* gets all the credit for the whole *the call is coming from inside the house* thing."

"Katie Cassidy was smokin' in that movie, dude!"

"*Not* the remake—the original one with Carol Kane as the babysitter." Brad just blinked and stared straight ahead. Adam continued, undeterred. "And even though everyone said that Carpenter was a fucking genius with the shot where the audience sees through Michael Myer's mask when he kills his sister at the beginning of *Halloween,* Bob Clark had already done that POV shit in this movie."

"POV? Huh?" Adam hoped Brad was good at sports.

"Point of view. *Black Christmas* came out four years before *Halloween,* yet everyone's always going on and on about how *Halloween* was the first modern slasher movie."

"Jesus, dude," Brad said from beside him, "you really know your shit when it comes to these old movies." Adam's cheeks flushed at the pseudo compliment. Brad wasn't so bad after all. Despite their age difference, Adam felt a connection to the kid sitting in the dark theater. He was about to ask him if he wanted some of his popcorn when Brad's cell phone erupted in a cacophony of expletive-laden rap music from somewhere in the darkness of his lap. He fished in his jeans for the phone, retrieved it, and looked down at the display.

"Shit. It's my girlfriend. Dude, gotta take this. Catch you some other time?" Brad's face glowed in the translucent light of the rapping cell phone as he looked at him expectantly.

"Yeah, sure," Adam said, dejected by the interruption.

Brad held up his right hand. For a split second, Adam thought he was challenging him to arm-wrestle, but then realized what was expected. They clasped hands momentarily, wrists meeting. Adam tingled at the momentary sensation of Brad's skin against his.

"Merry Christmas, dude." Brad said as he turned and walked away. Adam watched as he left, could hear him say hello to the intrusive girlfriend who'd disrupted their budding camaraderie. His words trailed off behind him as he went out the theater door.

Adam turned back to the screen. Claire was about to be asphyxiated by the sheath of plastic hanging in her closet, her last frantic gasp for air effectively shrink-wrapping the plastic to her panic-stricken grimace. Billy would then haul her up into the attic, where her corpse would sit in a rocking chair in the uppermost window of the sorority house, her lifeless eyes staring out into the dark wintry night. The image was grim and sad, yet Adam sat watching it with buoyed spirits. He couldn't be certain whether it was the movie, or his momentary connection to another person, or some residual sentiment of the holiday, but for the first time in a long time, Adam actually felt giddy and began to softly hum "Silent Night" as Claire rocked and rocked and rocked.

February

Brad wasn't behind the ticket window the next time Adam went to the matinee. Instead, he was greeted by an elderly woman with a swirl of bluish hair piled impossibly on top of her head. It resembled cotton candy. An image of Marge Simpson flashed through his mind and almost made him laugh aloud.

"One ticket, please," he announced, sliding the five-dollar bill toward her. Without a word, the woman took the money and returned a single ticket with his change.

"Thank you," he said and could hear the woman's barely audible grunt of acknowledgment as she looked past him toward the next customer in line. Adam stepped out of the line and scanned the crowd. He was actually glad Valentine's Day had fallen on a Sunday. His eyes scanned the sea of red- and pink-garbed moviegoers, but there was no sign of Brad.

His conscious mind chastised his subconscious for getting his hopes up. Despite the fact they hadn't spoken again since the Christmas matinee, Brad had nonetheless evolved into something of a friend over the past several weeks—at least in Adam's mind. Adam cheered Brad on during the remaining games of the Barnesville Barracudas, watching unseen from the bleachers as his fellow football players high-fived each other after a win and the cheerleaders swarmed about him as he walked off the field. He stood unobtrusively across the street from Barnesville High most mornings, straddling his clunker of a bike as he watched Brad pull into the student parking lot in the new BMW his parents must have given him as a present after his Christmas shift at the Liberty. Adam had even tricked Louie Carson into revealing Brad's street address one day after a matinee showing of *New Year's Evil*. He kept watch over his new friend, hidden behind the mammoth ancient oak tree across the street from Brad's house. He peered through the new pair of binoculars he got from Clement's Hardware and watched as Brad paced his bedroom floor talking on the phone, or lifted weights in the garage.

Adam thought about marching up to the front door and ringing the doorbell. He imagined Brad's mother answering the door, could almost see the look of skepticism on her face as she gave him the once-over. She'd wonder why a guy his age was calling on her son, might perhaps forbid Brad to see him.

No, it was better to remain cloaked in the shadows, keeping invisible sentry over his newfound friend.

He scanned the crowd outside the Liberty one more time before going in. He'd been convinced Brad would show for the matinee, that he'd remember their Christmas chat and come looking for him. Dejected, Adam walked into the theater lobby, paid for his Goobers, and entered the theater.

He stood for a minute, allowing his eyes to adjust to the darkness. The movie house had just gone dark, and the film would spring to life on the screen in seconds. He sat in the first seat to his left, hoping that by staying close to the door he'd be able to spot Brad if he came in late. Adam smiled. *Brad is always late for these things*.

The film began. Despite his eagerness for Brad to show, Adam soon lost himself in the movie, shrinking down in his seat in a posture from childhood. His eyes began to glaze over as the image of two miners played onscreen, with one miner turning out to be a woman. She tossed her long blond locks and gestured seductively to the other miner as she slipped out of the jumpsuit. Adam felt himself stiffen as he watched the woman stroke the tubing of the miner's breathing apparatus, the miner's breaths coming out short and hollow, Darth Vader–like, keeping time with Adam's own. He watched as the light from the miner's hard hat scanned the woman's face, traveling down her neck before stopping at the red heart tattoo just above her left breast. His stomach tightened in anticipation as the miner's hands began to shake. His own fists clenched as the miner grabbed the woman firmly by the shoulders and shoved her back roughly onto the tip of the waiting pickax. His mouth twisted in a mime of the close-up shot of the woman's red lips as they stretched into a long, pre-title scream.

Adam had a soft spot in his heart for crazy Harry Warden. He really dug the miner's outfit he used, even purchasing a gas mask just like the one Harry wore in the film. There weren't many opportunities to wear the damn thing, of course. He had only worn it once, in fact, that time last September when he finally hooked up with the chat-line guy who'd pleaded for a decapitation. But the guy hadn't liked Adam's chosen ensemble, had called him a freak.

The asshole called chat lines begging strangers to cut off his head, but he was the freak?

As the ill-fated youthful denizens of *My Bloody Valentine* went about their way prepping for the town's first Valentine's Day Dance in twenty years, Valentine's Bluff morphed into Barnesville. Adam wished they had a crazy Harry Warden, some deranged miner who'd go postal on the town with his pickax. He fantasized that all the town whores would get red, heart-shaped boxes delivered to their homes, eagerly tearing into them only to find decomposing human hearts inside. He imagined a simultaneous chorus of screams from across the town, imagined Harry Warden decked out in full miner's regalia as he walked down the center of town swinging his pickax. The whores would peer from behind the corners of their curtained windows, frightened by his power and terrified of the carnage he would unleash at nightfall.

The theater door swung inward in his direction, and bright light suddenly ripped Adam from his daydream. He recognized Brad, who seemed taller and more handsome than he remembered in simple jeans and a T-shirt. Caught up in his excitement, Adam forgot the movie and jumped up from his seat, startling the boy.

"Hey, Brad! I knew you'd come today." There was a startled sound from behind Brad, and a girl's head peered around his muscular frame.

"You *know* this guy?" came the girl's incredulous voice. She was shorter than Brad, pretty in a whorish kind of way. She smelled of her mother's good perfume and cigarettes. Brad looked momentarily disoriented, taken off guard by Adam's enthusiasm. He blinked several times, as if trying to place Adam in proper context.

"Yes, he knows me. I'm his friend Adam. We watched *Black Christmas* together. Tell her, Brad," Adam said in almost childlike tones, eager for the confusion to be behind them. Brad looked back at him, still blinking. Slowly, his expression changed as time and place found their respective spots on the shelf of his mind. His face contorted into a wrinkled look of disgust and contempt.

"This is the freak who made a pass at me when I was watching some piece of shit slasher movie last Christmas," he said to the girl without moving his eyes from Adam's face. Now it was Adam's turn to blink as his face went numb, his mouth slack-jawed at Brad's sudden viciousness. The little bitch behind him stepped out to stand next to him, emboldened by Brad's machismo. She giggled.

"What do you want, you fucking pervert?" Brad demanded. "Aren't I a little too old for you, dude?" Adam could feel a stir behind him as other patrons started to turn around in their seats to investigate the sudden ruckus at the back of the theater. He could only continue to stare at Brad's face, trying to comprehend the origin of the anger and rage that seemed to seep through every pore of the boy's skin. His cheeks suddenly felt flushed, his head heavy and throbbing.

"I…" His words trailed off, as if he were having a stroke.

"Get the hell away from me, you freakin' pedo," Brad said, pushing Adam backward. Adam fell back into his seat, stunned, as Brad and his little whore brushed past him and headed for the front of the theater. His eyes already burned from the tears welling up around their perimeter. He felt powerless to close his own mouth. His right hand went to the center of his chest where Brad's hand had connected roughly seconds before, and Adam could swear he felt the imprint of Brad's hand burned into this flesh.

Slightly breathless, Adam turned his eyes back to the screen. He watched through water-rimmed eyes as crazy Harry held Sylvia by her head, her arms and legs flailing as he carried her effortlessly backward toward the jagged water pipe jutting out of the wall. The demented miner gave the screaming girl one last lift and shoved the back of her head roughly into the pipe. And as the rushing water from the pipe mingled with Sylvia's blood and poured from her mouth like a macabre spigot, Adam's tears released, coursing down his cheeks in the darkened movie theater. He was ten years old again, and Brad had just ripped up his beloved comic books.

❖

May

Adam squinted in the bright spring sunlight as he emerged from the Liberty. He stood alone on the sidewalk in front of the theater for a moment, looked up at the brilliant blue sky, and inhaled deeply. The faint scent of freshly cut grass and spring flowers from the lawn of the municipal building across the street intermingled with the smell of car exhaust from the automobiles idling at the traffic light on Main Street. The last of the Episcopal church's Sunday services had let out; churchgoers were now making their way to the bakery to get the last of the crumb buns and fresh baked bread before old Mrs. Shindley and her daughters closed up shop for the day.

It was just after 1:30 p.m., and Adam had been the only patron in attendance for the Liberty's first matinee at noon. While moviegoers were likely to spend the more innocuous holidays like Halloween and Valentine's Day watching a slasher film, few could reconcile the sentimentality of Mother's Day with slicing and dicing. Still, he had a particular fondness for *Mother's Day,* and enjoyed spending time with inbreds Ike and Addley as they raped, tortured, and otherwise terrorized Abbey, Jackie, and Trina at the urging and bequest of their redneck mama.

Adam would take some good old-fashioned misogynistic sadism over trite Hallmark schmaltziness any day.

Adam started east down Main Street, stopping at an assortment of items gathered on the sidewalk at his feet. Their presence was out of place, the incongruousness of the display making it impossible to pass it by without looking. Several glass-ensconced candles, their wicks long ago burned down to nothingness, stood amidst a makeshift shrine. Cards with hopeful messages and prayers were wedged between bouquets of dried and decaying flowers and other trinkets—a teddy bear dressed in a football jersey, a high school yearbook, and several photos warped and faded by the elements. A solitary flyer with the headline *Missing* was taped on the wall of the theater above the display. A handsome, youthful face framed by thick golden hair looked out with promise on the world. Adam viewed the menagerie with indifference for a moment, his eyes scanning these tokens that expressed some collective sense of simultaneous hope and anguish. He cocked his head to one side, then shoved his hands into the pockets in his khakis and continued down Main Street.

He ducked in at the local Eckerd drugstore and returned to the sidewalk moments later carrying a flat paper bag and a small bouquet of slightly withered yellow carnations wrapped in cellophane. The floral pickings were slim this time of day, but these would have to suffice. Adam turned right onto Highland Street and walked the two remaining blocks to his destination.

He paused in front of the Barnesville Convalescent Center, admiring the exterior of the building long ago abandoned to disrepair. The nursing home was one of the glorious old-school varieties—not like the newfangled facilities that adopted that pseudo-Victorian look and almost blended into the neighborhood with wraparound porches and gables and turrets. No, Barnesville Convalescent Center stood defiant in its shabbiness—from its uninviting red brick façade punctuated by the occasional gutter hanging precariously off its roof, to the neglected grounds reduced to a few measly patches of crabgrass and a pot full of pansies planted by some well-meaning activities director who had probably long ago fled for greener pastures. Even the nursing home's choice to retain the far less aesthetically pleasing moniker of *convalescent center* bucked the popular trend toward sugarcoating old age and death: *healthcare facility, care center, nursing and rehabilitation center.*

Convalescent was a fitting term speaking honestly of the piss and shit and decay and dying characterizing such places.

Adam had chosen it for Elaine Mitchell because the ambience matched his mother's withered, feeble body and the sheer ugliness of her spirit. Following her stroke five years ago, he'd been offered several choices by a well-intentioned social worker at the hospital. She had spread out a half dozen or so brochures for him to peruse, launching into a polished discourse about how to pick a nursing home for a loved one. But Adam had barely heard the social worker's fluent dissertation on what questions to ask when considering such facilities when he spotted the cover of a brochure featuring the red brick building he stood in front of now. He remembered fingering through the other brochures, with their sunny shots of sprawling, manicured lawns and close-up shots of kindly old people smiling fondly at impeccably uniformed caregivers, and reaching for the one with no fancy catchphrase about caring for your loved one like family, but simply spelled out the nursing home's name in plain Times New Roman lettering with a dingy shot of the building underneath it.

"This one," Adam had said with uncharacteristic conviction, tapping the brochure firmly with his index finger. The social worker could only stare at him in disbelief.

"But perhaps you'd like…" she began earnestly.

"I *want* this one," Adam had demanded.

Defeated, the social worker had arranged for Elaine Mitchell's transfer to the Barnesville Convalescent Center on a snowy January morning five years ago. The nursing home proved to be a bastion of melancholy and degradation for its inhabitants. On good days, his mother was gotten out of bed. She was fed unappetizing pureed food while sitting at a half-moon-shaped table alongside five other residents as an overworked nurse's aide systematically went down the line and shoved spoonfuls of bland-looking glop into flaccid mouths. Sometimes the nurse's aide would forget to switch spoons, nervously glancing up to where Adam sat watching from the corner, offering a shrug of silent apology.

But Adam never complained about the care—which on good days was poor at best.

Adam was, in fact, one of the most popular family members who ever set foot in Barnesville Convalescent Center. The skeleton crew of staff nurses, nurse's aides, and activities director who called out bingo numbers in a droning monotone to a sea of semi-comatose residents staring off into nothingness seemingly admired Adam's loyalty to his mother. But the reality of his relationship with the caregivers at the Barnesville Convalescent Center was they cared less about the selflessness of his daily visits than they did about the fact that he appeared to turn a blind eye when he caught one of them slapping an unruly resident into submission or pilfering money from a newly arrived birthday card. Adam was indeed well-regarded—not as a model son, but as a silent co-conspirator in the ongoing perpetration of abuse and mistreatment at the home.

"Hello, Mother," Adam said tersely as he walked into the room Elaine Mitchell shared with four other residents. Today was a bad day, when staffing levels were critical, and his mother remained in bed wearing her bedclothes from the night before. He pulled a vinyl guest chair over to her bedside, set the paper bag and flowers down, and pulled a long length of tattered privacy curtain around the bed. His mother lay inert, her frail body perfectly centered on the twin mattress. A flimsy sheet covered her brittle limbs. Two sharp eyes followed him—the only part of her body she was still able to consciously control.

Adam sat down and pulled the chair closer, holding up the bouquet of carnations close to her face. "Look what I've brought you, Mother," he cooed. "You know what today is, don't you?"

Elaine Mitchell blinked at her son.

"Why, it's Mother's Day, silly." He laughed, tossing the bouquet onto the bedside table. "And today I have a very special treat for you, Mother." Adam looked down at her as if expecting an excited reply.

He regarded her for a long moment, trying to locate the vibrant, strong woman she once was. Despite the wrinkles and yellowed hair, the slackened jaw and sagging skin around her neck, he caught a glimpse of the old mean-spiritedness in her eyes. Although the shell was failing her, the mind stayed sharp and alert behind a voiceless mouth, sewn shut by the cerebrovascular accident that had set Adam free and turned the tables on her.

Now the wrath was *his,* playing out in painfully slow increments of time in this hellhole of a nursing home.

Adam picked up the paper bag and slid the thin comic book out reverently, like it was an artifact of priceless beauty. He gazed down at the cover, taking in the colorful images of superheroes and villains battling in the air above some futuristic metropolis while frightened city dwellers fled in panic. These characters were unfamiliar to him now; his beloved favorites were long ago relegated to the backburner to make room for the new and improved variety of superhero. *My superheroes.*

The ones unceremoniously shredded in an act of maternal carnage at the hands of the wretched old woman lying in the bed before him.

He looked up from the comic book at her, his eyes glassy with the emotional scars of years past. Elaine Mitchell met her son's eyes, her gaze momentarily triumphant before flickering into two opaque puddles of fear. She was in there, but the old self was caving into the new. Her new self transferred the power of the old self to Adam—restoring him, rejuvenating him, healing him.

Adam smiled down at his mother, opened the comic book, and began to read.

CAPTURING JOVE LUNGE
STEVE BERMAN

O h, how the cab stank. A rattling heater raised from the scarred seats the ghosts of dog-cheap cigars the driver must have smoked over decades. Like the one he was savoring now. Trapped in the back, Gus rolled down the window to let fresh air, cold and late January sharp, seep inside.

He regretted the boss insisting he take the train from New York to Providence rather than drive the Rover. Saul had sworn that the best way into this case was for Gus to appear down on his luck. Which meant a visit to a rag shop to buy some fellow's former Sunday best. Underneath his trusty pea coat, though, Gus's immense frame strained the suit's threadbare patches.

The cabbie took a turn too sharply. Brakes squealed as the car tires struggled to stay along the snow-covered road. The seams in Gus's sleeves tore as he stretched his thick arms to keep from tumbling about the backseat.

Gus whistled his appreciation when the house came into view. Saul had been square with him about the artist's taste: something out of a storybook, with lots of shingles, a crooked roof, and plenty of eaves. Gus expected Boris Karloff to be sitting on the front porch with his hands cupped around a steaming mug of joe.

The cab slowed on the cobblestone driveway, which circled a frozen fountain. The driver chewed around the stogie stub and muttered that he'd return the next night. Gus grabbed his bag and had barely stepped out of the car when the cab drove off, one rear door swinging like a canary's broken wing. Gus considered pitching a rock at the cabbie's back window, but he made it a point not to earn trouble while always anticipating it.

He'd have to demand Saul send him someplace warm and inviting for the next job.

A pair of custom-made knockers, brass fists gripping lightning bolts, decorated the gaunt doors. Their metal felt colder than a moll's heart when Gus struck them against the wood.

A few minutes later the door cracked open. One rheumy eye glared at Gus, who cleared his throat. "Yeah, Mr. Moiren is expecting me."

The door opened wider, revealing more of the dark-suited butler, a thin man in his late fifties with a blood-red eye patch hiding the worst of the damage suffered by the right side of his face. The man's rigid stance suggested he'd once served in the military. A Great War veteran, Gus suspected as the man moved aside for him to enter.

The butler accepted Gus's pea coat. "Master Moiren will receive you in the greenhouse."

"That ain't like the poorhouse, is it?" Gus made sure to bray like an ass. *Nothing's a worse tell than a man's laugh,* Saul always said, and if Moiren and the help thought Gus was a moron, it would make finding the girl easier.

"You may leave your bag here," the butler said as he hung the coat on a nearby rack. Gus counted the other coats. None looked like they'd belong to a spoiled rich girl, but that didn't mean Samantha Kingsford wasn't here.

A grandfather clock in the many shadows of the foyer chimed three in the afternoon. Mournful sounds.

The house's drafty interior wasn't much warmer than the outside. Most rooms weren't lit. Frost caked the windows. Gus rubbed his palms together. "All right, pally, lead the way." His breath rose in the air.

"This way," said the butler with the lift of a hand.

Rich men didn't impress Gus. They hid behind money—or used it as license to be vicious and petty. But Saul liked dealing with the wealthy. Men like Donald Kingsford, father to a wayward daughter who needed returning.

"Big enough joint for just Moiren and you." Gus paused to stick his head up the flue of a blackened stone fireplace roomy enough to roast a pig, like they did in Polynesia. But the hearth was cold. What good were such things if they weren't used?

"The master entertains on occasion."

"This be one of those occasions?"

But the butler said nothing. He didn't need to. Gus had already caught a whiff of perfume, expensive perfume, in the house's draft. And this house lacked any feminine touch, so he doubted there was a Mrs. Moiren.

No, Samantha Kingsford was here.

❖

When he walked into the massive space confined by a lattice of fogged glass and damp copper, Gus shook off the house's chill like a soaked dog. The humid air reeked, a bit like an outhouse in July, a bit like Brussels sprouts steaming on a plate. Gus had been born in the city; Central Park was the only spot on Earth with so much green. The closest he'd ever come to the jungle was admiring Johnny Weissmuller in that Tarzan talkie. But Moiren's greenhouse had taken a chunk of South America—or maybe Africa—and held it prisoner in Providence. Gus didn't spook much, but he knew he didn't belong any place surrounded by wild foliage.

A voice from on high called out, "Welcome." Gus looked up. Half-hidden behind shoots and wide leaves, a scaffolding covered part of the greenhouse wall. A man wearing a bruise-colored satin smoking jacket and a ridiculous red felt hat with a tassel stepped toward the railing. He held aloft a struggling rabbit for a moment, then dropped the animal down into the brush. "Our Jove Lunge, the Man of Daring, has arrived." Nestor Moiren—Gus recognized him from the photos Saul had spread over his messy desk—clapped with limp wrists.

"The name's Gus."

"As if it matters." Moiren's slippers echoed through the greenhouse as he descended the scaffolding stairs. "How are you finding Providence?"

"Cold."

"Yes. It is." Moiren had a puffy face, but thin lips. Gus had seen other men wear that same smirk, usually right before they threw lead around or tried to shiv you in the guts. "Did your man tell you what I require?"

Gus rubbed his square jaw. Saul had a number of guys working for him. Gus normally was called when the job required brawn and intimidation, not retrieving runaways. But Saul thought a guy playing off Moiren's fascination with muscle would have an easier time getting the girl back. "Said you needed some hired muscle."

"Indeed I do, but not the sort you're used to providing." Moiren turned to the butler. "I think the *Howl of Black Shuck* will do nicely."

The butler bent with an audible creak and left the greenhouse.

"That name I called you…Jove Lunge—"

Gus shrugged as he slipped off his jacket. Sweat had begun seeping down his back.

"—have you never read the Jove Lunge adventure stories?"

"Never made it past the race cards." Gus loosened his collar. "So who you want me to slug?" When people thought he was just some sap, they got lazy…and showed their hand sooner. Gus could tip a card, but he was no easy mark.

Moiren chuckled like a dying man's last wheeze. "A rare *Nepenthes,* but that comes later. Here we are." Moiren lifted a hand as the butler returned carrying a framed painting.

Gus paid little mind to art. He did appreciate the photos in *Iron Man* magazine. But those museums all over Manhattan were too quiet for his liking. Not that there was anything quiet about *Howl of the Black Shuck.* The hackles rose on the back of Gus's thick neck as he glanced at it.

One glance at the figure of Jove Lunge, his uniform flayed to shreds by the panther in his path, told Gus that Moiren liked his men strapping, all bulging muscle and taut sinew. Lunge held in one clenched fist an exotic dagger. When Gus examined the panther, he realized the beast wasn't a cat at all, but an immense black dog or wolf with blood-red eyes.

"I do love my work." Moiren motioned for the butler to withdraw, as if shooing an errant fly. "There are others, if you wish to see the gallery."

Gus shook his head. He wanted nothing more than to step out of the hot greenhouse and pour a cold beer down his throat.

"No? Pity." He took a few steps closer to Gus. "What I need from you is to pose."

"Pose?" Saul had shown Gus the covers. His first thought was, *How many boys buy the adventures of Jove Lunge, Man of Daring to jerk off to pictures of their heroes?*

Did their mothers find the books hidden beneath the bed and wish their husbands had even a tenth of Jove's stature?

"Yes, yes. One would think, after thirty covers, I would have committed to memory every display of hard muscle and tendon the Man of Daring possessed." Moiren stroked his lips a moment. "But I find it more satisfying to draw from life, capturing the moment."

"It's your spinach."

"An apt bit of jargon," Moiren said and rubbed a nearby leaf as large as Gus's head.

Gus bet the Arrow Collar Man never had done this. "So I should—"

"Unbutton your shirt, Mr. Lunge."

Gus did as asked.

"Stretch your arms wide. Curl them in. And...release. Yes, you may well be the best I have seen in some time. Lately I've received such poor offerings..." Moiren sighed. No, more like hissed.

"Now, rip your undershirt."

"What?" Gus looked down at the tight cotton taut over his torso. The front was damp with sweat, darkened by his chest hair.

"Rip. That. Undergarment. Now."

Gus shrugged and took hold of the shirt by the curve by his neck and tore. Worn fabric ripped apart in his fists.

A silken leash of saliva linked Moiren's parted jaws. The man's excitement was evident in his trousers.

"Don't you need your paints or something?" Gus asked. He brushed the front of his chest to tease the man.

"Yes, yes." Moiren's voice had softened to an awed whisper.

"Moiren. Moiren!"

The man's trance broke. "Oh, we can't begin painting now. The light fails. Too weak to illuminate the necessary daring. That will happen come morning. Besides, you have yet to meet my other guests."

❖

Once out of the greenhouse, Gus wiped the sweat from his chest with the ripped undershirt and felt like buttoning his shirt was akin to returning to civilization. The butler took him upstairs via a groaning staircase and down a dim hallway of closed doors. The butler stopped at the third. "This will be your room for the night. Supper is served within the hour. Proper attire is hanging in the closet." The butler turned a key in the lock. "Do not be late."

Gus anticipated a room decorated like a madam's boudoir, with plenty of pillows, dark furniture, and too much burgundy, like God spilt the wine all over the place—not a room with holes in the plaster walls, a sagging bed that belonged in a flophouse, and a pipsqueak in his undershirt, with his suspenders hanging down and a face full of lather by the water bowl and mirror. The kid held a straight razor. He could have stepped off the streets of New York, like any of the city gamins, swiping fruit, picking pockets, all the ways for a dirty squirt to learn the hard lessons life demanded.

"You don't look old enough to shave," Gus said as he threw his travel bag on the bed. Bad springs groaned. Sleeping on that would be rough.

"And you look like the lost son of Kong." Gus couldn't place the kid's accent but admired his moxie—though his eyes were wide, showing nerves. "The Empire State Building is thataway, big fella." The kid gestured at the window with the razorblade.

Gus strode over to the kid, who retreated in turn until he bumped against the slender table beneath the water bowl. Warm water sloshed them both, but most of it dripped down the kid's scrawny chest.

"W-What, you wanna see my diploma?" the kid asked.

"Who the hell are you?" Gus forced the kid against the faded wallpaper.

"Haven't you ever read a Jove Lunge novel?"

"Lemme guess. You're the shoeblack boy?" Gus grabbed the kid by the neck. The lather made the grip like catching an eel in water. He didn't want to strangle the kid, just make sure he knew who was tops. The razor dropped from the kid's hand to clatter on the floorboards. "Perhaps you should find another room."

"I-I can't," the kid rasped. "Moiren…"

"He put you in here?"

The kid nodded. Spittle frothed his pretty lips.

"Why?"

"Please…"

Gus released the kid, who collapsed to the floor, where he sputtered a while. Gus kicked the blade out of his reach, not that he looked like he had any spirit in him. "So?"

"Moiren didn't know if you'd rather have kitten or keister."

"So she is here." Gus wiped his hands dry on the towel.

The kid shrugged. "The girl? I just saw her once, when she came in." The kid rubbed his neck. "Moiren's sedan brought her."

"What's your name?"

"Carl. Carl Heim."

Gus nodded. "Okay, Carl, you better clean up. I don't share a bed with bums." *What kind of a job did I get into here?* he thought. *Nancies in a weird greenhouse wanting to paint me stripped down fighting boogeymen.*

❖

The dining room was long and narrow. Everything was dark wood and shining silverware, which reminded Gus of a coffin at a funeral. At least a fire roared in the fireplace chasing away some of the chill. Moiren, now dressed in a tuxedo and a Kraut's spiked helmet, sat at the far end of the table. Gus took a seat at the man's left. He fingered a knife and wondered if he could make the throw if he had to. He remembered that time in Red Hook...

"Ah, I see your oldest friend's son has arrived," Moiren said as Carl walked into the room. "Do join us, Timmy."

The kid cleaned up well. Some would even call him pretty, with that chestnut hair slicked and parted down the center.

"Mr. Lunge, I won't ask you to recount your time spent exploring Egypt with the professor who fell victim to the Blue Pharaoh's sinister death traps. I applaud your kindness at making Timmy your ward and constant companion on your more recent adventures."

"Hope you're luckier than your old man, Timmy," Gus said.

Carl took the seat directly across the table from him.

When she sauntered into the room, Moiren rose from his seat. The photographs of Samantha Kingsford Saul had shown Gus failed to capture her smoulder. Her hair might have been coiled flames. She wore a skimpy number that would have given the happiest of married fellas nervous ideas. Those red and plump lips savored, rather than breathed, the air. She was trouble, all tied up like a kid's Christmas present.

"Miss Samantha, how pleasant you could join us tonight."

"And who is she?" Gus asked. "Jove's squeeze?"

Moiren giggled a moment. "Oh, no. She doesn't have a part to play. At least not yet. That all depends on you, Mr. Lunge."

"I hope we're having steak. I just adore a good cut of meat." Samantha took the only empty seat, beside Carl, who glowered at her with about as much fondness as a mouse would to an alley cat.

"I haven't quite decided her role. She would make an excellent ingénue in distress. Or maybe a temptress playing a risky game. Yes, I think you would all agree—"

"I hope that the dress came free with the perfume." Carl rubbed his nose. She gave him a scathing look in return.

"Well, now that we are all here." Moiren gestured to the butler, who poured red wine for all. "A toast. *To Jove Lunge in the Jungle of Doom.* And to proving Oscar Wilde right. 'Life imitates art far more than art imitates life.'"

Gus brought the wine to his mouth, hesitated a moment, and trusted that the same iron gut owned by his father would keep him safe from mickeys. The wine tasted sour, but Moiren smacked his lips in appreciation. It must have been expensive, probably from France or Italy but kept dusty in the cellar for years.

"And what will be the feature course tonight, sir?" asked the butler.

"Mr. Lunge, as the guest of honor the choice is yours. Would you prefer the game hen—"

Samantha ran a finger around the edge of her wineglass. Gus felt something touch his thigh beneath the table.

Her stockinged foot, probably.

"—or the capon?"

Carl blushed and he looked into the fire.

Gus realized Moiren wasn't talking food. Was the man testing him? Could he suspect why Gus was really there, or was this simply a game for his amusement?

Neither sat well with Gus.

"Perhaps he would like a nice prawn, sir." Gus stiffened when the butler's long fingers stroked their way down his back.

"I'll take the capon." Better a familiar dish than one he didn't like prepared...

"No one ever picks the prawn," the butler said with a heavy sigh and returned to the kitchen.

Samantha wore a bored pout—what reckless rich girls like to try on when they've been turned down. Carl squirmed, almost like Gus had grabbed him by the throat again.

❖

After dinner, they followed their host into a drafty drawing room decorated—no, Gus decided that wasn't the right word—*marred,* or maybe cursed, by his paintings. A Jove Lunge broke the jaw of a masked man with a fierce right hook; another Jove strangled a man in an underground grotto's pool; a dangling Jove clutched the torn canvas of a dirigible covered in Oriental characters; Jove crouched, ready to pounce, behind an idol that resembled a leering squid while scarlet-robed men prepared to sacrifice a chesty dame in front. Each painting, each cover, was more reckless, more absurd than the one before.

Brandy was poured. Moiren struck a match to a pipe, one of those long affairs, with tobacco reeking like a bad fruit pie left too long in the oven.

The butler offered them cigarettes from a silvered case. Samantha reached over Gus's arm to take one.

"So, was it Daddy?" she whispered to him as the butler offered a flame.

"What?"

She leaned closer. "I assume it was either Daddy or James who hired you."

Gus began to suspect this wasn't the first time Samantha had strayed. "Lady, I don't know what you're talking about. Moiren hired me to be his hamfatter or model or something for the weekend." He glanced in the direction of his host, who had taken Carl aside to show him some etchings.

"I read those tiresome Jove Lunge books. He rescues the girl at the end. Every time, even when she's no good for him."

"Doesn't sound like Jove's a sharp fella."

"No. Doesn't. Some girls don't want to be rescued." She blew a stream of bluish gray smoke into his face.

"Isn't always up to the girl. Not when she's featured on the society page. All it does is make men wager on how fast and far they'll run. Like they do with horses on the racing pages."

She frowned. "Unless you have a sedan in your pocket, I'm not going back with you to New York, Mr. Lunge."

The reward for her return wasn't scratch, but Gus found himself curious why she was there. Couldn't be for the company—Moiren was one brushstroke away from being tossed into the loony bin. No, something was wrong, so he scrapped his original plan of grabbing her, kicking and screaming over his shoulder if necessary, and stealing one of Moiren's cars.

"So am I the only one here who doesn't appreciate art?" he asked.

A bored expression passed over her features. Even though Samantha knew the truth, she dismissed him as uninteresting. She seemed not to care if their host knew as well. Was that part of this entire game, or was she daring him to take her back home? And why, Gus had to wonder, had she run away to Moiren's in the first place?

❖

Gus sat up in bed in just his boxers, smoking one of his own cigarettes, not the awful tobacco Moiren offered. He was waiting to see who'd come through the door. Despite his being a gambling man, he wouldn't have wagered. Could be any of the lot.

The knob turned. The door opened a couple inches and the kid peered past the frame.

Maybe I should have played the favorite, Gus thought and motioned for him to come inside.

"Why'd you pick me? You don't seem a queer."

"Maybe I don't like uppity dames." He tapped a bit of ash over the side of the bed. "Or maybe I like kids that are scared of me."

"I'm not scared."

Gus patted the edge of the bed. "Then you better get over here."

Carl walked over to the bed and lifted the pack of cigarettes from the sheets. He tapped out one and set it between his lips. Then he plucked the lit cigarette from Gus's mouth to set his own smoldering. "You trust Moiren?"

Gus let loose a laugh. "Kid, I don't trust anyone." He stroked Carl's thighs through his trousers. He normally didn't play with rabbits, but the kid was begging for it. "Some don't worry me, though." Moiren, though, Gus had to admit, something about the man worried him.

"I asked Moiren why he—"

"Hired you?" Maybe the kid was no chump after all. "What'd he say?"

"That Jove Lunge had a connection with all his comrades. If Lunge didn't have feelin's for Timothy, then the paintin' would be insincere."

"And pairing us up is supposed to start feelings?"

"Like a couple of real nancies." Carl laughed, but he kept those brown eyes on Gus.

Yeah, begging for it. "I can feel you shaking."

"Am not."

Gus grabbed at the kid's crotch, squeezing tight, not enough to cause pain, but staking his claim. The kid definitely trembled.

Moaned a little, too.

"Maybe you don't trust me."

Carl reached out to touch Gus's bare chest. His fingers lightly tugged the curled hair, squeezed the hard slabs of pectoral muscle. "Honest, you're bigger than I'm used to. I think it would be like wrestling a bear."

Gus let go of the kid's crotch but grabbed his arm and pulled him down into bed, onto him. "Get ready to make me growl, kid," he muttered before his lips took on Carl's.

❖

While the kid slept, Gus slipped out of the bed. He opened his bag. His only change of clothing was a thick black sweater and dark trousers—he didn't intend to stay for breakfast. At the bottom of the bag was a pair of brass knuckles. He didn't like guns, delivering the goods over the last six years without having to resort to one. He slipped the heavy brass into a pocket.

He found the door locked. Not much of a surprise. He could force it easily, but that would be tipping his hand too soon. And he still didn't know where Samantha was staying in the mansion.

That left the window.

He glanced back at Carl. If Gus did find Samantha and did throw her into the back of whatever sedan Moiren kept in his garage, where would that leave the kid? A loose end. Saul hated loose ends. Gus wasn't fond of them, either. But coming back for the kid would be a mistake. You don't wager on a slow horse.

The window latch turned without effort and Gus stepped out on to the ledge. He was thankful that the bitterly cold night air lacked a biting wind. He inched along, wary of his step, peering into the other windows he passed, but saw no sign of Samantha.

As he neared one set of eaves, he noticed an old barn a couple hundred feet away from the house. Moonlight showed fresh footprints in the snow leading back and forth. That made Gus curious. He didn't care for the feeling—he wasn't paid to be inquisitive, he was no flatfoot or private dick—but everything about Moiren left him on edge. Not knowing what was in the barn seemed like a mistake. Mugs like him didn't outlive mistakes.

He jumped off the ledge, his landing cracking the semi-frozen surface of the snow, before rolling to his feet. He looked over his shoulder. The mansion remained dark and still.

The padlocked barn doors looked ready to collapse inward. Gus took hold of the latch. The muscles in his arms strained as he tore it free of the doors, which buckled but didn't fall.

Gus didn't step inside until his eyes adjusted to the darkness. The old scent of hay couldn't disguise a new odor. Musky, like a kennel—which meant some animal or animals, big and furry. His ears caught the rattle of chains from deeper in the barn. Cautious, but curious what the hell Moiren was keeping inside, he crept forward.

A moment before he noticed the crimson eyes high off the ground staring at him, Gus heard the rumble. A growl.

Heavy paws pounded the packed earthen floor of the barn. The heavy chain warned him, and he stumbled back, slamming against the doors, as massive jaws began snapping the air where he'd stood seconds earlier.

Black wolves aren't supposed to be the size of Packards.

A hand reached in through the cracked doors and pulled Gus back into the open. The shivering butler held a lantern. Moiren, dressed in a heavy fur coat, cradled an elephant gun in his arms. He wore another ridiculous hat, a Revolutionary War tricorn, and a tremendous smirk.

"So, Mr. Lunge, would you say this night is fit for neither man nor beast?"

"What is that thing!?"

The butler shut the doors.

"A *lusus naturae*. A *fantoccini* created especially for my art." Moiren looked over his shoulder at the house. "Shall we head back, or would you prefer to reenact something I painted ages ago?"

Gus nodded. He felt like someone had changed the landscape on him, tossing him off a map of the real world and into the pages of a nightmare book.

As they trudged through the snow, Moiren rested the rifle against his shoulder.

"Are you a good shot?" Gus asked.

"I've studied the male anatomy all my life. There are entry wounds that will never heal properly, leaving a man crippled for life. I suppose I could aim to be kind, but what sport is that?"

Gus's guts told him Moiren wasn't boasting. He no longer seemed like the silly fool Gus had thought he was. The danger level had just doubled. Gus paused and turned back to the barn. "How many Lunges have there been?"

The other two men stopped. The butler began counting on his fingers.

"I mean, have you ever used the same fella twice?"

Moircn wheezed that awful laugh. "Twice? My good man, I'd be astonished."

"Sir, might I recommend some brandy and Benedictine to warm us?" said the butler.

Gus thought a stiff drink might be the only thing sane waiting for him back at the house. The job wasn't going to be easy anymore.

"Were you frightened?" Moiren asked as he sipped his drink from a flame-warmed snifter.

"I think when you see a wolf the size of a city bus, you've every right to sweat a little."

"Well said. You are not only a man of action—scaling walls and trudging through my backyard tundra—but also a man of sense. Both admirable qualities in a hero."

"Heroes are short-lived."

"Oh, no, Mr. Lunge. You've faced some terrible things—the Hindoo Rahu, Captain Dream and his Zeppelin Marauders, even the Sons of Caqueux in Brittany…a favorite of mine, I must admit. Just picturing their weaving nooses from the sleeves of condemned criminals leaves me quivering."

"But they're only stories."

"*Only?* Your modesty is a disservice."

"But you know I'm not really this Lunge fella."

Gus looked at the butler, who gave a tiny nod of disapproval. No—of warning. Too late, because Moiren threw his snifter against the wall.

"You are Jove Lunge!" Moiren ran a hand through his hair, dislodging his tricorn hat. The butler picked it up and brushed the felt with his sleeve. "Don't you see…I need you to be him."

But Gus didn't see, didn't follow him…because the edges of his vision had grown cloudy. He looked down at his own glass and fell forward off the chair.

❖

The headache, the awful dryness in his mouth, the reluctance of his eyes to open wide enough to see right all told Gus he had one mother of a hangover. Only he couldn't remember having more than a glass. Guess his only inheritance from his old man wasn't proof against a Mickey Finn slipped into his drink.

He groaned and rolled over, felt someone warm next to him, cracked his eyes again. Some young guy, dressed like a Boy Scout, started rubbing Gus's stomach.

"Please tell me you didn't help me cross the street and into a bar."

The kid's hand drifted lower than Gus's waist. "I did my good deed. Twice last night. But today…"

Gus wiped his face with one hand. Despite the way he felt, the kid was managing to wake the rest of him. "Carl, right?"

The kid nodded. Looked even a bit hurt.

"Why are you dressed like that?"

"That butler knocked on the door an hour ago and brought us our costumes."

"Any chance he brought a cup of joe—or better, a beer?"

"Moiren wants us in the greenhouse."

Gus sat up and winced. Then other memories from last night came back to him. Sneaking outside. Seeing the largest mutt in the world chained up in the barn. The Mickey in his drink. The butler must have carried his unconscious body back to bed—not that the guy looked like he could handle a sack of potatoes, let alone a dead weight of over two hundred pounds. Maybe he'd had help. Gus looked at the kid. That guileless face smiled at him even as he stroked Gus's dick.

Maybe he wasn't so innocent after all.

"Not now, junior," he said, and took Carl's hand off him. He rose from the bed and went over to the washbowl. He dipped his head into the cold water to chase away the fog behind his eyes.

"Go down and tell Moiren that I'm not stepping into that vegetable soup he calls a greenhouse without breakfast."

Carl left. A few minutes later, the butler brought into the room a tray with cold meats and warm eggs. More importantly, there was a coffeepot.

"Do get dressed quickly. I've never seen the master so eager to begin painting."

I bet, Gus thought.

❖

The clothes were khaki, short-sleeved and short-legged. A bit snug around the thighs. The hard hat, which the butler insisted be referred to as a pith helmet, felt ridiculous. Gus missed his regular derby.

He followed after the butler on the way to the greenhouse when a *thump* stopped him. To his right was the drawing room, the door ajar. He opened it and saw Samantha resting atop the divan, one arm stretched down to the floor. A crystal tumbler lay on a damp patch of the Oriental rug.

"I'd watch what you sip here," Gus said, and sat her up. She looked pale, her eyelids fluttering like a caged bird's wings.

He glanced over his shoulder. The butler remained in the doorway, his face turned in the direction of the room's frosty windows. Decorum, or lack of interest?

"Mr. Lunge." Samantha rested her head on his shoulder. "Do...do you want to know my hidden...my...my secret?"

Her perfume had faded. Only by being so close against her flushed skin could he catch a trace of its former elegance.

"He promised me...Moiren said, 'Your father will never forget how I paint you.'" She slipped an arm around his neck, but the gesture seemed not to be seductive, but rather so she could lean against his chest for strength.

"Listen, I don't think you know the truth about Moiren's paintings." Gus thought back to the massive beast kept in the barn.

But she nodded, a sloppy, drunken gesture. "I want that cold bastard...Daddy to be...haunted."

Gus began to wonder if returning all those girls had been for the best. He'd never failed before. He could deal with Saul's fury at not bringing Samantha back, but he'd have to confront Moiren first.

The butler cleared his throat. "She's for later, Mr. Lunge. Master Moiren is considering...well, the unheard of. He thinks you may be worthy of two paintings. You should feel honored."

"Honored?"

The man adjusted his black jacket a moment. "Save the tempest for the greenhouse, sir. As for her—" The butler kicked the fallen glass under the divan. "She'll do for the sequel. *The Last Libation.*"

"Who writes these books, anyway?"

The butler gestured for Gus to return to the hallway.

"Damn it, who writes them?" Gus yelled. He wanted to grab the guy by his monkey suit's lapels and smash him through a wall.

"Don't you know?" When the butler grinned, his scar rippled like a snake across his face.

❖

Moiren stood by an easel in the heart of the greenhouse. He had traded one odd hat for another, a soft Frenchie number. His smock was stained, mostly in shades of an ugly brown. Gus told himself it had to be paint, not dried blood.

The surrounding plants were bloated and mottled. One had black thorns seeping a clear fluid that could have been tears. Another resembled a gigantic trombone or Englishman's pipe.

"I do hope you both come to appreciate my *Nepenthes rex.* I've spent the last decade cultivating it from seedlings found in the Amazon."

"Listen, pal, I think you should know I didn't come here to be your inspiration."

Moiren smirked. "The Marquis once wrote, 'Truth titillates the imagination far less than fiction.'"

"I don't know what your game is—"

"Art. Rooted in suffering is art."

Gus nodded at Carl. "C'mere, kid. Sorry, Moiren, but I think your guests have had enough of your hospitality."

The familiar click of a safety made Gus's head turn. The butler had leveled the elephant gun first at him, then at the kid.

"I have painted Lunge with bullet wounds in the past." Moiren lowered his voice, perhaps to sound soothing. "You will all be free to go once I am finished."

Gus cursed. He shouldn't care about some gunsel, but the way Carl looked at him, like a dog fearful it would be kicked to the curb, stopped him from tackling the butler. "Fine."

"Wonderful. Now, young Timothy, would you please take a few steps back."

Carl nodded and slowly shuffled backward until he bumped into the swollen body of one of the plants. Emerald vines snapped around his limbs and he was lifted off the ground. Carl struggled and fought to free himself but it happened so fast. The next moment the tendrils dropped the kid into the gourd belly. There came a splash and Carl began screaming, in fear, in agony.

"Not yet, Lunge," shouted the butler, who turned the rifle to Gus. An elephant gun would blast a hole through him.

"It's eating him alive!" Adrenaline rushing through his blood, Gus grabbed at several of the twisting, coarse vines, his ham-sized fists squeezing sticky fluid from them as he tore them apart.

"Yes, yes. Enzymes and mutualistic insect larvae and all that jazz." Moiren waved a paintbrush in bored annoyance, and then turned back to his canvas. "Now whatever happens, don't move."

A LETTER TO MY BROTHER, RELATING RECENT EVENTS WITH UNINTENDED CONSEQUENCES

CAROL ROSENFELD

D earest Rick,
I've gotten myself into a rather awkward situation. I hope you won't be angry with me; it wasn't my fault. Truly, dear.

You know how I am about trends: I was listening to torch songs while other girls were screaming for the Beatles. And I still haven't gotten one of those nuclear physicist phones like the one you have. When I drape myself on my chaise to chat with someone, I simply must have a phone cord trailing through the fingers of one hand.

A couple of years ago Anne Rice was all the rage and then this whole Twilight thing started and I simply could not understand the attraction, the excitement. But I thought maybe if I did a vampire scene with someone, I might get a glimmer of what all the fuss was about. You know what I mean by a scene, dear—make-believe for consenting adults. So I posted an advertisement on some list that begins with a C. Crone's List? No, that's something else. Anyway, I made it known that I was seeking an opportunity to play—*play* being the operative word— with a vampire. Meaning, of course, someone who found it stimulating to simulate a vampire. And I made my sexual preference quite clear.

I received a lovely e-mail from someone named Marty, offering to introduce me to the delights of "neck nibbling." Full sentences, no undecipherable acronyms or abbreviations, perfect spelling and grammar—I e-mailed my phone number and waited for Marty to call.

That night, while I was lying on the aforementioned chaise, the phone rang and someone with a low, sultry voice and some sort of East European accent began speaking. Well, you know how I am about accents; one word and I'm in a muddle, one sentence and I've melted into a puddle. Remember that exquisite Bridget from Dublin and my luverly Maggie from London? And Diana, that splendid Australian I had a fling with when we were in Sydney for the Olympics. Not to mention Merit, that divine Egyptian archeologist we met during our visit to the Valley of the Queens. If you don't remember Merit, I am sure you remember her brother, Minkabh!

Marty and I had an early dinner at a very good steakhouse. Thank heavens it was fairly dark inside, because Marty liked her—his?—but more about that later—steak rather rare, and you know I can't bear to see any red at all in my meat, just a tinge of pink. Well, she—he?—was very gallant—sort of a goth Fred Astaire. The cape Marty was wearing worked very well for the opera, of course—because sometimes a night at the Met is not unlike going to *The Rocky Horror Picture Show*: there was a man in full cowboy gear last year at *The Girl of the Golden West*.

After a wonderful performance of *Don Giovanni*, I invited Marty back here to our cozy penthouse on Central Park West for a nightcap. I remember raising my glass of brandy to my lips, but things get a bit vague after that. Actually, more than a bit. To be completely truthful, I can't remember a damn thing.

When I woke up the next morning the sun was so bright, I thought the ozone layer had vanished altogether, I simply don't understand these climate change deniers. I didn't feel very well. I desperately needed William Powell to bring me "pixie remover," as I believe it was called in *My Man Godfrey*.

But of course we don't have William Powell or David Niven, we have Winifred, who can, you must agree, be rather dour. When she came in with a vase of roses—so red, like drops of—no, I can't even write it, you know how I am about that particular substance—she looked insufferably censorious when she handed me the card. And there wasn't even a message; it was just a business card for a Dr. Vanessa Pearce that said: *Newly undead? I can help*. Well, I had no idea what to make of it, especially since I hadn't had any caffeine or carbohydrates. "What does this mean, Winifred?" I asked, handing her the card.

"It means, Miss Laura, that you've really gone and done it now," she replied. "And I'll not be helpin' you with your despicable, sinful prayin' activities." Well, of course that confused me even more. You know I'm not religious except for the occasional Beltane celebration.

I managed to sit up and noticed my pillow was stained with—that horrible red stuff. I thought Cleopatra might have scratched me while I slept; you know she deigns to share her pillow—which is in fact my pillow—with me. I went into the bathroom and looked in the mirror and there were streaks of—I don't need to spell it out for you, do I, dear? Knowing me so well, I am sure you can envision the scene: I put my hand to my neck, looked at my fingers, and fainted, as I usually do when confronted with—that-which-I-do-not-want-to-even-think-about-much-less-name.

When I came to I was propped up in bed. Winifred must have carried me there. She'd also bandaged my neck. Then she came back into the room with a breakfast tray.

As I was drinking my tea I became aware of some soreness and burning in a certain sensitive place—that is more than enough information for you, I am sure. And I had a flash of memory—it was no more than a flash, if it was indeed a memory and not a hallucination— of thinking how lifelike Marty's cock felt in my hand. Then the memory was gone. "Focus, Laura," I told myself. "You must focus." I was rewarded with another flash—a memory of hair. A lot of it. On a flat chest. I went through a checklist of places women might have hair: head, arms, under arms, legs, between legs. I said, "In general, Winifred, women don't have hair on their chests, do they?"

And she replied, a bit tartly, "No, Miss Laura, in general, they do not." I had to ask myself the question: Had I, without meaning to, slept with—a man? There came another memory, of a scratchy cheek. I'm sure you can appreciate my perturbation! I'm on the host committee of the Womyn-Born-Womyn with Womyn-Born-Womyn (WBW2) ball this year. Not for political reasons, dear, you know I'm not a separatist, but I have my eye on the caterer. She's from Georgia, and she is, indeed, a peach.

Later that day I found myself in the office of Dr. Vanessa Pearce. It looked like an ordinary therapists' office, except for the open coffin in the corner. I opted to sit on the couch. I do hope I won't have to sleep in a coffin now; you know how I love to sprawl out in my queen-sized bed and make angels on the satin sheets.

I got right to the point: "Do you mean to tell me that I'm a vampire now?" Dr. Pearce said denial was the first stage I would have to work through. "But I'm hemaphobic!" I said. (Do note the "e" and "a" vowels, darling! They make such a difference; I wouldn't want any confusion with that other horrible word.)

I thought perhaps I could just buy some of what I would need to drink in a sweet little container like those 187ml Pommery POP champagne bottles with straws I've seen young women drinking. I mean, almost no one—at least, no one we know—hunts and kills their own meat these days, so why should fanged folk have to attack someone for their liquid sustenance? The whole thing should be more civilized. Surely there must be some sort of artificial liquid that would have the same effect as the real thing? I must set up a foundation for research immediately.

Dr. Pearce recommended a support group for the newly undead, "Suck Buddies." I've already been to my first meeting. The idea is for your "Suck Buddy" to offer you support and encouragement during your first bite. It's a very nice group of people; we should have them over for dinner sometime. Or maybe not; I don't know if Uncle Percy could cope. I think his poetic sensibilities only extend so far.

At the meeting, they paired us up. My assigned "Suck Buddy" is Sunny Goldstein, an elementary school teacher. I feel so badly for her, because what on earth is she going to do about her fangs? Children do notice these things. At least Professor Lupin only changed into a werewolf once a month and that was at night, not during school hours.

When it came time to choose the one who would be my first, my initial thought was one of the supermodels, but I realized there's so little to them it's really not fair to drain them of any of the life-giving liquid that they have. And really, they look undead as it is, don't you agree? The Republican presidential candidates were an obvious choice, but I didn't think I could get close enough. Nor did I particularly want to. Then I saw that dreadful woman from the ninth floor of our building; the one with the stiff bouffant white hair and the perennially pink face, parading her miniscule yapping excuse for a dog. And I thought, "I could bite *her.*"

That night I dressed in black—sneakers, socks, jeans, turtleneck, leather jacket, and a watch cap. So unglamorous, but Sunny said, "You just have to get through that first bite, Laura; then you can make the whole thing your own. In fact, let's go shopping tomorrow to celebrate!"

I waited across the street from the apartment, in the shadows close to the entrance to the park. She walked into the park with the dog and I followed her, taking care not to step on any leaves, sticks, pebbles, or discarded trash. When she sat down on a bench while her dog was lifting one of its stick-like legs in the direction of a nearby tree, I waved one of Uncle Percy's linen handkerchiefs dampened with a dab of chloroform under her nose with my left hand and bent down. Sunny, who was watching from the wall alongside the park, whispered to me through the transmitter in my ear, "Laura honey, just close your eyes and pretend you're sipping tomato juice through a straw." And I did—I shut my eyes, chomped, and then sucked away. It was a nasty business; she wasn't tender at all. Still, I like to think you would have been proud of me. Is there anyone you would like me to bite, dearest? That dreadful man who keeps stealing antiquities? An ex, perhaps? We might as well get something good out of this.

I'm heading out soon to go shopping with Sunny, and will drop this letter in the mail on the way to my hat designer. I'm picturing something with a wide brim and a black lace veil.

The next time you see me, try not to be too horrified by the change in my appearance when I smile at you. I do hope you will still love me, as I am, and will always remain,

Your loving sister,
Laura

P.S. I am considering embellishing my new dental additions with what I believe is referred to as "bling." In the words of Lorelei Lee in *Gentlemen Prefer Blondes,* "I just LOVE finding new places to wear diamonds."

ALL THE PRETTY BOYS
MICHAEL ROWE

Dale saw the kid leaning up against a wall on Maitland, just in from Church Street. His first thought was, *Pretty boy. Very pretty.* Dale locked his motorcycle. He sat on the edge of the seat and lit a cigarette.

The kid looked about nineteen. High cheekbones, dark hair. Strong jaw. Blue eyes and long black lashes. There was a light spray of acne on the kid's forehead and some sort of scar—*a sports injury? a fight?*—on his chin, but otherwise his complexion was clear. The scar saved the kid from looking too completely delicate, or even girlish. Good body, lean and rangy. Coyote muscles. When he noticed Dale watching him, he ventured a tentative smile, then immediately looked away. He shuffled his feet nervously, then stood up a little straighter.

Across the street, Church was thronged with people, a riot of noise and color as it always was on Halloween night. Leathermen, drag queens, twinks, news crews from local television stations, and tourists from the suburbs jockeyed for available space with the most dramatically costumed revelers. The spectacle was entirely impossible to ignore. It called to the whole city like a siren. And yet the kid held back, just out of the light.

Vulnerable, Dale thought. He smiled. *New to the city? Maybe a hustler, or maybe just thinking about it.* The kid's jeans and boots were mall-cheap, and even from a distance Dale's expert eye detected that the jacket was vinyl. His hair was unfashionably cut, probably in some small town a long way from here. Definitely Derek's type, too. *Yes,* he thought, *he's the one.*

Dale pulled himself up to his full height of six foot four. He straightened his shoulders and walked over to where the kid was staring at him. The young ones always wanted to feel seduced, romanced, swept off their feet. Dale could do that. No sweat. Looking up, he smiled brilliantly, and the kid melted like they always did.

❖

The kid's slender arms were wrapped tightly around Dale's waist, fingers digging into his leather motorcycle jacket. The black October wind screamed past as they hurtled down the Lakeshore on Dale's 2002 Harley Fat Boy. In the distance, the low caul of clouds glowed with the first fingers of moonlight, and the harsher metallic smack of neon lit the black torrent of highway like phosphorus.

When you ride a Fat Boy you feel like God created asphalt just for you to glide over, Dale thought with familiar ecstasy. It could take ice, or heavy rain, and keep the pavement. Its engine roared like a mating cry. Whenever he started it up, it sounded to Dale like the guttural bellow of a powerful guy just before he shot. To Dale, riding was almost as good as sex. There was no bitch bar behind the seat, and Dale felt the kid's groin tight against his backside, his legs almost tucked under Dale's. He deliberately hit a couple of rough patches on the highway just to feel the kid's crotch vibrating against his back. Dale smiled beneath the visor of his helmet and revved the throttle. The bike shot forward into the night and the kid tightened his grip on Dale's waist.

"Nice bike," the kid had said back on Maitland, indicating Dale's motorcycle where it was parked. He had just arrived in Toronto from North Bay, was named Todd, and hoped to become a model—three facts Dale immediately discarded.

The kid had reached over and run his fingers across Dale's leather motorcycle chaps. "You always wear these? When you ride?"

"Are you into the bike, or into the chaps?"

"Both." The kid smiled winsomely. "I'm into older guys, too."

"I'm thirty," Dale said with mock outrage. "That's not old."

"You have a hot body." This time Dale could hear the lust beneath what the kid clearly thought was a sophisticated seduction on his part. He squeezed Dale's biceps, tentatively first, then with clear hunger. "Nice muscles." He reached up and touched Dale's thick, tanned neck. Reaching higher, he ran his fingers through Dale's black crewcut. Dale stood perfectly still, his eyes locked onto the kid's, and let the inevitable occur.

"You look like a cop," the kid said.

"You like that?" Dale said in a low voice. "You like that I look like a cop?"

"I don't like *cops,* but I like guys who *look* like cops. You're *not* a cop, are you?"

This time he sounded worried. Dale laughed, full and warm, and he felt the kid relax in response to the sound of his laughter.

"No, I'm not a cop." Then Dale threw out the bait. He paused. "I have a lover," he said. "He looks like a cop, too. You want to play with two cops?"

The kid barely hesitated. He put his palm on Dale's leathered thigh. "Will you leave the chaps on? And the jacket?" His breathing quickened with desire.

Dale smiled. "Always," he said. "My lover wears leather, too. We never play without it."

"Cool," the kid said with studied casualness, his voice suddenly tighter and an octave higher. "Where do you live? Nearby?"

Dale indicated the bike with a backward nod of his head. "Hop on. I'll show you."

When the kid hesitated, small-town admonitions about the big bad city at night likely echoing in his relatively empty nineteen-year-old head, Dale wrapped his arms around him and kissed him roughly and possessively on the mouth. When he felt the kid melt into his body, pressing closer, forcing his tongue clumsily into Dale's mouth, he knew the kid was his for the taking.

The house was dark when they pulled into the driveway. Dale cut the engine and dismounted. He removed his helmet and tucked it under his arm. He turned and took the kid's helmet from him. The kid's face was pale, his hair askew. But he looked euphoric.

"What'd you think?" Dale asked. "Did you like it?"

"Loved it," the kid replied. Then, shyly: "It was my first time. I'd love to go again sometime." The streetwise veneer was momentarily abandoned, and Dale saw softness. This was somebody's son a long way from home. He felt a sudden stab of guilt, sharp as a shard of glass. He dug his nails brutally into his inner palm and focused on the pain. When he thought he could barely take it, he squeezed again, harder, till white supernovas exploded behind his eyes and he felt sticky blood in his palm when he pulled his fingers away.

Then he was back in control, and the kid had seen none of it. Dale winked at the kid, dead sexy again. "I'll take you home," he said. "Tomorrow morning. You'll be able to see the sun rise over the lake."

❖

"Where's your lover?" The kid sounded like he was falling asleep. He lay back against the cushions of the couch. He took another swallow of the beer. He grimaced. Dale sat across from him, very still. The light from the hallway gleamed against the leather of his chaps. "You said he'd be here, and it's been, like, half an hour." The words were slurred. "What was his name again?" *Wuhwush hish namagen?*

"I told you. His name is Derek. He's downstairs, changing," Dale said. "He'll be ready for you very soon." Dale looked out the window at the dark lawn and the spreading moonlight. "Let's get you out of those clothes."

Dale stood up and walked over to where the kid was sprawled and began to undress him. The kid's eyelids fluttered as he tried to focus on Dale, then they closed. The beer bottle dropped from his hand and rolled across the floor, the dark amber liquid foaming, staining the rug. Dale leaned down and listened to the kid's breathing. He wasn't sleeping yet, but he was close. Dale finished undressing the kid and then lifted his naked body into his arms. He crossed the living room floor and entered the kitchen. The moonlight was growing brighter and he could see the floor very clearly. He kicked open the door to the cellar, feeling a gust of cold air wafting up from the room far below the cellar. He smelled dampness and mold, and something darker and sweeter underneath that. Dale shuddered and instinctively pulled the kid's body closer as though to warm it, to protect it.

In the sky above the city, the full moon reached its zenith in the October sky, heavy purple and black clouds parting like stage curtains. He knew the moonlight would just now be shattering across the dark waters of Lake Ontario. Dale pictured it pouring down like molten metal.

In the basement *below* the basement, he knew Derek could more than imagine it, he knew Derek could *feel* it. After all these years as lovers they could practically hear each other's thoughts. The cheap Mexican Rohypnol he'd slipped into the kid's beer would have done its work by now and he'd be unconscious. Dale had learned, over the years, that it was always easier for the boys when they didn't see what

Derek finally looked like by the time he was ready to come up from the basement to meet them.

Most of the time, Derek *did* look like a cop. He was better-looking than Dale. All their friends said so. Much better. Usually.

Yeah, Dale thought. *He's changing all right.* At least he'd told the kid one truth tonight.

"Happy Halloween," he whispered. He kissed the kid's forehead as he laid him on the cold basement floor near the trap door like an offering.

All the pretty boys, Dale thought. He could barely remember their faces. But in a way, he loved them all. They fed his love. *What was his name? Todd? Tom? It hardly matters now. It's better that I don't remember.*

The sounds from the sub-basement became louder. Dale heard a frustrated, low whining, then, a roar of purest animal hunger, not unlike a mating cry, followed by a volley of blows that made the floor tremble. Dale backed away from the trap door. He thought he heard Derek's voice for a moment, calling his name. Then it was gone, lost in the rising crescendo of bestial fury. The kid lay motionless where Dale had left him, sleeping deeply, oblivious to the sound of the trap door splintering. In a moment, the night would become unspeakable.

He was definitely Derek's type.

The kid smiled in his sleep. His arms moved reflexively as though he were still holding tight to Dale's waist, still on the bike and trusting. A thin sliver of drool trickled from the corner of his full bottom lip. To Dale, asleep, he suddenly looked much younger than nineteen.

Dale prayed it would be over quickly this time, for the kid's sake. He didn't even realize he was weeping. Sometimes love really did hurt. It hurt a lot.

THE ROOMMATE
LISA GIROLAMI

You have to get used to the noise. At first, it all sounds the same, like the constant droning of static that you might wake up to if you left the TV on in the middle of the night. But you can train your ears to listen past the white noise. As perfume becomes less noticeable the longer you're around it, the static falls away and sounds begin to punch through.

The paranormal experts call it EVP, short for electronic voice phenomenon. The belief is that ghost voices, while sometimes not discernable to the human ear in real time, can be caught on audiotape and then played back and heard through the white noise. These voices are not humanly generated, but electronically produced when a spirit is using the energy around it to manifest sound.

I didn't believe it at first, but I was convinced to try it one night.

I live in a house that was built in 1908. It's a California Craftsman bungalow that has been my home for the past year. Shortly after I moved in, I noticed that the house seemed to have a life of its own. At first, I thought it was charming; the squeaking floors and the popping and creaking noises made me feel as if I were part of its history.

Things were fairly normal for the first eleven-plus months. And then I began dating Nance Crawford. She was a medical equipment salesman and had just moved into town. We met at a grocery store, of all places. We both liked Camembert cheese. She always came over to my place since hers was in a bad part of town and she said she was in constant battle with cockroaches.

Since she was new, she didn't have any friends, but integrated easily into my circle.

I remember that it was the night after Nance and I met when I was lying in bed alone, just about to fall asleep, and my bedroom door started to open. The windows were all closed, so I knew it wasn't an errant breeze. I watched it slowly opening, creaking slightly as if announcing its intent. It finally stopped, making a tapping sound as it touched the wall. I lay there staring at it, wondering how that could have opened. Ten seconds later, the door closed and latched.

I sat up, stunned that whatever momentum that opened the door had somehow reversed itself.

I'm no scholar in physics, but I don't think that's supposed to happen.

The next day, I told some coworkers about it and one of them was convinced I had a ghost in the house.

I laughed it off but he shook his head and said, "Just wait. More things will happen."

And more things did happen.

In that week, I saw a shadowy figure walk the length of my hallway and watched every door open and close on its own at least once. Finally, I tried this EVP stuff.

I bought a digital recorder and, like my coworker had instructed me to, I asked questions, leaving silence in between in case there were answers. I asked a lot of questions and heard nothing but static. Then, as if my ears had grown accustomed to the background noise, I heard something. I had just asked, "How are you?" and played it back. There was a faint voice but I couldn't make out what it said. Excited, I replayed it over and over. On the fifth or sixth time, the word became clear. "Other."

I was surprised and a little scared. Was this a ghost? Was it standing right next to me or behind me? And what did other mean? Over the next week, when I wasn't out with Nance, I was using the recorder. I'd gotten a number of responses, all being of few words in length: the answer "I am with you" or "I am here" when I asked who was opening doors, and, after I greeted my paranormal entity by saying, "nice night we're having," getting the response, "cold."

Things were going really well for Nance and me. In our second week of dating, she was over at my house quite a bit. She didn't have to work that much because she had already met her sales quota. And the night we first had sex was amazing…up to a point.

It wasn't Nance, really. Things were going great up until the middle of the final act. That is, she was between my legs and doing all the right things, but all of a sudden, I heard a loud thump and she raised her head, yelling, "Fuck!"

She picked up a book that lay on the bed next to her. I was confused because the book hadn't been there when we started.

"I just got hit in the back of the head with this," she said.

"Really?"

She looked at me, glaring. She must have been skeptical about my response.

"I didn't move it. It's been on my dresser," I said, which was behind her, about four feet away.

"Things don't just fly through the room." She rubbed her head, clearly not happy.

"They kind of do," I replied, not really wanting to admit that the house seemed to be alive.

But I told her about the activity in the house and explained the recordings I'd been doing.

"So these EVP things you do, is that what was causing all this other activity?"

"I'm not sure. I think so."

"It's evil," she said. "All of it. Evil." Needless to say, she didn't stay that night.

After she got dressed and left, I lay there in bed wondering about her last comment.

The house was very quiet.

I got the tape recorder out. It was the first time someone had been hurt by the house. Granted, it was only a knock on the head, but nevertheless, it was stranger than the normal strange.

I clicked the Record button and asked, "Are you evil?" I knew I might be inviting the equivalent of a Ouija board monster into my house, but I had to ask.

An answer came. "Ancy. DonDan Yells."

What the hell did that mean?

I turned up the gain, to increase the sensitivity of the audio segment that had the EVP.

"Ancy. Dondan Yells."

"What am I supposed to do with that?" I asked.

There was no answer.

"Is your name Dondan?"

Nothing but static.

So I said, "Are you just having fun making nonsensical words?"

This time, a clear answer punctuated the white noise. "Kill you."

I dropped the tape recorder and moved away from it.

It had been amusing up to that point, but now I was spooked. Did the ghost want to kill me?

Sleep didn't come that easily but by morning, I was happy to get up and go to work.

Nance was over a lot in the next few days and I tried to forget about the last transmission. It seemed the stakes had suddenly changed, and I didn't know why. Was it another voice from out there that had commandeered the recorder? Doubtful, because it sounded exactly the same as the voice I'd always heard.

And what did "Ancy. Dondan Yells" mean? Was it someone's first name? Last name? Was it the name of a place? I searched Dondan on the internet and got, literally, six billion eight hundred million hits for Don Dan.

When my girlfriend knocked on the door later that evening, I shut off the computer and let her in. I could tell right away that she was in a solemn mood. I poured her some wine, led her to my couch, and as we sat, I asked her what was wrong.

"My checking account. They've put a hold on the direct deposits of my monthly paychecks because they're from out of state."

"Really?"

"Yes." She took a rather large swig from her glass. "I'm overdue on my hotel bill and they want to kick me out."

"Hotel? I thought you had an apartment."

"I did. That is, until they kicked me out for the same reason. My checks weren't clearing."

"That's horrible. I'm so sorry, Nance."

She cuddled up to me. "I can't use my credit card because it's a business account."

"I could loan you some money, I guess." I said this mostly because she didn't have any other friends and she needed help. I added "I guess" because it had come out of the blue and we had only been dating a little over two weeks.

"Would you? Really? I hate to ask."

"You didn't ask. I offered."

Nance put down her glass and stood. Taking my hand, she led me to the bedroom, where she promised she'd thank me for my generosity. I didn't quite get the thanks I was hoping for because this time, a long-stemmed candle somehow unlodged itself from a holder on my nightstand and whacked her in the temple. And I happened to have my eyes open when it levitated and flew through the air. Part of me wanted to laugh because it was so damn surreal, but I also felt a tremor of shock and disbelief at the bizarre occurrence.

"What the fuck?" she yelled. And this time, she got off the bed. "This house is fucked up!"

I could do nothing but open my mouth and raise my hands in a sort of "I'm sorry" grimace.

"You've been playing around with that EVP stuff, haven't you?"

"A little..."

She picked up the candle from the floor. "Why?"

"You made a comment that you thought it was evil, so I was trying to find out."

"If it's evil? Of course it is!" She shook the candle at me. "Don't mess with that shit!"

"I'm sorry, Nance," I said. "I won't anymore. Just come back to bed."

With a bit more coaxing, she did. We talked for some time, both of us not really wanting to turn off the lights. I told her about my childhood, growing up in town, playing hide and go seek with my two brothers, and eventually attending college here as well. She talked about moving around a lot as a kid, with no father and a drunken mother who beat her repeatedly. The two stories were so diverse that I felt bad for her. Maybe there was a way to find common ground.

"What's your favorite ice cream?" I said.

She looked at me a moment and replied, "Vanilla."

"Mine's chocolate. Favorite color?"

"Black."

Black? "Blue. Middle name?"

"Dawn," she said.

"Mine's Maria."

"Best subject in school?"

"Science."

"Ah! I was bad at science. Mine was art."

"Listen, I'm a little tired. Do you mind if we shut the lights out now?"

"Sure," I said. And she immediately curled up to my side and was asleep before I could count to twenty.

I lay there, thinking about her childhood and how bad it must have been. So many abused kids get so messed up in life. They turn to crime or destroy themselves with drugs and alcohol. Nance seemed to have turned out pretty well.

Nance Dawn. I tried out her first and middle names in my mind. It sounded a bit odd. Maybe she'd been born Nancy Dawn. That sounded more logical.

I remembered a little friend named Nancy from first grade who had been called Nancy Pantsy. She hated being teased. Maybe Nance had been teased as well and changed her name to just Nance. Nancy Rancy. Nancy Fancy. Ancy Nancy.

I stopped my rhymes. Ancy. The EVP had said "Ancy. Dondan Yells."

Ancy. Dondan.

Nancy Dawn.

Strange coincidence, I thought. Or was it? The ghost obviously hadn't taken a shine to Nance other than to use her as target practice. Or, at the very least, didn't want her and me to do the deed.

Was there a connection?

Luckily, Nance was sound asleep, so I quietly got out of bed, grabbed the recorder, and made my way to the back of the house. Once in the laundry room, I stood by the dryer and turned the recorder on.

"Dondan, are you there?"

I played back the tape.

"No," it said.

I chuckled. "How can you not be there and answer?"

No response.

"Do you dislike Nance?"

"Kill you."

I jumped. There it was again. Hearing the disembodied voice throwing out such a threat was chilling.

I shook off the fright and said, "Why do you want to kill me?"

"No."

"No?"

"Ancy. Dondan Yells."

I shook my head. Damn.

I listened again. It was pretty much the same as when I had heard it before. Being the longest string of words I'd recorded so far, I tried to make sense of different versions of what I'd heard.

Ancydon. Ancydondan.

Ancy. Don. Dan. Yells.

I stopped, suddenly taken aback.

Nancy Dawn Daniels?

What was Nancy's last name? Certainly she'd told me, but sheepishly, I admitted that I'd forgotten it. I silently scolded myself for bedding a woman whose name escaped me so easily. I made my way back to the bedroom, trying to avoid the creaky floorboards I was becoming accustomed to. Her very large and heavy satchel lay on the dresser and, stealthily, I lifted her wallet out of a side pocket and peered at the driver's license through its plastic sleeve. Nancy Dawn Edwards.

Okay, not the same name.

Placing everything back, I went to my den and flicked the computer on. As it warmed up, I unplugged the speakers so the bleeps and dings wouldn't wake Nance. It felt a bit awkward, looking up a name that I'd heard from a ghost. But there were too many strange things happening and, anyway, what harm was a little surfing? I typed in what I thought the EVP was telling me, Nancy Dawn Daniels. I blinked at the top twenty or so hits.

I clicked on the first listing. A local Columbus, Ohio, newspaper said that a Nancy Dawn Daniels had committed the murder of a local woman. There were no pictures but the article went on to say she hadn't been caught.

What a creepy coincidence. But the name certainly had to be a common one.

The next listing was from Philadelphia and the third was from Memphis. They both cited the Columbus murder and called Nancy Dawn Daniels a serial killer who had swindled women she'd become lovers with and when they began to figure things out, she had killed each of them before moving on. So far, the articles said, she'd murdered victims in seven cities around the U.S. I read on to find that Nancy Dawn Daniels was currently at large.

The Memphis article had a link for photographs, so I clicked on it. The first was of the Memphis victim. She was pretty, with blond hair and a winning smile. The next was the Philadelphia victim. Five more clicks and I had seen all the women this killer had left dead in her monstrous wake. I clicked again.

I stared as my body grew cold and my ears began to ring. The woman staring back had shorter hair but there was no mistake that this same person was currently lying in my bed.

I had to get out of the house and call the police. I immediately closed the computer window and when I jumped up, I came face-to-face with Nance.

"What are you doing?" she said. I barely heard her because she held a menacing-looking butcher knife that hadn't come from my kitchen.

There was no reason to answer her. She'd seen the computer screen over my shoulder.

We were both dressed in underwear and T-shirts but I had never felt more naked and vulnerable.

"This is an unfortunate circumstance," she said, scaring me with eyes black and malevolent.

My pulse raced and I knew I had to do something, so I pushed her as hard as I could and dodged to the right. She jabbed downward and caught my arm with the blade of her knife. Bleeding and frightened for my life, I made it to the kitchen, but she was right behind me.

I was able to grab my own knife from the counter, one that was much smaller and wouldn't outreach hers. My blood splattered and I knew the cut was deep.

She stopped about three feet from me. I could tell she was thinking about her next move and then she let out a big sigh. "This changes things, of course. Now I'll need your credit cards and checkbook. Oh, yes, your ATM card and PIN number as well."

This was the evil that the ghost tried to warn me about. Nancy Dawn Daniels was evil personified.

"And don't think about screaming," she said. "I'll slice your throat open so that the only noise you'll be able to make is the expulsion of the last bit of air from your—"

A silver flash came from the left and, before I could register what it was, hit Nance in the head. One of the pots that hung from my pot rack had somehow freed itself and clobbered her. She bent over a moment but before she could stand, two more pots flew by me and struck her. She went down on her knees, head down, but her knifed hand stabbed at the air right in front of me. She was desperately trying to attack, but the kitchen suddenly erupted in retaliation. The drawers opened and silverware launched out, stabbing her all over. The cabinet doors flew open and dishes pummeled her, each one breaking as it connected with her skull and shoulders. This time, it was her blood that splattered the cabinets and the floor and even me.

Now both of her arms were flailing as she tried to fend off the attack. I was pinned against the sink with no way to escape without her stabbing me in her frenzy. Her butcher knife kept me from trying to kick her, but I was also too surprised at what was occurring in my kitchen to think of much. Blood started to dribble from her wounds as the onslaught of tableware and plates sliced and gashed more holes in her. Finally, everything had been emptied from the drawers and cupboards and everything went eerily quiet.

She was on her knees in a heap on the floor. The knife I was holding was the only object that hadn't assaulted her, and I gripped it as hard as I could.

She raised her head. Her eyes were bloodied and her hair matted grotesquely against her face. The look she gave me was of confusion and anger. Slowly, she raised her weapon and I knew she was going to take one huge swipe at me.

Something like an electrical charge suddenly made my hand begin to buzz and the pain made me loosen my grip on the knife. And just as quickly, the knife flew out of my hand and impaled itself in her chest. Her eyes grew so large, I thought they would pop out. As if in slow motion, she fell forward and I heard the horrible, wet scrunch of the knife skewering her even further as she landed face down at my feet.

I stepped over her, holding my arm to stanch the blood flow. I called 911 and sat at the table to wait for help to arrive. After a moment where my brain tried to make sense of what happened and failed miserably, I turned the recorder on and said, "Thank you."

When I played the tape back, there was no response.

The strange door openings and other paranormal occurrences have stopped. I've tried the recorder since but with no results. I suppose I should be happy, but I admit, I miss my invisible roommate.

FILTH
'NATHAN BURGOINE

W hat are you doing?"
Noah froze. The voice was calm. He looked up and saw his father on the stairs. He'd obviously come home straight from work. His father was still wearing his mechanic's overalls, the ones with his name on the white patch over his heart. Jake, though everyone called him the Judge.

It wasn't done out of camaraderie.

Noah hadn't heard the door, hadn't heard the Judge hit the third step, which always squeaked.

Had he?

His dick didn't soften. The magazines—health magazines, muscle magazines, wrestling magazines—were scattered around the workout bench, opened to the pages he'd chosen. His jeans tugged low, his dick in hand, Noah looked at his father and thought, *I should have heard the squeak.*

"You…" His father looked down, looked up, looked directly at him, at his cock—and now it did deflate—and swallowed.

"You are full of filth," his father said, his voice a gavel crack in the cool basement. Then he turned and went back up the stairs.

Noah shook as he stuffed himself back into his jeans and tugged his shirt back over his head. He tidied the magazines, stacked them by the bench with his weights. Then, knowing he couldn't stay down in the basement forever, he went upstairs into the kitchen and waited for the first fist to fall.

❖

"Remember when Miss Matthews said that if we didn't learn calculus, we'd never make it to university?"

Noah glanced at Simon. He didn't reply, but as always, Simon took eye contact for agreement.

"She was wrong," Simon said and raised his arms, laughing. The two young men were mopping the floors of the University Center, after hours. The hallways were dark, and they worked amid Simon's constant chatter, even though Noah rarely said a word in return.

"I think I'm getting smarter already," Simon said and went to pour out and refill the bucket they were sharing. Simon had fixed earlobes, Noah noticed. Recessive trait.

Noah swallowed.

When Simon left, Noah regarded the wall of notices in front of him. Rooms for rent. Furniture for sale. Tutors. There was a calculus study group meeting on Thursday, Noah noticed, and thought about pointing it out to Simon when he got back, but it would only encourage him. His eyes froze on the next poster.

"Come On Out!" it declared in bright pink letters. "Lesbian, Gay, Bisexual and Transgendered coffee night at Bittersweets!" There was a date, and a time—next Saturday.

"What you reading?" Simon was back.

"Calculus," Noah said, his voice dry. It might have been the first thing he'd said all night. He pointed to the study group notice.

Simon laughed. They got back to work, mopping and scrubbing. Every stroke made the bruises across Noah's stomach burn and ache. He wished he could split open his own belly and spill all the bruises out onto the floor, and mop them up forever.

❖

"We need to talk."

Noah had perfected the art of being still. When his bedroom door had opened, he hadn't moved. He lay on his bed, reading a library book without really remembering what was on the previous page.

"Noah."

Noah put the book down, slowly. Carefully. He met his father's gaze without any attitude, eyes open to the conversation, no facial expression that could be considered sass.

"Yes?" Noah said. It had taken years to perfect that "yes." Polite without sarcasm, attentive without fear, confident without brashness.

"You're not right," the Judge said. "You're not right with the Lord." Noah noticed the Bible in his father's hand, and swallowed.

"There's filth inside your blood," his father said. "Evil. Legion. You've got to pray. I love you, son."

Liar, Noah thought. But it didn't show on his face. Instead, he said "I will."

His father watched him, pale blue eyes freezing him. Noah curled his thumb against the palm of his left hand, which was hidden from the Judge's view. He squeezed it against himself, willing himself not to look away, not to flinch, not to say anything more. The thumbnail was sharp against his skin.

"What are you reading?"

Noah held up the book. His father took it. Cold blue eyes measured the title, then the back of the book. It was a classic—*Moby Dick*—one he knew his father had never read. He'd chosen it on the merit of its own reputation. It would pass the Judge's scrutiny, Noah believed.

Queequeg had been unexpected.

His father handed the book back to him, saying nothing. It passed.

"Dinner will be in half an hour," his father said. "Put that away, and pray until then." He handed Noah the family Bible. "I've marked passages."

Noah nodded.

The Judge watched him open the Bible, turn to the pages where the little scraps of paper with their numbers waited for him. To the Judge, they were like coordinates for redemption, Noah knew. They were talismans to cure the sickness in his blood.

Noah began to read. His father hovered at the door a moment longer.

"Draw it out, Noah," the Judge said. "Draw it out."

Noah nodded and said the word his father wanted to hear, the way he wanted to hear it.

"Yes."

❖

He dreamed of ships, of tattooed skin that smelled of musk, the taste of salt. Strong arms gripping him while the world tipped one way, then another. Tongues—scalding hot—licking against hard skin in a dark cramped place.

Noah woke with a strangled cry, and knew at once he'd had an orgasm in his sleep. His hands ached—he'd had his fingers clenched into fists for hours, he knew, and this time he'd even bitten his tongue. He spat the blood into his empty water glass and curled into a tight ball, his stomach still sore from the bruises, his tongue stinging, and the dampness on his boxers already growing cold.

The filth in his blood, he knew, wasn't going away. It was only getting worse. Like Legion, it was endless, and as far as he could tell, there was no Jesus coming to cast it out. He pressed his hands against his stomach, making his bruises burn and hurt.

"Get out," he said quietly. "Get out."

Something moved.

He unfurled himself and reached out to his lamp, swallowing another cry before he could wake his father. The light snapped on and he blinked away the momentary blindness. He looked through the sheets—ignored the wet spot—and shivered. He reached for the lamp again, to turn the light off, and froze.

A cockroach crawled along the edge of his water glass. He watched it for a while, unsure, then quietly slipped out of bed and lifted the glass. The bug unfurled large, clear wings from under the mud brown carapace, but didn't leap or fly away, content, it seemed, to crawl along the rim of the cup. Noah went to his window, and opened it, then shook the glass until the cockroach fluttered its wings and flew off into the night. He closed the window again and looked at the glass.

It was clean.

❖

The sign was still there, and Noah looked at it again. He knew the coffee shop.

"You thinking of going?" Simon asked.

Noah jumped. "What? No!" He hadn't heard him come back with the bucket. He flinched, rubbing his stomach.

Simon laughed. "I'm not a fan of calculus either, remember?" Then he frowned. "Are you okay? You sick, maybe?"

Noah shook his head. He noticed Simon's earlobes again.

"You keep rubbing your stomach," Simon said.

"Just a little hungry," Noah lied.

Simon regarded him. "You wanna maybe grab a beer after? Get some wings or something?"

They'd be done by ten thirty.

"I gotta head home."

Simon nodded. He was used to Noah not coming.
But Noah's eyes flicked back to the paper.
He wasn't working Saturday.

❖

He'd tried to cover and do the laundry, but the Judge wasn't fooled by Noah's altruistic desire to do one more chore. Noah had tried to lie, blaming a spill of ketchup as the motivation—a rookie mistake, something he should have known better than to attempt—and the Judge's blue eyes had seen right through him. The lapse in the night had been bad enough, the lie another. The first blow had taken him in the stomach, as always—the next had struck his face.

It was rare his father's judgments landed somewhere visible. The first punch had dropped him to his knees, the second had laid him low.

"Pray," his father had said—and there was a tremble in his voice, so Noah lay completely still, fighting the urge to curl up, to spit out the blood, to cry, to make any noise at all. "Beg the Lord to cleanse your unworthy flesh and blood."

His father had left, and Noah had slowly risen. He'd winced all the way to the bathroom and looked at his face in the mirror. Eyes such a dark brown they were nearly black, the cleft chin—it was hard to look at himself.

Filth.

His lip was cut—just slightly. He wiped it, watching the blood blossom and spread on the tissue, then closing his eyes.

In his room, he curled up on his bed and rocked back and forth.

"Get out of me," he said, voice trembling. "Get out, get out, get out…"

There was a buzz. Noah opened his eyes and saw the bee orbiting the bed in lazy circles. He frowned, but gingerly got to his feet and opened the window. The bee looped twice more and flew out into the warm summer air.

With a jolt, he realized it was Saturday.

❖

The coffee shop was only about half-full, but to Noah it felt like a crowd was pressing into him from all sides. He held himself still, controlled his voice as he ordered a black coffee, and sat by himself at one of the small tables. There were women and men—and one woman Noah thought might actually be a man—in the coffee shop, and some of them had their arms around each other. They were laughing and talking in loud voices.

Noah wrapped his hands around the coffee cup, letting the heat scald his palms, and closed his eyes.

"Are you here for the LGBT coffee night?"

His eyes snapped open. There was a red-haired man smiling at him. Recessive trait.

"Yes," Noah said. It came out unsteady, the syllable broken in half. Years of practice ruined.

"I'm Rory," the red-haired man said. He held out a hand. Noah took it on reflex, and they shook.

"Noah," he said. He'd intended to lie, and suddenly couldn't.

"Come join us at the back," Rory said. He picked up Noah's coffee and led the way. Noah followed.

Rory was slim, but masculine. Noah liked how the man's eyelashes were almost a gold color. He had a small dent in his chin—everything about him was somehow clean, and normal. When Rory put the coffee down at a table with two women, Noah sat, and Rory sat beside him.

"Guys, this is Noah," Rory said. "Noah, this is Kate, and Jan. They're the co-coordinators at the LGBT Center on campus."

Kate was willowy, Jan was dark. They both smiled and said hello.

"You in first year?" Kate asked.

"I mop the floors after hours," Noah said, more truth pulled out of him against his will. "I saw the sign." A wash of shame filled his aching stomach. They were all university students. Smart kids. Not high school dropouts who still lived with their fathers and mopped floors. He shouldn't be here.

"See?" Jan said. "This is why we put up signs. People read them." She smiled at him. "Glad you could make it."

Noah felt light-headed.

Rory looked at him. "Is this your first...uh, coffee night?"

Noah nodded. His voice was gone. He saw Rory understood.

"Relax," Rory said, and took Noah's shoulder for a brief squeeze. "You're doing fine."

They spoke around him, but included him with their eyes and gestures. Slowly, as the evening progressed, more people introduced themselves, or were introduced to him, and though he never quite relaxed, Noah managed a kind of calm patience. The evening would end, and he would go home, he knew—and nothing would have changed.

When people finally began to drift away, Noah rose.

"Heading out?" Rory asked.

Noah nodded. "Yeah."

"Did you need a ride?"

"It's not far. I walked." It would take him nearly an hour.

Rory regarded him for a long moment. "Here," he said, and pulled out a pen and a small white business card from his shirt pocket. He flipped it over and wrote on the back. "Give me a call, and I can put you on the e-mail list for the events and stuff."

"Or he could sign up at the website, and you wouldn't have to give him your number," Jan said. Kate shoved her shoulder, and the two young women laughed.

Rory was turning red. Noah felt his fists clench with shame—but they weren't laughing at him. They were including him, somehow.

"Thanks," he said, taking the card. His hands were shaking. Outside, he flicked two ants from his fingertips and saw that he'd cut his palm with his fingernails. Another ant ran across the back of his hand, and he watched it, entranced by its small orange body.

❖

"Where were you?"

The Judge had been waiting. Noah fell silent, regarding those cool blue eyes carefully.

"I went for a coffee," he said.

His father's eyes didn't blink. He met them.

"Where did you go for coffee?" he asked.

"Just Tim Hortons."

"Liar." No change in inflection. "Where did you go for coffee?"

"It was just a little place downtown," Noah said. "In the Market."

"Then why did you lie?"

Noah's voice failed. There were no good reasons beyond the truth, and the truth would never do.

"I…I don't know…"

The punch came blindingly fast.

❖

The kitchen floor was cool, and he let his cheek rest there until he could control his breathing and hadn't heard his father's steps on the floor above for a while. He slowly rose, his stomach burning, and the side of his head full of a dull ache. He reached up to his temple, and his fingers came away wet. He looked at the blood on his fingertips.

There was a tickle on the side of his head. He shook his head—which made the floor blur and his gorge rise —and a small group of flies took off. He lurched to the sink and threw up, while the flies landed around the room. Their buzzing fell silent.

He poured water into the sink and watched the vomit disappear down the drain. When the water ran clear, he could see his own reflection in the metal of the sink, distorted and dull. Dark eyes.

You are full of filth, he thought. *Pray it out.*

There was a steak knife in the sink. He reached for it, wrapping his fingers around the handle and lifting it from the cool running water. He looked at the edge of the blade and forced himself to breathe.

The cut was shallow, but the sting made Noah wince. The palm of his hand filled with blood.

And more.

The edge of his vision blurred, but he held on to consciousness. He'd always known. Always believed.

The Judge was right.

Noah put the blade in the sink. He pulled the white card from his pocket with his good hand—the card was crushed now, but still legible—and put it on the counter. He kept his cut palm held out before him, and with his unhurt hand he picked up the phone. He dialed, and waited. It went to voice mail, but the greeting was obviously Rory's voice. He waited for the beep.

"You're very handsome," Noah said. "I like your hair. I'm sorry I won't be at the next event."

Noah hung up the phone, watching the maggots writhing in the blood on his opened hand.

Then he picked up the knife again and went upstairs.

❖

"Mom had blue eyes."

The words surprised the Judge, and in some small corner of his mind, Noah felt a surge of pleasure in that.

"What?" his father asked.

"Mom had blue eyes," Noah repeated. "You have blue eyes. So I have to wonder, who do you think she fucked to get a child with brown eyes like me?"

The Judge's neck turned red. "Stop right now. Get out of this room," he said. He rose from his chair.

"How long did you know?" Noah held up the knife. There was blood on the blade, and for the first time, Noah saw the Judge falter.

"What are you doing, Noah?" he asked. Noah let the maggots fall to the ground, and the Judge looked at them, uncomprehending. Noah's palm itched as more of the bugs struggled to get free.

Noah drew the blade across his forearm, hearing his flesh part under the knife.

"Noah!" the Judge yelled and stepped toward him. Noah dodged back, slicing himself again.

"Get out," Noah said and cut himself again. Blood welled.

The Judge leapt at him—always faster than him—and gripped his wrist, twisting it back until the knife fell from his grasp. Noah cried out.

"Stop it!" his father yelled. "Noah, stop it!"

"I am," Noah said.

The buzzing took the Judge aback, and he glanced at Noah's arms with confusion until the first of the wasps flicked their wings free from Noah's blood and landed on the back of the Judge's hand. It stung him, and he swore, letting go of his "son" and stepping back.

He stared at the wasps on Noah's forearm, mouth open.

"What…?" he began, but the next wasp landed on his forehead. The Judge swatted it away only to feel two more land on his arm. A third on his cheek. Another on his neck. Noah raised his arms and watched wasp after wasp push through the slashes on his arms, burrowing free from his skin and flying at the man who'd raised him. Their wings buzzed as their brilliant yellow and black bodies landed and they drove their stingers into the older man's exposed skin.

His father was now spinning in a circle, and slapping and swatting at the insects and screaming as they stung him again and again. The Judge tried to move to his bedroom door, but Noah closed it, and the older man—now nearly covered in a swarm of the clinging yellow and black insects—bounced off the wood and fell to the floor, leaving a smear of crushed insect bodies in both places. He rolled over and over, screaming a high-pitched wail of panic and pain and fear. Noah leaned against the wall, the loud buzzing noise receding as the world grew dull around the edges. His fingers were cold and numb. The knife fell from his fingertips. He slid along the wall, into his father's bathroom, feeling his flesh twitch and warp as the wasps drew themselves out of his wounds. He closed the bathroom door and slid down to his knees.

His father had stopped screaming.

Noah closed his eyes and was gone.

❖

The ceiling of the room was white. Noah blinked a few times and rolled his head to the side with a monumental effort.

Rory was sitting in a chair. When he saw Noah's eyes were open, he smiled.

"I always hated my hair growing up," he said.

Noah frowned.

"You're in the hospital," Rory said. "Your neighbor called the cops when he heard...uh..."

"Wasps," Noah said.

Rory nodded. "Somehow a swarm got in your house."

Noah shifted in the bed, trying to raise his head. A jolt of pain shot through his stomach, and he looked down, realizing he was in a hospital gown. He looked at Rory and saw it in his eyes.

"They could tell what he'd done to you," Rory said, and there was a mix of anger and sadness in his voice. Noah brought a hand to the side of his head and felt bandages there. His lip had been cleaned. The palm of his hand was bandaged as well, and an IV had been inserted. Where he'd slashed at his arms, long strips of white cloth covered him.

Rory was still watching him.

"Why are you here?" Noah asked.

"They found my number on the kitchen counter, and they called me, asked me if I knew you." Rory bit his lip, struggling. "Noah...Your father...he died."

"He wasn't my father."

"But I thought...The police said..."

"Grade eleven biology," Noah said. "Three years ago. Right before I dropped out. My eyes. They're brown. My mother had blue eyes. He had blue eyes. And my chin, my earlobes...Pretty much impossible." He paused. "I asked him. Before he..."

Noah's voice trailed off. He closed his eyes.

"Hey," Rory said, and Noah heard him get up. A moment later, Rory was holding his hand—the one that he hadn't sliced open—and squeezing.

"I'm full of filth," Noah said, so quietly he wasn't sure he'd said it at all until Rory's other hand was on his shoulder.

"No, you're not."

Noah opened his eyes. Those golden eyelashes were wet.

"I like your eyes," Rory said.

Noah just looked at him.

"I'm gonna go find the nurse, okay?" he said.

Noah nodded.

Rory leaned in and kissed his forehead. When he rose, Noah watched him leave the room. Outside, an older man was looking in with a scowl on his face, sitting in one of the chairs in the hallway. He wore a patient gown himself and was hooked up to an IV stand. He met Noah's gaze and shook his head, disgusted.

Noah worked the bandage free on his cut palm, and rubbed his thumb into the cut until he felt wetness. The spider that crawled out from between his fingers was shiny and black, with a bulbous body marked with a blood-red hourglass. He felt it crawl across his hand to the sheet, and then it vanished down the side of the bed.

When the older man began to call for help, and doctors and nurses began to raise their voices in the hall, Noah closed his eyes, let out a deep sigh, and went to sleep.

Saint Louis 1990
Jewelle Gomez

Gilda was more than alive. The 150 years she carried were flung casually around her shoulders, an intricately knit shawl handed down from previous generations, yet distinctly her own. Her legs were smooth and mocha brown, unscarred by the knife-edge years spent on a Mississippi plantation, and strengthened by more recent nights dancing in speakeasies and then discos. The paradox did not escape Gilda: Her power was forged by deprivation and decadence, and the preternatural endurance that had been thrust upon her unexpectedly. Her grip could snap bone and bend metal, and when she ran she was the wind, she was invincible and alone.

Tonight, hurrying toward home to Effie, she walked anxiously, gazing at the evening skyline. It sparkled like Effie's favorite necklace, which plunged liquid silver between her dark breasts. The image pushed Gilda faster through the tree-shrouded park. She glanced over her shoulder at the shadowed sidewalk behind her, where the light from the street lamps was cast through shifting leaves. Little moved on the Manhattan avenue at this late hour, but Gilda knew danger was not far behind her.

Gilda had not seen any of her siblings since she'd escaped slavery more than one hundred years before. Their loss was so remote, Gilda was always surprised when an image of them arose in her mind. It was the same with Samuel, whose face she could not banish now. Not a relative, but a blood relation, Samuel had haunted her path since they'd met in Yerba Buena just before the turn of the century. The town had been exploding with prosperity, much like New York now. Gold almost coursed down the hills into the pockets of seamen, traders, bankers, and speculators, until its pursuit became a contagion.

Gilda easily remembered her first impressions when she'd met Samuel: greed, selfishness, fear, and jealousy. That volatile blend had swirled through Samuel's eyes like mist from the Bay. Even when he'd smiled, Gilda knew he despised her. Her femaleness and her blackness were an outrage in his eyes. It was this peculiar amalgamation of feelings that turned Samuel into a dangerous man. The surprise of seeing him again tonight had left Gilda feeling chilled and sluggish. She walked slowly turning over in her mind every word he'd said in that angry encounter, trying not to let his sudden appearance alarm her.

When he'd stepped from the darkened doorway on upper Broadway Gilda had been preoccupied with getting home. Samuel appeared abruptly in front of her, giving an elaborate bow as if it were still 1890.

"The not-so-fair Gilda lives, I see," Samuel had intoned, the taut agitation of his voice unchanged after almost one hundred years.

"Samuel," Gilda answered simply, as if she were greeting him in one of the Yerba Buena salons they used to frequent. She said no more but shifted her weight in preparation for his attack.

"Gilda, why so pugnacious? I'm only looking up an old friend."

"What do you want, Samuel?"

"I've just stated my intention. One would think you'd be more solicitous of past acquaintances."

"As I recall, our last encounter was less than friendly."

"Those of our blood are fewer than used to be, Gilda. We must learn to make peace with each other. We greeted the turning of this century in each other's company; I thought perhaps we might do the same for this millennium which is on everyone's lips."

Gilda had watched his eyes as he spoke. They still glittered with the sullen anger he'd always harbored. Samuel's dark blond hair was masked almost completely by a narrow-brimmed hat which he wore at a rakish tilt. His wiry build rippled with tension beneath a raincoat with a short cape. The affectation made his shoulders appear much broader than Gilda knew them to be. She tried to push into his thoughts to discern the truth of why he'd sought her out, but he carefully blocked her. Samuel shared blood from the line of those who'd brought her into the life, yet he was as different from those she counted as family as night was from day.

"For some reason, Samuel, you've always felt I cheated you. It's as if I was the favored child and you were somehow left out. I don't know why you've fixed this sentiment on me, nor do I care."

"You will care, Gilda my girl."

"I only care that you stop leaping into my life as if I owed you some form of reparation."

Samuel's bellowing laugh was riddled with strands of his hatred. Two men lingering in front of the metal-shuttered doorway of a bodega had glanced in their direction nervously then ambled up the street to another spot. Gilda recalled the way he'd always clung to the idea that he was the victim, even when he was inflicting pain.

When they'd first met, Gilda was new to their life and still learning the mores and responsibilities of her power. But she understood immediately that Samuel was one who believed in nothing but his own gain, his own life. And wherever he'd fallen into error, he found someone else to blame. They were connected by blood that had turned sour, and Gilda was weary of trying to clean Samuel's wounds.

"The follies of your life are your own. Leave me out of them," Gilda said. The chill of her disaffection made her voice flat.

"Fine. If you insist. I'd always thought there was fairness about you, Gilda. I'm sure I'm not mistaken."

Samuel had turned on his heel and disappeared into the darkness, leaving Gilda to continue on her way home with a rising sense of ill-defined dread. Samuel had drawn her into battle twice in the past century. She had no doubt he intended to do the same again, sometime soon.

She veered off Broadway down to West End Avenue, where grass sloped gently downward from the city street to the brackish river. The soft flowing of the water played in her ears, obscuring the city sound to her left and stirring her already bubbling uneasiness. She focused her attention to steel herself against the discomfort of the running water of the Hudson River so she could enjoy the textured darkness of the tree-lined avenue and try to rid herself of the image of Samuel.

Ahead of her, hidden from the streetlight by the shadows of a thick maple tree, Gilda saw a man leaning against the park fence. Her body tensed, but she felt no fear. It wasn't Samuel. This was a mortal, in his twenties, strongly built and obviously up to no good. He wore a sweat suit several sizes too large, but that did not conceal his muscled arms from her. A knit cap was pulled down over his brow to hide his dark features; it only exposed his vulnerability to Gilda. Gilda slowed her steps momentarily, and then thought: *He's just a man.*

A surprise flood of anger washed over her. She'd only recently understood such anger could be hers. Her mother, Fulani features hemmed into a placid gaze, had not been allowed that luxury. She'd been a slave, admonished to be grateful. As a child Gilda had not understood: The master, who owned all and was responsible for everyone, never showed anger; his wife, whom he pampered and worshipped oppressively, was angry all the time. As was the overseer who regularly vented his anger on black flesh. But blacks were not thought to have anger any more than a mule or a tree cut down for kindling.

Gilda looked quickly behind her and saw several apartment dwellers moving casually past their windows, and a couple approaching a little more than a block behind her. No sign of Samuel, but the young man stood ahead of her under the maple, his intentions leering out from behind an empty grin.

Gilda's step was firm. She wondered what drove men—black, white, rich, poor, alive or otherwise—to need to leap out at women from the darkness. As she walked past she noted the sallow quality of his brown skin. He spoke low, almost directly in her ear, "Hey, Mama, don't walk so fast."

Gilda continued on, hoping he would take his loss and shut up.

He didn't. "Aw, Mama, come on. Be nice to me."

The wheedling in his voice scraped and scratched at her. That sound had been the undercurrent of every encounter she'd had with Samuel over the past century. His demands for her help, his threats to harm her, his pleas for her sympathy were all delivered in the same calculated, pitiful pitch; devised to take advantage of their blood relationship.

We're connected by blood, too, Gilda thought as she felt the young black man waiting. She understood that the poverty she saw around her ground people into hopelessness. She herself fought each day to resist the predatory impulse that promised to ease her feelings of desperation. In the man before her she recognized his surrender to that impulse. Like Samuel, he reeked of his enjoyment of power over someone else he considered weaker, unworthy; his assault in the dark was the substitution for truly taking power.

Anger speared her, leaving a metallic taste in her mouth. Where were the words for what she felt?

Gilda stopped and turned to him, smiling as she remembered the words of an irate Chicago waitress she'd overheard decades before: "I am not your mama. If I were, I would have drowned you at birth."

She walked on. He caught up. "Why you bitches so hard. Come on, sistuh, give me a break!"

Gilda continued walking. She had no desire to let her anxiety about Samuel push her to end the night with angry blood.

"Come on, sistuh, let me see that smile again." With that he seized her arm. His grip would have bruised another but Gilda shook free easily, leaving him off balance. In a smooth reach he snatched at her close-cropped hair, hoping to pull her into the darkness.

The image of Effie, waiting in their rooms, her sinewy form concealed in shadow, flashed through Gilda's mind. A low moan sounded in the back of her throat. She could almost feel her slim fingers clenched around his neck, snapping the connection to the spine. She replaced that sensation with the memory of a hot night thirty years before—Florida in 1950. She'd been sitting in an after-hours club watching the fighter show how he'd whipped a Tampa boy who said boxing was just a "coon show." His precision was awe-inspiring. As was the care he showed the young boys who clustered around him outside the club, waiting in the wee hours for a glimpse of their hero. More than his fists, he had craft and commitment that seemed saintly when he looked down at the boys who worshiped him.

Gilda smiled again as she raised her left fist in perfect form and smashed it into the man's jaw. He fell unconscious to the cracked pavement, half-sprawled on the thin city grass.

Gilda lifted him from the street and held him to her as the couple she'd seen earlier passed by. Once they were several paces away she lowered the man to the ground so he sat against the maple tree. She knelt low, hiding him from the street, and smoothly sliced the flesh behind his ear with her fingernail. His eyes opened in shock, and Gilda held him in the grip of her hands and her mind. He was pinned against the tree, its rough bark biting into his shirt as Gilda rummaged amongst his thoughts. Confusion replaced shock, then rage followed. Unable to move, the young man bellowed internally. His ideas were petty, self-centered, ignorant of any world except the small circle in which he traveled. The history Gilda knew, the triumphs she'd seen all meant nothing to him. He was so tainted by the hatred and fear others had of him he left no room inside for anything but that. Gilda had not felt so unrelated to a mortal since she'd taken on this life. In his eyes she observed the same deadness she often saw in Samuel's: They always looked inward, were always scavenging. They never really saw.

Gilda pressed her lips to the cut. Blood had begun to seep out onto his sweatshirt. The flesh was soft and smelled of sweet soap. Gilda could imagine the boy he'd been, when he was still able to picture himself a part of the larger world. She drew her share of the blood from him swiftly, barely enjoying the warmth as it washed over her. His anger began to swell inside her, wiping away the sensation of his youth. She was engorged yet continued taking the blood, unable to stop, feeling no need to leave something for him.

At the final moment she pulled back, lifted herself from his neck, and looked into his almost dead eyes. She touched his nearly empty mind, searching for a tiny space where there was no anger or hatred. She found too many places seared white with disappointment turned into rage. And then, a small moment where a treasured memory was hidden opened up. There she planted the understanding of what it could mean to really feel love toward a sister, and from that love find a connection to the rest of the world. In the shallow cavern of his thoughts she left him that one sensation to live for, to strive for as she held her hand to seal the wound. His pulse was faint but soon became steady. She lifted him gently and rested him on the park bench, placing his arms casually behind his head, as if he were only napping. She drew the cap back so it rested on the crown of his head but left his dark face open and smooth in the dim light. His lips were no longer curled in a smirk but rested partly open, ready to finally speak. She could see the young man he'd been, the young man he might still be.

As she rose to leave, Gilda was glad she had such a good memory. "Yeah, Joe Louis was a heck of a fighter," she said aloud.

She knew it would not be so simple with Samuel. A century of bitterness and jealousy, left over from times even Gilda couldn't remember, festering fuel. She looked down at the young man and hoped his bitterness would end here.

Gilda continued downtown, her sense of dread building. Samuel's words were like a prickly burr against her skin. Turning them over, back and forth Gilda searched for reasons Samuel would return at this particular time. The young man she'd left on the bench had probably lived all of his life under the sour message implying his worthlessness. He made victims of others out of ignorance. *Not just ignorance. Vanity!* Gilda thought. She probed the air around her looking for Samuel's thoughts, trying to discern his presence. She perceived only apartment dwellers and the homeless who slept in the park. It was a kind of vanity that drove both Samuel and the young man. They could not stand to be one of many, but only one—always alone, always outlawed. And that fooled them into thinking they were on top.

Her recollection of the last time Samuel had burst into her life did not comfort Gilda. For a moment it had seemed as if he'd forgotten their past, had learned to appreciate his special place in the world. He'd appeared in much the same way as he'd done this evening, with no warning, on a public street. Then he'd been more devious, trying to lull Gilda into a sense of goodwill. Her wariness had lingered and was proven justified. The battle between them had gone on for several hours, leaving both with gruesome injuries. Gilda had not wanted to fight him, or to kill him. It had been a draw and Samuel had retreated when he understood that Gilda could not be easily destroyed. Gilda shuddered. *There can be no fairness in a fight between us,* she thought.

Fair. The word resonated in Gilda's mind; there was something about the way he'd said the word several times. She felt the skin of her entire body become an antenna tingling with input. And then she understood. Samuel had said she was not fair—not light-skinned. Then he'd said there was "fairness about you." He was talking about Effie. In some cultures, the name Effie meant "fair." Effie herself had told Gilda that when they first met. Samuel had come to hurt Gilda, just as she suspected, but he'd do that by hurting Effie.

A flame of terror shot through Gilda's body, dispelling the chill that had settled on her. She now knew why the image of Effie had shown her in shadow. Anger pulsed through Gilda, leaving no room for caution. She knew Effie had powers at least as strong as her own, yet fear for Effie's safety seared her heart. She pushed a warning through the air toward their home as she turned swiftly southward, then disappeared inside the wind blowing off the river.

❖

Manhattan lay glittering like a sequined scarf, floating on the coastal waters of the Atlantic. Lights from the street, apartments and office buildings flickered in the darkness, multiplied by their reflections off the glass of windows, storefronts and shiny cars. Yet night was wrapped tightly around the city and its chill penetrated Gilda. She moved so quickly she was invisible to anyone looking down from one of the windows of the towering apartment buildings of Riverside Drive. The rustle of leaves was the only sign that she passed through the night air. A pedestrian out for an evening stroll by the river would feel only the brush of an unexpectedly warm breeze. But Gilda was a whirlwind of emotion as she sped downtown to the danger she knew was also hurtling through the night toward her home.

Gilda's thoughts were a kaleidescoping blur. She glimpsed the calm and elegant face of Effie, her brow furrowed with concern, then an image of the home they shared in lower Manhattan, with its startling murals of foreign cities created by her dear brother Julius. The almond-shaped eyes of her tenant, Marci de Justo, who'd become almost as close a friend as those of her blood. Vivid sounds of Celia Cruz and Ismael Miranda wafting down from Marci's audio speakers out over her backyard garden like a warm mist usually welcomed her home. The faces of Sorel, Anthony, Julius, and Marci—the men in her life—floated through her mind. Gilda often laughed at the image of the incongruous quartet. Her fear that a fifth, Samuel, was about to destroy all she held so precious swelled in her throat, almost choking off the air to her lungs. She pushed herself to move even faster.

Gilda easily recalled earlier threats Samuel had made—in the ninety years they'd known each other there had been many. They were usually accompanied by vengeful attacks, in the dark, from behind, under cover of innocence. But this time it had been a veiled hint, so subtle Gilda wondered if she was imagining the menace she felt when Samuel had spoken her name.

"The not-so-fair Gilda lives, I see," Samuel had said casually, as if he were simply observing the movements of a bug beneath his feet. Samuel continued to be the threat he'd always been. In less time than it took to think Samuel's name, Gilda had traversed the four miles downtown and was standing outside the door of her garden apartment. Located in a renovated brick building she'd owned for twenty years, the rooms provided both the privacy Gilda required and a natural place in the rhythm of the neighborhood that nourished her as much as the blood that maintained her long life.

She listened and was startled to hear such quiet enveloping the building. Peering at the two tall windows that faced the street and then through the intricate paintings Julius had applied to each pane, she saw the warm amber glow that bathed the front rooms. She unlocked the wrought iron gate that shielded her door and entered the spacious parlor.

As she'd come to spend more time with Gilda, Effie had added her own influences to the sparely decorated room. Fresh flowers sat on the low cherrywood table in the center. A piece of Kente cloth was draped over the back of the overstuffed sofa and a small painting by Julius now hung between the tall windows. Gilda looked around, satisfied with her home, which seemed the same as usual.

She drew in her breath and listened more closely: Around her she heard the muted noises of her tenants, and directly above, it sounded as if Marci were enjoying a romantic evening with soft music. But in her own flat she sensed no one. As she reached for the key to unlock the sleeping room, her hands trembled with anxiety; "no one" could mean "no one alive." She flung open the heavy metal door, which was paneled to look like oak, and was relieved when it crashed against the wall and revealed an uninhabited room. The thick silk of the oriental carpet glistened in soft light, the yellow satin comforter rested on the sleeping platform where the soil of Gilda's home state was mixed with that of others of her family. Her eyes burned with the memory of the ritual blending—dark earth sprinkled together and sown into layered pallets that allowed any of her family to rest in this place in safety. The wave of emotions was for those whose earth blended here with hers and for the many whose did not.

Gilda closed and locked the door, puzzled. Earlier she'd been certain she'd sensed that Effie was in danger. Samuel's fearsome cruelty had shone in his eyes, brighter than sunlight; and Effie had seemed to be his focus. She opened the door to the garden, clinging to the hope that it, too, would be unchanged. She rushed out to the small patch of roses, rhododendron, and the queenly evergreen. Turning in circles, relieved and frustrated, Gilda saw nothing to either support or alleviate her fear. Danger was still near; Gilda knew it with all the molecules of her blood, but where?

She looked up at Marci's open windows. The shades were pulled down. A pale red glow emanated from inside, where music played softly. The red light was a sign that Marci was entertaining. Gilda watched the shadows on the window for a minute listening, but despite the music the room was cloaked in intimacy. Then Marci appeared at the window, snapping the shade up and lifting the window.

"*Hermana,* what are you doing down there? Is there something?" Marci leaned low out of the window, his shoulders swathed in a pale yellow silk blouse.

"I was just wondering where Effie might be." Gilda held her voice steady, letting it float on the air, falsely casual.

"Sister, she don't come up here with no red light, you know that." Marci laughed as the picture tickled him. "She was there, then she went out, downtown, I think."

Gilda marveled at how Marci could tell which direction people walked when they left the building, even though his apartment faced the back. He had a preternatural connection with all the tenants, listening to them, their needs, and their troubles. The mother hen of the building, he offered his vibrant wisdom spun from the practical Puerto Rican reality of his childhood and grounded in the ancient Taino spirits. It amazed Gilda how each of the tenants accommodated their own reluctant reliance on a Puerto Rican drag queen who'd made them his family when his own had rejected him. As the men around him succumbed in greater numbers to the unnamed disease Marci traveled across town, to the Bronx or Queens to help out bar acquaintances and old friends indiscriminately. He dispensed *mafongo* and advice liberally to everyone as if his thick stew and experiences were a universal resource.

In the years since she'd acquired the building, Marci had become her guide to the mortal world around their home. His music, the smell of his food, the love he showed for her and their building had made it a place of easy rest.

"Gotta go." Marci's voice sparkled in the night air.

"Hey, I thought you were single as of last month?"

"Not tonight."

"Marci…are you being careful?"

He looked down at Gilda, affecting the face of a wounded child.

"Manuel de Justo," Gilda said solemnly. She knew how much he hated anyone to use his given name. *"Ten cuidado!"*

"Of course, I am the soul of careful." Marci's long lashes lowered modestly as his lips curled in a brilliant smile and he withdrew inside.

What a strange existence, Gilda thought. She warned her friend to be cautious of blood that had become dangerous in this decade. Around them young men had begun to sicken and die so quickly Gilda was uncertain how severely even she might be weakened by the infection. But her heightened senses enabled her to easily detect any illness and sidestep its perils. She'd helped tend to many and still the affliction, just like her own nature, remained a mystery to her. She looked up at the window but saw no more movement in the ruby light. Quiet blanketed the building and Gilda felt afraid again.

She returned to her living room, beginning to trace the energy of Effie's route in the air, then noticed the slip of paper sticking out from beneath the vase of yellow roses:

Sorel and Anthony are back.
Cocktails.
E.

Excitement flooded Gilda, pushing thoughts of Samuel from her mind. Sorel and Anthony, who'd helped her learn her way through the world of their kind, were her blood family, bound to her as surely as her mother who'd died in slavery on a Mississippi plantation. Effie, who was newer in Gilda's life, was also part of this family, now linked with dozens of others around the world. She again raced through New York's city streets, this time her fear mixed with anticipation. The one gift from the confrontation with Samuel was that it had evoked the memory of Joe Louis. Gilda had always savored that brief time when she'd known him. She visualized his power and sense of community sometimes just to keep his face in her memory. The kids who admired him thought he was a saint. But he'd been better than that.

When Gilda stood on the corner of the lower Manhattan street where Sorel and Anthony maintained their establishment, she slowed to savor the feel of cobblestones beneath her feet. She could sense the three of them inside together, safe.

It had been almost a decade since Sorel and Anthony had made the difficult journey across the Atlantic to visit old friends and places they'd not seen for over a century. The moments Gilda spent apart from her family always seemed to fly by, yet they weighed on her heavily. She'd not yet learned how to let the years pass and trust in the future. In that way she felt too much like Samuel, who also clung to the past. His rage at Gilda from almost a century before was as fresh for him as a new wound. The woman who'd betrayed him for Gilda had been dead longer now than she'd been alive. Gilda pushed the memory away from her, just as she wished she could do with Samuel.

The door of Sorel and Anthony's small bar was set right on the street, the ground level of an ancient factory which they owned. On the outside the door was covered by a modest sheet of metal, like many which lined the block. The seventeenth-century carved wood from Spain that was attached to the interior side of the door made it hang heavily in the frame. Once inside, Gilda leaned back on the intricate, hard forms, which pressed into her back as she breathed in deeply.

Sorel, in evening wear accentuated by a gold embroidered vest, sat in his booth holding Effie's hand. The bar was appointed like an elegant pub: wood paneling, coats of arms, gleaming crystal. The bar had deeply padded stools with backs; two were now occupied by people familiar to Gilda. The four booths, other than Sorel's, were empty.

Anthony, not wearing his usual apron but a blue silk suit, poured the wine expertly. Champagne for Sorel, a deep red for Effie. Gilda nodded a greeting at the thin, dark man behind the bar who'd worked with Anthony and Sorel since they'd opened the establishment long ago. He proffered her a champagne flute in a fluid movement. Gilda didn't break her stride as she took the glass and continued toward the dark green leather upholstered booth at the back.

"Ah, at last." Sorel rose from his seat, his rotund body moving lithely. His pale, delicate fingers encircled her large brown hand. "My daughter. I've missed you like sweet air."

Gilda never knew how to bridge these chasms. So much time seemed like only moments, yet their emotions were full. If tears had been possible for them their eyes would have been brimming. Instead they squeezed each other's hands, letting the magnitude of their happiness pulse between them.

When Gilda sat next to Effie her body completely relaxed. She looked up into Anthony's sardonic gaze.

"So you are still drinking this poor excuse for wine?" he asked, nodding at the champagne flute.

"Anthony, you know I take after Sorel in that regard. The champagne grape has captured my soul almost as assuredly as Effie."

"Effie at least does not leave the blood sluggish."

"Thank you, Anthony." Effie's light voice carried a music of its own, distilled from hundreds of years of travel. She sipped the red wine through smiling lips. Gilda brushed her finger across Effie's mouth, enjoying the warm fullness, savoring her relief at seeing her safe. Her round dark face was just as it had been for more than three hundred years. Her tightly braided hair curved across the crown of her head like a dark halo. She was petite and seemed to be swallowed up by the deep leather banquet. As their skin touched Gilda sensed, not for the first time, Effie holding something hidden inside her. She pushed the sensation away and enjoyed her relief.

Sorel watched Gilda recognize a secret place inside Effie, and wondered how they would weather the coming years. He and Anthony had spent almost two centuries of living together, striking a balance between the separations they both appreciated and their desire to experience life side by side. The separations, sometimes weeks sometimes years, were part of the growing process for them. Living on one's own developed survival skills and helped each one of their family to stay connected to the world and not withdraw into safely guarded enclaves. It was within those isolated clans that the deadly patronizing attitude toward mortals was cultivated. Those like Samuel, who took no responsibility for his existence, thrived among those isolated circles. Within them they reinforced each other's weaknesses and fed on dreams of power. Each decade he grew thick with paranoia and the blood of terrified victims slaughtered like deer in season.

Sorel understood how difficult the separations were for Gilda and had tried to help her understand how important they were. Their life needed air as much as it needed blood. As he held her hand he could feel both her joy at his return and the edge of anxiety that anticipated his next trip. More than a hundred years had passed since Gilda's enslavement and the death of her mother under its brutality, yet she could still barely withstand separations. Every journey away from her was a move toward abandonment. This was another lesson Sorel was confident Gilda would learn in time. As he'd held Effie's hand, he sensed her compelling need to move back out into the world. The lesson would be brought home to Gilda soon.

"We have so much to tell you about the land we left behind. It has changed, as you can imagine."

Laughter burst from Gilda and Effie, knowing that the last time Anthony and Sorel had seen France, Marie Antoinette was about to be led to the guillotine.

"But you have things to discuss with us, I believe." Sorel took a sip from his glass, then sat back in the booth. Effie turned to Gilda, seeing the thoughts behind her eyes for the first time. Effie's blue-black skin glistened in the soft light that bathed the room.

"What is it?" Effie's voice was low and even as the muscles in her body became alert. Her tiny figure became a tight coil of energy as she took in Gilda's concern.

"I don't want to spoil your homecoming," Gilda said, looking up at Anthony. She could feel him not waiting for her to speak but probing her mind.

"Samuel." Anthony spat the name out.

"Yes."

"Samuel? I'd hoped we were done with him," Effie said, her voice as hard and sharp as a steel dagger.

"He came to me tonight. On the street. Again. Full of syrup overlaying the vinegar."

Anthony drank from his glass, set it down firmly on the table and walked away. The set of his back told them how angry he was.

"Did he make threats again?" Effie asked.

"Not directly. He said something about seeing in the turn of the century together as we had in the past."

"He is a bit early," Sorel said, trying to mask his anxiety. "Off schedule as is his usual."

"But he made several references that worried me. He kept using the word 'fair' in odd ways. Not so odd really, just repeatedly. I didn't think anything of it at first. Then he disappeared with such a sense of bemusement I was…" Gilda stopped, unsure what to say. She looked to Effie, whose brow was wrinkled in thought; then at Sorel, who looked alarmed. He'd known Samuel longer than any of them and understood that Gilda's concern was not misplaced.

"Why does he continue this? Eleanor used him and tried to use Gilda. She's been dead for almost a hundred years!" Effie spoke her anger aloud before she thought.

Sadness settled on Sorel's face like a carnival mask. In her mortal life Eleanor had been like a daughter to him. The sunny face of curiosity and hopefulness all of them struggled to hold on to. Her spirit was as golden as the hills of Yerba Buena where miners dug for precious ore. Her selfishness was so strong it had infected Samuel.

"He's always blamed Gilda. Even Eleanor's death can't release him." Sorel's voice deepened with sorrow. Everyone was silent as he closed his eyes. His beautiful hands rested lightly on the table as the image of Eleanor sprang to life in his mind. The way she tossed her auburn hair had remained unchanged from the time she was five until the day she died—haughty and vulnerable at the same time. Sorel could almost feel the brush of it against his hand. But the picture he examined behind his eyes also revealed the glint of petulance in hers. Many of their blood acted deliberately cruel or brutal, and Eleanor had done both. Yet there'd been no meanness in her. She'd cared deeply about everything, in the moment. Samuel and Gilda had both entranced her. But her most enduring care was for herself and her whims.

He'd brought Eleanor into their family impulsively. She had

repeated that same mistake with Samuel, then abandoned him in pursuit of others. It didn't matter to Samuel that Gilda was only one of many lovers she preferred to him.

Sorel opened his eyes, no longer able to bear the shining clarity of his memory. "I'll call him to me, make him see some sense."

"Sorel, this isn't your responsibility," Gilda said. She too remembered the feel of Eleanor, as well as all she might have done to keep Eleanor by her side. But she'd refused to accommodate Eleanor's profoundest desire—Samuel's death. "He was Eleanor's error in judgment, not yours."

"If we follow lineage, he is my mistake, too."

"Don't blame yourself." Effie spoke from many more years of experience than even Sorel. "At some point, troublesome people have to take responsibility for their own actions."

"Samuel is not someone we can assume will recognize good sense, even if it's pointed out to him," Gilda said. "This time there'll be no avoiding him."

"I'm afraid you're wholly correct, Gilda." Anthony had returned to the table carrying a small wood box. Gilda was startled by the way the hardness in Anthony's voice mirrored Effie's. It was as if they knew a secret no one else could comprehend and they meant her to follow their lead without thought or sentiment.

The box sat ominously on the table. It was rough-hewn but had three finely made bronze clasps. Anthony sat down beside Sorel, whose usually jovial expression was unreadable.

Gilda stared at the box, unwilling to focus on what lay inside it.

"I think we can manage Samuel," Effie said.

"I'm sure you can," Anthony said, "but with this you both can avoid undue—"

"Please stop talking as if Samuel were a cockroach I'm going to squash under my boot. That's just how Samuel thinks!" Gilda's voice rose with emotion. "We spend so much of our time learning to respect life, to live beside mortals and share the world in a responsible way. Don't talk about disposing of Samuel as if he'd never been human, or one of us."

"Samuel listens to no one," Effie said, her anger tightening her throat. She pushed her glass away from her and locked Gilda in her gaze. "Everywhere we turn there are the angry ones, full of rage with no idea how they got that way. They have some vague idea of injustice and a hunger for redress. And nothing else."

"Not all of us can cast off our sorrow easily," Sorel said.

"Samuel's life is a poison to all of us, whatever his sorrows. And we are the ones who hold the responsibility for him, no one else." She finally looked away toward Anthony. "All of you know his hatred for Gilda."

They were silent in their assent. She went on, unable to let her feelings remain unspoken: "If it means not having to weep dry tears while I scatter the ashes of any of you...I will incinerate Samuel."

Effie's anger was a wave of fiery air in the room. Gilda had never seen her so implacable.

"But how can we say he's irredeemable? Eleanor may have made a poor decision, but we can't compound it." Gilda's voice was tight with pleading. "She cared enough to bring him into our family. We have to give him some chance."

They could feel the others in the room straining not to appear to hear their conversation, but the words would be as clear to the other patrons and the bartender as if whispered next to their ears. The clink of ice in glasses and the movement of the air around the room punctuated the rising emotion.

"Samuel was a choice she regretted almost immediately," Anthony stated. "He's tried to harm you more than once. Don't sentimentalize."

Gilda inhaled deeply, not willing to embrace the idea of destruction. "Tonight coming home, I encountered a young black man much like Samuel. Bitter, disappointed. He assumed by attacking me, maybe raping me he'd make himself a man. Have something to share with his brothers. Something the white man couldn't take away from him." Gilda hurried as she felt them resist her story. "I know many men who look at women like they watch sports. I'm not sentimentalizing anything. When he touched me I could have killed him, tossed his body in the river, and few would have noticed his absence. But inside him was a boy who'd been hurt. When I was able to find that clear space I could help him. I know we can't always help. But when do we stop trying?"

It was at these moments that Sorel felt most weary and at the same time most proud. "If you want to handle Samuel on your own," he spoke softly, "I won't interfere. Not yet." He pushed the box across the table back toward Anthony. "But I assure you neither Anthony nor I will hesitate to protect you."

Gilda sat back in the booth and said: "Let's not talk about this anymore, then. I think Samuel is simply succeeding in making us give him attention. I imagine he's repaired to one of those establishments in this town where blood is spilled and mortals are tortured, braying with smugness that's he's frightened me."

Gilda didn't believe the words even as she spoke them. Nor did anyone else at the table, but they let the conversation turn to Sorel and Anthony's trip to Europe. The anxiety remained at the table, seated silently with them.

❖

Effie and Gilda walked northward toward home slowly, enjoying the sporadic lights of lower Broadway and the people who moved around them. As they got closer to Chelsea, Gilda felt her muscles tense, anticipating the danger awaiting her. She saw that Effie, too, was listening with her body.

"I don't think I've ever known such fear. Not since I escaped the plantation as a child," Gilda said almost in a whisper.

"Yes. There is something about being hunted silently that never leaves the blood."

"I can't deliberately kill him. I made the choice to let go of my mortality, but not humanity."

"I understand that, Gilda. But you need to understand Samuel has given away his humanity."

"I don't believe that."

"Then why did you rush home in terror?"

Gilda's hand went automatically to her throat, but she could not answer Effie. She did still feel him clawing at her and could, if she let herself, still sense his murderous lust pouring through his hands into her as he tried to rip her life from her. Yet Gilda clung to the possibility of his goodness as desperately as he'd gripped her throat.

"He let go finally, and so must you," Effie said, expressing no regret for listening to Gilda's thoughts. The remaining blocks to their home were traversed in silence, neither Effie nor Gilda speaking or thinking.

The glow of their windows was a lighthouse, guiding them to a comfortable berth after turbulent emotions, many still unspoken. Once inside they shed their clothes and with it the scent of fear. They both listened to the building as always, assuring themselves that each of the tenants was safe. The apartments were wrapped in sleep except Marci's, where the stereo still played softly over the energy of desire.

"He must be in love!" Gilda said with laughter.

"This is news." Effie unlocked the door to the sleeping room and pulled the comforter back. The soft sheen of the black satin sheet that covered their pallets was inviting in the light of the candle Effie lit.

"He was wearing that yellow blouse that looks so beautiful on his skin when I saw him earlier this evening." Gilda followed her. "And grinning like a Mardi Gras mask."

"That sounds like love," Effie said and reached out to pull Gilda down to her.

"Your affection for Eleanor, your feelings of guilt for not staying with her, have made Samuel a cause you cannot win. I don't want to leave here worried that you'll end your life in a foolish battle with him."

Gilda stiffened in Effie's arms, but Effie held on to her. The truth of the moment raced between them like an electrical current. Gilda had known even without the words. Sorel and Anthony spent most of their days and nights together. But often they separated for months and sometimes years. Bird, who'd helped bring her into this life, who'd known her even before they did, had traveled unceasingly, stopping only occasionally to look into the face of her daughter, Gilda. Each of them had told her this was their way to maintain the sense of anticipation and wonder at life. To keep returning to the world alone, seeking to learn from mortals, gave them a connection they'd never get keeping themselves secluded and apart. But Gilda still didn't know how to manage the long days when she had no one to lie with and feared she never would.

The natural pattern of eternal life frightened Gilda; it felt too much like an abyss. When she was a child she'd watched the overseer carrying her mother's body from their room. She understood it was no longer her mother, but now simply a "thing" just as the slave master had always insisted. At that moment she'd been consumed by knowing she'd never see her birth mother again. A huge vacuum had opened in front of her, sucking her into a breathless, infinite hole that she'd spent her subsequent years running from.

"It is our rhythm of living, my love. We are always together, even when we part. You've seen that with Bird, Anthony, Sorel. Good heavens, even with Samuel!" The sinewy muscle of Effie's arm held tight. The years Effie had spent wandering the world far outnumbered those of Anthony and Sorel. She enjoyed the many lives she'd touch as time passed and knew that Gilda would never be at ease until she too fully accepted the change in perspective that was necessary to them.

Gilda rested her head in the soft part of Effie's neck at her shoulder. She couldn't deny what she knew was true. When she'd raced home in fear for Effie, she'd known then that the time was near for Effie to return to her travels.

"When?" Gilda asked.

"Let's not talk with our voices now," Effie said and covered Gilda's mouth with hers. At first Gilda could not respond; the ashes that would have been tears filled her mouth and eyes. Then the heat of Effie's lips drew her. Effie leaned backward onto the bed, her small breasts appealing in the dark. She pulled Gilda down to her. The moist earth shifted gently beneath them as Gilda let her weight press into Effie.

The desire they held for each other was heightened by the imminent separation, and for the first time Gilda could let herself feel anticipation of that moment when they'd see each other again.

Gilda stopped resisting and her desire pinned Effie to their bed. She thrust down, feeling Effie's body meet hers. This was the first woman she'd ever made love to with the fullness of desire. She remembered so many fleeting touches, moments when desire floated around her like bright bubbles until she wiped them away into the air. Now she wanted to breath them in as she did when drinking Sorel's beloved champagne. With Effie she'd learned to open, to meet the needs of her body that ran just as deep as blood.

Pushing her knee between Effie's legs, Gilda straddled her tight thigh muscle and set a rhythmic pace that kept time with their breathing. Each inhalation drove them deeper into their hunger for each other. When Gilda felt they were both ready she slipped inside Effie, gently letting the tide of their desire guide her. The muscles in Gilda's arm tightened to solid cords as her thrusts grew more insistent and Effie's embrace tightened. Their bodies pulsated on the firm pallet in a rhythm both old and new. The sound of their breathing and the wetness of Effie's body rocking on Gilda's hand filled the locked room. Everything around them was forgotten until Effie exploded into Gilda's hand. Gilda's body stiffened as she continued pushing harder. She thrust against Effie, feeling every texture of her skin and feeling nothing at all except the wave crashing inside her. She muffled her final scream in the pillow at Effie's head.

The room vibrated with the passion that they'd released into the air. A damp mist floated above them as they both lay still until their breathing steadied.

Effie touched the softness of Gilda's close-cut hair and was pleased to sense the change in Gilda's understanding. The worry had sat uneasily on her for weeks. She'd used all her energy to shield Gilda from the conflict she felt. Now she was able to open.

Gilda pulled the comforter up around them and they drifted into the rest that usually claimed all of them in the pre-dawn hours. After only moments of listening to Effie's breathing slow to almost nothing, Gilda, too, was no longer awake. Their room was steeped in darkness maintained by the painted windows and heavy drapes that hung in front of them. Their rest was not governed by a diurnal clock, but ebbed and flowed with their energy. Night was their natural milieu and daylight could drain their energy, but no hours were unavailable to them.

Just before the sun pushed against the covered window Gilda's eyes opened. She stared into the inky air, uncertain why she was suddenly alert at that moment. The house remained quiet all around her. Too quiet.

Gilda reached out for Effie, who pulled herself back from sleep.

"He's here," Gilda said in a low hiss.

Effie was awake and reaching for her clothes within the moment. They both stepped into pants and sweaters as they listened to the air around them.

"The music," Effie said as she realized she could still hear a soft guitar from Marci's apartment above them. Without speaking Gilda and Effie bolted through the doors and out into the hall. They moved silently up the stairs afraid of what they'd find. Samuel was there. Using his powers, he'd shrouded Marci's room so nothing could be perceived except the record on the stereo. They stood outside the door for only a second, then Effie twisted the knob off silently, the brass wrinkling between her fingers like paper before she dropped it to the floor. Gilda pushed the door open to Marci's living room, which glowed in red.

At first Gilda thought the walls were awash in blood but realized it was the lamplight that usually shone down into their yard. The shade moved against the open window where a figure stood. Samuel stepped forward, his face twisted in hatred. The torn yellow silk of Marci's blouse lay at his feet. Gilda looked quickly around the room. On the far side, across the plush couch he'd been so proud of, Marci lay sprawled, blood still draining onto the floor from his wound.

Gilda ran to Marci and knelt on the floor. Around his head, blood had soaked into the cushions of the couch and then pooled on the floor beside him. His eyes fluttered behind his lids. Gilda's anger rose through her throat.

"You didn't even take his blood. You spilled it like sewage!" Gilda pressed her hand to the wound in Marci's neck, hoping to stem the flow before it was too late.

Effie took a step closer and looked over at Marci. "I don't know, Gilda."

"Forget about him," said Samuel the satisfaction clear in his voice.

"You were here with him, weren't you? When I was in the yard?"

Samuel's laughter was not mirthful. "Of course. The little slut was wiggling with glee. I could have slaughtered him right then. But I wanted you to see."

"No, Samuel, I think you wanted to be punished," Effie said, her voice unnaturally even, as if she were in a trance.

Samuel was startled, as if he'd not noticed her before. He tried to move but found his limbs were sluggish.

"Marci...de Justo! That's who you meant when you said "fair." Gilda spoke her realization aloud as if it might reel the hours back in and she could save her friend.

"My fight is with Gilda." Samuel almost shouted at Effie.

"And what is that quarrel?"

"She knows."

"An unarticulated complaint is an answer withheld. Speak!"

"Gilda knows."

"An answer withheld is an embrace of ignorance."

Samuel's face was filled with as much puzzlement as fear each time Effie spoke.

"He's barely breathing!" Gilda spoke as she clenched her hand tightly around Marci's neck.

"Careful. Press your lips to the wound."

"No! This isn't Marci's choice, I..."

"Do it, gently let your fluids mix. But take nothing from him, listen inside."

Samuel watched Gilda bend toward the small body. He doubted Marci could be revived without an infusion of blood and he believed Gilda too timid to give Marci life that way. He smirked in satisfaction that finally he'd found his revenge.

"Ignorance is a dull knife." Effie moved closer to Samuel, her muscles rippling like electricity under her clothes. Samuel thought he heard a noise in the yard below but was afraid to turn his eyes from Effie.

"All I wanted was peace," Samuel said, his voice a narrow whine that grated in the air.

"You wanted Eleanor to love you. She didn't! Can't you understand that? She didn't love anyone but herself," Effie said. She could feel Gilda's energy flowing through the room and sense Marci regaining consciousness. "Pull back!" she shouted.

Gilda raised her head and wiped Marci's blood from her mouth. The tiny portion of her blood she'd shared would give him the strength he needed. She would nurse him through the moment when he might have hunger without drawing him into their family against his wishes.

She stood, placing Marci tenderly back onto the couch with his legs raised on pillows. *"Mi hermano,"* she murmured to him softly to quiet the terror that returned with his consciousness. The wound had closed and she could feel fresh blood, enlivened by hers, coursing through his veins. His skin took on a more natural color as he struggled to open his eyes. Gilda rested her hands on his forehead, willing him into sleep.

"She wouldn't leave us in peace," Samuel said to Effie as if that explained their friend bleeding on the couch.

"Peace is most difficult to endure, one of my teachers was fond of saying," Effie said as she moved closer to Samuel. His eyes hardened; he was unable to understand why he couldn't move. Effie held him in her gaze, not letting her anger or disgust distract her.

"You will now have peace," she said as she clasped her two hands together as if to pray. Her swing curved smoothly up through the air; her blow knocked Samuel back against the window frame, cracking the wood. She hit him again as he bounced forward, and the glass shattered. He struggled back toward Effie.

"No!" Gilda said, her voice rising out of the deep place she'd always run from. The thick, guttural tone was like broken ice showering around them. Gilda's stride carried her across the room before either Effie or Samuel saw her move. Samuel reached out with both hands for her throat as if he could silence her voice. Gilda dropped to her knees, eluding his grasp, and yanked Marci's ruined blouse from beneath his feet. The tear of the cloth reverberated in the room. With the shredded material gripped between her clenched fists Gilda rose, swinging upward. Her blow caught Samuel under his chin and she could hear his teeth clamp shut through the flesh of his tongue. This time he fell back through the window as the shade snapped open.

In the few seconds of his fall Samuel still smiled, the blood of his severed tongue creasing his face. He was certain he could not be hurt by a two-story fall onto a garden. In his years he'd survived much worse.

At that moment Anthony took a step away from the artfully carved box on the ground, off the carefully laid flagstones and into the path of Samuel's descent. He raised a broad silver dagger. His pale skin glistened in the darkness of the yard. The shining metal and colorful gems that adorned the handle caught the hint of morning light that peeked over the horizon. The muscles of Anthony's arm were taut, holding the silver dagger before him. He admired its beauty just as Samuel's spine made contact with the tip. Anthony released his hold as Samuel's body swallowed the blade and crashed to the ground. He lay on the grass, the hilt driven into the ground, the bloody blade gleaming from his chest. Samuel's eyes opened in disbelief, and then were empty.

Anthony looked up at the windows that surrounded the yard. All were dark and unoccupied except for Marci's, where Gilda and Effie looked down at him. "You will have peace now," he said. He pulled an edge of Samuel's coat up to protect his hand as he gripped the blade of the knife and wrenched it downward, opening Samuel's chest. He then pushed the hilt deeper into the ground. Blood flowed like a stream into the roots of the evergreen. Anthony ripped at Samuel's clothes, removing them and his shoes, which held his protective soil. He then stepped back into the shadow of Gilda's garden door and watched morning break over the city.

Gilda and Effie locked Marci's door, leaving him cocooned in sleep until they woke him. When they stood beside Anthony at the garden door they clasped each other's hands, which were slick with blood.

"His life was much too long, Gilda. He didn't have the spirit for it," Effie said.

"I'm sorry it ended here." Anthony spoke softly.

"We saved Marci, that's a balance, I think," Gilda answered.

"More than a balance," Effie added.

"Do you remember Joe Louis?" Gilda asked Effie.

"Of course. His power was amazing!"

"He'd have loved your swing." Gilda laughed.

"I think you might make the college team yourself," Effie said.

They retreated into the house as the sun took over the sky. Before anyone could look from their windows, it had turned Samuel's body into ash, leaving only the dagger in the soil. From above, its silver gleam looked like the tilted arm of a sundial greeting the day. Although windows were painted and the curtains were already drawn, Effie tugged at their hems as if to fasten them more tightly.

"Come," Gilda said as she removed her clothes. After washing off the blood of their enemy and of their friend, the three climbed into the wide bed where the two women had made love only moments before. Pulling the gold comforter up, Effie, Gilda, and Anthony turned to fit into the curves of each other's bodies. Each left the other to personal thoughts: Anthony remembered a time over a hundred years earlier when he'd helped the young Gilda wash away the filth of the road in a deep copper tub. At this cleansing tonight, he saw that naïveté was no longer a veil between her and the real world. Effie's mind drifted over the roads she might follow now that Gilda had her own path.

Gilda was at first startled that Samuel's death was a relief more than a burden. She'd watched the muscles of his face soften and his eyes lose their hardness, finally understanding he'd locked himself inside a torment that had only this release. She fell into sleep planning to clean Marci's rooms before awakening him, wondering where she'd find him a new silk blouse. They were all at rest before the sun's rays tapped at the shuttered windows.

BLACKOUT
JEFFREY RICKER

It had been snowing for two days with no end in sight. Jason looked out the living room window at four-foot drifts piled against the garage. The howling wind rattled the windows. He shivered, stubbed out his cigarette, and lit another one.

The house phone had gone dead an hour ago. Cell phone reception was mediocre at best and nonexistent inside the house. At least the electricity was still on. He had a drawer full of candles, and the woodpile was well stocked. He was as prepared as he could be. His power was usually the first to go out and the last to come back on. Last winter, they couldn't get the garage door open and had only firewood, candles, and cold cuts for ten days.

The howling wind eventually died away. Upstairs, the floor creaked, and Jason nearly dropped his cigarette. The house had been built before the turn of the last century, and he'd never gotten used to its shorthand of creaks and rattles: the ticking of the radiators, the buzz of the hall lights.

It wasn't the first time the house had startled him.

❖

Get out of my house.
"Did you hear that?"

"Hear what?" David asked. He poked at the fire, stirring up sparks as he repositioned the logs. Satisfied he'd arranged the fire just so, he stood up, arched his back, and took his wineglass from the mantel. At the same time, a gust of wind swept against the house, and the fire flickered in time with the lights. The windows rattled. Upstairs, the floors groaned again. Jason shuddered and glanced up toward the ceiling.

"Sometimes," he said, "it sounds like someone's walking around up there."

"It's just the wind," David said, brandishing the poker like a sword. "Fear not, fair maiden. I'll defend you."

That had been last winter, not long after they'd moved in.

A year before David died.

A house in the country had been David's idea. He'd grown up in a small town and missed having the rhythms of the natural world close to his front door. He didn't mind the hour commute to and from the city every day, and Jason could freelance from anywhere. It was hard to resist when he saw David's face light up at the moment their real estate agent brought them through the front door that first time. Even when they drove up to the house, David got more and more excited as the trees on either side of the driveway drew close overhead.

"This is it," he'd said, "I just know it."

"We haven't even seen it yet." Jason hoped David would stay patient long enough to bargain for a decent price—they were asking too much, and it had been sitting on the market more than six months. The house had been kept in good shape and modernized while remaining true to its original design.

"So, who were the previous owners?" Jason asked Lydia, their Realtor—an older woman, relatively new to the area herself, a city refugee for the past three years. Mercifully, she wasn't as perky as other real estate agents he'd had the misfortune to meet.

"Dan Richards? Widower, lived in the house for forty years. His wife died about three years ago. Unfortunately, she was the nicest thing about him, from what I hear." Lydia leaned in close. "He was a holier-than-thou son of a bitch. I can't imagine why anyone would stay with that bastard for as long as she did."

David didn't hear her estimation of the former owner, having disappeared into the kitchen. When he returned, the expression on his face was as far from poker as possible.

"It needs updating, but it's *huge*."

"Size queen," Jason muttered under his breath. Lydia giggled.

❖

Why do perverts like you get to live and my wife doesn't?

"Lydia never met Dan before Abby died." Jane Babbage said this when she dropped in two weeks after Jason and Dan moved in. Jane was their nearest neighbor (if a neighbor they couldn't see through the dense curtain of trees could be called a neighbor). David was already back to work and getting used to the lengthy commute, while Jason spent half his day working and the other half unpacking. When he heard the knock on the kitchen door, he thought it might have been a woodpecker. Instead, he opened the door to a small, elderly woman in an orange corduroy field jacket, who smiled and held up a basket of muffins.

"Welcome to the neighborhood," she said brightly. "Well, actually, we *are* the neighborhood."

Jason took the basket. The muffins were still warm. He invited her in for coffee.

"He was absolutely devoted to her," Mrs. Babbage ("Please, call me Jane") said of Dan Richards while they waited for the pot to brew. The muffins were carrot and walnut; Jason polished off three of them while Jane filled him in on the details of the Richards' lives, Abby's cancer, and Dan's abrupt change.

"He just got mean, like an old dog who's lived too long. We tried to stay friends, but after a while it was too much of a strain." She fiddled with her coffee cup, rolling it between her palms. "Eventually, he just wouldn't answer the door, even when we knew he was in here. Then no one saw him in town for over a week, we finally called the police, and they told us he'd died in here."

Jason shuddered, and Jane stopped playing with her coffee mug and covered his hand with hers. "Oh, listen to me, telling you these horrible things. Mark's always saying I have no filters."

"It's all right," Jason said, though the house seemed darker now. He was certain it was just his imagination. Still, he got up and turned on the light over the kitchen table, even though it was only early afternoon.

❖

"That was his dream home, not yours," Katie said. "Why are you still even there?"

Katie was David's sister. She'd called him just about every day since the funeral. Jason wondered why she still cared.

"It's not that easy," he said. "I can't just leave here."

"Oh, of course it is, and of course you can." He listened to her exhale forcefully—she was a smoker too—and pictured her pacing the short distance from her studio apartment's front door to the kitchen (if you could call the row of appliances along the opposite wall an actual kitchen). The last time he and David had visited, they'd stayed in a hotel.

When he was quiet on the line for a beat too long, Katie added, "Hell, just come visit for a few days. I know my place is the size of a postage stamp, but we can spend most of our time out and about anyway. It'll do you good to get away from there for a while."

"It hasn't even been a month," he said.

"Trust me. That's long enough."

They'd had that conversation last week. He'd intended to take her up on her offer—he'd been thinking about it earlier that weekend, but now, with it snowing like hell, thoughts of getting away gradually contracted until he just wanted to wait out the storm.

❖

You're going to hell, you filthy sinner.

Things started going wrong when they began to redo the kitchen the following fall. It was a big, open, airy room, but had barely enough cabinet space for David's pots and pans, and the upper cabinets were too shallow to accommodate their dinner plates. Too much wasted space, David said. Later that summer, he had plans drawn up for a center island and new cabinets along two walls. They moved the refrigerator and the microwave into the dining room, and contractors got to work ripping out the old fixtures.

The house started getting drafty after that. David never seemed to notice, but Jason kept walking through sudden chills and breezes in odd places. Sometimes they were strong enough to rustle curtains or set a ceiling fan's string pull to swaying, even when the fan wasn't on. It never seemed to happen in or near the kitchen, where the contractors were busting things up. Instead, the draft was strongest in the bedroom or while he was walking down the second-floor hall.

"You want me to start a fire?" David asked. Jason had just put on a hoodie and had the hood up over his head. It was only September, and too early even to be thinking about that sort of thing. Nevertheless, Jason nodded.

The breezes got stronger as the renovation went on. They'd come rushing toward Jason out of nowhere, then stop, abrupt as a slamming door. He and David turned on the heat, kept a fire going in the fireplace as often as possible, and Jason pulled out the winter clothes a couple months early.

It was worst when David was at work and Jason was alone.

Jason was at his desk in the second-floor office, around three thirty in the afternoon, three hours before David got home. Jason tensed when the contractors left the house. Then it was just him and whatever was making that breeze. He went around the first floor and opened all the curtains, turned on the radio, opened the back door and let in the cool air through the screen door. Still, when he walked down the second-floor hall, he could feel that breeze sweep past him, and he knew it wasn't because the door downstairs was open.

He tried to concentrate on the laptop screen in front of him, but the breeze settled into a chill across his shoulders and neck and wouldn't leave him alone. He shivered, hunched his shoulders, and pulled the collar of his shirt higher. The chill drifted away.

The door slammed. Jason spun in his chair, bumped into his desk, and sent his coffee cup crashing to the floor. He stared at the now-closed door and listened to the house creaking in the breeze—and tried to convince himself that he wasn't hearing footsteps moving down the hall.

❖

"You don't seriously think the place is haunted, do you?" David asked. They'd just finished dinner, and neither of them was in a hurry to get up and clear the table.

Jason shrugged. "It's an old house. The old guy died in here. If he was as much of a bastard as Lydia made him out to be, I guess it wouldn't surprise me."

David all but rolled his eyes. "I can't believe we're discussing this like it's even possible."

"I don't know how else to explain it." Jason knocked back the contents of his wineglass and checked the bottle for more. He refilled his glass.

"Could it have been one of the construction workers maybe opening a door in another part of the house? You've said yourself how drafty this place can be."

Jason shook his head. "This was no draft. And the guys had been gone at least half an hour before the door slammed."

Jason could tell David wasn't convinced. "I wonder why I haven't seen or felt anything. You've always said I had an extra sense when it comes to picking up on things."

Jason smirked. "I didn't say you had an extra sense. I said you were overly sensitive."

David, scowling in mock anger, balled up his napkin and threw it at Jason, who caught it and dropped it on his empty plate. He got up to clear the table.

"You don't suppose someone could have come into the house while you weren't looking?" David asked. "Maybe the contractors left a door unlocked?"

"We never lock the doors anyway," Jason said. "Besides, who would bother? We have exactly one neighbor, and you practically have to drive to get to their house. The only other people who come by are the contractors and the mailman."

Jason crammed the paper plates in the trash can and let the lid bang shut. He'd have to wash the wineglasses in the bathroom sink. Hopefully the kitchen would be done soon. He was getting tired of eating off paper plates.

"Out of the way, concealed from view, and not heavily trafficked sounds like a thief's dream come true. I guess it's a good thing I bought the gun."

Jason nearly dropped the wineglasses. "You bought *what?* When?"

"A couple weeks ago. It's in the nightstand upstairs."

"You might have told me before you brought a deadly weapon into the house."

"Well, I'm telling you now." David got up, took the wineglasses from Jason, and headed to the bathroom to wash them. "We live in a secluded place where it'd take the county sheriff a long time to respond if we were in real trouble."

Jason scowled. "When you talk like that, it makes me wonder why we moved here in the first place."

"We could always move back," David said.

"Not on your life," Jason snapped without thinking. He would have loved to go back, actually—their friends all promised to visit, but would they really? If he and David did move back to the city, though, they'd have to deal with insane rents for postage-stamp-sized apartments, crowds, neighbors.

On second thought, he didn't want to go back.

Besides, they'd just shelled out a small fortune for the kitchen, so they should at least take the time to enjoy it.

"I just wish you wouldn't play devil's advocate so much," Jason said.

David carried the now-clean glasses to the one finished piece of countertop in the kitchen, where he upended them on a dish towel. "Well, if I don't play devil's advocate, then that means the house really *is* haunted. That, or you've lost your mind. I'm not sure which of those options I prefer—especially since I just told you there's a gun in the house and if you're crazy, you might shoot me in the middle of the night."

"Don't even joke like that!" Jason said, though David had a grin on his face the whole time. He drew Jason into a kiss that clearly meant business, and they went upstairs.

Jason didn't tell him that even when they were in bed, with David underneath him, he felt the chill settle across his shoulders. Long after David was snoring away next to him, the cold lingered.

❖

That was a week before the contractors finished the kitchen. Two weeks before David died. It was late October, not quite Halloween, but a sudden cold snap blasted the East Coast, and Jason couldn't stop his teeth from chattering.

"You sure you're not coming down with something?" David asked. He was getting ready to go out and restock the woodpile. In the past week they'd burned through most of their supply.

"The only thing I think I'm coming down with is frostbite," Jason said. He lay wrapped in a blanket on the sofa, the fireplace blazing. David put a mug of tea on the coffee table and kissed Jason's forehead before heading outside.

Jason stared at the flames waving madly in the fireplace. David left the TV remote in reach, but Jason couldn't muster the strength to reach for it any more than he could reach for his tea.

Outside, the chain saw revved up. Next spring, they wanted to put a garden on the other side of the driveway, and David planned to take down some of the maples and spruces to make room. The thought of more firewood actually warmed Jason up for a moment, and he drifted off.

He dreamed of a fly buzzing by his ear before he woke up. The fire had died down to embers, and the living room was dim in the slanting late-afternoon sunlight. He sat up and reached for his mug, which had gone cold. He could still hear the fly—which, he realized, wasn't a fly. It was David's chain saw, and it had been running a long time.

He set the mug down and got to his feet. His first instinct was to go outside and see what was wrong. Because something was wrong, he was sure of it. Even more than that, though, he didn't want to leave the house. As long as he stayed inside, everything might be fine.

The chill at his back goaded him forward, though. It taunted him into the foyer, rustled the curtains over the sidelight as he fumbled with his boots, and snatched the door out of his grasp and banged it open.

Felled, the tree seemed larger than it had when it was upright. It lay across the driveway, and the yellow-leafed crown extended all the way into the main yard.

The tree's massive trunk also lay across David. From the front porch, Jason could see David's feet and lower legs, the right one twisted at an odd angle toward the other part of David that Jason could see: his right arm, hand gripping the still-running chain saw.

We should have hired someone to do that, Jason thought in the instant before he screamed David's name and bolted across the yard. He jammed his hand in his pocket for his phone—pulled it out, fumbled, dropped it, picked it up again. He had to call 911, though he could tell even without seeing David's face there was no hope.

He stared at the screen—*No Service,* it said, and he screamed again, this time a wordless noise of anguish and frustration. He ran down the driveway toward the road, where he knew he could get cell phone reception. He could have used the landline, but the memory of that cold breeze in the house propelled him down the drive.

Jason made the call and raced back up the driveway as quickly as he could—skidding to a sudden halt. He could have sworn he saw a man standing in the entryway, far enough back to be mostly concealed in shadow. When he stopped and looked, *really* looked, all he saw was darkness.

He wasn't sure how long he stood there staring before the steady burr of the chain saw cut through his fog. He turned away from the house and took a few halting steps toward David.

Jason knelt by the chain saw and carefully slipped it out of David's grip, which was still surprisingly strong even in death. Once he shut off the saw, the quiet slammed into him. It was that hour of golden light typical of perfect fall afternoons, the sun filtering through the trees in yellow, orange, and red, the breeze more refreshing than chilling.

It hardly seemed like the sort of day when someone would die.

From where he sat on the ground, Jason couldn't see David's face. Did he look surprised? Were his eyes still open? Was his expression contorted in his final moment of pain? Maybe his eyes were closed and his expression serene. Jason didn't want to know. He picked up David's hand, the skin already cool, and stared at the sunlight through the trees. He did not look toward the front door.

❖

Returning to the house after the funeral was strange. Jason spent two weeks with David's parents. His own parents had come all the way from Missouri. The endless parade of relatives and mourners left him little time to think about the house. Buffered by the abundance of love and caring, he wondered if he'd just imagined the baleful aspect of that place in the woods.

He hadn't. The familiar, oppressive gloom settled on him like a sigh as soon as the front door closed. Jason dropped his bag on the floor and stared down the hall. The stairs rose on his left, the second floor sunny and bright. All the leaves had fallen from the trees while he was gone, and the late-afternoon sun, stark and cold, streamed in the windows. The mail was piled on the hall table along with a note from Jane. Mark had cut up the tree and hauled it away.

Good. Jason didn't want it in the house, even if only to burn it.

He went into the living room. The curtains swayed gently in a draft, though he supposed that could have been from opening the front door.

He doubted it, though.

❖

It took the old man's ghost—and Jason was sure it was him—a while to work up his energy. Jason spent the afternoon putting away his clothes and cleaning out the things that had gone bad in the fridge. He didn't feel like making dinner, but he did open a bottle of wine while he began boxing up David's clothes.

Somehow, he managed to do it without bursting into tears, the first day in two weeks that he'd remained dry-eyed. He set aside a few things David's parents had asked for, as well as some watches, pieces of jewelry, and purely sentimental items—pictures, a couple of books, an old stuffed teddy bear—he thought David's sister Katie might like. He took all the photos with David in them off the walls, cleared picture frames from shelves, and put them away. He couldn't bear to look at them, not now. At his bedside Jason kept the first picture of David he'd taken—at the beach, his hair still wet, face and chest bronzed and gorgeous. Jason put it face-down in the nightstand drawer.

David's fingerprints on the house still surrounded him, though, and Jason *wanted* to believe he could feel David's presence, but in truth all he felt was chilled, and it dawned on him the house had grown colder since he started on his task. When he finished taping the last box shut, it was dark outside, the wine bottle was empty, and he was too tired to bother with dinner.

Sleep came fast, a small mercy that kept Jason from dwelling on David's absence from the other side of the bed. Not that his dreams afforded him any refuge. David dominated them, though later Jason only remembered snippets, frames from a movie: David turning to tell him something, David swimming toward him in a glass-sided pool, David running toward him through a forest of falling trees, their impacts making the ground shudder, and one final massive tree directly behind David tumbling straight toward him.

Jason sat upright, not sure what had woken him up, only that *something* had roused him out of sleep. An echoing filled his ears, though he couldn't remember the sound that had produced it.

He heard it again. And again. It sounded like someone was slamming every door in the house. Jason fumbled for the nightstand drawer, his hands in the darkness finding the gun. He flipped off the safety and pressed his back against the headboard, the gun aimed at the bedroom door.

He waited. Adrenaline overpowered his sleepiness, and his hands didn't shake as much as he'd thought they would. The slamming doors grew more distant—they were downstairs now—until eventually they ran out of doors to slam.

He sat up all night staring at the bedroom door.

When it was finally light the next morning, he went out. Every door on the second floor was shut. He knew when he went downstairs, he'd find the same.

❖

You're next, faggot.

Jane called on him at least twice a week, sometimes every other day. Sometimes Mark came with her and busied himself with whatever needed doing—raking leaves, winterizing the lawnmower, stocking the woodpile.

"You look thinner," Jane said. It was not a compliment. "When was the last time you took a shower?"

Jason pondered and shrugged. "What day is it?"

She sent him upstairs to clean up, even going so far as to follow him and lay out clean clothes. He closed the bathroom door and turned on the shower, and stood under the spray until he remembered what he was supposed to be doing.

Showered and dressed, hair still damp, he went downstairs, the breeze following until his foot hit the last step and he headed for the kitchen. Glancing in the living room along the way, he noticed the blankets and pillows he'd scattered across the sofa were now folded and in a neat pile on the ottoman.

"Why have you been sleeping on the couch?" Jane asked. She was at the stove sautéing something, and a pot of water boiled on the back burner.

"Leave him be if he wants to sleep downstairs," Mark said. He sat at the kitchen table and cradled a mug of coffee. Jane scowled at her husband but said nothing. She turned back to the stove.

Jason didn't tell them that he was sleeping on the sofa, not because he couldn't bear to be in the bed he used to share with David—though that was certainly true—but because the chilling breeze that lingered over his shoulders, ruffled curtains, and slammed doors had whipped into a full-blown gale two nights before, strong enough to sweep books and candles off dressers and nightstands and topple the peace lily in the corner of the bedroom. Jason had raced downstairs and taken refuge in the kitchen, curled up on the floor and clutching the biggest knife from the butcher block. After that, he'd made his bed in the living room and couldn't bring himself to go upstairs until Jane practically pushed him into the shower.

Jason sat at the table and poured himself a cup of coffee. Mark gestured toward the back door. "Supposed to be a big storm coming up the coast, so I've got your woodpile in pretty good shape."

"You don't have a whole lot in the refrigerator, honey," Jane said, not turning away from the stove. Jason wondered what she was making; he could smell garlic and onions. "I have to go to the store later. You want us to pick up a few things for you?"

"Thanks, that'd be nice," he said. That meant they'd be back later in the afternoon, and it seemed important that they should return soon.

In spite of everything that had gone on before, he hadn't been afraid of the house until now. David's accident could have been just that—an accident—and not related to the spectre intent on bedeviling just him, but he wasn't sure he believed that anymore. And the odd whispers he thought were just voices in his head…maybe they weren't.

Jane placed a bowl of spaghetti with meatballs in front of him and another at Mark's place. She returned with a basket of garlic bread and her own bowl, and sat down.

"Eat," she said.

Jason was about to point out that spaghetti was an odd choice for breakfast until he glanced at the clock. It was one thirty in the afternoon. He didn't have any meat or pasta in the house; Jane must have brought all the ingredients with her.

"Thanks for making lunch," he said. He wasn't hungry, but he ate it anyway. "Did, um…did anyone ask you to check in on me?"

A glance passed between Jane and her husband. Mark paused with his fork above a meatball before looking down and spearing it. "Guess the jig's up," he said.

"We would have come by anyway, but your sister-in-law said at the funeral she was worried about you coming back up here all by yourself."

"I'm fine." He didn't sound convincing even to himself.

Mark leaned in. "Bullshit, son," he said, his tone low and gentle, the way he might have talked to a spooked horse.

Jason let his head drop over his bowl. He'd been so preoccupied by the ever-present chill pursuing him throughout the house, he hadn't given much thought to David. He let out a sigh.

The chill entered his body then with such force that Jason dropped his fork. His hands trembled as he brought them to his chest, where it felt like a blizzard raged.

Jane looked on the verge of tears when she reached for Jason, then gasped and almost snatched her hand away.

"Mark, he's ice cold. Go start a fire." She took Jason's hand in both of hers and began rubbing vigorously. He clenched his jaw to keep his teeth from chattering. "Are you coming down with something, hon?"

I'm coming down with a ghost was what he wanted to say, but he didn't trust his teeth to keep from clacking together if he opened his mouth. Instead, he just shook his head. Once Mark had a fire raging, Jason and Jane moved to the sofa and Jane threw a blanket over his shoulders.

"I'll bring you your lunch, hon," she said.

Jason stared into the fire and wished more than anything that he could feel warm again. He'd been cold ever since David died, even before that, but watching the flames twist and lick at each other, he couldn't help but remember the warmth he had drawn from David, trails of heat that David had been able to trace with his fingertips across Jason's skin.

Heat he breathed into Jason with a kiss.

He *did* feel warm then, remembering that. A band of heat draped across his shoulders and trailed down his chest, as if a pair of arms encircled him. Jason smiled at the memory of David doing just that, often when Jason stood cooking at the stove. Jason would lift a fork or spoonful of whatever he was making for David to try. David would have a taste, make approving noises (even if it wasn't very good) and leave a kiss of the flavor on Jason's cheek.

Jason burst into tears, the want for that feeling forcing its way out of him. He drew his legs up and hugged his knees into his chest, the sobs coming in gulps and hiccups. He hadn't even cried this hard in the days around the funeral. It scared him. He squeezed his eyes shut to try to stem the tears, but still they came.

He felt arms encircle and hug him close, and he felt someone else sit on the sofa and hug him too. He opened his eyes, expecting to see Jane and Mark on either side of him, but there was just Jane, rocking him gently and stroking his hair. Mark stood by the fire, twisting his hat in his hands and staring at his feet.

"Son," he said in that low, mournful rumble of a voice, "I really think you should get out of this house."

❖

Jason didn't leave, though. He promised he'd call the Babbages if he needed anything, and Jane said she'd come by with the extra groceries. But then the wind picked up, steel-gray clouds shut out the sky, and the snow began falling. Before long the driveway and the yard were covered. Soon it was coming down so hard he couldn't see beyond a few feet outside.

The warmth bled away gradually until he was once again shivering, even though he stood in front of the fireplace. By evening, the snow had piled up to the first step on the porch. Jane called to apologize for not dropping by with the groceries. They couldn't make it up the hill to his house, even with four-wheel drive. They'd come tomorrow, she said.

The next day, it snowed relentlessly. The wind rattled the windows and pushed drifts up to the third porch step. Jason wasn't sure how deep it really was. The tiny boxwood shrubs lining the stone path were barely visible humps beneath the snow.

He slept in the living room again, left the TV on so he wouldn't hear whatever walked upstairs at night. He slept fitfully and tossed wood onto the fire when he woke periodically, opening more wine as he finished off each bottle. He knew he was drinking too much, but it was the only way he could shake off wakefulness. If he dreamed, he barely remembered it. He recalled nothing more than a whispering voice, the words indistinct, buzzing at his ear.

He left every first floor light burning through the night, but when he woke up, the foyer light above the stairs was out. When he walked into the entryway to check it out, the first thing he noticed was a sharp, gasp-inducing shock of cold, like he'd just stepped under an icy showerhead.

The second thing he noticed, when he turned toward the stairs, were his clothes scattered up and down the length of the staircase to the second floor—shirts, trousers, underwear, even ties and suit jackets were flung, twisted and in some cases shredded. The second floor itself was encased in inky blackness. How could it be so dark up there? Had he closed all the curtains yesterday?

Even so, there should have been *some* light.

He didn't linger to consider this. The cold soon became too much, and he ran back to the living room and the comfort of the fire.

He kept away from the hallway and the foyer, limiting himself to the kitchen, living room, dining room, and half bathroom in the back. If he really needed to leave, he'd have to go out through the kitchen. He couldn't imagine it was colder outside than it was in the foyer.

The phone went dead first. By lunchtime, he still hadn't heard from Jane Babbage. He picked up the phone to see how they were doing and just to hear a voice besides the ones on TV. The silence that greeted him was flat and stunning; he nearly dropped the phone. If he needed to call, he'd have to use his cell phone, which never worked in the dead zone of the house.

He looked out the window. No way was he going outside any time soon. The power went out sometime after Jason found the unopened pack of Marlboro Lights in the kitchen junk drawer. He hadn't smoked in years, but he must have packed them when they moved. How old were they?

"Fuck it," he said and opened them. He'd already finished off the last bottle of white that day, and he'd just cracked into the red. Back in the day, he always said drinking and a cigarette were why he had two hands. Falling back into the habit took no effort at all.

But then the TV screen went blank and the lights flickered—once, twice, and out. Silence hung heavy in the house, while outside the wind whistled past the windows and moaned in the distance.

At first, he couldn't distinguish the whispering from the sound of the storm outside. Gradually, it became clearer, not enough to make out actual words, but impossible to ignore.

Don't listen to it, he thought, kneeling to put another log on the fire. The whispering buzzed like a gnat, though, and he found it hard to resist looking toward the foyer, afraid of what he might see waiting there.

Jason headed for the kitchen and the mudroom where they kept their heavy coats, hats, and gloves. He'd need to head toward the road if he expected to get a cell phone signal. Bundled up, he checked his pocket one last time for his phone and opened the door.

The snow came up to his knees in some places, and what was still coming down stung his face as he plodded down the hill. When a bar of signal finally popped up, he called Katie.

"You're *where?*" she asked, the connection clear enough to telegraph her disbelief. Or maybe she was just yelling *that* loudly. "You get back inside right now."

"I can't get any signal in the house and the landline's gone out. Listen, I was thinking maybe you're right and I should get out of here for a while...if your offer for me to visit still stands."

"Of course it does, but why did you have to go outside in the middle of a blizzard to tell me this? Is something wrong?"

Here it is, he thought. *She's going to think I'm crazy or—* He couldn't come up with an alternative.

"There've been—things happening. In the house. I can't explain them. All the doors slammed a few nights ago. I know that sounds crazy, but they were open when I went to bed, and I woke up in the middle of the night and heard them. And then the house has been getting so cold, even with the heat on and a fire going." He paused a moment before adding, "And I've been hearing something, like someone whispering things to me."

She was quiet for a long time. "What kind of things?" she asked, her tone careful.

"I can't tell, but I figure it can't be good."

She breathed deeply, and he could hear that even over the storm. "Listen to me," she said, her voice surprisingly calm. "You need to go back inside now, no matter how frightening it is. You stay outside and you'll freeze to death." Jason started to protest, but Katie cut him off. "After we get off the phone, I'll call the Babbages and ask them to come get you as soon as they can. But you have to go back inside first."

She wouldn't hang up on him until he agreed, and she even stayed on the line as he walked back up the hill until finally he lost her signal. It was impossible to see his footprints in the driveway. When he made it back inside, the house provided little warmth.

He wasn't surprised.

❖

He kept the fire going. It was the only thing keeping the ghost at bay, he was sure of it. Jason wondered how long the snow would keep falling, how long the firewood would last, whether the Babbages would come for him before it ran out.

He was also down to his last two bottles of wine. Drinking didn't make him feel any warmer, but it made him mind the cold less and made it harder to focus on the whispers that were a constant drone now, even when he retreated to the kitchen. He lit every candle in the living room and got more out of the kitchen drawer. All he had to do was make the firewood last until the next morning and keep the fire going in the meantime.

It didn't turn out that way.

He remembered the tail end of the dream he was having. David was once again running through the trees, which were falling behind him again too. Once again, Jason stood on the front porch, watching helplessly as David raced toward him. This time, he wasn't alone on the porch—but he also knew he really, *really* didn't want to look at the figure standing to his left. When the big tree once again started falling directly at David, Jason averted his eyes.

The man looked older than old. Few details of his appearance registered clearly except for the halo of receding white hair, the leathery wrinkles in his sunken cheeks, and—when he tilted his head to return Jason's stare—the blackness of his eyes.

"You're doing this," Jason said, gesturing toward the falling tree. "Stop it."

The man smiled and opened his mouth wide, impossibly wide, as if he were a snake about to devour prey. There were no fangs, though, no forked tongue, not even a normal mouth. It was nothing but blackness. He exhaled a frigid wind that howled louder than the crashing of the tree that flattened David.

Jason awoke to darkness. He was lying on the floor near the fireplace, which had gone out, and the room was frigid. He couldn't breathe. Hands pressed against his throat, fingers an icy vise digging into his skin. The whispers, insistent before, were now clear.

"This is my house."

Jason reached for the hands even though he couldn't see them. Touching them was like touching cold fire. He tried to scream but could only draw enough air for a croak. He flailed in the darkness, trying to find anything. He knocked over an empty wine bottle and heard it rolling away. Before it was out of reach, he grabbed it by the neck and swung upward. He heard the crack of glass against bone and the hands released him.

Jason stumbled drunkenly toward the stairs. Going out in the cold would surely kill him, not that it was much warmer inside. But the gun was upstairs.

How do you shoot a ghost, though? Jason wondered.

He barreled into the darkened bedroom, a sliver of moonlight through the window barely lighting his way. Memory drew him to the nightstand where he yanked the drawer open too quickly, spilling its contents onto the floor. He heard glass breaking. He flailed for the pistol he knew was there, shards pricking his fingers until he found first cold metal, then the rubber grip of the handle.

Jason rolled onto his back, turned toward the bedroom door, and raised the pistol. Before he pulled the trigger, David's first instruction when he was teaching Jason to shoot came back to him, the words as clear as if he actually heard them right then: *Use both hands.*

Jason fired. In the brief flare of light from the barrel, he saw a man in the doorway.

He fired again, the sound deafening him. The man was in the room now.

Jason fired a third shot. The man was at the foot of the bed. His face was gray and lined. He looked old, but the darkness in his eyes looked even older.

Jason fired one last time. The man's hands were reaching out toward him when something *(someone?)* darted from Jason's left side and rammed into the figure. In the darkness Jason heard what sounded like a scream, but it could have been the sound a tree makes when it topples over. Wind, arctic cold, swept through the room as the sound grew deafening.

Leaving the gun behind, Jason ran for the bedroom door. He continued down the hall and half ran, half fell down the stairs, arms outstretched, bouncing off the handrail as he tripped and sprawled in the foyer, pain stabbing his knee. Ignoring it, he swayed to his feet and flung open the front door. The blast of snow and frigid air staggered him briefly, but he felt the wind at his back propelling him down the front steps and into the snow. He got up, staggered down the walk—maybe through the yard, he wasn't sure where he was going—then weaved to the left just before he ran headlong into a tree, hooking it with an arm and boomeranging around it until he slumped to the ground. Behind him, it sounded like two wild cats fighting as consciousness sank beneath a blanket of snow.

❖

Jason awoke on the sofa. Mr. Babbage stoked the fire, and as Jason stared at him through half-open eyes, Jane came in with an armload of blankets and a mug of tea.

"Mark, he's awake." Jane set down the tea and then knelt beside the sofa. She unfurled a blanket and settled it over him. "What happened, hon?"

Jason tried to sit up, but even pressing his hands against the sofa cushions beneath him made his fingertips burn. He gave up and leaned back again. "I could have sworn someone was in the house last night. The power went out, and then they tried to break into the bedroom—"

"Why did you go outside, though?" she asked.

Jason tried to remember, but his memory of the night before receded even as he tried to pull it closer. He shook his head, and she patted his arm. "It's okay, hon. Just try to relax. Your sister-in-law called. She's coming up to get you as soon as the roads are clear."

He reclined on the sofa and turned to gaze out the window. The snow had stopped, and the sunlight reflecting off the white-covered yard blinded him for a moment. He closed his eyes. Later, he'd think about calling Lydia and putting the house on the market. He'd pack a few things and go stay with Katie for a while, even if her apartment *was* the size of a closet.

That could all wait, though. For the moment, he lay back and tried to remember the last time the house had been so bright.

CRAZY IN THE NIGHT
GREG HERREN

Danny probably would have never moved from his apartment on Constantinople Street—if it hadn't been for that damned thunderstorm.

It wasn't that it was such a great place—it was far too expensive for as small as it was, frankly, and he was well aware of that. But rents had gone through the roof after Katrina, and he needed a place to live. He could afford the rent, of course, that wasn't the problem with it. He just felt like he was being gouged every month when he wrote the check to his landlady, whom he called "that greedy bitch" to his coworkers and friends so often that no explanation was necessary. But he hated the hassle of moving—of getting services turned off and on, of packing and unpacking—and he hated the search for a new place most of all. So every month on the first he simply gritted his teeth, wrote the check, and gave it to that greedy bitch with a phony smile plastered on his face.

The forecast that day had been for rain, but between May and November the forecast every day was "hot, humid, chance of rain," but he took an umbrella with him when he left for work at the Monteleone Hotel that particular morning. He was so busy once he got to his office that he didn't know it turned dark as night outside when the rain started around one in the afternoon. The loud crack of thunder did startle him, breaking through the intense level of concentration he'd focused on the conference contract he was putting together, trying to remember things from the phone conversation with the conference organizer and swearing at himself for not writing down every request she'd made.

He walked out to the hotel lobby and saw Royal Street filling with water, and the doorman had come inside. *At least it's not a tropical storm,* he thought with a sigh of relief as he headed back to his office, *because that would suck.*

But the storm did manage to dump twelve inches of rain on New Orleans in slightly less than two hours, despite not being a tropical storm. That would be problematic in any city, but for New Orleans, built on a swamp below sea level and surrounded by water on every side, it was catastrophic. Despite the efforts of one of the best pumping systems in the world, the streets flooded. The residents of the city could only watch in helpless horror as the dirty brown rainwater rose and rose. Cars attempting to make it through the bayous the streets quickly became were inundated with water and engines stalled. Lightning knocked out power in most of the Uptown part of the city, and the power flickered a few times at the Monteleone.

Around three in the afternoon the storm passed and the sun came back out as though nothing had ever happened. In less than half an hour, the pumping system kicked into high gear and the dirty water disappeared. The only evidence that it had ever been there was the stalled cars, the mud and dirt and debris on the sidewalks and in the gutters, and the unlucky ones in low-lying houses pushing dirty water out of their houses with mops.

As Danny drove home from work that night, past dead cars pushed out of the streets up into parks and neutral grounds, his relief that his small overpriced apartment was on the second floor grew—until he turned down Constantinople Street and saw the enormous live oak that had crashed into the front of the building.

He parked, and stared in horror. He could see clearly into his apartment from where he was standing. His hands shaking, he fished his cell phone out of his pants pocket and called his boyfriend. Matthew came right over and spent a few hours with him in the wreckage, finding what was and wasn't ruined—almost everything was.

Finally, Matthew shook his head as the light faded and said, "Come on, babe, let's go over to my place. You can stay with me for now."

For now.

Too emotional and upset to say anything else, Danny just nodded.

But it rankled, as it always did.

They'd been seeing each other exclusively for just over a year—but God forbid Matthew even *consider* the frightening possibility of asking his newly homeless boyfriend to move in with him.

Matthew always begged off about making any kind of commitment, giving him a sheepish grin and an apology. He always claimed a long-term relationship that had ended really badly made him commitment-shy, and with some space and time he'd "get over it, I promise."

Much as Danny loved him, he couldn't help but wonder if he was wasting his time.

For two weeks he waited for Matthew to ask him to make his stay permanent, but he waited in vain. Once the settlement check was in his hand, he told Matthew in bed that night he was going to start looking for a place.

"Well, don't just grab the first place you see," Matthew said, slipping his arm around Danny's waist and pulling him closer. "You're welcome to stay here until you find the right place, you know."

He was glad it was dark, so that Matthew couldn't see his face.

He started looking the next morning on his drive to work—looking for "for rent" signs on his way downtown, cursing Matthew under his breath. It wasn't like there wasn't plenty of room in Matthew's house—he even had a spare bedroom, if it came to that—and since almost everything Danny had owned was water-damaged, it would be relatively simple. Everything he owned was already in Matthew's house. *But no, we can't have that, can we?* he thought angrily as the light at St. Andrew changed and he headed down Camp Street.

"Maybe it's time to just end this," he said out loud as he reached for his travel mug. He took a sip of coffee, stopped several cars back from the light at Melpomene. He was so wrapped up in his anger at Matthew he almost missed the cup holder—almost dropping the mug and making an enormous mess. He carefully set the mug down and just happened to see through the passenger window a For Rent sign hung on a massive live oak on the other side of the sidewalk. He bent down and leaned over, peering out the window. The house was a beautifully restored Victorian, painted green with brown trim. There was a wide front porch, whose roof made a balcony for the second floor. Hand-lettered with a black Sharpie in the long white rectangular box beneath the words *For Rent* was written: *2 bedroom upper, 1600 square feet, central heat and air, washer/dryer, modern kitchen, call Linda 555-0890.*

He typed the name and number into his phone just as the light turned green.

He called as soon as he got to the office, and made an appointment to see the place over his lunch hour.

It was perfect. The apartment took up the front half of the second floor of the house—each bedroom had two windows opening out onto the balcony. The kitchen was, indeed, modern—all the appliances were new, as were the front-loading washer and dryer, which sat in a small room Linda, the real estate agent, said "could be used as a walk-in closet, a pantry, or just storage." The bathroom was art deco, and everything in it was new. The floors were polished, shining dark hardwood, the ceilings were fourteen feet above the floor, and the living room was enormous. Beautiful brass chandeliers hung in the center of each room, with energy efficient bulbs screwed into the lighting fixtures just below the broad wooden blades of the ceiling fans, which matched the dark floors. There was a driveway that led to off-street parking, behind an electric gate.

And the house was right across the street from Coliseum Square, a beautiful old park with classic-looking street lamps and ancient live oaks. The St. Charles parade route and streetcar line were just a couple of blocks away, and he was much closer to work. He was almost afraid to ask the monthly rental price, and almost fainted in shock when she quoted him a number that was $200 less than the ruined apartment uptown.

"I'll take it," he said without even having to think twice about it, pulling his checkbook out of his back pocket. "When can I move in?"

"Whenever you want," she replied, producing a lease out of her briefcase. "It's available now."

Once he signed the lease and wrote her a check for a deposit and first month's rent, she handed over the keys and a remote control for the gate.

"Why is the rent so cheap?" Matthew asked that evening as he walked around the empty apartment, stopping at one of the bedroom windows facing the park. "As big as this place is, they should be able to get double what they're charging you—a balcony and a view of the park?" He shook his head. "It's almost too good to be true, you know?"

"There always has to be something wrong, doesn't there?" Danny stood in the living room, thinking about where to hang his Herb Ritts prints before remembering they'd been ruined. He spoke absently, without any malice.

"What's that supposed to mean?" Matthew walked back out of the bedroom with his two thick black eyebrows knit together and his round brown eyes narrowed. He folded his arms in front of him. He was wearing a white ribbed tank top, and crossing his arms made his thick chest bulge over the neckline.

"It's not supposed to mean anything. All I was thinking was, you know, after being overcharged by the bitch for so long, maybe I earned some apartment kharma." Danny looked at him, at the heavily muscled thick folded arms, the narrow waist, the jean shorts clinging tightly to his muscular upper thighs, and wondered if anyone could see inside the curtainless windows. He walked over to one of the side windows and looked out. No, they were much higher up than the nearest neighbor's windows. He moved toward Matthew and slid his arms around his waist, cupping his buttocks. "And I'm really glad I was lucky enough to find this place before someone else did." He kissed Matthew's lips, which were tightly closed at first and resistant.

But after a moment, Matthew's arms went around him and his lips parted.

They broke in the new apartment right there on the hardwood floor.

Danny took a week off from work and spent two days driving around the city, buying new furniture and new prints, sheets and towels and a phone, a television and kitchenware. It was the first time he'd ever moved into a new place and actually had the time to think about where things should go. He decided the bigger bedroom, the one to the right from the street, would be his bedroom and he would turn the other into a combination office/guest room. He bought curtains and hung them, deciding to make his bedroom dark blue and the guest room in earth tones. Late Thursday afternoon the bed arrived, and after the deliverymen left, he put the sheets on and made the bed. *Tomorrow,* he decided, *I am going to start living here.*

He usually spent Friday nights at Matthew's.

Maybe it's time I start putting some distance between me and Matthew, he thought as he straightened the new Lindsey Smolensky print he'd bought that morning and hung in the living room.

At least until he decides if he wants to get serious, or whatever it is he wants. I'm tired of waiting.

He made dinner for Matthew on Friday night while Matthew was at the gym, and the kitchen felt like it was *his* in a way the one on

Constantinople Street never had. *In fact,* he thought as he sliced onions for a salad and to put in the jambalaya, *that place never felt like home the way this one does.*

He'd given Matthew a gate key, and he'd just finished putting everything into the big stock pot and given it a big stir with a big wooden spoon when he heard the key in the dead bolt just before the apartment door opened.

"Christ, it's hot," Matthew said, pulling his sweaty T-shirt over his head and bunching it up in his big strong hands. Sweat gleamed on his thick muscles. He'd shaved his torso again that morning apparently, because there were red bumps in the deep cleavage in the center of his chest. "And you're making jambalaya? Are you crazy?"

"It's your favorite," Danny replied, a little resentfully. *You always criticize me,* he thought, *nothing's ever right enough for you.*

Matthew slipped off his shorts and underwear, coming up behind him naked. He snaked his arms around Danny's waist and started kissing the back of his neck. "Smells great to me," he said.

"You're all hot and sticky," Danny complained as Matthew tugged at the button fly of his shorts.

"Let's get stickier." Matthew slid Danny's shorts down, sliding his right hand inside the front of Danny's underwear.

"Matthew—" Danny tried to push Matthew away as his traitorous body responded to Matthew's hand. Matthew picked him up bodily, kissing him. Danny put his arms around Matthew's neck as Matthew carried him into the bedroom, setting him down on the bed like he weighed nothing. He tried to sit up but Matthew pushed him back down on the bed, tearing off his shirt. Before Danny knew it he was naked, and Matthew was kissing him all over his chest, nuzzling at his nipples, and Danny just gave in to it, as he always did.

Afterward, Matthew fell asleep and Danny slipped on his shorts. He opened the big window and stepped out onto the balcony to smoke a cigarette. Matthew hated him smoking, and Danny had pretty much quit but still sneaked one every now and then. He looked out at the park and relaxed. The apartment was beautiful, and the view of the park was spectacular. The live oak was far enough from the house so if it ever was blown into it, it probably wouldn't damage the house too much—the porch would keep it away. He wondered for the millionth time where things were going with Matthew. They loved each other, got along great, the sex was amazing, and they'd been together for over a year. Why was Matthew so uninterested in taking their relationship further? *If only I had the nerve to give him an ultimatum,* he thought, looking in through the window at Matthew's sleeping body, and yet again the sheer beauty and symmetry of Matthew's muscles made him catch his breath. He turned back away from the window and watched a man playing Frisbee with a Jack Russell terrier in the park. He finished the cigarette and tossed it, slid the window open and went back into the kitchen to check on the jambalaya. It was almost ready, and when he walked back into the bedroom, Matthew was getting dressed. "I don't think I'm going to stay for dinner, after all."

Annoyed, he said, "You're going home?" He couldn't believe it. His first night in the new apartment, he was making Matthew's favorite meal, and he was bailing?

"I gotta go let the dogs out." Matthew pulled his shirt over his head and tucked it into his shorts. "You can come sleep over." He smiled. "You can put the jambalaya in a bowl and we can reheat it. What do you say?"

Danny bit his lip and counted to ten. It was an ongoing bone of contention between them. Matthew always used his dogs as an excuse for never staying at Danny's, but that had been in the cramped old place—he'd thought now that he was in this beautiful new place it might be different. They had fought about it so many times that Danny didn't feel like getting into it again. "I was hoping you'd stay with me on my first night in a new apartment." He closed his eyes. Why had he said it? The fuse was now lit.

"I can't, you know that." Matthew shook his head. "I'd still have to go let them out in the morning."

"Fine." Danny walked back into the kitchen and turned the burner off. *I won't cry, I won't cry, I won't,* he repeated over and over to himself as he took the stock pot off the burner and started spooning it all into a plastic bowl. When Matthew tried to kiss him good-bye, he turned his face and Matthew's lips brushed his cheek.

"Whatever." Matthew rolled his eyes and went out the door. Danny shut the door behind him, pleased he'd resisted the urge to slam it, and turned the dead bolt. He opened a bottle of wine and found an appropriate play list on his iPod—Anita Baker, Toni Braxton, and old Gladys Knight—and hit "shuffle." *I'll just stay by myself in my beautiful new apartment and drink a bottle of wine and have myself a good cry with my girls,* he told himself. It was getting dark out, so he went around and turned on the lights. The dark had always made him uncomfortable. He wasn't afraid of the dark—but being alone in it always made him nervous. When the apartment was sufficiently lit, he sat down on the couch with the wine.

A few hours later he sat up on the couch. The wine bottle was almost completely empty and his head was spinning. *I shouldn't have drunk all that on an empty stomach,* he thought, staggering into the kitchen. The plastic bowl with the jambalaya in it was still sitting there on the counter. He ate a few spoonfuls—it was pretty good, if he did say so himself—and drank a glass of water. Still a little bit drunk, he walked around turning off the lights in the apartment. He went into the bedroom and picked out his clothes for the gym the next morning, draping them over a chair, and put his shoes on the floor in front of the chair. After plugging in his Mickey Mouse night-light, he got undressed, sliding naked into the sheets that still smelled of Matthew's musk. He wrapped his arms tightly around himself and turned off the light on the nightstand.

The alarm clock glowed 3:17 when he sat up in bed groggily. *Why did I just wake up?* he wondered as his eyes adjusted to the light. *Was there a noise or something?* He sat there, still, listening. Nothing. He heard nothing.

Then he realized the only light in the room was the reddish glow of the alarm clock.

He turned on the light, annoyed. If the bulb in the night-light was blown, he didn't have another. He climbed out of the bed and walked over to the socket.

"What the fuck?" He leaned over. The night-light was lying on the floor. He knelt down and picked it up. He distinctly remembered plugging it in, the warm glow it cast as he had closed his eyes. How could it have worked itself loose in the night? He plugged it back in. Once again, Mickey lit up, and he got under the covers again. He listened for a few moments, but heard nothing but the occasional car driving past on Camp Street.

He turned out the light and went back to sleep.

It seemed like he had just fallen asleep when the alarm started its highly annoying buzzing. He smacked at it and got out of the bed. He half staggered into the kitchen and started the coffeemaker before walking into the bathroom and brushing his teeth. His head ached a bit, so he started the shower—he always felt better after a shower—

and walked back into the bedroom. He glanced over at the night-light, which was still securely plugged in. *I must have been REALLY drunk and didn't push it all the way in, and the vibration of cars driving by worked it loose during the night,* he thought, making another mental note to always make sure it was securely pushed all the way into the outlet. He got a fresh pair of underwear out of the dresser and walked back into the kitchen. He poured a cup of coffee and walked into the bathroom, yawning. He got into the shower and felt the hot needle spray start to wake up his body. Once he washed thoroughly and vigorously, his fair skin turning red not only from the heat of the water but from the scrubbing he gave himself, he got out, dried himself off, and walked into the bedroom to get dressed, then sat down on the chair to put his shoes on.

He picked up the right shoe and stared at it.

"What the fuck?" The entire back of the shoe had been gnawed away. Angrily he threw the shoe across the room. It hit the wall with a loud thud and made another, softer thud when it landed on the floor. He picked up the other shoe—it was fine.

No wonder the rent was so cheap.

Rats.

He got another pair of workout shoes and headed to the gym.

He called Linda the minute he got back from the gym.

"I'm telling you, Danny, that there are no rats in the building." Her voice was so sweet and honeyed over the phone he worried he might develop diabetes. "Pest control comes out once a month. No one has ever reported mice, rats, or even roaches in the building, and you know how rare it is not to have roaches in an old building like that."

"Would you like me to bring my shoe over to your office?" Danny felt himself starting to get angry. "I'm telling you, something chewed the back of my shoe off."

"Maybe it happened in your old apartment, or at your friend's. Didn't you tell me he had dogs?"

"I think I would have noticed when I got the shoes out last night." But she had him doubting himself now—Matthew's dogs *did* chew things all the time; he'd often had to rescue shoes and other things from them.

"Maybe you would, maybe you wouldn't have." She went on. "Did you pay that much attention?"

He started to say *of course I did, you moronic bitch,* but stopped the words before they came out. Maybe he hadn't paid that much attention—he'd drunk almost an entire bottle of wine. It was possible that it could have happened in the old apartment—after all, who knew what all got into the place after the tree smashed the building open? It could have been Matthew's dogs. He hadn't been to the gym the entire time he'd stayed at Matthew's.

But he was almost completely positive the shoe had been fine the night before.

"I'll call the exterminators out, if it'll make you feel better."

He knew he was being patronized, and as much as he wanted to tell her to fuck herself, he didn't. "That would be fine, Lisa," he said, hoping his tone was as smooth and honeyed and phony as hers, and hung up.

He spent the afternoon running errands, and Matthew called him while he was picking up his dry cleaning. Sounding contrite for a change, Matthew actually apologized for running out on him and offered to take him to dinner at their favorite restaurant—Byblos on Magazine—to make up for it, and to a movie afterward.

Maybe—maybe he's starting to come around, he thought as he drove home.

It was a happy thought.

He was on his second margarita when he felt sufficiently relaxed to tell Matthew about his shoe.

Matthew frowned. "Did you have the shoes at my place?"

He sipped his drink. He loved margaritas, and licked at the salt on the rim. "Of course I did—everything that was salvageable was at your place."

"Toby might have done it. He's been chewing things lately." Matthew frowned. "I don't know why he suddenly started doing that."

"Then it looks like you owe me a pair of shoes."

Matthew smiled at him and rubbed his foot up Danny's calf. "Care to take it out in trade?"

They never made it to the movie.

It was almost midnight when Danny got home from Matthew's. They'd had a fight, again. Matthew wanted him to stay over, and for the first time, Danny had refused. He was proud of himself. He hadn't given in the way he always had before, and stuck to his guns. The drive home had calmed him down a little, but he still felt some righteous indignation.

He walked into the kitchen and opened a bottle of wine. The pleasant buzz he had been feeling from the margaritas—and from the post-sex joint they'd smoked—had been burned off by the anger.

Why should I stay here when you won't stay at my place? Danny had asked as he got dressed.

I can't stay because of the dogs. You KNOW that.

Fuck the dogs.

Matthew had exploded then, screaming obscenities. And even though Danny was also angry, he struggled to stay in control and not shout back at him. He actually felt a little triumphant. Matthew was usually so calm and cool, nothing ever bothered him—but tonight Danny had finally gotten through his reserve and touched a nerve. As he filled a wineglass, he smiled to himself. *Nice move, not losing your temper.* He patted himself on the back. *Now he'll feel like a complete ass and have to apologize.* He walked into the bedroom, kicking off his shoes in the process, set the glass down and began to undress. He picked out his clothes for Sunday and laid them over the chair, then got out another pair of shoes and set them in front of the chair. He sipped the wine and went over to plug in the night-light.

It wasn't there.

He frowned. He looked on both sides of the dresser, behind it, and finally underneath it. There was no sign of it anywhere.

Where is it? he wondered, opening drawers to see if it had maybe somehow fallen inside one of them. Every morning when he unplugged it, he always set it on top of the dresser so it would be easy to find that night, even if he was shitfaced falling-down drunk. This was the first time it wasn't where it was supposed to be. He went back out into the hall and turned the light back on. *Tomorrow, I'll have to get a new one.*

He got into bed. *Damn, I've had Mickey since I was a kid* was his last thought before falling asleep.

Matthew called and apologized the next morning, and while Danny accepted the apology he turned down the dinner invitation that came with it.

"I think I need some time to myself," he said, his voice level and reasonable. "You really scared me last night."

"I'm sorry, Danny, really." Matthew sounded like he was going to start crying at any moment.

"I know, Matthew," Danny replied before hanging up.

He smiled.

He spent the day shopping at the mall in Metairie. He had lunch at the food court and splurged on some new clothes at Macy's, a new outfit to wear to the office the next day. He bought himself some other things courtesy of his Platinum MasterCard, and went to see a movie before treating himself to dinner at Houston's.

It was getting dark when he climbed the steps. The staircase light was out. He fumbled for his keys in the darkness, and when he managed to get the door unlocked he stumbled over a box. Putting his packages down, he picked it up. It was a Nike box. He opened it up, and nestled in the wrapping paper was a pair of incredibly expensive workout shoes he'd been coveting for a long time, but had never been able to justify spending that much money on shoes. He smiled and was reaching for the light switch when he heard the sound from the bedroom.

It was a small thump.

Not much of a sound, kind of like the sound of a shoe falling off a shelf, and his blood ran cold. He opened his mouth but his throat was completely dry, his vocal cords frozen, useless. *Someone's in the apartment* was his first fevered thought. But how could they have gotten in? Everything was locked up, and the apartment was too high up for someone to have climbed up the porch and come in through the front windows. Facing a busy street the way the house did, surely someone would have noticed…He reached for the cordless phone and stepped back out into the hallway and called Matthew.

"There's someone in my apartment." he blurted out in a whisper as soon as Matthew said hello.

"What? Danny?"

"There's someone in my apartment," he whispered furiously. "I just got home and opened the front door and I heard a noise from the bedroom. Twice. I heard it twice! I just grabbed the phone and came back outside!"

"I'm coming over. Call the police." Click, dial tone. Feverishly he dialed 911, gave the details to a bored-sounding operator, and tiptoed back down the steps to wait for the cavalry.

❖

"You're sure you heard something?" The cop was overweight and had a mustache. He looked down at where Danny and Matthew's hands were entwined, and momentarily sneered before his cop mask dropped back in place.

"I heard a noise, twice." Danny dropped Matthew's hand.

"Well, all the windows are shut and latched from the inside. No sign of forced entry on the outer door, and you said yourself no one has come down the stairs since you called us." The police officer scratched his head. "Are you sure you didn't just think you heard a sound?"

"I heard it twice." Danny's voice rose, and he realized he was shaking.

"All right then." The officer turned to Matthew. "You might want to stay the night with your friend, he seems to be nervous."

"He can't. He has *dogs*." Danny spat the words out, walked past the police officer and up the stairs. He passed another police officer on the stairs. The apartment was ablaze with light. He walked inside, resisting the urge to slam the door and let out a primal scream. Instead, he went to the refrigerator and got the wine bottle. He was on his second glass when the front door opened.

"What the fuck is going on around here?" Matthew's voice was soft, gentle. He walked toward Danny. "First you pitch a hissy fit about some shoe being chewed up. Then you won't stay over last night. And now this!"

"What are you trying to say?" Danny took a big gulp of wine and poured more into the glass.

"Are you mad at me for not asking you to move in with me?" Matthew stepped closer to him. "I didn't ask you not because I didn't want to—I just know how you feel about the dogs, and—"

"Get the fuck out of here." Danny set the wineglass down carefully, trying to keep his hands from shaking.

"But these blatant attempts to get attention, Danny, I have to say, you're starting to make me wonder about you."

"Get the *fuck* out of here."

"I mean, are you okay?"

"Get the fuck out of here!" He screamed the words so loudly that he was surprised the windows didn't blow out.

"I'll go." Matthew backed toward the door. "But I'm really starting to think you need to get some help." The door slammed behind him.

"Fuck you." He picked up the wineglass and drained it. He refilled the glass. *Maybe I am going crazy,* he thought as he gulped down the wine and refilled the glass again. *All this fuss and bother over a shoe. Maybe I am hearing things. Maybe I'm just going crazy. Maybe I am just trying to get attention, Matthew's attention, maybe that is what this is all about, I'm mad because he didn't ask me to move in with him, and—*

Fuck that, he thought. *I am not crazy. I did hear something. Something chewed up my shoe. And where did my night-light go?' Where's Mickey? I didn't just leave it somewhere different.*

There's something in this apartment.

That's crazy.

Maybe I am cracking up.

He finished off the glass of wine and rinsed it out in the sink, recorked the bottle, and put it back into the refrigerator. He turned off the lights and went into the bedroom, carefully getting undressed. He picked out the clothes he would wear the next day and put them on the chair before lacing up the new shoes Matthew had bought him and placing them on the floor by the chair.

The light went out.

He uttered a half scream before he could stop himself. *Just a blown bulb,* he told himself, shivering slightly. He groped his way out to the hall and flicked the switch.

Nothing.

There was a sound, so soft he could barely hear it. Goose bumps rose on his arms, the hair on the back of his neck standing up. He stood completely still, ears straining to hear, his heart pounding, his breath coming quickly, in and out.

The sound had been in the bedroom.

Where the fuck is my flashlight? he wondered, his mind quickly flashing through the process of putting new things away, seeing himself putting silverware in the drawer, extension cords, light bulbs, the hammer, the screwdriver—all of that was in the storage room where the washer and dryer were.

He heard it again—a soft noise, just a little thump, like a book falling over on a bookshelf. *What the hell?* He was starting to shiver.

Get out of here, I need to just get out of here, it's stupid to just stand here in the dark, listening, it's nothing, it's just an old house settling, all old houses make noises, there's nothing in the bedroom, my imagination is just working overtime, call Matthew and apologize, this is so stupid...

The bedsprings squeaked.

He screamed and ran for the front door, not caring about getting his keys, he wouldn't be able to find them in the dark anyway, his mind racing. *Just get the hell out of here, there's something in there, I don't*

*know what, but there's something in the bedroom, I am not going crazy,
I am NOT GOING CRAZY! I am not, I am not, I am not, I am not, I am
not going crazy, there's something in there...*

He tripped and fell headlong, crashing to the floor with a loud
thump, his head banging on the floor, the breath knocked out of him.

There was a rustling sound from the bedroom, a kind of scuttling
noise, coming out of the bedroom, into the hallway.

He began to sob as he scrambled to his feet, his head ringing and
aching and thumping, the breaths coming in gasps as he headed for the
door in the darkness, the dark clinging to him, as though not wanting to
let him free, he was almost there—

Something grabbed his ankle.

He screamed.

❖

"This is how I found him," Matthew said to the paramedic. "I just
came by to see if he was okay, and he was just sitting there on the floor,
staring into space, all curled up."

"And he hasn't spoken?" The paramedic looked at Danny, who
was just sitting on the floor, his arms curled around his legs, rocking
back and forth, eyes blank and staring.

"Not a word."

Two of the paramedics helped Danny to his feet. He went along
with them, obeying their commands, and then they helped him onto a
stretcher. Matthew watched, his eyes filling with tears as they began to
move the stretcher out of the apartment. When they reached the door,
Danny looked at Matthew, and for just a moment his eyes seem to
focus.

"Dark," he said clearly, and then his eyes swam out of focus
again.

ORDINARY MAYHEM
VICTORIA A. BROWNWORTH

1.

The fascination began when Faye was a child. The darkroom, the red light, the big black and white timer that made a loud ticking noise as it wound down, the trays of liquid that turned the paper into pictures as her grandfather moved them back and forth with his fingers or a pair of big wooden tongs with plastic on the tips. She would sit on the high stool in the darkroom and watch as the paper came out of the big yellow boxes and then slid into the white pans of fluid that had that slightly acid smell that reminded her of the dead mice they sometimes found near the basement door.

Her grandfather never spoke to her when they were in the darkroom. He just moved from tray to tray, making the papers swim gently in the liquid that glowed red in the light. When the timer went off, the images would begin to appear on the paper: jagged pieces of clothing, a half-formed face, a disembodied leg, the flail of an arm. When the completed pictures finally came through, he would pull the photographs out of the fluid and hang them by the corners with little wooden clothespins on a thin piece of rope that ran the length of the darkroom.

Then he would take a magnifying glass and look at each picture. Sitting behind him, Faye would see an eye bug out, or a mouth go askew, or the side of a face puff up. In the hazy cast of the darkroom light, everything looked red, everything looked as if it had been soaked in blood.

Some of the photos her grandfather would mark with a silver pencil that came out white in the corner of the pictures, which were still wet—she could see they were wet, which made the images swim together. Some he left alone. There was a small black fan that ran all the time, back behind the trays. The photographs would move ever so slightly on the line, but they never blew around, never touched each other. When they were all hung up and all checked, or not, with the silver pencil, then the red light would go out and the door would open, and he would tell her they had to wait for the photographs to dry. Sometimes she would look back to see what was there, but the room was dark without the red light and she could see nothing at all. It was all black inside.

Later, they would sit at the kitchen table together and her grandfather would set things out on a big piece of yellow oilcloth. A dozen or more little white glass pots with heavy, dark, oily paint in them. Reds, magentas, purples, and blues that looked like small organ meats with their thick, gelatinous consistency. The greens and yellows seemed like mold or fungus, but without the thick furring at the edges she had seen sometimes on rotting food. The paints smelled sharp, a smell she could never place because it wasn't like anything else.

Her grandfather would give her little pieces of his canvas board and a pencil and three pots of her own and some Q-tips. He let her draw and paint while he sat bent over the black and white photographs, slowly turning them to color. He would twirl tight little pieces he tore off cotton balls, dip them gently in the thick paint, and paint the photographs with the delicate details their owners wanted.

Faye would always watch him before she started her drawings. Watch the slow, meticulous way he twirled the cotton and how carefully he worked on the linen photographic prints. Sometimes he would take a cotton ball and rub it over a photo to make the color softer and lighter. She always noticed how red the lips were. From where she sat they always looked like wounds in the faces of the people. Deep gashes that would never, ever heal.

They could do this for hours—sit at the table with the white pots and the cotton and the photographs—without speaking. When the photographs were finished, he would slide them into sleeves of parchment paper and put them in the cabinet behind where the cameras and tripod were kept until whoever's photographs they were came to pick them up.

Sometimes, when no one was watching, Faye would open the door to the darkroom and turn on the red light. She would set the timer and slide pieces of paper from the yellow boxes marked with big letters, OPEN IN RED LIGHT ONLY, into the trays of fluid. She would sit on the stool and wait, but no images would appear in the trays. She would think about what images they would be: She would squint her eyes the way she had seen her grandfather do over and over and she would imagine the pictures.

The images she saw always looked like slices of bodies, half-finished faces, torn shreds of clothing. And always, they were bathed red, like the darkroom light, like blood, like the gashes of mouths her grandfather painted on the photographs. When she closed her eyes, they were still there: the charnel house images that were the bits and pieces from the pans of liquid. When she closed her eyes, the red light still burned behind her eyelids and pulsed, like a vein, until she turned off the light and left the room.

2.

Later, when Faye was sent away to the convent school for girls, she was often called to Mother Superior's office for this or that minor infraction. At first, in the early days, she felt fear, but soon she began to like the trips from the building where her class was to the one where Mother Superior's office was. She liked the solitude, she liked the opportunity to explore. She would walk across the schoolyard, stopping briefly at the grotto with the sleek, despondent Virgin Mary standing within the hewn gray stone recess. Faye would stare up into the face of Mary and wait to see if she would speak to her like she had to the children at Fatima or to St. Bernadette at Lourdes. Sometimes there would be leaves at the feet of the Virgin and other times she would find small dead things—rodents or birds, because the grotto was set into a wooded area and there were feral animals, foxes and racoons and cats, that came out from the trees to kill.

When she found dead animals, Faye would pick them up with leaves or sticks and take them to the bushes and lay them on the ground. She kept a notebook of sketches and each time she found a dead animal, she would draw it later, trying to remember exactly how it had been when she'd found it—if the neck was broken, if the mouth was open in a final scream, if it had puncture wounds or missing parts, if it was stiff and cold, or still limp and warm. Sometimes, when there was more than one, she would arrange them together on piles of leaves, sort of like a burial pyre she had seen in a book. She wasn't sure exactly what it was she was cataloguing with the drawings, but she knew they were important and she knew they meant something, so she was meticulous about them and would look at them later to be sure she had gotten everything right. She never killed anything herself, but she was always grateful that it was she who had found the dead things and not someone else. It was like a secret between herself and God. Or so she imagined it was.

After Faye left the grotto, walking back down the slate path and on toward the high school building where Mother Superior's office was, she sometimes heard crying. She was never sure exactly who it was, but it always seemed to come from the same place, the music rooms where one of the nuns, Sister Anne Marie, would compose different kinds of music for the girls to sing at the regular musical events that were held at the school. The place was named for St. Cecelia, the patron saint of music, and so music was a major part of the school's activities. Faye thought Sister Anne Marie was probably the person she heard crying. She thought it must be hard to love music so much but never be able to choose what music you listened to because nothing here was a choice, it was all up to God, or so they were told every morning in catechism class.

Sometimes Faye would walk closer to the place where the music rooms were—the small, two-story cottage across the stretch of lawn from where the grotto was—because she liked Sister Anne Marie. Faye thought she was nice, but sad, and there didn't seem to be anything that made her less sad. It was always the same—the sadness. Sometimes, when the nun played the piano for them in music class, she looked different. Not happy, exactly, but something else— glowing. Like the angels in the pictures in the catechism books. Music made her glow. But Faye knew that there was something else, she just didn't know what it was. But she was sure that was who was crying, because another time she had seen Sister Anne Marie in the grotto, on her hands and knees in front of the Virgin Mary, her forehead touching the ground. And she was crying then, too, and hitting the slate of the grotto with her hands, slapping it over and over again, pounding it with her hands flat against the rippled gray slate. She was saying something, but Faye could only hear certain words. The only ones she was sure she heard were "sacrifice" and "terrible" and "killing."

Faye had stood behind a bush near the grotto and watched. When Sister Anne Marie got up, there was blood on her hands, and little bits of leaves and twigs had stuck to them. She had looked at her hands and then she had turned and looked back at Mary. When she turned back around, Faye could see that the expression on her face was exactly the same as Mary's—sad. Very, very sad.

After Sister had walked away and gone back to the music rooms, Faye had gone up to the spot where the nun had been. The slate apron in front of Mary had smears of blood where Sister Anne Marie had been. Faye could see the mark of her hands on the slate—a thick, dark red gore. She had bent down and touched it, had rubbed her fingers together, feeling the consistency of the blood mixed with dirt and a little bit of leaf matter. Faye had taken out her notebook and pressed the blood onto a page, wiping the blood off her fingers onto the paper. Then she had closed the book and stared up at Mary for a long time.

There was a fire escape that ran down the side of the building where the music rooms were. Once there had been a fire drill and Faye had heard the alarm and one of the girls hadn't known it was a drill and she had started to cry, saying that they were all going to be burned alive and it would be like going to hell. Sister Anne Marie had looked at Faye with a look Faye didn't quite recognize—some kind of distress. Faye thought she was upset because Faye's parents had been burned to death in a car crash, but Faye knew all about that. About the blood and the smoke and the flames in the snow and probably screaming. She was sure there had been screaming, because one day she had turned on the stove in the kitchen at her grandparents' house and put her hand in the flame and held it there for as long as she could, until she started to scream, involuntarily. Her grandmother had come running in and grabbed her hand out of the blue flame and put it under the cold water of the tap, then she had put ice on it. Faye's hand had turned red and there had been blisters on her fingers and she had thought how terrible it had been for her parents in the car, screaming, with no one to come and pull them out. But now she knew what it would be like, the fire. Now she knew.

Faye had turned to the girl and said, "There's no blue flame. There's no smoke. There's no blood. So we won't die. And it won't be like hell, because there would be snow, too, and flames in the snow, and there's no snow."

The girl had stopped crying, but she still looked scared. Sister Anne Marie had stared at Faye, then. Her eyes seemed wider than before. The look on her face was strange, Faye thought. And not much different from that of the girl.

3.

Outside Mother Superior's office, the big parquet off the closed door of the room had a row of hard, straight-backed chairs along the wall. Faye was supposed to sit and fold her hands in her lap with some semblance of the contrition she never felt, but instead she would walk up the steps to view the alabaster statue of St. Cecelia that lay on a white marble slab at the landing of the stairs, beneath a stained-glass window depicting the appearance of Mary to the children at Fatima.

The body was life-sized and lying on what looked like a stone coffin of the sort she had seen in the old cemeteries she'd gone to with her grandfather. She was mesmerized by the statue of the fallen saint, and never failed to touch it, even though that was forbidden and the nuns would slap you if they caught you. The young saint lay on her side, as if she had merely fainted, like some of her classmates did when they were fasting, and someone had placed her on the closed tomb and arranged her body there, as if she were sleeping. But Cecelia, the patron saint of the school, wasn't sleeping, Cecelia had been struck down by an infidel—there were three deep slices in her neck.

Faye always slid her fingers into the crevices where the wounds were, wondering, because she was fascinated by the lives of the saints and read as much as she could about them, what it had felt like to die that way, to have your head nearly sliced off, and to have fallen dead so openly, with the wound of your death exposed to everyone who passed. Her parents had died that way and Faye always thought death should be more private. That's why she always moved the little dead animals she found near Mary's statue in the grotto to a more secluded place.

There was no blood on St. Cecelia, of course. Just a vast whiteness of the body. The lovely face, eyes closed, the folds of her garments, and the three telltale wounds spread open on the neck, open so wide that a young girl's fingers could slip into the spaces, but not quite fill them. Faye would wonder if Cecelia had tried to hold the wounds closed. She didn't think it was possible, but she wondered.

Other times Faye would forgo the statue for her other fascination: the science library that was always open and empty whenever she was there—she had never seen the high school students inside, even though she knew it was used for the biology lectures. She had several years to go before she was in the high school. She wondered if the mysteries of the science library would be revealed then.

The room was very large, yet had no windows. Faye thought maybe they had been closed up, like in one of the Edgar Allen Poe stories, because the things in the room shouldn't be seen in the light, or from the outside by someone peering in. There was a smell that layered itself over the whole room that would make you gag after a while and she thought that was why the room was always empty and the sliding wooden doors were always open. She knew what the smell was—it was formaldehyde, the same smell that she remembered from the funeral home when her parents were killed. It was a smell that got caught in the back of your throat and lay there, until it was really hard to breathe and you had to get as far away from the smell as you could because the smell was always attached to death and it might be able to take your breath with it. Or so she thought.

In the room, on one side, the floor-to-ceiling bookcases were filled with books, all stacked neatly with the edges out to the end of the shelf the way the nuns had taught them books must be shelved. But on the other side were the jars. These were stacked from the floor to about a foot or so above eye level, so that none of what was inside could be missed, yet not all could be seen. Most were of a uniform size—about a gallon, Faye thought, envisioning the plastic milk jugs at home. Some were smaller, like the jelly and jam jars her grandmother would put up at the end of the summer.

All the jars were filled with a murky yellow-green liquid that looked like the bottom of the creek near her house where she would take the dog on Saturdays after confession and where you could see the small fish swimming under the flat rocks. But though the liquid was the same, the contents of each jar were different.

Faye thought of this as the experiment room. The jars were the most compelling thing in the school, to her—after Mary in the grotto and St. Cecelia on the marble slab. She often thought Mary or Cecelia could easily come back to life if the right miracle occurred, the kind of miracle they were always talking about at school. But she was certain nothing in the jars could come back to life, and uncertain if they had ever even been alive. Faye was surprised these things were even allowed in the school, since they all seemed as if they came from Satan and could never have been created by God.

All the things in the jars were dead, of course. Some she knew what they were—frogs and toads, some split apart and floating, their eyes open and staring out from the jars. She also knew the nematodes, because she'd studied about them and about the salamanders. There were some other slithery things—large, fat worms and little garter snakes. But the other things, she wasn't sure. One looked like a baby with a huge head that curved away from the body that seemed shrunken and too small—how could it ever hold that head up? The eyes of the big-headed baby were a milky blue and were set into a too-pink and somewhat bloody socket. There was something that looked like a tiny pig that had been skinned or had never grown a skin, Faye wasn't sure. Like the frogs, it too was splayed open and the eyes had rolled back in the head, exposing only the whites. The legs stuck out in front, like it was reaching for something, and the mouth was open, and Faye could never tell if it looked like it was smiling or screaming.

The most disturbing jars held things with more than

one head. A rat, a frog, a kitten, another animal that looked like a fox, but wasn't. A baby alligator. A squirrel. These had all been sliced open and had an eerie comedy/tragedy look to the different heads. In the kitten, an eye had come loose from the socket and floated out a little on a shred of skin that looked like a stalk. If you moved close to the jar, the eye would move and turn a little toward you. Faye didn't like to think about the two-headed kitten with its floating eye.

Faye could never tell what was in the jars on the highest shelves and she had never dared to drag one of the big chairs over to stand on to see what was in them. The higher the shelf, the more horrifying the contents of the jars, so she always imagined that the ones she could not see were the ones that held the things that weren't meant to be seen, the things that she was certain had not come from God ever, but which were like the bits and pieces of bodies she had seen in the photographs in her grandfather's darkroom: Things that it was best never to know about. Things that held mysteries it was better not to have revealed.

Faye wondered why there were never any students in that room, and she thought maybe it was because those things weren't really meant to be seen, but were there as a warning, just like the statue of St. Cecelia. All those things were meant to warn the girls at the school to be careful, to do what they were told, to stay away from places where blood drenched body parts and kittens lolled with two heads and floating eyes, and someone could strike you down with their knife and slice open your neck so deep, you could never close it up ever again.

Whenever Faye thought about these things, she would stop looking at the jars and walk over to the chairs and sit, positioned so that she could see both the jars on the bookshelves and St. Cecelia lying, bathed in the colored light from the stained glass, and wait for Mother Superior to call for her.

4.

It never seemed like a big leap from those early days in the dark room and running her fingers through St. Cecelia's wounds and cataloguing the science specimens to where she was today. Faye

Blake was born to photograph carnage—or at least that's what she would say to slightly appalled friends and colleagues from the time she was in college until now. Once she was on her third drink it was easier to explain how she'd been mesmerized by the red light of her grandfather's darkroom or transfixed in a kind of religious fervor by St. Cecelia and her Reliquary, as she had come to refer to the science library, and how both had propelled her to her career—or her fate. Faye was never exactly sure what she should call what she did. She knew there was nothing else she could do; she'd never tried, but she didn't have to. She was meant to do what she did from the very first time she'd sat on the stool in the darkroom. She was meant to do what she did from the very first time she had felt St. Cecelia's wounds or gazed up into the contents of the jars in the science room. Some of the girls she had gone to school with had become nuns. Not many, but a few. She had become—this—but it was a calling, nevertheless. Of that, she was certain.

The squeamish were put off early by the baldness of Faye's statements about her work and why she did it, but others were, naturally, intrigued. The wrong sort of men and the wrong sort of women were drawn to Faye and Faye herself had no flair for the normal, so she dove in, wondering sometimes if she was looking hard for the kind of end that had befallen St. Cecelia and was destined to ignore every bit of what the nuns had taught her about circumspection and restraint. When Faye thought *restraint* she thought of people bound and gagged and waiting for something terrible to happen. She never thought of holding herself back from whatever it was she wanted to do. *Restraint* was a form of punishment, it was sitting waiting for Mother Superior, it was *not* going home with the woman with the switchblade in her boot, it was choking back everything.

Then perhaps Faye would simply end up like her parents—dead from a drunk-driving accident on New Year's Eve, blood and flames running hot red rivulets into the snow, the car crumpled like leftover gift wrap from Christmas.

Faye tried to care about what might happen to her, tried to think about the danger, tried to lean more toward normalcy, but it seemed counterintuitive to what she wanted from her life and the work that she also considered her art and which was inextricably linked to what she did when she wasn't drawing or photographing. She wanted to catalogue those things on the upper shelves, the hidden horrors she had never been able to fully glimpse. Faye knew there was more than the two-headed kitten with the floating eye or the flayed-open pig with its hideous gaping mouth. There was how they got there in the first place. She had known all along those things weren't created by God. What she hadn't known was that it was people, not Satan, who had filled those jars and thought nothing of it as they did so. Once she understood that, Faye wanted to be the artist who shocked and appalled and drove people from galleries with their hands over their mouths, unsure if they were going to scream or vomit or both because she had shown them something of themselves that they wanted to see, couldn't wait to see, were in fact desperate to see and even excited to see, but which revolted and horrified them nonetheless.

Just as Faye's fascination with her grandfather's darkroom and the dead things she found at school had started soon after her parents' deaths, Faye's career had followed a similarly clear-cut path. After college, Faye had started on her quest simply enough, doing the kind of photojournalism that won awards and which no one thought of as voyeuristic because it had purpose and meaning. Art was always her end game, but she wanted that foundation of sincerity first. She wanted to tell her stories, but she never wanted to be perceived as a monster just because she wanted to roll back the rock to see what slithered underneath. After all, Faye was merely moving the rock and showing what was beneath it—she was doing what she had always done, recording the deaths of the little creatures with as pinpoint accuracy as she could, but she wasn't doing the actual killing. Faye didn't create the things no one wanted to see—and it wasn't because of her that they couldn't keep themselves from looking. Everything Faye had photographed from the time she had gotten her first camera at eleven when the notebooks and drawings were no longer enough had led her in the same direction: show the wounds deep enough to lay a finger in, examine the jars on the uppermost shelves, see if the bodies really do come together in the trays of developer, or if they were never whole in the first place, if it was always the fleshy, gore-streaked, blood-soaked shrapnel of human carnage, of what people can do to each other when no one else is looking.

In an interview after her first big award, after she had chronicled the impact of an arson fire on a small town where several hundred people were trapped in a theater for a children's Christmas pageant and the charred bodies had been laid out on the snowy sidewalk like some horrific holiday display, Faye had told the reporter that it didn't faze her to detail what people were capable of because she knew everyone, given the right circumstances, could do the most unspeakable things and have no conscience about it whatsoever. Faye had leaned forward and looked directly into the face of the interviewer as she explained how the person who had set that fire had done so deliberately, had put two-by-fours through the door handles, had poured the accelerant all around the building and then lit the match—knowing there were three hundred people inside, more than a third of them children, and that it was a week before Christmas and everyone in the town would be touched by the tragedy.

"We're all capable of killing," Faye had told the reporter, who was older than she by at least a decade and clearly unnerved by what he had hoped was merely her youthful candor and artistic bravado.

"The question is, *why* would we kill? To save ourselves? To protect someone we loved? Or just because we wanted to know what it was like to watch the blood or breath run out of someone else? Or because we've come to love the sound of other people's tormented screaming?"

That first award had led to others, because the stories had gotten grislier and more provocative and sometimes it seemed that only she had the stomach to tell the tale—the stomach and the interest. Faye was always interested.

Faye covered other terrible events—fatal fires, multiple killings. She had been the first photographer on the scene of a freak accident when an 18-wheeler carrying steel pipe had lost its load on the West Side Highway where it wasn't even supposed to be. Lengths of pipe had flown off the rig, doing damage as they went. Two lengths shot through the windshield of the cars directly behind the truck. One driver had been decapitated instantly, his head flying into the seat behind him. The EMTs had found it later, on the floor. In the other car, a passenger had been impaled. The steel pipe had gone through his chest just above his heart, skewering him to the car seat. It had taken over an hour to cut him free, and even then a piece of the pipe protruded from his chest as he was lifted onto the gurney. Five other pieces of pipe had flown over onto the sidewalk, killing three dogs and fatally injuring their owner, who died later at the hospital.

The paper's photo editor had looked at Faye's photographs and then at her.

"Good stuff," he'd said, then added, "for a horror movie. No way we can use these. What were you thinking? Decapitation? Impaling?

Dead dogs? Really, Faye? We'll use the first one. The rest you can take home for your scrapbook. And remind me never to look at *that*."

She *had* taken the photographs home and filed them. The paper had gone with her first shot of the truck and the splayed pipe with the windshield behind the truck smashed through, the headless body obscured. But before the other photos had left the paper, the buzz had gone out about them. Everyone on the city desk had made sure they got a look at them. Just as Faye knew they would.

That was why the darker assignments had continued to go to her, because everyone knew she'd photograph anything. Then her editor changed. He thought her photos had a whole other level of potential and he wanted to let her run with her gut and his own voyeurism. "People's right to know, Faye, people's right to know."

That was how she'd been sent to do a series she thought might get turned into a book about children dying in the San Joaquin Valley in central California. A piece had come over the wire about a disease cluster and deaths linked to pesticide poisoning from run-off into the well water in the towns surrounded by the lush, endless fields of cotton, soybeans, strawberries, grapes, almonds, limes, roses, and carnations that spun out in a little hub of perfect produce and collateral damage from Fresno.

"Fresno is a hellhole of a town," her editor had told Faye. "But it's one of those places where a lot happens off the page. Let's get it on the page. There's something there and I know you'll find it."

The story was going to be in the paper's magazine section. Nothing like dead and dying kids when you were having your Sunday breakfast or coming home from church. As she tracked down her sources for the pesticide poisoning exposé, Faye was caught in the endless web of contradiction that was the Central Valley: unremittingly beautiful and gut-wrenchingly grim. It was blazingly sunny every day and by eight a.m. it would be 100 degrees as Faye drove from one small town, Pixley, to another, Waco, and then onto a series of other small towns. Then she would go over to Bakersfield, then back to Fresno. Eighteen-hour days cataloguing things that would make most people scream and run from the room. In each place Faye went there were dead or dying children, their parents' faces always uncomprehending, unable to cope with the idea that the only work they could get hired to do was killing off their children, slowly and terribly.

Faye had sat in a tiny oven of a house where a shiny little white coffin festooned with gaily colored woven crosses was displayed in the center of the room. Its tiny occupant was a bald and wizened four-year-old girl in a white frilly dress reminiscent of the First Holy Communion dress Faye herself had worn at St. Cecelia's. This girl in the coffin was the third child in her family to die from the cancer that came from the work her parents did in the fields.

When Faye had taken the photographs of the weeping mother and inconsolable father as they sat next to the tiny coffin, the father's arm draped protectively around it, she had remembered being at the grave site after her parents' deaths. Her father's secretary, a trim young woman with fluffy blond hair and big, dark sunglasses had been standing in the snow with a friend, visibly weeping. But when Faye's parents' coffins—side by side—were being lowered into the frozen ground, the woman had cried out and run to the edge of the big, gaping hole with the green, fake-grass tarps next to it, and had called out Faye's father's name over and over, a white rose in one gloved hand and her arms outstretched, as if she were trying to grab the coffin to her. The friend who was with her had tried to pull her back, murmuring to her to calm down, but the woman had pulled away, slipped on the muddy side of the hole, and fallen onto the coffin. She had gashed her cheek on one of the brass hinges, and blood gushed from the wound and onto Faye's father's coffin as she lurched into the open grave.

A collective gasp had gone up among the mourners and the priest had looked around as if someone else might be able to fix what had gone wrong at the burial and make everything proper and sedate again. He had glanced at Faye, who had been in a kind of shock since her parents had been killed and she had been staying at her grandparents' house, waiting to go back home.

Faye's grandmother had put her hand over Faye's eyes like a kind of visor—not tight, but just like a shield, as if she were keeping a too-bright sunlight away from her, even though the day was gray, and she had whispered, "Poor girl," and Faye had wondered if her grandmother had meant her or the woman who had been hurt. But before the woman had been lifted out of Faye's father's grave by some of the men at the grave site, blood coursing down her cheek and onto the front of her ivory coat, Faye had seen the look on her grandfather's face as he watched the sad, macabre scene.

It was excitement. He had licked his lips and his eyes had sparkled, but not with tears, like her grandmother's, but a different kind. And

Faye had been glad her grandmother had covered her eyes. She hadn't wanted to see more.

5.

After Faye had photographed the little girl in her coffin, she took photographs of the boy with no arms or legs, whose mother had tended the roses and carnations in the fields near Waco until just a few days before her son was born at the hospital in Fresno. The woman had gone mad when she had seen her egg-shaped baby, all round and sweet, but missing so many of his parts. The boy's father had fled back to Mexico, clutching his rosary and the thick cross around his neck, hoping God would forgive him for whatever it was he had done to create a monster even the Chupacabras would be frightened of. The grandmother had told Faye the story while the boy, now five and very lively, rolled around in the dirt and laughed, crawling on his stomach like a lizard in the hot sun and telling Faye funny stories in Spanish while she took his picture. Faye had thought, just briefly, that he could have been one of the things in the jars back at school, floating dreamily in the murky yellow-green fluid in a perpetual limbo state while St. Cecelia's mutilated body watched over him from her alabaster slab.

After Faye had photographed the little lizard boy, she had driven back to Fresno, heading to the morgue to photograph the bodies of children waiting for autopsy. According to the coroner, seven children between the ages of two and eleven lay on trays in the morgue, all allegedly dead from the cancers caused by the pesticides. Their bodies could not be released to the families until the investigation was over. And that could take weeks.

It was late—after nine p.m.—when Faye arrived at the morgue. The coroner had agreed to meet Faye at nine, and as she grabbed her bag and cameras out of the car, she was suddenly aware that it was nearly fully dark and that the parking lot was empty of all but a handful of cars. Faye wasn't one for foreboding, but she didn't want to stay. She didn't like this place, and she hadn't even gone inside.

There was no security at the door and Faye just walked through, following the black signs with arrows sending her in the proper direction. It wasn't a large building and the heat of the day hung in the halls. Faye had been so aware of the heat on this trip. The blazing sun, the lack of shade anywhere due to the omnipresent fields of this or that crop. Fresno was a small city and towns around it were hamlets with nothing but convenience shops and beer outlets and dollar stores here and there. The poverty was like the heat—oppressive and endless, rolling over everything.

The morgue building was the hottest place Faye had been that day. Hotter even than the little house with the corpse in the dining room. As hot as the dusty yard where the boy with no arms or legs had slithered in the dirt. She had hoped for the chill of institutional air-conditioning, but there appeared to be none. She felt like heaving.

The building smelled like most morgues Faye had been in—a heavy layer of formaldehyde covered everything, but underneath you could still smell the semi-sweet acid stink of rotting bodies. She knew that smell. *Decomposition.* It had been with her since childhood. Since the mice at the door of her grandparents' basement. Since the basement itself, that one time she had gone down and found all those things, right before she'd been sent off to St. Cecelia's for school.

As Faye got closer to the autopsy room, she began to gag. The rotting smell had overtaken everything. She wasn't sure she could stay. She couldn't imagine how anyone could work here.

The double doors in front of her opened, and a middle-aged man with graying hair and glasses greeted her. Classical music—Brahms, perhaps—played at a moderate volume, though not loudly enough to drown out the sound of the refrigeration unit that banked almost the entire wall across from where Faye and the coroner stood.

The room was that institutional yellow—the color of a faded manilla envelope, meant at some point to be cheery, no doubt, but in the glare of the fluorescent lights, with the black squares of night-dark windows set up above the sight-line, it just looked raw and ugly.

It was a surprisingly large room, yet still only a third of the size of the morgue in New York, but then there would be fewer bodies here. A scale like you'd see at the produce market hung from the ceiling in the corner next to a blue-cushioned examining table of the sort in doctor's offices. Faye wondered what live person was being examined here. On the white paper sheet sat an open book and a cup of coffee. Perhaps it was for the living after all.

The other wall held an array of sinks and cabinets, and in one there were jars like the ones that had been at St. Cecelia's, only these held organs that she recognized right away. Organs for dissection. Organs to explain what should be inside each body splayed open in the Y-shaped wound that exposed it all. Organs that held nothing but knowledge—no hidden message, like those jars at St. Cecelia's.

The coroner introduced himself and led Faye to the opposite corner where there stood a series of stainless steel tables with sheets covering what lay beneath. Flies buzzed in the room and occasionally sizzled in the blue light of the bug zapper that hung in a far corner. Too far away from the bodies, Faye thought.

It was time to start taking pictures. She started to put down her bag when the coroner grabbed her arm and shook his head violently. "Don't do that!" he exclaimed, grabbing her bag before it touched the floor. Faye looked at him quizzically and he pointed down at the floor. As she looked, the floor, a dull yellow-gray linoleum, appear to move. Everywhere there were maggots—so many, that Faye wondered how she hadn't heard the squish as she stepped on them, walking through the room. The music and the refrigeration unit had drowned out the sound, but now as she stepped back, involuntarily, she heard it, and it made her feel nauseous.

The coroner led her outside the double doors to a bank of chairs eerily reminiscent of those outside Mother Superior's office. He took her bag and placed it on one of the chairs. He explained that the excessive June heat had caused a worse outbreak than usual of maggots.

"I had to leak the story to the news," he told her. "They're everywhere. They're in the walls, inside the tiles on the ceiling. It's better now, at night, but during the day they drop on us from up there while we're working. They're infesting new bodies, there's so many larvae. It's interfering with autopsies, time of death, that kind of thing. We don't know whose maggots are whose."

Faye had turned to look at him and saw a small white worm inching across the collar of his lab coat. She reached out and flicked it off with her finger without thinking.

"There's probably more inside," he said, his face unsmiling. "I don't even look anymore because I feel them crawling on me all the time, whether they're there or not. Should we go back in? I think you should leave your bag here."

Faye stood, took out the camera she wanted, and zipped the bag closed. She checked it for maggots. Nothing. They went back in through the double doors. She began taking pictures of the floor, then the far wall, which was alive with maggots. She looked up, but couldn't see any on the ceiling. "They tend to withdraw at night," the coroner told her. "I never see them on the ceiling then—just on the floor and the walls."

They went back over to the tables and he drew the sheets back as Faye took shot after shot.

Every small body was crawling with maggots. On the smallest, a girl of twenty-eight months who had died of neuroblastoma, maggots crawled in the incision in her skull and all along the Y-shaped cut in her chest. Faye could tell they were eating the flesh because the areas near the stitching were raw and macerated and pulling away from the thread, showing bits of bone beneath.

A little boy of about five had maggots coming out from under his eyelids and, as Faye photographed him, maggots crawled out of his nostrils. The coroner stifled a sound and Faye turned to look at him. He told her, "It wasn't this bad earlier. They start with the softest flesh, the maggots do. So the eyes and the mucosa go first."

Faye turned back to the tables. The oldest child, an eleven-year-old girl who had died of kidney cancer, was the only one of the children with hair. Maggots crawled along the black ringlets and came out from inside her mouth. The coroner moved to pull the sheet down further, but Faye stopped him. "We know what's happening down there, I think," she said, and continued to take shot after shot of the children on the remaining tables.

The coroner re-covered each body, then took Faye over to the corner of the room, where a cabinet filled with more jars stood.

"These are the organs of the victims," he told her, as he opened the cabinet. "We had to preserve these to keep the maggots away. We'll need them if there's a lawsuit, and I'm sure there will be. But you can see the effects of the cancers. These are the organs of old people, not children. These are monstrous. It shouldn't be like this here—" and he had waved his arm out toward the tables with the sheets. Faye saw a maggot moving along his belt, under his white lab coat when he raised his arm.

Faye had stopped shooting for a moment when he had said that— *monstrous*—and had looked at him for a second before she resumed photographing the oddly shaped and discolored organs in the jars. *Monstrous*.

When she was finished, Faye thanked him for his time, and for showing her the organs as well as the bodies. She added, as a courtesy, that she hoped an exterminator could kill the maggots.

"You know what we say here," he told her as she was leaving, "the worms crawl in, but they don't crawl out." Faye thought of the childhood rhyme. She couldn't smile, though. She just needed to leave.

She said good-bye and strode to the car. In the bushes next to where she'd parked, she vomited several times. She stomped her feet on the ground to loosen any maggots that might have traveled onto her shoes or the cuff of her pants, then wiped her feet hard on the grass, getting as much of the squashed maggots off as she could.

6.

As she worked on the story, there were more children—dead and alive—one almost dead. Too many. In the end, Faye put together a disturbing tale told in a montage of photographs about more than twenty sick, maimed, and dead children. She had juxtaposed them with the beautiful flowers, lush fruits, and pristine bolls of cotton that were the other side of the pesticides. She had a jar with maggots in the center, the white worms crawling over the side, moving toward the food and flowers. Perfection always came at a cost, she wrote in her copy. Because there is always collateral damage in any war and this one, the war on bugs and fungi, was killing kids.

Faye had spent nearly five weeks on that story. After it was complete—or as complete as it could be, since it was a story with no ending—Faye had driven up to San Francisco before she flew back to New York. She needed to get away from those lush but deadly fields and from the oppressive heat.

Her editor had told her to take a week, "Get some R and R, you need it after this. A tough one, I know."

But he hadn't known. He'd had no idea.

7.

It was night and the house was quiet when Faye left her bed and went downstairs to the darkroom. She had a little flashlight that she kept under her pillow so she could read under the covers after she was supposed to be asleep. She almost never fell asleep without reading. And she often woke from bad dreams, dreams about her parents' accident, dreams in which her grandfather's photographs were moving on the thin clothesline, dreams in which the clothesline itself was drenched in blood and the black fan was on fire and the darkroom filled with smoke the way she imagined her parents' car had done when it crashed, down near the river on New Year's Eve, and then caught fire. Faye would try to scream in the dreams, but no sound would come out.

Faye opened the door and turned on the red light. Photos hung from every part of the clothesline. She knew they were dry because the little fan was going and it had been hours since her grandfather had been in there while she did her homework at the kitchen table and he had done all the work alone, without her, and her grandmother had been down the street, at church, playing bingo.

Faye went over to the photos and shined her flashlight on them, one by one. The photos were all black and white— her grandfather hadn't gotten to the color part yet. But as she looked at them, she wasn't sure if or how he would color them.

The first photo was of a woman with half a face. It was what Faye's grandfather called a portrait shot: Just the woman's head and shoulders. Or part of her head. It wasn't the kind of half-face Faye saw when she looked over her grandfather's shoulder as he brought the magnifying glass up to the still-wet photos, or the bits and pieces she saw when the paper was beginning to become a picture in the tray of developer. In this photo the woman only had half her face. Her forehead and eyes were normal—smooth and with sleek eyebrows and eyes that looked like they might be blue or maybe green, like Faye's were. The lashes were long. Her hair wasn't light, but wasn't dark, either. Faye thought it was probably light brown or maybe a darker red color.

The rest of her face wasn't face anymore. There was a big hole where her nose should have been and then her teeth were half there and half missing, like when you saw a skeleton in a book. Around where her mouth should have been was a lot of muscle-y flesh. It looked raw and open, like it had just been sliced, like meat. It looked like the lamb's heads that hung in the Italian Market at Easter when they went down to get the roast. If the photo hadn't been black and white, it would have been red like that meat, Faye was sure, but there was no blood, just the raw, wounded, cut-open parts.

The next photo was the same woman, but this time her

eyes were closed and Faye could see that there were cuts over her eyes on the eyelids and there were streaks there, like blood, and the one socket looked hollow underneath, like her eyes had come out, too, like the bottom of her face was gone. The other eye socket looked squishy somehow, like the eye had been rubbed out and little bits of it had pushed out and been left on the eyelashes, which looked thick and matted on that side.

The photograph after that was different—the eyes were also closed and flat and in this one both had been squeezed out and there were more pieces littering the eyelashes. The flesh of the face was all there in this one, but the mouth was open, wide, like the woman had been singing, or maybe screaming. And the tongue was out, but in pieces, like a snake tongue—cut down the middle so that it went in two different directions.

The next few photos were of different women, all with their eyes closed and all with cuts on their faces and pieces taken off—a nose, lips, a section of cheek. One had slices all up and down the face with sections of flesh taken out, kind of like bread from a loaf. All the faces looked raw and meaty, like the first woman, but there wasn't blood running in the photos. It just all looked dark, like when Faye would open the white pots of paint and it looked like thick blood in the pot.

Faye didn't know why these faces were like this, and they scared her, but she couldn't stop looking at them.

The last six photos were of more women. The first one had her eyes open and her mouth was open, too, like she was surprised. She was standing outside somewhere—on a street, but not really near anything. There weren't any stores around, just a big long brick wall with writing on it that didn't say anything and then the sidewalk and it looked like it was night, but it was really bright where she was standing.

The woman was wearing a really tight dress and had her hair up on her head and she had big white earrings on and really high heels and a little funny short jacket. She looked frightened and she was half-turned, like she was going to run away.

In the next photo, it was the same woman, but in this one she was against the brick wall and she looked like she was crying. She had her hand up to her face the way people in movies sometimes do, with the back of her hand against her mouth and her palm out toward the camera, like the way women scream sometimes. This picture was more of a head shot, but you could see down to her breasts. In this picture you could see her dress was torn a little in the front and one of her earrings was gone, and her ear looked bloody where the earring should have been. It looked like it had a little rip in it, like the skin was torn.

In the next photo, the woman had a big cut on her face, like some of the other women, and her one eye was closed and looked darker than the other one. She wasn't on the street anymore, but was in a room somewhere, and she was sitting on a small bed. She was still wearing the short dress, but there was a rope tied around her ankles and her hands were in her lap and she had rope around her wrists. She was sitting really still and her mouth was closed because there was something tied over it and there was also a big cut on the front of her dress where her left breast was. It was dark in the spot there—her dress was a light color—and it was flat, not like the other side. There was something round and dark on the bed next to her. It looked like it might be her breast, just there on the bed, instead of on her chest.

Now the photographs really scared Faye and she wanted to stop looking at them. They were like pictures out of a scary movie and she wasn't usually allowed to watch those, because she had the bad dreams and her grandmother said they reminded her of the trauma, but she wasn't exactly sure what the trauma was, just that it had something to do with her parents dying and her coming to live with her grandparents in the little house with the darkroom and the sign out front about the photographs.

Faye didn't want to see the other pictures, and she thought she should go back upstairs to bed, but now it was like she was reading a story and she wanted to know how it ended. But after she had looked at all of them, after she saw everything that was there, and all the bits and pieces and all the dark spots and all the things that were lined up on the bed like when you fold the laundry and put it away in your drawers only this wasn't anything like laundry, Faye wished she hadn't looked. She felt funny—scared and sick and like she might throw up. She went to the door and turned out the red light. She closed the door behind her and turned off her little flashlight. She went into the kitchen in the dark and got a glass of water. She drank all of it and it sloshed around in her stomach and she thought she was going to throw up. She stood over the sink and made a little choking sound, but she didn't vomit.

When she turned to go back upstairs to bed, she saw her grandfather standing in the doorway, in the dark. She stopped and stood still and waited.

"It feels that way at first," he said, his voice soft and low, because it was night and dark and Faye's grandmother was sleeping. "Sickening. But then it feels different. So different. And when you sit here"—and he pointed to the kitchen table—"when you start the painting, it seems good. It seems really good. And you feel proud of the work you are doing. Because it is, you know, art. And art is always beautiful and important, no matter what the subject. No matter—" He stopped speaking for a moment and stared at her, then he said, "One day you'll understand, even if you don't right now."

Faye never spoke. She never asked about the photographs or what they meant or why the women had lost their faces or their eyes or their breasts or why one had been cut open on the little bed and everything inside her had been taken out and laid around her like...something Faye couldn't quite describe.

Faye didn't say anything. She just stood there, looking at her grandfather standing in the doorway. She wondered if her father had known about the photographs. She wondered if her grandmother knew. She wondered if someone else should know about them. Someone other than her.

And then her grandfather had stretched out his hand to Faye and she had walked toward him and they had gone upstairs together, each to their own room. Faye had lain in her bed and thought about the pictures for a long time, especially the ones where the pieces were on the bed, laid out around the body, and the way the woman's legs were spread apart and the thing that had been between them. She thought about what the pieces were and what it meant that they were there, on the bed. She still felt sick, but not as sick as before. She thought about what her grandfather had said and how she didn't understand what it meant. Then she rolled over on her side and she had gone to sleep.

8.

Faye had taken that week's vacation her editor had offered, staying in San Francisco the whole time. She'd settled into a boutique hotel on Post Street where she was near enough to everything that she could walk, take a cable car, or, if she absolutely had to, drive. She'd driven up from Fresno on a Friday and taken a long nap before ending up on the Castro after eleven, drinking gin martinis because she'd never liked vodka all that much, and waiting for this one or that one to sidle up to her as they always did. Faye liked women and they liked her even more. They liked what they thought she was—they liked what she had learned to project since her days at St. Cecelia's, since her days in the darkroom, *Calm*. She'd patterned herself after the saints she'd read about in those early years. Not the acts so much as the demeanor. Faye was always unfazed. In the clubs, Faye was always just sitting on the bar stool, looking, watching, seeing. She didn't need to be eager. Not being eager drew people to her.

The ones who liked her most were the tough ones, the ones who wanted to pin someone pretty to the wall or the bed—white, black, Latina, and Asian butches with shaved heads or faux hawks, with body art and piercings everywhere that mattered. In San Francisco, Faye had spent her first three nights in three different beds, but hadn't found what she was looking for. She had walked through the Mission District and Pacific Palisades and back. She'd gone from bar to bar, beginning and ending at the Lex, beginning and ending with the same kind of women.

On the fourth night, Faye had stayed away from the Castro and the Mission and had worked her way from her hotel toward Chinatown. She'd had a fruity, too-sweet drink with the clichéd umbrella and pineapple and cherry skewer in it at the tiki bar off Union Square with the Asian hostess. The place was a combination overpriced tourist trap and mob hangout. When Faye had walked from her hotel to the bar, she was pretty sure she was looking for more things to photograph, or some kind of trouble, she just wasn't sure which. Time felt like it was standing still for her since she'd left the dead and dying children behind in the San Joaquin Valley, with the bougainvillea landscaping along the highways between one pretty little coffin and another.

Maybe she just needed to get back to New York.

She'd walked down Market Street late the night before, after two, after she'd exited the bed of the scrappy little Latina butch she'd left the Lex with around eleven. She'd gone to the Tendernob, the most crime-ridden place she could find in San Francisco, because it wasn't New York and there wasn't enough danger for her—or at least she hadn't been to the city enough times to know exactly where to look for it, although everyone said the same thing: *Stay away from the Tenderloin, stay away from the Tendernob.* And so she had taken her camera down Market, over to Sixth, then back to Little Saigon, but there was nothing to see—homeless men, addicts, tranny prostitutes looking for dates or just money, a man who said he was a priest trying to talk people off the streets and into shelters. She watched an older Chinese woman trying to catch one of the night pigeons that were always down there whenever Faye had been in San Francisco, but she hadn't caught it and both she and the woman gave up that game.

Faye had walked around for a few hours, until it was getting light. This was the place, the Tenderloin, now working its way into gentrification like everywhere else, that Dashiell Hammett had written about in *The Maltese Falcon*. How could it be less dangerous now than it was then? Or had Faye become inured to danger because after her parents' deaths, her grandparents' house, and St. Cecelia's, everything else had seemed so close to normal, even children burned to death in a Christmas pageant or children poisoned in their mother's wombs?

Faye had left and gone back to her hotel to sleep, the only photographs from her sojourn those of a petite Asian prostitute with a knife strapped to her thigh, the Chinese woman chasing the pigeon, and in the dark recess of an open doorway, the man dressed like a priest getting a blow job from a Latina transsexual.

❖

Faye and the Asian hostess, Shihong, had sat talking and then left the tiki bar together and headed to Chinatown. Faye had always liked it there—had liked the smells and the guttural sounds of languages that weren't English or Spanish. It was big and strange and seemed more like Hong Kong than San Francisco. It wasn't like New York's Chinatown—it was its own city, the biggest Chinatown in North America, the most foreign place Faye could find stateside. The rolling night fog, the closeness of the water, the hilly streets—all added something, an aura, an atmosphere, Faye couldn't quite place, but she liked being there. She liked feeling completely anonymous.

Shihong had led her through the maze of alley-like streets off Grant Avenue, after they had walked through the Dragon Gate. Shihong had pulled her into a darkened doorway and kissed her, hard, and Faye had felt the sleekness of the satin dress she wore as she ran her hands down Shihong's body. Then Shihong had taken Faye to a place where she had ended up buying several animal netsuke, a dark little shop where no one spoke English and where she was the only customer.

Afterward they had stopped for more drinks and Shihong had told Faye about Chinatown, *her* Chinatown. "No *Joy Luck Club*," she had said, her soft voice surprisingly rough. "No PG movie. Look around you—no money, many secrets, lots of darkness. So much, I could never leave. The secrets become you, don't they?"

Shihong had looked straight at Faye and stretched out her hand to Faye and Faye had taken it, wanted to kiss it. *The secrets become you.* Faye decided to tell Shihong a story about secrets, a story she had only told one other time, to Sister Anne Marie. Shihong listened, without moving, except to sip from her drink. But when Faye finished telling the story, Shihong had looked at her, stared with an expression Faye, who was so good at reading other people's faces, couldn't quite discern. Then Shihong told Faye about a black market shop she thought Faye might want to see, "a shop that sells secrets," she said, "a shop not"—she had briefly turned away from Faye—"for everyone. There are two Chinatowns, you know. One for tourists, one for us. I take you to the one for us."

They had left the bar, wending their way through the fog and a series of alleyways. Along the way Shihong would stop and pull Faye into a doorway here, an alcove there, and kiss her, hard. The kisses were hot and violent and Faye's mouth felt bruised from the force of them. But she didn't pull away. There was a kind of heat emanating from Shihong that Faye didn't quite understand, but she wanted to see where it went. Even if it took her to a place she didn't know.

The two women kept walking, Shihong slightly ahead, her hand in Faye's, almost as if she were pulling her along, until they reached a small shop on a tiny street, the name of which Faye had not seen—the streetlight over the sign was out. The name of the shop was written in Chinese characters—no English translation. Shihong had rung a bell and an elderly woman in traditional silk pajamas had answered the door. She and Shihong had spoken in whatever dialect they spoke—Faye had no idea, some kind of Cantonese, she assumed. She also could not discern the tenor of the conversation—was it friendly or rancorous? Shihong had lowered her voice while the old woman had raised hers. Faye had thought for a moment that she should leave right then—run, in fact, since the door was still open and she was fairly sure she could find her way back to Grant Street and out of here. The Castro was one thing. She had felt equal to the women she had bedded in the past few days. The Tenderloin had been the same thing—she spoke that language, always had. But here—here she was in a foreign country and one where she stood out; she was nothing like anyone, here, especially not here in the old part of Chinatown where some things clearly had not changed in the hundred and sixty-odd years since this place had been established.

Faye edged back toward the door. It was definitely time to go. She needed to be back in New York. This was not the place for her.

But just as she half turned to leave, the old woman reached into the folds of her trousers and pulled out a key, pressing it into Shihong's hand and folding the fingers over it. She then turned toward Faye, bowed quickly, and shuffled away. Faye had been disarmed by the bow, chiding herself for being nervous. This was an old woman, not a threat. She remembered the feeling of dread she'd had at the morgue in Fresno. And in the end that had just been heat and maggots. Nothing dangerous. Nothing irreparable. Just an unpleasantness. Plus, she and Shihong had had a chemistry over drinks and with those kisses that was real, not fake.

Faye looked at the woman as she disappeared up a staircase to the side of the shop's interior and wondered for a moment whether her feet were bound—it had only been a little over fifty years since that barbaric practice had ended. Faye wished she'd paid closer attention. She knew that was a photograph she would like to have, although she wasn't sure she could have asked for it.

Shihong shut the door behind them and locked it with the key in her hand. She took Faye's hand and Faye shook off her momentary fear as Shihong pulled her forward into the dark recesses of the shop. A dim amber light glowed beyond the doorway as they walked through a room made narrow by high stacks of shelves on one side of the pathway they were walking. On the other side were glass cases, like in a jewelry shop. Faye couldn't really see anything in the dim light. Everything was dark—the wood of the shelves, the things on the shelves. The lights in the glass cases were off. She couldn't discern where she was or what was there. Shihong stopped suddenly and turned toward her.

"You saw her," she told Faye, referring to the elderly woman. "Now you see why I cannot leave this place. This will always be my home."

Faye nodded, but wasn't sure what Shihong meant. Was this woman related to Shihong? What was this place, exactly? Did Shihong live here? Faye flashed for a moment on the classic Roman Polanski film and wondered if perhaps she had stepped too far into the wrong story by coming here, to Chinatown, with this woman she'd known for barely three hours who had picked her up at a mob bar and had now locked her into a shop with no English name, a shop that held God-only-knew what.

Shihong reached up above the two of them and switched on a small light. It illumined the shelves directly in front of them. On the shelves were rows of jars. For years Faye had never seen anything like that room at St. Cecelia's. Now, in the space of a few days, she'd been treated to the anomalous organs in the Fresno morgue and whatever this was. Just as at St. Cecelia's, these jars were above Faye's head, not at eye level. The fact that she could not see them made her anxious suddenly, and she thought again that she should leave. She looked at Shihong, questioningly. The woman tossed her head back, her black hair whipping behind her, her long earrings making a light tinkling sound as she did so.

"You said you like to uncover secrets," Shihong said in a tone Faye could not decipher. "Here are secrets. What do you think now?"

Faye had stepped back, away from the shelves, and looked up. She stared at what was arrayed all along the shelves. Faye, who was never unfazed, had gasped, her hand flying up to her mouth, stifling the scream that threatened to escape. She turned toward Shihong, but she was no longer there.

❖

Faye had left the unnamed place many hours later, her left wrist sliced raw and open with a rope burn and bruises and dried blood. Her bag was heavy and full as she heaved it over her shoulder. In her right hand she gripped the netsuke and her jacket, both smeared with what looked like blood and something else—maybe little bits of flesh. She remembered what Shihong had told her when Faye had asked what her name meant in Chinese.

"The whole world is red," Shihong had told her.

❖

When Faye got back to the hotel, she changed her reservation and packed. She stopped at the post office on her way to the airport and mailed a large package. Then she flew home to New York.

9.

After the first time, Faye would creep downstairs to the darkroom in the middle of the night when she was certain even her grandfather could not hear her. She had begun to wait for the nights when she had seen him take the little pill from the bottle in the kitchen on the shelf over the sink. She had learned to make the trip without her flashlight, so that even that weak whisper of light wouldn't disturb her grandparents—although it was her grandfather she didn't want to wake.

She would go into the darkroom and close the door before she turned on the red light. The photographs were always the same: Women. Several at a time. The progression of the pictures was always the same—wounds to the face, smashing of the eyes, torn pieces from the lips, nose, cheeks, ears. There was always one with the frightened look who ended up tied on the bed in the room Faye didn't recognize. But each new time she came down to look, now, there were more pieces on the bed. And this time, there was something new.

It was the ninth photograph on the line. Faye wasn't sure why she always counted the photographs, but she did. The ninth photograph had a woman in a chair at a table. She was wearing a dress and the skirt was pulled all the way up, to where her underwear should be. She had something over her eyes and something over her mouth and the thing over her mouth had a big dark spot on it. Her head was down, like she had fallen asleep at the table.

She was tied to the chair at the ankles and her legs were open the way Faye's grandmother told her never to sit. Where her underwear should be was a dark spot and that spot was on her dress right there, too. On the table was a plate and a fork and knife and a glass with something dark in it. The plate had something on it, too, but Faye wasn't sure what it was.

All the other pictures were of plates on the table and each one had something else on it, something Faye had never seen before. It all looked like meat, but not meat they ever ate here. The last photograph was back at the little room with the bed. The woman who had been sitting at the table was lying on the bed and her dress was ripped and there were pieces taken out of it all over. On the bed next to her were the plates, all of them with the things on them that looked like meat, but Faye wasn't sure.

She stared at the photos for a long time, going back and forth and looking at all of the things on the plates. Then she knew what it was she was looking at: the things on the plates were the things that were inside her operation doll. They were the organs—the heart, the liver, the kidneys, the intestines, some other things she didn't think were inside the body in the operation doll.

Faye looked at the photographs again. Then she turned off the light and shut the door. She went into the kitchen and sat down at the table. The light from the back porch was on and a small shaft of it came through the window onto the table, onto her pajama legs as she sat in the chair and thought about what she had just seen.

She got up to go back to her bedroom. When she got to the door of the kitchen she turned and looked at the table and chair again. It was the same as the one in the photographs. Suddenly, Faye felt really hot and her heart started to pound fast, like when she was scared. Then everything went dark as she fell to the floor.

10.

Another Christmas, three years after the arson fire and six months after Faye had taken the photographs of the children in the Central Valley, a young woman, distraught over a breakup and too upset to head home for the holiday, had thrown herself from the subway platform in front of the train. She'd been sliced nearly in half, yet remained alive beneath the train. Faye had been only a few blocks away, still at the newspaper, and gotten the call from the city desk to go down and see if she could get some shots. The city desk editor was always looking for the story that no one else had, and he and Faye got along really well because those were the stories she wanted, too. He always saw Pulitzer on everything and he'd say to her, "This has Pulitzer written all over it, if you've got the 'nads. Whaddaya think? Can ya do it?"

He liked talking like that, like it was 1940 and she was WeeGee being sent down to take flashbulb shots of dead gangsters lying in the street in the meat-packing district with the kind of equipment her grandfather had once used, instead of the small Nikon with the SIM card that was even more like magic than everything that had been in her grandfather's studio when she was growing up.

So Faye had gone. In fact, because it was two days before Christmas and a Friday night, she'd been the only one around for the shots. The EMTs and firefighters who were cutting away at the train car above the woman wouldn't let the TV crews down—too much equipment, too dangerous. But Faye, lean and lithe and agile enough to leap down onto the tracks without getting in anyone's way, had been there with her little camera. She'd crawled down to chronicle what the woman thought—prayed—would be her final moments as rescuers worked above to free her. Faye had talked to her the whole time, talked while the whine of the torch and the crunch of the shears had cut and cut and cut around her and the woman, whose name was, in an irony too bald for Faye, Esperanza, told her the story of why she jumped in front of the train and how much she wanted to die.

Faye had photographed the aftermath, too. She couldn't catalogue the sucking sound as what was left of the young woman was pulled off the tracks, or the smell of charred flesh and other offal that rose up off the place where the woman had been under the train, but Faye took shot after shot as the EMTs got Esperanza onto the backboard and strapped tourniquets and put pressure bandages on her, hung the IV that they hoped—or maybe didn't—would keep her alive, and pushed morphine into the drip.

Faye just kept shooting—the IV bag streaked with blood, the blue and yellow vial of morphine, the silver-foil warming blanket to try to prevent the shock that had set in an hour before, the expressions of fear, pain, and something else Faye couldn't name on the face of Esperanza and the faces of the EMTs.

As Esperanza had been lifted up onto the platform, Faye had kept on shooting—photographing the EMT whose job it was to collect the body parts left behind in the hope—*esperanza,* Faye thought—that something might be re-attached if the woman made it into surgery before she died. An arm sheared off at the shoulder, a leg in two pieces, a slab of flesh with shredded muscle and mangled bone, something else red and pulpy that Faye couldn't identify. All of these went into plastic bags and coolers filled with cold packs, then were handed back up onto the platform, like this was some creepy Christmas tailgate party, and all the while, Faye kept shooting photo after photo.

The woman hadn't died. Esperanza had lived, missing an arm, a leg, part of her shoulder, several ribs, and a section of pelvis on the side where she'd been sliced apart by the train. The excisions had left her with just a sheer covering of skin over that half of her body, so that some of her organs—a lung, a kidney—could almost be seen through the bluish-pink layering of muscle and flesh that resembled uncooked chicken. The woman's hideous deformity remained a constant reminder of her momentary misery and sudden desire for the obliterating death that never came after all.

Grateful that Faye had been down there on the tracks with her, Esperanza had allowed Faye full access to her recovery, and the photo essay, *A Cry from the Tunnel: Woman on the Tracks,* had become a coffee-table book that one critic called "art of the creepiest, most intrusive, most voyeuristic, most repugnant sort. Even Nan Goldin or Diane Arbus wouldn't touch this stuff. We really don't need to see everything, just because it's there," he had written. Faye had smiled a grim smile when she had read that, telling her assistant, Sonja, who had brought the review to her with trepidation, "But that's the whole point—no one wants to touch it. Yet the organs are still going to be pulsing just below the skin, aren't they, whether we want to see them or not?"

Other reviews had been laudatory, but had more than hinted at the dark side of Faye's artistry and one had gone so far as to mention Faye's parents' deaths as a possible foundation for what the critic had called Faye's "addictive and addicting response to the grisly and profane."

There had been a book signing downtown, which was well-attended, and Esperanza had been there in her wheelchair, with a cousin and some guy she had met in rehab. There had been a big party after at Locande Verde, in the Greenwich Village Hotel, that had packed the restaurant, but Esperanza had left after the signing and Faye hadn't tried to stop her. Faye and Esperanza both knew she should have died. Faye wasn't sure how long it would be before Esperanza tried to kill herself again. Faye only hoped this time she would be successful.

After the party, there had been the inevitable—some had gone home and others had wanted to keep partying. Faye had taken a cadre off to dance at Henrietta Hudson because even the boys were welcome there, although she never went for the boys, just the tough girls.

The night at the club had gone late and Faye had wanted to see the river when she left, not quite drunk, but barely sober, after some quick and unexpected finger-fucking sex in the bathroom with an assiduous publicist from a rival publisher. She'd taken a cab to the meat-packing district. Faye didn't live down there anymore, but when she had, on Horatio Street, she had woken up nightly when the trucks had rolled in and some nights she'd gone to the window and stood, just to watch the big hunks of flesh and bone travel from one place to another, bodies of animals hanging from big racks, just like clothing in the garment district.

This night Faye got out of the cab near her old apartment and just walked. She wasn't sure what she wanted to see—the river or the meat—but she wanted to see something that wasn't there at the book signing or the party or the club. The meat-packing district was all trendy now, with the High Line and the Hotel Gansvoort and the old slaughterhouses turned into lofts. There were only eight or nine meat-packers left and none of the edgiest S&M bars that used to be there, like the Mineshaft. And yet she still wanted to go, still wanted to think about what it had been like when she did live there, before gentrification took over. It hadn't been that long—not even ten years.

She pulled her camera out of her bag and walked away from the river and toward where the trucks would be unloading the meat. It was almost four a.m. and she was looking for flesh—dead flesh, cut slabs of flesh, chunky, meaty flesh, and the commingling smell of blood. And something else Faye couldn't quite name. Maybe, if she kept looking, she would find it.

11.

Faye's grandmother had found her on the floor that night, awakened by the sound of her small body falling, catching the side of a chair as she went down. She had lifted Faye up off the floor and as Faye came to, had asked her what had happened. Faye just stared at her, but said nothing. She knew she should tell, but what was there to tell, really? She sat in her grandmother's lap on one of the chairs where the woman had sat. Which one was it? Which one had she been tied to? Which one had her organs on the plate in front of her? And how could she live without her organs? Faye's operation doll was empty when the organs were out on the floor when she played with it in her room. Was the woman empty, too?

Faye couldn't think about any more of it. She wished she hadn't looked at the pictures because now that was all she could see—the pictures and the table, the chair and the woman, the plates and the organs. Were they the same plates that her grandmother put down at breakfast and dinner? Was the meat they were eating the organs from the woman?

Faye felt hot again, and sweaty. Her face was burning hot, like she was in the sun. She wanted to go to sleep. She wanted to forget about the pictures. Her eyes started to burn and she felt tears coming down her face.

Her grandmother felt her forehead and whispered, "Oh, you're burning up. No wonder you fainted. Let's get you to bed."

She had carried Faye upstairs herself, then, not waking her grandfather to come and get her. Her grandmother had laid her on the bed, on top of the covers, and gotten clean pajamas and told her to put them on. She had left the room and come back with a washcloth. She wiped Faye's face and the cloth felt cool and now Faye was sleepy and not thinking about the pictures anymore. Her grandmother got her into the bed and covered her up, still wiping her face with the washcloth.

"Are you feeling better, dear? I know this is all very hard on you. I'm not surprised you're sick. Things will be better when you go off to school. It will be new and strange at first, but it will be good for you, you'll see. How do you feel now?"

Her grandmother had looked at Faye, her face full of concern and caring. Even in the dim night-light, Faye could tell she was worried.

"I think it was the meat," Faye said. "I think the meat from dinner made me sick. I don't want to eat it anymore.

Please don't make me." And Faye's eyes had filled with tears and her grandmother had stroked her hair.

"Well, we'll have to find something else to feed you, then, dear, won't we? But for now, no more meat until you are better, okay?"

Faye had slid down under the covers and put her head on her grandmother's lap.

"Thank you," was all she said, and then she fell asleep.

12.

After Esperanza and the book and the controversy, Faye had more cachet at the paper. She went into the editorial meeting a week after the book party and asked if she could do something really different. Faye wanted to do a two-part series on women in Congo and Afghanistan.

"These wars are endless," she had said. "And the women are the primary victims. Our readers know about these places—think of all the African immigrants here in New York," she had argued. "And we're still in Afghanistan. Even if we leave, nothing will have changed there for women. It will still be the most hellish place on Earth after the DRC. Give me three weeks. I'll get you something no one else has. Hell, I may do the stuff in Afghanistan in a burka."

Faye had detailed the stories of gang rapes and acid burnings. She pulled up the page of facts from her iPad that she'd compiled with the help of a woman she knew at an NGO and read off the string of ritualistic mayhem: 15,000 rapes a month in DRC. Hundreds of acid burnings in Afghanistan. Women raped and eviscerated on their way to get water in the bush. Women raped and then stoned to death. Women flayed alive. Women tortured with unspeakable brutality and no one paying attention. No UN sanctions. No invasions. Nothing.

Just so much killing.

"You understand," Faye told them, leaning forward and looking at each of them, "these are going to be photographs no one else has, stories no one else has. But it's going to be ghastly and hideous and no one in this room is going to want to look at these photographs, let alone our readers. But we have to make them. We have to make them."

When Faye had finished detailing all the ways a woman could be mutilated in the service of war, she knew the assignment was hers. Not for the right reasons, of course, but hers, nevertheless. She could practically see the word light up on everyone's forehead: *Pulitzer.* It was a done deal. She knew it would be.

It was easier than she'd expected: The main thing was the vaccinations and buying some long scarves and that burka. The latter had been a bizarre experience in a small shop in Jamaica Heights. The shop window was filled with mannequins that were dead white, covered in various dark-colored burkas, some with a fabric that had a pattern woven into it that could only be seen up close. Inside the shop, the mannequins were just the same: Only the white slit where the eyes should have been showed, giving each mannequin an eerie look, as if the burkas clothed ghosts. An unconscious metaphor, Faye thought, considering that under the burka, all women became invisible.

Faye left New York for Kinshasa ten days after the editorial meeting. Standing in her apartment a few hours before she took the cab to the airport, she thought, this was the last one—the last story. She was going to leave the paper after this. She was going to put together a show that would be a retrospective of her life's work. Faye already knew what she would title it: *Ordinary Mayhem.* She was already writing the copy for the book that would follow it.

Faye walked into the small room that served as her studio and shut the door behind her—force of habit. She closed the blackout shade on the window over her work table and walked to the old apothecary cabinet that stood against the far wall, behind the door. There were curtains over the glass doors in a deep burgundy red. Inside the cabinet, on the six shelves, were a series of jars in different sizes. She stood and looked at them for a time, then reached in and touched one, then another. She took out one of the largest jars, walked to the table, and put it down. She sat in the chair, looking at it, then reached for her notebook and wrote a few sentences.

On the wall opposite her table were photographs—rows and rows of photographs. She stared at them, then made more notations in the notebook. The book about Esperanza had just been a start. Soon she would have that show. The gallery exhibit—that was going to reveal a completely different side of her work. Not just the photographs, but the other things. It would definitely be mixed media. She had already had several offers from gallery owners. She had chosen one at the edge of SoHo—still trendy, but enough money to get her what she wanted in the end. The notoriety and the attention.

For a brief moment she thought of her grandfather, the darkroom, the other things. She thought of Sister Anne Marie. And of that night in Chinatown, with Shihong.

Faye felt cold. She looked at her watch. Then she got up and put the jar back on its shelf. She closed the cabinet again, locked it, and left the room.

It was time to go to the airport.

13.

It was summer before Faye went into the darkroom again at night. Her grandfather would invite her in during the day, but Faye only went in after she had seen people in the studio and she'd seen the photographs being taken. Then she knew what would be on the floating pieces of paper in the trays. Then she knew she wouldn't be sick. She wouldn't see the women, or the table, or the pieces of the women on the beds and on the plates. She thought about these things all the time, but there was no one to tell about them, no one to talk to. When he went into the darkroom, her grandfather would wink at her, like they had a secret between them. And they did—Faye knew now that if her grandfather had taken those photographs, it was like everything else he took photographs of: the weddings, the graduations, the prom pictures, the family portraits. He arranged everything. She could almost hear him saying to those women, "Now lick your lips and tilt your head up."

And then what had he done? And where had he done it? And why?

There was something so strange for Faye about the secret. She knew it—she'd figured it out that night at the table, and then she fainted, because it made her sick to think about it. Yet she wasn't afraid of her grandfather. Every night he would kiss her before she went to bed and it didn't scare her, it didn't even make her feel creepy. Sometimes she thought she'd made it all up in her head, that it never really happened. But then he would wink at her and she would think that it had to be because of the secret, because he knew she knew and that it was something they shared.

He told her over and over that he would give her a camera in a few years so that she could take her own pictures. "You'll see things, and you'll want to photograph them," he told her. "You'll want to see them over and over again. Because even though you have the memory of something, seeing it again, having the picture—it's just like being at that place or doing that thing all over again. And it makes you feel—" He had stopped talking for a moment and she saw the look on his face. He was remembering. He was remembering the women and the parts and the table. And she had to look away. It was better if she looked away.

But he had started talking again, and had told her that until she had a camera, she should draw pictures of things she saw that meant something to her. She should keep a notebook. And he had given her some special pencils that were very sharp and in a little box. They were different colors and he had told her to try to make the colors match the things she saw. He had also given her a little notebook. It had thick white paper in it with no lines and it had a spiral binding so she could tear out the pages if she wanted to.

Then he had taken her out back, into the yard, and he had said, "Look at this, you should draw this," and he had pointed at the edge of one of the flower beds.

Faye had looked and there was a small dead shrew there. Its eyes were open and so was its mouth. It looked like something had surprised it all of a sudden. Then Faye looked closer and she saw that it had a tear in its stomach and some of the guts were out on the ground. She didn't want to look at it anymore, but her grandfather said, "Now go inside and draw the shrew. Draw everything you saw. Because then, when you want to remember it, it will be right there for you to look at."

Faye's grandfather had been looking down at her as she bent over the flower bed, and as Faye looked up, she could see his face, all excited. What she didn't know was whether he was excited about the dead shrew or about her drawing it.

❖

Faye still remembered the night when she had fainted in the kitchen and her grandmother had taken her upstairs. It had been cold on the floor, but she had still felt really hot. She'd stayed in bed for almost two weeks after that. There had been a trip to the doctor who had told her grandmother that Faye was suffering from trauma, just as her grandmother had been saying all along to her, to everyone. The anguish over her parents' deaths, plus being uprooted from her home—it had all been too much, the doctor told them. Faye's immune system was worn down, the doctor said, and she was prey for infection. He had given her grandmother a prescription for some pills that Faye had to take for two weeks, to make the infection go away, and before they left the office, a dark-skinned woman in a bright pink uniform with little smiling animals on the shirt had taken three glass vials of blood from her arm.

The doctor had also said that Faye needed to be back in school. That too much time had passed—"It's been several weeks since the accident"—and she might end up being left back a year if she didn't return. He recommended tutoring if there were problems adjusting to the new school in a different borough.

"I know Brooklyn is like a foreign country to her," he'd told her grandmother, "so whatever we can do to help the transition. This is, you know, compounding the trauma."

He also recommended a therapist. "She needs to talk to someone, talk it out," he had said, while he rubbed Faye's shoulder like she was a cat.

Faye had started at St. Cecelia's on Valentine's Day. The school was different from her other school—there were only girls and nuns in habits taught all the classes. A priest came every morning and gave Holy Communion to the girls who were old enough. Faye would have her first Holy Communion in May. She was sorry her mother wouldn't be able to see that, because she had wanted to make Faye's dress. They had talked about it at Christmas, before the accident.

St. Cecelia's had girls who went home and girls who lived at the school. Faye wasn't sure why some girls lived there and the rest of them did not, but she thought maybe it would be nice to live there, with all the other girls and the nuns. Maybe it would be different from her grandparents' house. She hoped it would be. She hoped it would be more like home. Or at least different. She was ready to leave her grandparents' house now. She was ready to go someplace else.

The school year had gone quickly. Faye hadn't fallen behind like the doctor had said; in fact, she was recommended to skip a grade. She'd had her First Holy Communion and had stood at the altar rail with the other girls in her white frilly dress and thin white veil. Her grandmother had given her a rosary with pearly beads and a little white Missal as a present and her grandfather had taken her picture and she had watched him develop it in the darkroom after.

She had spent part of the summer at a camp for Catholic girls and she had made things and gone hiking and caught frogs. In the mornings there was Mass and then there was swimming and lunch and activities in the afternoon. Faye had made some friends, including a girl, Rosario, who would be in her new grade at St. Cecelia's in September. Rosario didn't have a father, either, although her father wasn't dead. She just didn't know who he was. Rosario lived with her grandparents, too, because, she said, her mother was "sick on the drugs" and she couldn't take care of Rosario anymore.

Faye was looking forward to seeing Rosario again. Now it was late August and Faye had been back at her grandparents' house for more than two weeks. It was another week before school would start again. It was hot in her little room, which used to be her father's room when he was a child, and the fan just whirled around, but didn't make anything cooler.

Sometimes Faye would go downstairs and lie on the floor in the kitchen because the linoleum was cool and her grandmother kept everything so clean, she didn't mind being on the floor. She would take the pillow from her rocking chair and put it under her head and sleep there until it got light.

This time when she went downstairs, she stopped outside the darkroom door. She stood still for a minute. She could hear the black fan whirring inside. She could imagine the photographs moving slightly on the clothesline. She could imagine the cut-up women in the pictures, too.

Faye went into the kitchen and put her pillow on a chair. Then she went back to the darkroom and went inside.

14.

The story in Congo was different from anything else Faye had done. The place was hot and steamy and breathtakingly beautiful. That was the text. The subtext was like all subtexts—something totally different. The war that wasn't a war in Congo was an unending nightmare from which no one could awaken, least of all the women whose lives Faye had come to chronicle. Everything had been shunted off to East Congo, so that people could act like nothing was happening in the rest of the country.

Faye had never seen things quite as terrible as what she saw in Congo and she had to find ways to make the story new, to make a war-weary readership care about the women and girls who were being gang-raped and eviscerated on their way to get water or wood for fire or just right in their own homes, as they lay sleeping. Faye was keeping notebooks again—this was no place for an iPad or a cell phone vlog. As soon as she got there, she knew there was another book here. A big book. *An important book.* Because Faye knew that even though people didn't really care what happened to these women, they'd still want to pore over their suffering and examine every hideous detail. She could see them turning her photographs this way and that to see every bit of the horror and still feeling just a little disappointed that they couldn't see more.

It was just like when she had taken those photographs of the rig that spilled the steel rods back in New York. Everyone wanted to see the decapitated driver, blood and spinal fluid spurting from the place where his head should be, jagged bits of bone and spine and strings of sinew all splayed out like rebar twisted in cement when a building is demolished. Everyone wanted to see the guy screaming, pinned to the seat of his car with the steel pipe, his mouth open in one continuous howl as he tried to pull himself free. Or the dogs, flattened next to their owner, intestines protruding from one, brains spilled out from another. Everyone wanted to see mayhem juxtaposed with the most tranquil of settings. A simple weekday dog walk turned into carnage. That's all there was in Congo—the simple walk turned into carnage, set against the most postcard-beautiful background.

Faye had met with a woman, Martine, in Kinshasa. Martine worked for the NGO Women for Women and Faye had talked to her on the phone while she was still in New York, setting up the itinerary for her trip. Martine was very dark-skinned and slight, but elegant—she seemed much taller and more imposing than her actual height implied. The scarf wound around her head was a muted blue fabric with black flowers outlined in it. Her skirt, which fell almost to her ankles, was of the same material and she wore a white blouse that looked like a T-shirt, but was a thin linen with white embroidery. She wore no jewelry. Martine told Faye to remove her earrings, watch, and the thin silver bracelets she wore on her left wrist.

"They will tear the earrings from your ears, should they catch you," Martine said, almost matter-of-factly, as if it were a foregone conclusion that Faye would be ambushed and injured. "They do that. And the watch and the bracelets they will notice first. Just put them away. You don't need to know the time here, anyway. It is all the same hour."

Martine had traveled with Faye to eastern Congo, which was, Martine said, the rape capital of the world. "We give out numbers, but we can't really count. On one weekend, 16,000 women were raped. So many of these women have been raped more than once. By the time they come to us, it is all over for them, they believe. So much has happened. They feel destroyed, like ghosts, yet still drawing breath."

Faye and Martine had gone to South Kivu province, then to a rural refugee center outside Bukavu, where rape victims were cared for by Catholic nuns and medical personnel from Doctors Without Borders. The building was low and flat and spread out over a wide space that was lush and green. A low-hanging mist furled around the center and in the near distance Faye could see the hills of Rwanda rolling out over the horizon. Below them lay Lake Kivu. It was an incredibly beautiful landscape. If only you didn't know what lay beneath as well as beyond, for the legacy of the Rwandan genocide was what had bled over into the DRC.

As they entered the building, Faye felt dread take her over: it was like the morgue in Fresno—a bad feeling, a grim, heart-pounding foreboding. She began to sweat; a slight faintness gripped her briefly. Maybe this trip had been a bad idea. Maybe she wouldn't be able to do what she had hoped. It was only a few days and the handful of people she'd talked to had made her sick with their stories. And how to explain such extremes of violence against such a serene—no, breathtakingly beautiful—landscape? This was exponentially worse than the pesticide poisoning story. Worse than Esperanza. After all, Esperanza had tried to take her own life. Tragic as it was, that young woman had been driven by her own demons, not someone else's.

Martine led Faye down a wide, open hallway to a very large room that served as a ward for women recovering from gang rapes and the surgeries required after. As they neared the room, a hideous smell began to waft toward them. Faye coughed and Martine said, "I know, I should have warned you. The smell—it is awful, you see. I would give you something to put under your nose, but it does not help. I have tried all of it…"

"What is it, the smell?" Faye asked, trying not to gag. She had stopped walking down the open hallway toward the room. She wasn't sure what was beyond the doorway. The place was surprisingly quiet. Too quiet. Preternaturally quiet. She reached in her bag for an Altoid. The intensity of the mint would help deaden the smell—and calm her gagging.

"Urine, feces, blood. There is always some rotting flesh, no matter what the doctors do. The gangrene, it can set in quickly, the wounds are so severe. That is the smell that lingers most, the smell of what is already dead. The things that have been done to these women—" Martine drew her hand across her face. It came away wet. "What they tell you when they get here, what they describe—"

She turned toward Faye, looked directly at her. Martine's eyes were the deepest brown, almost black; Faye could hardly discern the pupils. Martine reached out her hand, placing it on Faye's shoulder. Her grip was shockingly tight. Painful. Faye wanted to shake it off. She was reminded of Shihong, in Chinatown.

"Make them show you," Martine said, her voice almost a whisper, her face moving closer. "Of course, that means you will have to look, but make them show you. People must see what goes on here. It is hell here. It is the very worst of hell. Make them show you."

They had entered the room and Faye had steeled herself, biting into the mint and feeling the burning heat of it on her tongue. It would keep her focused, that mint. She'd keep putting them in her mouth as long as was necessary.

The room was long and open. The ceiling was low. Windows ran the length of each side of the room. It reminded Faye of the dormitory at St. Cecelia's. Only this was a ward and the paint wasn't the bright white of St. Cecelia's with its tidy little stenciling of blue crosses near the ceiling. The paint here was shiny enamel of the sort that had been used decades ago, and was probably filled with lead. It was a pale blue and here and there where the paint was scraped off, a sweaty effulgent plaster showed through; it looked like infection. The floor was painted concrete. There were drains in different places. In more than one spot, blood pooled on the floor, flies and other insects buzzing over it.

Everyone on the ward was hovering just this side of death. Twenty-four beds—cots, really—twelve on each side, lined the walls. The beds were low and very flat—thin mattresses with no pillows. Each had a colored sheet but nothing else.

Some women lay in a fetal position, others lay completely flat. Still others lay as if they had been thrown onto the beds, their legs and arms askew. Most had IV bags, a few also had bags with blood. There were none of the accoutrements of a twenty-first century medical ward for what Faye presumed was the intensive care status of these patients. No heart monitors, no oxygen, no nurses, no call buttons.

Some of the beds had another person tending the woman. A mother, a sister, an aunt. No men. No children.

No one seemed to speak, but there was, Faye realized, a low susurration throughout the room—a collective sighing between patients and their caregivers. Occasionally there was a moan.

Martine explained what Faye would see when she got closer. They began with a woman named Jetta. She was one of the women sprawled on her cot. She had not one but two IVs, each running into the place where her arms should have been.

Martine spoke to Jetta in a language Faye did not know, and then the story began to be repeated—Jetta looked at Faye and Martine repeated in English what Jetta told her.

They had come for her at night, late, after midnight. She was alone, her husband had gone to care for his ailing father. It was just Jetta and her younger son and daughter. The older son was with his father. There were five of them—*five, imagine, five*—she said. Jetta started to cry then, and Martine, who was sitting close to her, where her family should have been, began to stroke her forehead.

Jetta continued, explaining how they had threatened to rape her daughter and her son—*they are only children, they are only children*—and so she consented. Or so they told her husband, later. But what she had done was beg them for the lives of her children. There was never any consent. Never.

They made her children watch—time after time, in all the places. She was torn apart. And when it was over, they cut off her arms. *"One for each child,"* they told her, and had tossed the arms at the feet of each child. She could still hear their terrified screams. She could still hear her own screams. *"We were like animals, in our pain,"* Jetta said. *"Like animals in the bush, tearing each other to bits."*

Two neighbors had crept up because of the screaming and had slipped into the house after the men had left. *"I owe them my life,"* she said, because they had kept her from bleeding to death and had brought her here.

Six more women consented to talk to Faye, to let her take pictures of them. The stories were each of unbelievable torture. Two women had also lost limbs, five had lost their uteruses, because of knives being used on them, or the barrels of guns. All would need catheters for the rest of their lives because of the damage that couldn't be repaired.

One woman, Yvette, had lost part of her bowel. She had been pregnant when they took her, and so they had cut her open after they raped her and killed her baby, hacking it to pieces in front of her.

"I will never have a child, now," she cried. *"I will never have a husband. I will only have this—"* and she had pulled up her shirt and revealed a webbing of raw, red scars against the dark skin and at the center, a tube leading out to a small bag filled with a thick dark fluid. *"This is the baby I care for now, now that my child is dead, my husband has gone."*

Each woman had allowed Faye to photograph the scars, the missing pieces—one woman's breasts had been sliced off. Faye had them turn their faces away, so they would not feel humiliated, but Yvette had said no, she wanted to be seen.

"Let them see what they did to me. Let them see the pieces of me that are missing—my baby, my heart, my soul. They think they saved me here at this place. And they are kind, they want to help. But I died with my baby. I am a ghost, just a ghost—but a vengeful ghost. So show them, show them my face. Let me haunt them for all eternity."

Faye thanked each of the women, one by one. And then she and Martine went outside where Faye walked as far from the center as she could, put both hands over her mouth, and screamed.

15.

There was another woman Martine wanted Faye to see, but she wasn't on the ward. She was in a cottage off the main building with three other women. Faye said she wasn't sure. She felt shaky and something else, she didn't know what it was. *Déjà vu,* yet that wasn't possible.

Martine was talking to her. "We have to keep the worst ones separate," Martine told Faye. "Sometimes it is better if they do not share their stories. These women are so fragile, and some of these stories—well, you will see."

Faye wasn't sure what could be worse than the evisceration of Yvette and the murder of her baby. What could be worse than having your arms cut off and tossed at your children's feet while they—and you—screamed? What could be worse than five men, or seven men, or nine men and your insides coming out of you?

Vandana sat in the corner of the small room in a straight-backed chair. There was no one else in the room, which held a small cot, a plastic dresser, and a fan. There was a thin pillow between her and the chair. She was looking out the window, which faced the Rwandan hills. It would soon be dusk and a spiral of insects whirled in a column just outside the window.

Vandana didn't turn when Faye and Martine came into the room. She said, *"It is so beautiful here, but I never want it to be night. I want to be where it is never, ever night."*

She didn't turn until they were standing next to her and Martine said something softly, and Vandana turned toward them, then.

Her face was in two halves. On one side, a pretty, twenty-something woman with full lips, high cheekbones, and a dark, sparkling eye. On the other side, a reddish brown welt of a scar ran from an inch above her eyebrow, through where her left eye should be, and down to her mouth, which had been sliced at the corner, leaving another scar that ran from the corner of her mouth, up her cheek, to her ear, which was gone, sliced clean off. She was missing part of her hand on that side as well. Her eye socket was concave and the scar ran in a Y-shape over it.

Faye began to feel hot. Her heart was pounding now, too, and the blood rushed in her ears.

"I've been waiting for you," Vandana said, *"I've been waiting to tell you everything, since I have so little to show you. You cannot photograph what is no longer here."*

Like all the other women, they had come to Vandana's house at night, the soldiers, or whatever they were, she wasn't sure. *"They all call themselves soldiers, but what are they really? Just monsters. Nothing but monsters. They are the things you feared as a child, that you begged your mother and father to protect you from in the dark, in the night. But there is no protection now. The monsters, they are free to do as they please. They are free to be monsters, monsters."*

As Vandana began to tell her story, Faye felt herself recede from the room—this story had a familiarity to it that at first she could not place.

Vandana's entire family had been home the night the men came. They had broken through the door and there had been no time for hiding. Vandana, her husband, her mother, her two small children, her brother and two sisters—eight of them in all—had been asleep.

Her husband had been trussed up right away. It was, they told her, his job to watch. They had tied him to a chair with rope, Vandana said.

"And then they made a meal of us. I am the only one left—what is left of me."

Faye looked at Martine, but Martine said, yes, that was what she had said.

Faye had been half sitting on the edge of the dresser across from Vandana. She stood up, but felt unaccountably dizzy. Martine reached out her hand to steady Faye, a look of concern on her face. Then Vandana said something which Martine translated as, *"I understand. I wanted to run as well. I still do, but there is nowhere to go, no escape from this—"* and she had gestured over her body with the mutilated hand.

Faye moved to the cot on the other side of Vandana, the side where her eye was missing and her face raw. She sat at the edge of the hard little bed, thinking that anyone who had been through these things deserved more comforting places to rest. She wanted to lay Vandana in a thick feather bed, let her be comforted by the enveloping softness.

The story continued. There had been eleven soldiers—eleven monsters. They had been young and particularly sadistic, Vandana told Faye. They had begun by killing her mother outright.

"They took her head off." Vandana said it succinctly. A tear rolled down her face on the side where the eye was. It had happened quickly, but not without suffering.

"They said nothing. They just pulled everyone up from the floor. They tied up my husband, put something in his mouth so he could not speak—or scream. Then the one soldier—" Here Vandana stopped speaking. Faye leaned forward. Vandana had closed her eye. Her mouth was tight. She was clenching and unclenching a piece of the fabric of her skirt in her remaining hand.

She opened her eye and her lips parted, then she began to speak again.

"This one, this one who looked like someone's lost child, he just took the butt of his rifle and hit her so hard in the side of her head that her eye came out, it fell onto her cheek. And then as she grabbed for her eye, she didn't even have time to scream, really, another one, a taller, bigger one, older—he took a machete and sliced right through her neck. He did it with such force that her head came off—completely off. The children were screaming, my brother and sisters were screaming. My mother's head landed near my husband's feet—his bare feet. Her hair had fallen over one foot. You could see my husband's mouth try to scream, but he couldn't, because of the thing they had stuffed inside."

Martine coughed several times at the end of this part of Vandana's story. Faye continued to sit at the edge of the cot. A reel of pictures flashed through her head. Outside the little cottage, the sounds of the compound could be heard—as if this were any other place, as if this were any normal day, as if the stories Faye had heard, the stories Martine must have translated into English and French several times over, were not the stuff of sheer unmitigated horror, did not call up, as Vandana had said, the childhood images of monsters.

"They silenced my brother first. A third soldier grabbed him from behind and slit his throat like a goat's. The blood just pumped out like I have seen at the well here. After that, well—it became so ugly."

Vandana leaned forward, then stood. She turned toward Faye, but spoke to Martine, asking her if Faye was ready to take the photographs. Faye picked up her camera and Vandana untied the fabric that was knotted at her left shoulder but draped around her body like a long sarong.

The light green fabric was embedded with a faded blue and red print—flowers, maybe. Faye wasn't sure. But as Vandana's garment drifted to the floor, Faye bit hard on the mint in her mouth.

Under her left arm, the arm without the hand, chunks of flesh had been removed. Inside her thighs, more flesh had been cut away, as had part of the soft mound where her pubic hair should have been. Vandana turned around, as if she were showing Faye a new outfit she had gotten, and Faye saw that her buttocks also bore the marks of cutting, and her back had been flayed open and sewn back up, inexpertly, as if in a great hurry.

Vandana moved closer to Faye, who had been taking shot after shot. Faye stopped and looked at her and said something. Faye looked to Martine, who said, "She wants you to look closer. At the wounds."

Faye stayed where she was, as the naked woman moved toward her. Faye thought about all the times naked women had come toward her in just this way and how none of those times had been anything like this. She wondered if she would think of this the next time she was with another woman. She hoped not.

Vandana was right in front of her now and she began to point— *"La, la, la,"* she said as she pointed to her thigh, her arm, her pubic area. It was then that Faye saw. The chunks of flesh hadn't been cut away, they had been torn away—by teeth.

"I told you," she said, *"they made a meal of us. This is only part of what they did. There is so much more."*

16.

Faye wasn't sure why she wanted to go into the darkroom again. She already knew she didn't want to see whatever it was that was hanging from the clothesline. But she opened the door anyway and went inside.

The red light came on when she flipped the switch. She saw that there were photographs, but she didn't look at them. She held her left hand at the side of her eye like she was blocking bright sunlight. She didn't want to see what was there.

Faye had never been in the basement of her grandparents' house before. The door had a big bolt across it and there was usually a chair in front of the door. Once, Faye had asked her grandfather what was down there and he had said, "Mice. Mice and the furnace. And darkness. There's a lot of darkness. It can swallow you up, you know. You don't want to go down there. Trust me. It's not a place for little girls."

As Faye began to move the bolt back, she could feel her heart pounding again. She hoped she wouldn't faint like she had in the kitchen that last time. But she wanted to go down to the basement. She wanted to see what was there. She *needed* to see what was there. Something one of the older girls had said when she was away at camp had made her think about the photographs and her grandfather, and now, the basement.

The bolt didn't make any noise when she pulled it back, which surprised her. She had thought it would be loud and make a grating noise or a clanging sound like the black iron gate in front of the house that she would sometimes swing on until her grandmother would come out and just say her name, "Faye," and she would stop and come inside.

On the wall at the top of the stairs was a big white light switch. It was round and ceramic. When she flipped it, a light went on at the bottom of the stairs. It wasn't a bright light, but it wasn't red, either.

The stairs were made of a rough-looking wood. Faye went down two, four, six steps, and then stopped. She could see into the basement now if she crouched down and looked to the right, where it was open.

There were boxes all along the walls and the tiny windows that Faye recognized from where the garden was. There were some other steps that led up to the door that was on a slant that was in the garden, too. It had a big bolt across it like the one upstairs. She could also see the heater—what her grandfather called the furnace. It was silver and black metal and had big round tubes coming up out of it.

In the center of the room was a table, like the one in the kitchen. There were two chairs, one on either side, and the table was set, like there was going to be a meal. In the center of the table was a jar—a really big one, like the one her grandmother had that was blue and white china and had "flour" written across it in pretty writing. Faye couldn't see what was in the jar from her spot on the stairs.

In the corner there was a long wooden table—Faye knew it was a workbench because her father had had one in her old house when her parents were still alive. At the end of it was something Faye couldn't quite see.

She got up from the step and went down the rest of the stairs and over to the workbench. There was a chain above it that turned on a light. Her heart was beating really fast now and she wasn't sure if she should pull the chain or not.

She put her hand on the chain, closed her eyes, and pulled. When she opened her eyes she saw it.

At the very end, near the wall, in the darkest corner of the basement room was a vise. It was just like the one her father had at his workbench. But her father's had always had pieces of wood in his, wood being pressed together for something her father was making—a shelf or a little table or bookcase. Once, there had been the leg of a chair that kept falling out of the socket in their dining room.

Her grandfather's vise was turned tight, just like her father's had been. But inside the two metal pieces there wasn't wood. There was a lady's head, pressed between the two metal pieces at the sides above the ears.

Faye thought she was going to scream, but she didn't. She felt hot and her heart still pounded and her face got flushed and sweaty. But now she wanted to look at it. She went closer.

The skin wasn't like skin anymore. It was all dried up and wrinkly. The hair wasn't soft-looking, either. It was long and a reddish color and some of it was wound around the part of the vise that gets turned. Where the eyes should have been were just holes that were black around the edges and the mouth was all sewn up, like the mouth on her Raggedy Ann doll that Faye's mother had made for her.

Faye reached out to touch it, but changed her mind. She pulled the chain and the light went out. She walked toward the table, to see what was in the jar, but decided she didn't want to know. She wished she hadn't come down here, but at least she knew what was here now. It was one of the places where the pictures got taken. Because as she was going back toward the stairs, she saw the little bed against the far wall, behind the stairs. The little bed where the women in the photographs would be.

She had seen enough. She went back up the stairs, turned out the light, pushed the heavy fat bolt back across the door, and left the darkroom without looking at the pictures.

She went into the kitchen and washed her face and hands, then she got her pillow and went back upstairs to bed. It was just beginning to get light.

17.

Vandana had put her garment back on. Faye watched as she managed despite the missing hand to deftly twist the fabric around her mutilated body and tie it over her shoulder using her other hand and her teeth. She sat back down in her chair and resumed her story. Faye wasn't sure she could hear more, but Martine was looking at her with the look she had given her before, when she asked her to "make them show you."

The story Vandana recounted was pure nightmare. Her brother's body had been cut open and his organs had been cut out. The men had shoved the hot pieces of flesh into the hands of everyone in the room—her sisters, her children, her. They had been ordered to eat—the liver, the kidneys, the heart. And when they didn't or couldn't, the soldiers had begun to do their worst. Atrocity after atrocity. Vandana's four-year-old daughter had been raped, then killed. Her sisters had both been disemboweled while they were still alive, one soldier raping her youngest sister while her guts pulsed onto the floor. Her six-year-old son's head had been cut off, like her mother's had been. Her husband had choked to death in front of her when he vomited into the rag they had stuffed in his mouth.

Vandana had been the last. They had sliced at her back when she had tried to run and cut off part of her left hand. She'd been raped by all of them, her rectum ripped open, her vagina prolapsed outside her vulva. They had torn bites out of her flesh as they assaulted her—tearing bits of her buttocks and breasts and vulva. They thought she was dead when they left—everyone else in her family was. She wished she had been, but she was still writhing in her own blood, feces, vomit, and urine when her aunt found her the next day. She'd been brought here, barely alive, and saved. Although for what, she could not say.

"They took everything. What you see here is all that is left. They wanted us to eat each other and when we wouldn't, they made their meal of us. I scream every day as it begins to get dark. Every day I relive the nightmare as dusk falls. Now that you know my story, perhaps I will not have to live much longer. I miss my husband and my children. I miss my family. I know they are waiting for me. I only hope they are in the light, and there will be no more darkness." Vandana pointed out the window to the setting sun, an incomparably postcard-beautiful sunset that bled out onto the lush greenery beyond the cottage, and said, *"Soon it will be dark and I will live it all over again, until dawn comes. So you see, I was not saved. Not saved at all."*

She began to weep and as Martine went to her, a woman came in dressed in a white nun's habit, murmuring softly in the same language Vandana and Martine had been speaking.

Martine whispered a thank-you to Vandana for her time and her story, and kissed her on her good cheek, while the nun prepared some kind of medication for her. Martine and Faye left. As they drove back to Bukavu proper, Faye was silent. Martine talked a little, explaining how these were actually common stories. Many of the soldiers now tried to force cannibalism on their victims as a way to defile them and shame them, making them unfit for this world or the next.

Faye listened, but said nothing. She kept hearing Vandana saying, *"They made a meal of us."*

She and Martine rode the rest of the way in silence. Martine said they would spend the night there, in Bukavu, at the hotel.

"We cannot drive around at night, you see," she said, looking away from Faye. "It would not be safe. This is not a place to be a woman. Not at night. Not on the road. The roads have been bad since the war, and it is easy to break down, and then..." Martine's voice trailed off.

"Tomorrow we will go back west. I will arrange for us to get to Kinshasa. I think you have your story, now, don't you?"

That night they had stayed at the best hotel in Bukavu, the Orchids Safari Club. The place was small, but lovely. Faye thought it could have been in any resort town in the Bahamas or the Virgin Islands—someplace where the only horror outside the hotel grounds might be the poverty of the island residents. The view of Lake Kivu was extraordinary, even as it had gone almost dark, and for a moment in this place filled with European and East Asian tourists, one could believe that nothing bad was happening outside its walls.

But peculiar rules reminded Faye that all was not right in Congo. There was no eating outside, despite the gorgeous view from the veranda. There was no room service. The rooms were simple, but luxurious compared to what Faye had just seen. Yet there was an atmosphere that reminded Faye of the Graham Greene novels she had read in college. Why was there even a hotel in a place like this, with so much happening beyond the gates, just down the bad road Martine had spoken of, all rutted and gnarled? Faye recalled the scenes from *Hotel Rwanda,* and remembered how the deadly legacy of colonialism lingered. She wondered, as she watched the other guests in the dining room, most of them speaking either French or some kind of Arabic, if they knew that somewhere not far from where they ate, later that night, people would be forced to eat the still-pulsing organs of their families just before they were murdered in their own homes.

❖

Faye had not expected to have Martine walk toward her bed in the hotel room and stand there, as if waiting to be invited in, but it was not an unwelcome surprise. As she stood, dropping her thin robe onto the bed, Faye saw her perfect, unmarred body, the skin smooth and dark, devoid of scars or burns or teeth marks. That was more of a relief even than the orgasmic sex itself. Faye wanted to look at Martine, feel every bit of her body, the wholeness of her. Faye hadn't had sex with anyone since the night of the book launch and the release felt good, surprisingly intense, given the day they had shared. Neither of them cried, though. Faye thought perhaps the sex took the place of tears.

Later, as they lay in Faye's bed, Martine told her that she had been gang-raped three years earlier, by four men who had stopped her at a roadblock when she was driving from one care center to another. "They didn't cut me, they didn't burn me. They let me live. I didn't get pregnant. But I could never imagine being with a man ever again after that. Because, you see, I had seen these men before—many times. They ran this same road block for nearly a year before they raped me. How could they see me all those times, how could they smile at me and let me pass and then one day pull me from my car and drag me into the bush until I was bloody and act as if it was simply expected? How could I be sure that another man might not turn into a monster before my eyes? How could I risk having a child with a monster?"

Faye had held her, stroking her arms and making the small susurrations that are not actual speech, but which sound like comfort. Faye had thought about telling Martine a story, but then she remembered Shihong in Chinatown, and said only, "It's good that you told me. Someone else told me that the secrets become you. And they do. That's not always a good thing."

❖

In the morning they had dutifully pretended nothing had happened between them beyond a comforting exchange. After having a meal in the dining room and then walking out onto the veranda and looking at the lake, they had gone on to the airport and flown back to Kinshasa.

But that night, the night she had spent with Martine, Faye had had a series of progressively more terrifying dreams. The dreams had stayed with her after she awoke. Even when they had reached Kinshasa, the images still lingered. Faye wanted to go back to New York. She didn't think she could go on to Afghanistan now. She called her editor. She'd have to do the second part, Afghanistan, later. This was a lot to process and she wasn't feeling all that well, she told him—water, developing world, she knew he understood. She tried to keep the shakiness out of her voice. She wanted to get out of this place. The contradiction of the physical beauty and what she knew lay beneath was too extreme, even for her, the photographer who never cringed, never flinched, never stopped recording the darkest of images.

Faye booked her flight, then she called Martine from her room at the hotel. She had asked for a room on the top floor—for some reason she felt safest there, as if soldiers would work their way up the flights if they invaded in the night, and it would be easiest to attack on the first or second floor, rather than the tenth. She asked Martine to spend the night with her before she left.

"You understand—I don't feel safe. It's not that I expect you to protect me, and we're in Kinshasa now, anyway, and this is a big city, as big as New York, and I know I'm being paranoid. But I just don't want to be alone."

Martine had talked to her on the phone, trying to reassure her. Telling her the kind of historical facts one tells a tourist—that Kinshasa was the second-largest city in Africa. That it was the largest French-speaking city in the world—that legacy of colonialism, again. That Faye should try to absorb the lush beauty and not be fearful because Kinshasa was civilized, truly. It's not like they were in the bush. And anyway, tourists came all the time to see the gorillas. She was safe at the hotel. She really was.

But Faye knew Martine was reciting from childhood memory and that knee-jerk thing that Faye herself always felt when people talked about the dangers of New York. But this was not New York and she had just spent days looking at the torn-apart bodies of several dozen women. Faye was beginning to understand why Vandana began to scream as night fell.

❖

Faye fell into a deep sleep after the sex with Martine. This time it was Martine who held her and Faye felt that sense of safety she had hoped Martine would give her.

Then the dreams came.

18.

After that first summer, Faye had been grateful when school started and she could see Rosario again. She liked being out of her grandparents' house. She liked being in the crisp blue blouse and navy blue skirt of her uniform. She liked the music at the school and she liked running her fingers through the cuts in the neck of St. Cecelia as they walked down the steps to the assembly every morning after Mass. If she couldn't be in her real home with her parents, she could be here. In the afternoons she would go to the grotto and pray to the Virgin Mary to make her parents come back, even though she knew God didn't give people back once he took them.

Faye started to bring little gifts to Mary—a flower, a pretty leaf, a drawing. She knew that in the Bible there were animal sacrifices, but she didn't want to kill anything. She wondered if the lady's head was still in the basement and if that would count, but she didn't want to go down there again, she didn't want to touch it, and somehow she knew it wasn't the right thing to do—that God might actually punish her for that. If not for stealing, then for whatever had happened to the lady, because Faye never told anyone and she knew, she really did know, that she should have told someone.

If she'd told anyone, it would have been Sister Anne Marie. Sister had been very kind to her since she had come to St. Cecelia's and Faye felt like she could tell her things.

It was October when Faye was helping Sister Anne Marie at lunchtime by clapping erasers outside on the fire escape and sweeping the leaves that gathered around the door to the little music cottage where they had choir every other afternoon.

Faye could tell Sister Anne Marie was trying to get her to talk about her parents, but Faye didn't want to. She had already talked to Rosario at camp that summer about her parents and Rosario had been really strange to her afterward. So Faye hadn't said anything else and Rosario had stopped being weird and Faye began to understand what her grandmother meant when she said, "We don't share family things outside the house, Faye. It's not proper.

You understand what proper means, don't you?" And Faye hadn't. What she did know was that secrets were supposed to be kept, not shared. That's what her grandmother meant.

But Sister Anne Marie wanted her to share secrets with her and Faye thought it would be different, because Sister was a nun and Rosario was just another kid, like she was. Rosario had her own family secrets and always felt bad after she told them to Faye. But Faye was better at listening than Rosario was, so she always knew to look solemn and nod her head and not say anything but maybe just put her hand on Rosario's shoulder like her grandmother did with her. That always seemed to work. So Rosario kept sharing her secrets and Faye just kept listening.

Faye liked autumn. She liked the leaves and the crisp air and the way everything smelled. She liked that it was mostly gray outside and windy, and that she had to wear a jacket and that her hands were always cold. She liked Halloween and Thanksgiving—or she used to.

She stood by the door with the broom in her hands and she was surprised to feel the tears running down her face. Sister Anne Marie came and took the broom away. She shut the door and led Faye to a small bank of chairs behind the music stands and they sat down. Sister asked Faye what was wrong, but Faye didn't say anything. Then she said, "I would have brought the things from the basement to the Virgin if I thought they would bring my parents back, but I don't think they will. I don't want to kill any animals, but that's what they do in the Bible. I'll kill something if I have to, to bring my parents back, but I really don't want to. I brought other things, but I think I'm supposed to kill something."

Sister Anne Marie had looked away for a moment and her hand had flown up to her face in the same way as the women in the photographs Faye's grandfather had taken. She turned back to Faye and said, her voice a little funny, "Why do you think you have to kill someone, Faye?"

"In the Bible there's always animal sacrifice. A lamb or a goat. Or a calf. Or some doves. I don't even know where you get those things in Brooklyn. I don't think it's the same if you get them from the Italian Market where they are already dead and in the butcher shop. But I would get one if I knew how. I would do what Abraham did if it would save my parents, the way it saved Isaac."

Sister Anne Marie had looked different then—the scared look on her face had changed to a worried look. She had talked to Faye about her parents and said that they couldn't come back, but that Faye would see them later, in Heaven.

Faye had told her that she wished she had died with them, that she wished she could live at St. Cecelia's with the girls in the dorm. That she had liked being at camp, that she didn't want to be at her grandparents' house anymore. Then she told Sister about the photographs and the table and the things on the plates and the head. She knew this was what her grandmother had meant about not telling secrets, that it wasn't proper. But Faye knew that even if the table and the plates and the things on the bed weren't real, the head was real. And now that Sister knew, maybe she would let Faye come and live at St. Cecelia's all the time with the other girls who were orphans, like she was.

Faye hadn't planned any of this. She hadn't planned to tell Sister Anne Marie about any of the things she told her. And now she couldn't take it back. All she could do was say again, "I think I should live here. I think it's what my parents would want. I think that's why I am supposed to go and pray to Mary every day. Because then she will intercede like the priest says, and if my parents can't come back, then I can come here, instead."

❖

It was almost Halloween when Faye had first seen Sister Anne Marie slapping her hands on the slate outside the grotto until they were bloody. It was almost Thanksgiving before she told Faye that she was going to talk to Faye's grandfather and "get to the bottom of this."

That day, that first fall day when Faye had been crying, Sister had asked her again and again about the photographs and everything else. She had asked Faye about the doctor and the medication and when Faye had fainted and been in bed and all of that. She had asked Faye if she understood what she was saying and Faye had told her yes to everything and said that she didn't go into the darkroom anymore now that she knew what the photographs were, because they frightened her and sometimes they made her sick and that she didn't eat meat anymore because of what she saw on the plates and she thought that was what was making her sick—the pieces from the ladies in the photographs that her grandfather took that were on the plates and then maybe in the refrigerator and then on the plates. Their plates, the plates they ate from every day.

Sister Anne Marie had left the room then. She had told Faye to stay there and she'd be right back, but Faye had heard her in the lavatory outside the music room, throwing up and making gurgling noises and running water in the sink and when she came back her face was red and she looked like she had been crying.

"We'll find a way to fix this," was all she had said then, and she had put her arms around Faye and held her really tight. Then she had sent her back to class.

19.

In the dreams Faye had on her last night in Congo, she was running through the lush rainforest of Kivu, trying to save Martine. Faye had been in the Land Rover with Martine, but then they had hit something—a great gaping hole in the road—and Martine was no longer in the car with her. It was late in the afternoon, nearly evening, just as it had been when they had left the care center after talking to Vandana, and the shadows had begun to fall as the sun set. Faye had gotten out of the Land Rover and had gone searching for Martine. She had tried to call her name, but no sound would come out of her. So Faye ran, looking near where the car was stuck in the big hole in the road, then further and further into the rainforest.

In the dream, Faye was out of breath from running, and she could hear her own breath and her heart pounding in her ears as she ran. She was frightened, as frightened as she'd ever been, because there was no one near where she was and she couldn't find Martine and she knew she had to find her, had to find her, something had happened to Martine, *where was she?*

Faye had fallen, then, as she whirled around in a circle trying to see everything she could before it got dark, trying not to lose sight of the road so she didn't get lost among the trees and plants. She could hear the insects and the birds and some small sounds of shrews or weasels or whatever ran along the ground here in this place she knew almost nothing about.

She had fallen, tripped over some plant or root or something and when she fell, everything around her was wet. But it was always wet in the rainforest, that was why it was called rainforest, she told herself, as she tried to get up out of the wetness. It was then that she realized the wetness was blood and the ooze of entrails and damp, gory pieces of bodies—hands, feet, ears, a head, then another head, all crawling with maggots and worms and other slithery things she couldn't identify, didn't want to identify.

She had tried to scream, had put her blood-drenched hand up to her mouth and seen that maggots were dripping from her hand onto her legs. She had felt the pressure in her lungs of screaming, but no sound would come out. She could feel her lips pulled tight across her teeth, her mouth wide, as wide as it had ever been, but no sound, no sound at all came from her, none at all.

❖

It was after that when Faye began to get sick. Very sick. So sick that it took her over a week once she was back in New York to understand how sick she was. She was sick with images that would not go away, sick with remembering. She lay in her own bed, in her own apartment, paralyzed with fear, paralyzed with the photographs in her head that just kept flipping by like when she was at school, back at St. Cecelia's, and the nuns would run the little round carousel slide projector that had been there forever and the girls in her class had all giggled because it seemed so old-fashioned. The images in Faye's head ran like that—over and over, clicking past, and then starting again. She was literally reeling from the intensity and how many pictures there were in her own personal memory card—hundreds, hundreds, how had she taken all these photographs, how had she seen all those things?

It wasn't just Bukavu she was remembering.

It was Chinatown, it was Fresno, it was Esperanza lying under the train, it was the accident with the decapitated man, it was the fire in the theater at Christmas and all the incinerated children, it was St. Cecelia's. It was her grandparents' house. She was remembering it all now. And then, one night, she was awakened by her own screaming.

20.

Sister Anne Marie had made up the little bed for Faye at the end of the row in the junior dorm at St. Cecelia's. There was a small table next to the bed that had two little drawers in it. On the table was a little wooden crucifix, but it was just the cross, there was no Jesus on it.

The bed was small. A single bed with a flat wooden headboard. It was low to the floor and Faye thought there wasn't even room for there to be someone her size under it, let alone a monster.

There were fourteen beds in the room, which was on the top floor—the fourth floor—of the dormitory. All the girls in the junior dormitory were twelve years old and younger. In the senior dormitory, the girls were teenagers. There were more of them—thirty in all. The first floor had a big living room kind of room with chairs and sofas and a TV and there was a kitchen and a dining room.

When Sister Anne Marie made the little bed for Faye, she told her that she would be staying there from now on. She said that she had spoken to Mother Superior and that Faye shouldn't worry. She was going to see Faye's grandfather "This very day," and from then on, Faye would be what she called "a ward of the State."

She patted the end of the bed when she had finished with the sheets and the dark blue blanket and Faye sat down and Sister sat next to her. "We will pray now," she told Faye. "We will pray for your parents, who are in Heaven, and for your grandmother, for Jesus's forgiveness, and we will pray for the salvation of your grandfather's soul. And we will pray for...those women in the photographs."

Faye wasn't sure what Sister meant about her grandparents, but she said the three Hail Marys and the two Our Fathers with Sister, out loud.

Sister pulled a little box out from under the bed—it was cardboard, but flat. She put it on the end of the bed and opened it and inside were pajamas and underwear and a pair of slippers and a thin robe.

"These are for you. They are yours now. You can wear them tonight when you go to bed. In the drawer here"—and she had opened the top drawer in the little table—"there is a toothbrush and everything else you need. I'll have Theresa show you everything tonight. You know her, she's in the fifth grade. She sleeps in the bed next to yours."

Sister Anne Marie put the underwear in the second drawer, along with the robe, which she folded very flat. She put the pajamas underneath the pillow and put the slippers on the floor under the bed, by the table. She looked at Faye, still sitting on the bed, and then she came over and put her arms around Faye.

"St. Cecelia will watch over you, Faye. She will. She was brave, like you."

Then she had taken Faye's hand and they had gone downstairs. Faye had sat in a window seat with her notebook and watched as Sister Anne Marie walked down the walkway to the end of the driveway and turned down the street, toward the bus stop that went to the subway that went to Faye's grandparents' house.

Faye never saw her again.

21.

More than a week had passed since Faye had returned to New York and she had barely left her apartment. She had stayed away from the newspaper, she had stayed away from friends, she had stayed out of her own studio. Faye had told her editor she was ill, really ill, some kind of parasite, she never should have eaten that food, and that she was being treated, but that she was too weak to come in.

Faye said she'd e-mail him photos to look at in a few days, but he told her to rest, they had time before the story ran, two weeks, maybe more, wiggle room, don't worry. Faye told him she had a rough draft of the copy, but thought she might need help from rewrite. "The pictures don't tell the whole story," she'd said as she thought of the chunks of flesh torn out of Vandana's body and what Vandana had told her. "For the first time, the pictures really don't tell the whole story."

❖

On the eighth night after she was back, Faye woke up drenched in sweat and screaming. She picked up her iPhone, Googled a number, and called the suicide hotline.

"I want to be dead," she said to the woman who answered the phone. Her voice was flat, monotonal. It held none of the hysteria she'd awoken with. She repeated, "I want to be dead. I *need* to be dead." And then she had hung up before the woman could say anything at all.

22.

Before she had left for the DRC, Faye had been planning her exhibit. Every night she had spent a few hours in her studio, ambient music playing as she sorted through boxes of notebooks, memory cards, negatives, and actual photographs. She had gone to the cabinet time after time, taking out this jar or that. She had been writing the copy to go with the exhibit, knew exactly what she wanted, had already settled on the gallery, signed the contract, knew that very little was missing. When she returned from this assignment, she'd have everything she needed.

It was time to reveal the upper shelves, time to tip the jars open and let the contents spill at the feet of the those who came to be titillated by mayhem, time to show what happened when St. Cecelia didn't die, yet the wounds didn't close, either. Time for the screaming to begin.

23.

Theresa had shown Faye around the dormitory that first night. Faye had thought it would be scary, but it wasn't. The girls in the junior dorm all laughed a lot and threw things at each other and then Sister Mary Margaret had come in and told them to "simmer down" and "get ready for bed," but she was kind of laughing with them and then said, "I mean it, now," and tried to look stern, but it didn't work, but the girls started to get ready for bed anyway, because they didn't want Sister Mary Margaret to get mad.

Faye had fallen asleep right away, before she even finished all her prayers, and she hadn't woken up until Sister Mary Margaret came back for them in the morning.

The police had come to St. Cecelia's just after dinner two days after Sister Anne Marie had left to go to Faye's grandparents' house. Sister Anne Marie had never come back to St. Cecelia's, and Mother Superior had reported her missing.

The police had sent a detective over to the dormitory

and Sister Mary Margaret had come to get Faye because the detective wanted to talk to her, to ask her what she had told Sister Anne Marie.

They had all gone into a little room off the living room in the dormitory, the room that Sister Mary Margaret called the office. There was a desk and three chairs and a lamp and a big, plain crucifix on the wall over the desk. Mother Superior sat down behind the desk and Sister Mary Margaret sat in one of the chairs and had Faye sit next to her. The detective, who said, "Call me Tom, Faye, my name is Tom," asked her about different things—her parents, if she was sad, if she was angry.

Faye said she prayed a lot for her parents to come back, but that she knew that couldn't happen. She said she wasn't sad as much, now that she was at St. Cecelia's. Then she said she knew she should be sad about not being at her grandparents' house anymore, but that she really didn't like it there, that at first it was okay, because of the darkroom and the people who came to get their pictures taken, and painting with her grandfather in the kitchen. But then there had been the ladies in the photographs and the things on the plates and the head in the basement and she didn't want to eat meat anymore and it just got harder and harder to be there and easier and easier to be here, at St. Cecelia's, and that since she was really an orphan anyway, she should be here, it's what her parents would have wanted, she was sure of that, really sure, because there was never anything but wood in the vise at her parents' house and there was that lady's head with the sewn-up lips and no eyes in the vise at her grandparents' house and Faye just knew, she really just knew, that wasn't at all right.

Detective Tom had been writing things down on a little notepad. Sister Mary Margaret had been holding Faye's hand while she talked, but after Faye started to talk about the photographs, she had squeezed Faye's hand really hard and then let it go. Detective Tom was leaning against Mother Superior's desk and Faye couldn't really see Mother's face. But Detective Tom had stopped writing after a while and had just looked right at Faye while she talked.

"I never looked at the jar on the table," Faye said, at the end. "I just really didn't want to see any more. Sister

Anne Marie said she would get to the bottom of things. She said it would all work out."

Detective Tom had turned and looked at Mother Superior then and tilted his head toward Faye as he said, "We need to talk now, without the child."

24.

After Faye had called the suicide hotline, she had gotten out of bed, gotten dressed, pulled on her coat, and left the apartment. It was nearly two in the morning, but it was New York on a Thursday and even though it was biting cold, there was always somewhere to go, places where there would be people. Faye needed people. Faye needed noise and music and even though she hated it, maybe even cigarette smoke. Faye thought if she just had a drink in a bar with a lot of loud music and people shouting and laughing and dancing and smoking and drinking, she wouldn't kill herself.

At least not tonight.

She wouldn't go to the river and drown herself, which was how she had decided to die. She already knew from a myriad of stories she'd covered what *wouldn't* work—she couldn't throw herself in front of a car or a subway. She couldn't take pills or hang herself. She couldn't jump from her apartment window. She didn't want to take anyone else with her, anyway, not now, not tonight. She had enough blood on her hands. Faye just wanted a drink and some inane conversation and someone to give her a reason not to die, even if it was just temporary. She needed to stop seeing the slide show that wouldn't stop running in her head. She needed someone else's story or pictures to run for a while. She was prepared to be the best listener ever. If only for this one night.

❖

When Faye woke up, it was nearly dark again. She looked at the clock—quarter to five. How had she slept so long—ten, twelve hours? She didn't remember coming home, but she also didn't remember dreaming, so she didn't care if she'd gotten plastered or even with whom. She hadn't slept without nightmares since that night in Bukavu nearly two weeks ago with Martine. She lay in her bed, trying to think.

She vaguely remembered being in one of the Irish bars near Penn Station. She'd liked those bars when she had first been working at the paper. A lot of retired cops hung out there, along with a few errant IRA types, and some low-level criminals and mobsters. It was as good a place as any to get a drink, or get drunk, and she got to listen, because she was always looking for a new story then, or even an old story that could be brought to life in a new form—replete with photographs.

Faye knew she'd been in a cab, though going to or from the bar or even what bar, she couldn't recall. Faye sat up slowly—she felt slightly dizzy, as if she'd had way too much to drink. She had an awful taste in her mouth and what felt like pieces of food. Ugh—had she gone to sleep with food in her mouth? Or had she vomited from drinking? Her lips felt dry and cracked. She walked—staggered was more like it—to the bathroom, turned on the light, and looked in the mirror.

Her mouth was crusted with blood and there was blood on her left cheek and blood on her neck and ear. She spat into the sink and bits of what looked like meat splattered the porcelain. Faye hadn't eaten meat since she was seven and living at her grandparents house. She felt like she was going to vomit. Faye turned on the faucet and as she did, she saw she had blood on both hands. Her nails had blood under them and as her heart began to pound, she saw she had blood on her shirt and blood on her thighs. She turned off the faucet and got into the shower, still in her shirt and underwear. But as she reached for the faucet there, she saw blood on her feet, blood pooled on the floor of the tub, blood leaking from somewhere behind her.

Faye felt hot and dizzy and she could feel the air pressing up out of her lungs, but she didn't scream, couldn't scream. She turned and pulled back the shower curtain.

There, behind the shower curtain, up against the edge of the tub, lay the crumpled body of Sister Anne Marie. Her throat was slit and gaping, the blood thick and gelatinous around the wound. Her habit was cut apart in different places—one of her breasts had been cut clean off. Her side was open, just like the pictures of Jesus, and her liver had been cut out. Her habit was pushed up to her waist and blood was congealed on her thighs and between them. Her face had not been cut, but her eyes were open wide and had the blue fish-eye film of death over them. Her mouth was open and askew and there was blood on her teeth and lips, but Faye did not see a wound. As she leaned closer, though, she saw that Sister Anne Marie's tongue had been cut out. Inside her mouth was filled with clotted, pudding-like gore.

Faye stood there, her feet covered in the pooling blood, staring at Sister Anne Marie's body, at what had been done to her. She reached over to pull down her habit, to cover her up, automatically crossing herself as she did so, but as she moved forward, making the sign of the cross, she slipped in the blood and fell into Sister Anne Marie, Faye's face up against hers, her lips almost on the dead nun's.

❖

It was Faye's own screaming that finally woke her.

25.

Sister Mary Margaret had taken Faye out of the office in the dormitory and led her back to the living room. Theresa had gotten up and come over and asked if she was okay and Faye had just nodded, but hadn't said anything. Faye knew something was wrong, she knew that something had happened to Sister Anne Marie and she was afraid—afraid it was her fault and that she would never see Sister Anne Marie again.

After a while, Detective Tom had come out of the room with Mother Superior and they had walked to the front door together and walked out onto the enclosed porch. They were talking very low and both of them looked serious. Faye couldn't hear anything they said. From where she was sitting, Faye could see Mother Superior put her head down and put her hands on her face and shake her head. Detective Tom put his hand on her shoulder and said something. Then he left. Mother came back in, motioned to Sister Mary Margaret, and they went into the office together and shut the door.

❖

Sister Anne Marie never came back to St. Cecelia's. There was an assembly and Mother Superior spoke to everyone and said there had been an accident and Sister Anne Marie was not coming back to St. Cecelia's. Mother told them that they might hear things, other things, but that was what had happened. There had been an accident.

She said it was very sad and it was all right for them to feel sad and they could cry if they wanted to, but they should remember that Jesus was taking care of Sister Anne Marie now and that she was safe and loved and in Heaven.

There was a big rustling in the room and murmurs and Faye could hear the sounds of some of the girls starting to cry and there were whispers among the older girls.

Mother looked very pale and tired as she stood on the little stage where Sister Anne Marie had put on the recitals and musical events. She knew that people weren't supposed to lie, but she knew Mother Superior was lying. She knew that there hadn't been an accident. She knew that Sister Anne Marie had gone to her grandparents' house to make sure that Faye never had to go back there and now she was gone. Faye thought about Sister Anne Marie praying with her in the dormitory, sitting on her bed with her and hugging her and she wished she had never told her about her grandfather and the photographs and the lady's head. Faye didn't want to cry, but she did anyway. She wanted to see Sister Anne Marie. She didn't want to think about what had happened to her. She couldn't think about what had happened to her.

Mother Superior told them they should all pray for Sister Anne Marie. Right now, they were going to pray for Sister Anne Marie, "Hail Mary, full of grace, the Lord is with thee, blessed art thou among women..."

26.

Faye hadn't quit the newspaper and now she knew she wouldn't. She'd intended to when she got back from the DRC and Afghanistan, but she'd never gone on to Afghanistan as planned—it had been too much. That story was still waiting for her and she still wanted it. She'd learned that ordinary mayhem was her *metier* and she knew she had to follow it, no matter what.

It had taken nearly all the pre-production time they'd had for Faye and her editor to lay out the Congo story. He had looked at the photos— she'd culled just under a hundred for him to look at—and he had looked at them for about fifteen minutes and then had abruptly gotten up and left the room.

When he came back, he hadn't looked directly at Faye, but had gone back to the light table and said, "Powerful stuff, Faye. More powerful than I expected. I have to think about what we're going to use here. Give me some time—go do more work on the copy. It needs to be pristine for this one. I don't want rewrite involved. This is all you here. All you. I want to showcase this. People remember the other stories—that girl in the subway and the kids being poisoned. They want to hear from you. And you were there—rewrite wasn't there. So just tell it. Lay it out for us. The part that's not here, whatever that is. You know, I don't."

Faye had gone home to write, but had ended up crawling into bed and trying not to dream.

❖

The day after she'd had the nightmare about Sister Anne Marie, Faye had finalized the date with the Tribeca gallery owner she'd signed the contract with for her show and had begun to put it together. Now she had a clear picture of the show in her head. She was ready. She went down to the gallery and met with Nick Allingham, the owner, and his assistant, a young woman with fluffy, white-blond hair and dramatic tattoos who went by the unlikely name of Persia, just Persia.

Nick was clear: He wanted a gag order on the show until the opening. Only he and Persia were to see the photos and what Faye was calling "mixed media" pieces. There was also a video installation piece that Persia had put together of Faye's previous work. It was going to be fantastic. For the first time since she'd returned from the DRC, Faye felt okay. More than okay, actually. Maybe the nightmares were over for good. Maybe that was what the work was for—to keep the nightmares at bay.

Nick and Faye both knew the show was going to generate the kind of attention that Andres Serrano's *Piss Christ* and AIDS artist David Wojnarowicz had garnered. Nick was calling Faye "the new Mapplethorpe" in press releases and on the gallery's website, which made Faye cringe. She didn't want to be derivative of anyone else. Faye reminded Nick that Mapplethorpe never developed his own photographs and that they were all staged, whereas hers were real— *cinema verité* of the most visceral sort. She knew she sounded petulant when she said it—a diva artist of a type she'd never aspired to be. But it was out there.

Nick shrugged. But Persia, who despite her studied vacant look was clearly brilliant, the video installation was spectacular, said that they—Faye, Nick, the gallery—needed to be prepared for backlash. And also to expect it.

"Sure, this mayor isn't going to go all Giuliani on everyone and try and shut the place down, but this is intense. People always think they really want to know," Persia said, her unnaturally green eyes sparkling with something Faye thought was pure rage. "Oh yeah—they all think they want to see what's hiding underneath the rocks or what's hidden behind those blue drapes at the scene of an accident or behind the yellow police tape at a crime. They think it will broaden them and expand them and put them more in touch with humanity, but they really don't want to know because they really can't, you know, *process* it. They're really just voyeurs and can't admit to it. They just want to get off on the sickness of what's in the darkest recesses of everyone's twisted psyche. I mean think about how many people buy the art work and memorabilia of serial killers. *Serial killers*. Imagine."

Faye had begun looking at something in one of her portfolios while Persia was talking, but when she said *serial killers,* Faye had snapped to attention and looked directly at her. But Persia was just spewing—she hated the insincerity of the majority of what she called New York's "art predators" and just kept ranting.

The rest of what she said, Faye had always known. She'd known it since the very first time she'd actually looked at the photographs of the women hanging on the clothesline in her grandfather's darkroom. She'd known it when she had been unflinching on the subway tracks with Esperanza. She'd started to feel it, really feel it, when Shihong had shown her everything in the little shop in Chinatown. That still made her shudder. But Faye had never felt it as deeply as she had when she had been in the DRC. That feeling, which she'd had every day and night since, was the feeling that Persia was talking about. Once you knew for sure what other people were capable of, once you knew the horror was more than nightmare, once you knew what *true* horror was and that there was nothing supernatural about it—no vampires, no werewolves, no things that went bump in the night—but that it was as real as it gets, that it was what Vandana meant when she said "monsters," then you could never look away again.

Ever.

All three of them—Faye, Nick, Persia—wanted to be prepared for whatever the response was, but they also wanted the initial shock to be dramatic. Persia said she wanted people to feel like they'd been hit hard when they first came into the gallery. Nick knew the kind of reviews Faye's other work had received and he was hoping for an even more dramatic response to this show. He was hoping for a sellout opening where all Faye's work was sold and people put in orders for more.

Faye was exhibiting the most brutal of the DRC photos—ones that the paper said they simply couldn't run, even in the magazine. And then there was everything she had gotten from Shihong when she'd been in Chinatown, and the contents of her apothecary cabinet at home. There were the photographs she had taken years before, of the jars at St. Cecelia's and of St. Cecelia herself, lying on her alabaster slab, with her neck sliced open. Those were the photographs she had taken with her first camera and developed herself, they were her own private retrospective, she realized now.

But there were also the other photographs, the ones that no one had ever seen, that even Nick hadn't seen yet and which would be in the show as a surprise. A stunning surprise, Faye thought.

❖

The nightmares had stopped after that last dream about Sister Anne Marie, the one that had been so intense, so real Faye had actually tasted blood in her mouth, but then realized she had bitten the inside of her cheek from fear in her sleep. When she woke up there was fresh blood on her pillow.

Faye had called Martine a few days later. They had talked for a while and Faye had felt better. She realized that getting back to work was the best thing. She was already planning her trip to Afghanistan. A soldier had just gone nuts over there and killed over a dozen civilians, some of them children. He was decorated, but on his fifth tour of duty. He'd already had a traumatic brain injury in an IED attack. The day before he went out at night and shot up a series of homes in the village near the base, he'd watched a friend get blown up in front of him. Body parts had landed in his lap. If he'd been a foot closer, it would have been *his* body parts strewn across the roadway.

Faye had called a friend, a reporter, over in Kabul and asked what else there was to know. He'd told her that there had been some "unpleasant stuff" at the base where the soldier had been—another soldier had gone home on leave and lit his wife on fire and killed himself. A few other suicides, really grisly ones. Another couple murders. "It's a bad situation—you just can't keep sending these guys out to kill every day for years and years and think they're going to stay anything like normal, you know? They become killing machines. Put them back in their own society and they can't cope. They *need* to kill. If you want stories, I've got stories. Let me know when you're coming."

And Faye, who had been so sure before she'd gone to the DRC that she was leaving the paper, leaving the images behind, had felt the lure again. This time she would be prepared, though. She knew that. This time she'd be safe from the carousel of images. The gallery show would take care of all that—it would be cathartic, an exorcism. It would lay it all out. The ordinary mayhem she'd lived with since the night her parents burned alive in their car in the snow on New Year's Eve. Faye thought she was okay now. Faye thought she was safe.

27.

Faye had stayed on at St. Cecelia's until she graduated. A decade of moving between the floors of the dormitory. A decade of leaving talismans for the Virgin Mary in the grotto. A decade of being friends with Rosario and Carmen, Alicia and the three Theresas. A decade of prayers. A decade of photographs. A decade of running her fingers through the slices on St. Cecelia's neck every morning on her way to Mass. A decade of knowing she was Mother Superior's special project, because Mother Superior knew what no one else had known.

Mother Superior and Detective Tom had told her that Sister Anne Marie had had an accident when she had gone to Faye's grandparents' house. They had told her there had been a fall down a flight of stairs, a broken neck, a twisted body on the basement floor. Things like this happen sometimes, Mother Superior had told her in the little office, while Detective Tom had looked off to the side, not meeting Faye's eyes. But Mother Superior had looked like she had been crying. Mother Superior, who was in charge of everything, had looked scared.

That night Faye had prayed until she fell asleep. Prayed for Sister Anne Marie, who had been her friend, and who had protected her. Prayed for Mother Superior, who had told Faye lie after lie because she knew the truth was too awful to bear. Prayed for Detective Tom, because he had found

Sister Anne Marie, and Faye knew what that meant. Prayed for her grandparents, because she was afraid they would go to hell and never see Jesus. Prayed for herself, because as she had sat in the little office, she had felt like Detective Tom and Mother Superior were both afraid of her, and if they were too afraid, Mother Superior might not let her stay at St. Cecelia's. Mother Superior might call Detective Tom, and he might put her in jail. Because they knew she knew. They knew Faye knew about everything. Maybe, Faye thought, maybe they thought that she was part of it.

And maybe, maybe, maybe, she was. Which was why she had to pray.

28.

A couple of nights before the opening, Faye was lying in bed, trying to sleep, trying not to think, trying not to worry that it wouldn't be a success. She had begun taking sleeping pills ten days after she'd gotten back from the DRC. The morning after the night when she'd wanted to kill herself, when she couldn't remember what had happened and she'd awakened from the terrible dream about Sister Anne Marie, she'd made an appointment with her doctor, gotten some Ambien and hoped that it would work. And it had—she'd slept through night after night with barely a dream. Until that last night.

Faye wasn't sure at first if she was awake or asleep as she sat on the floor of her studio, the sharp halogen beam of the little gooseneck lamp beside her the only light in the room. On the floor around her were bits and pieces of things she was taking to the gallery—the last-minute touches she'd been considering and reconsidering since the last exhibit and the book about Esperanza. These were things she'd been putting together since she'd first decided on what she wanted the exhibit to be. These were, she thought, the subtly horrifying nuances that would complement the photographs.

Faye turned her head—she thought she heard something in the other room—and she saw the apothecary cabinet was open and the contents were in different places around the room. Not turned over, but out from their shelves. Faye didn't remember taking them out, but she knew you could do things on Ambien that you didn't remember. Her doctor had even warned her about that before she had written Faye the prescription. Faye's friend Dorcas had taken Ambien and ended up driving to Connecticut to an ex-girlfriend's house in her underwear and almost getting arrested.

Open in front of Faye was her oldest notebook—the one she had kept that first year at St. Cecelia's. On the verso page was a drawing—a really good drawing, actually—of a dead squirrel. Faye stared at the details: the throat had been torn apart, probably by one of the feral cats that roamed the school grounds and the woods just beyond. The squirrel's eyes were open and in the drawing, the mouth was open, too, and the teeth were bared in what Faye now knew was the death scream. It was a child's drawing, but it had a surprising verisimilitude to it. So much so that Faye thought back to Detective Tom McManus and wondered what he would have thought had he seen it. Would he have reconsidered letting her stay at St. Cecelia's?

On the opposite page there were several rough dark smears and at the bottom of the page, in Faye's careful, looping, second-grade cursive was the notation: *Sister Anne Marie's blood from in front of the Virgin Mary at school.* Faye could still remember the day she had seen Sister Anne Marie at the grotto slapping her hands on the slate until they bled. She could still feel the texture of the blood mixed with dirt and leaves when she had touched it on the cold, slate path.

Faye closed the notebook and stood up. She walked to the window and opened the blackout drapes. She looked down onto the street six floors below. Would she die if she leapt from the window? What if she went out backward? Was she more likely to smash her head irreparably if she went that way? Would she be more assured of "dying instantly," as they said? She thought about the people jumping from the towers on 9/11, their bodies ablaze. She thought about the immigrant girls jumping to their deaths from the Triangle Shirtwaist Factory, their hair and skirts on fire. She thought about those little parchment Amaretto papers that flew up at the end when you lit them in a restaurant after dinner. Maybe she should set herself on fire first. Maybe someone would take a photograph of her as she sparked through the air to the ground below. Maybe she would set the timer on one of her own cameras first, before she did it, so it would be recorded in real time.

Faye opened the window. A rush of cold air hit her. The air smelled like snow, but there had been very little snow that winter. She sat on the edge of the sill, listened to the sounds of Manhattan below her, and thought about just leaning back, how easy it would be. She thought it might be like falling backward into a pool. She thought it would be quick. She thought she should just close her eyes and do it. But when she closed her eyes and started to lean back into the air, into the cold embrace of the winter night, she felt a hand, strong, on her arm, pulling her back. She opened her eyes, startled. There was Shihong.

"I don't think you want to do that," Shihong said in her low, whispery, slightly accented English as she pulled Faye back into the room. "Not when I've brought you these for your exhibit." Faye half-stumbled back into her studio and looked toward where Shihong was pointing.

On the long table across from the window were four jars—four of the same jars Shihong had shown her in that black-market shop in Chinatown. And now when she saw them, just as she had then, Faye couldn't keep from screaming.

This time she did not wake up. She wasn't dreaming.

29.

A few months before the end of her senior year, Mother Superior called Faye into her office. Faye had watched different classmates brought in for what other girls had always called the "separation" talk. The girls who were orphans could stay at St. Cecelia's throughout the summer after their graduation, but they had to spend that summer looking for work and a place to live if they weren't going to college in the fall. St. Cecelia's gave every girl a small stipend when she left the school. Still, over the years a few had ended up staying at the school and working there. Three girls who were in the high school when Faye was in eighth grade had actually gone on to become nuns.

Faye was going to college. She had gotten financial aid to NYU. But she was not eager to leave St. Cecelia's. She felt safe there, protected. She had let herself be sheltered. There were the things she knew and the things she didn't want to know. There was nothing Dickensian about St. Cecelia's. She loved it there. She loved Sister Mary Margaret, who was like a den mother to the girls in the dormitory. She loved the strength and calm of Mother Superior. She even loved the Latina nun who had taken Sister Anne Marie's place with the music, Sister Fatima Dolores.

In the ten years Faye had spent at the school, she had never climbed on a chair or a stepstool to see what was in the uppermost jars outside Mother Superior's office. She had never gone into Manhattan to search the newspaper files at the public library with the stone lions out in front to see what she could find out about Sister Anne Marie's death, or even about what had happened to her own grandparents. Mother Superior had told her, after Sister Anne Marie's disappearance, that Faye wouldn't be seeing them again, that legally she belonged to St. Cecelia's now. She had told Faye that there were some rules that her grandparents had broken and that there would be some punishment involved, just as there was at St. Cecelia's. That was all she said, and over the years they had never spoken about it again.

Until the day Faye went to the office for what she thought would be the separation talk.

It was a chill gray day in late March. The daffodils were in full bloom by the grotto as Faye walked that same path she had taken every day she had been at the school. She had stopped and said a small prayer to Mary just as she always did. She listened for a moment, as she had continued to do all these years later, listened for the sound of Sister Anne Marie crying in the music room when she thought no one could hear. Sister Fatima Dolores never cried. She was relentlessly cheerful, always humming, always smiling. Faye never thought of her as Sister Anne Marie's replacement. She just thought of her as someone else. But Faye still listened for Sister Anne Marie. She couldn't help it.

Mother Superior opened the door to the office and another girl, one of the Theresas, slipped past Faye. Her head was down and she only murmured "Hi" to Faye without looking at her as she walked hurriedly away. Faye looked after the retreating girl and then turned to Mother Superior, a questioning look on her face. Faye hadn't thought the separation talk was going to be that bad. Her stomach flipped a little as she walked into the office and shut the door.

She'd been in this office many times over the years. She'd memorized it—from the spare black crucifix to the small glassed-in cabinet with the prayer books to the oval print of Raphael's *Madonna of the Streets* that hung opposite Mother's desk.

"You know we have a separation talk with all the senior girls who live here, right, Faye?" Mother began. Faye nodded and Mother continued.

"Ours will be a little different, dear." Mother had reached across the desk then and held out her hand toward Faye. Faye reached back. It was strange and somewhat unsettling. Faye had never remembered Mother touching anyone except shaking the hands of parents. Mother only grasped her hand for a minute, then let go.

"I have something for you. I don't want you to take it to the dormitory and I am not altogether sure I should even be giving it to you. But it belongs to you, so you should have it. And since you will be leaving here soon—" Here she paused and looked toward the small window, then back at Faye. "You need to have it before you go...out there." Mother waved her hand in the direction of the world outside the window, the Brooklyn neighborhood outside St. Cecelia's protected little enclave.

"We've never talked about this, but now we have to," she continued. "We have to talk about Sister Anne Marie and your grandfather."

Faye hadn't realized how straight she'd been sitting in her chair, her hands folded in her lap the way they'd been taught by Sister Mary Margaret. Now she gripped the arms of the hard wooden chair. She could feel her heart racing.

"I don't want to talk about that, Mother, if you don't mind. I just don't..." Faye had that hot, dizzy feeling she'd had so many years ago at her grandparents' house. She didn't want to feel like this. She wanted to leave. She had actually started to get up out of her chair when Mother said, "Please sit down, Faye. We have to talk, whether either of us wants to or not."

And then Mother began. She bent over and picked up a white cardboard carton, the kind that Xerox paper came in, with a lid on it. Neatly printed on the side was FAYE ELIZABETH BLAKE and Faye's old address, the one she had with her parents. Faye felt tears pricking behind her eyes. She didn't want to cry. She wanted to leave.

"I haven't looked in this box, Faye," Mother Superior said, and Faye believed her, although she couldn't imagine how Mother had kept her curiosity at bay all these years. Maybe, like Faye, she really didn't want to know what was inside. "I'm sure there are things here that could be upsetting. And I would prefer, given what happened with Sister Anne Marie, that you not discuss this with your friends, even though you may want to. It's especially important that you not say anything to Rosario Lopez or Theresa Flynn, as they are both already in a somewhat unstable situation." Faye thought about how Theresa had been when she had left Mother's office a few minutes ago. She wondered what was wrong.

Mother continued, "Whenever you want to look at the contents of this box, let me know, and I will provide a space for you to do so. I think that it would best if you do that here or across the hall in the biology lab."

Faye thought about the appropriateness of the jars of horrifying things as she looked through whatever it was that was in the box.

"We have never discussed this, but I think you have known this whole time that Sister Anne Marie did not have an accident." Mother looked at Faye and got up from behind the desk, came around, and stood in front of Faye.

Faye could feel a fine film of sweat break out over her whole body. She felt clammy and cold and her teeth started to chatter uncontrollably. She didn't want to hear this. It was time to go. She got up out of the chair and moved toward the door, but Mother was faster and put her hand against the door, keeping it shut, before Faye could open it.

"Please..." was all Faye said, her hand still on the doorknob, her back to Mother.

"You must hear this, Faye, because you cannot leave here not knowing. Other people know. They know out there. They know and it's quite possible when they hear your name or where you went to school, that someone will say something to you. Someone will ask you if you are the girl whose grandfather murdered the nun and...well..."

It was out now. There was no taking it back. Faye didn't even feel it when her body hit the floor. She was already unconscious.

30.

The gallery looked perfect. The bottle-green velvet drape on the front window was pulled across. It would be pulled back only after the gallery opened at seven. In the window, centered in front of the drape, was the poster that Persia had done for the show. It was the photograph of the bodies of the children in the morgue in Fresno, with the maggots, along with Faye's name and the name of the show, *Ordinary Mayhem,* and the gallery and the dates. The photo was black and white and the titles were in a dark blood-red—Persia's idea, naturally. That this was the least disturbing of the photos in the show struck Faye as she walked into the gallery. There were small programs printed up in a stack with the same image on them and inside, a statement by Faye about the content of the show and the meaning of the work.

Faye had hung everything herself early that very morning. She had asked that Nick and Persia not be there and they had agreed. A long red satin drape had been strung across the photos on each side of the gallery on a little pulley. The drapes would be pulled away once everyone had arrived at the gallery. Faye had also arranged all the other pieces on the series of tables that Nick had provided for her. The tables were covered with pieces of velvet in a dark claret and black. Even Nick and Persia had not seen what was underneath. The show was going to surprise them as much as it would the public. Persia had wanted to see, but Nick, who always seemed permanently bored, was obviously excited by the idea that here was something that might stimulate his jaded palate.

At the back of the long room was a table with various canapés of the most chic New York kind. The bar stood at an angle to the food. It all looked splendid. There was a display of flowers in dark reds, with a series of rather frightening-looking greens that reminded Faye of *Little Shop of Horrors.*

"When do you want to take the drapes off the tables, Faye?" Persia was sleek and alien-looking in a tight, black silk *Chinoise* dress with impossibly high black platform shoes and one long black earring that dangled to her shoulder. She looked magnificent, and not for the first time, Faye thought perhaps she should have invited her home before this. After the show, Persia might not be as interested as she had seemed during the preparation.

"What do you think?" Faye asked. "Should we have an unveiling after people arrive or do it now, for you and Nick and the waitstaff and then cover everything over again? We have a half hour. What do you think? Do you think people will hear the screaming from here?" Faye didn't laugh when she said this and she thought she saw Persia flinch involuntarily. For the first time, Faye felt apprehensive. She knew what was under the little drapes. She knew even the cynical Nick and the cool aesthete that Persia was would be unsettled. Maybe they should wait until there was an audience and do it all at once. Like ripping off a bandage.

"I say let's do it now," Persia said, looking around for Nick, who was on his cell phone in the back, a glass of red wine in his hand. "I want to see what's going to slither out from under the rock."

31.

Faye lay flat on her bed in the dorm staring up at the little blue stenciled crosses. She was still in her uniform. It was almost dark and the only light was the small one on the little table near the door that led to the landing at the top of the stairs. She hadn't wanted to take the box Mother had given her. She hadn't wanted to look inside. She hadn't wanted to remember the things she had spent ten years— most of her childhood—trying to forget.

But Mother had wanted her to take it. She had waited ten years to give it to Faye. And she clearly wanted Faye to have time to recover before she went off to college. But how could she ever recover from this, from what Mother had told her? From what was in the box?

❖

After she had fainted, Mother had brought her around with smelling salts. Faye remembered that her mother had had the same old-fashioned bottle on her dresser. Faye had wanted to take the bottle from Mother and hold it, the sense memory of her own mother, her dead mother, her burned-alive mother, was so vivid in that moment. But instead she had pulled herself up off the floor and sat down in the chair in front of Mother's desk and started to cry.

It hadn't been what she had wanted. She had spent all these years being brave and controlled and leading as close to a normal life as she could for a girl whose grandfather had killed women and whose grandmother had known and said nothing. She had tried to be a good student and pray every day and make friends and not seem like the displaced orphan girl who kept herself cloistered like a nun behind the walls of St. Cecelia's. But Mother had blown that safe façade apart with her box of who-knows-what and her declarative statement that Sister Anne Marie, Faye's first friend, her protector, her second mother, had been murdered by her grandfather.

And now all she could do was weep. Ten years of weeping. She wanted to wail and claw at her own skin and tear her clothes, like some biblical hysteric, but she didn't. She just sat, her head on her arm on Mother's desk, weeping.

Mother stood over her, stroking her hair. They stayed like that for ten, fifteen, twenty minutes. And then as suddenly as she had begun to cry, Faye just stopped. She pulled a tissue from her uniform pocket, wiped her face, blew her nose, and stood.

"I'll take the box now, Mother, and go across the hall if no one is there." Her voice sounded hollow and scary, even to her. Mother walked around the desk, picked up the box, and handed it to Faye.

"I would say perhaps now is not the time, but I don't think there will ever be a right time, my dear. I am sorry. Please knock on my door when you are finished and I will keep the box here for you." Mother opened the door for Faye and led her across the hall to the creepy room that had fascinated and repelled Faye since she'd first come to St. Cecelia's. Faye put the box down on one of the marble tables next to some beakers and turned toward Mother, who said, "I'm going to pull these doors shut, Faye. Please don't let anyone in. And remember, you have done nothing wrong, and God loves you as His own."

With that, Mother had pulled the double doors out from the wall and closed them, leaving Faye alone with the shelves of jars filled with horror and the box filled with still more.

Faye had involuntarily made the sign of the cross before she opened the box. But when she looked inside, at first it all seemed anticlimactic.

Inside there appeared to be nothing but a big stack of thin, opaque paper envelopes of the sort her grandfather used to put the finished photographs in when he gave them to clients. But as Faye began lifting them out, she saw what they were. Strips and strips of negatives. Hundreds of them. Perhaps as many as a thousand. And at the bottom of the box, several small notebooks and a small stack of the little paintings Faye used to do at the kitchen table when her grandfather was coloring the photographs. Faye looked at the first few envelopes and saw that they were labeled in that silver pencil that her grandfather used. She sorted through the pile until she found the envelope she was looking for, the one she knew would be there, even as she hoped it wouldn't.

The photographs of Sister Anne Marie.

Faye thought about whether or not she should look at the pictures, thought about whether or not she should read the notebooks. But she was seventeen now, not six and a half, and she had experienced more than most adults ever would—she knew that, even though she had spent all these years pretending that those things had happened to someone else, a different Faye, not the Faye who had always lived at St. Cecelia's.

She slid the negatives out from the envelope and the whispery crackle of the paper sounded shockingly loud in the sterile quiet of the science lab. She closed her eyes for a moment and thought of Sister Anne Marie as she had last seen her, angry and determined, beautiful and strong as she had walked away from St. Cecelia's for what would be the last time, intent on protecting Faye from her murderous grandfather. Faye had loved Sister Anne Marie. Without her, Faye knew she would be dead, knew she would never have learned that she could ever be safe, that there would always be women to protect her and hold her and keep her from the kind of harm the women in the photographs her grandfather had taken could not be protected from.

Faye held the first strip up to the light, and the gasp that escaped her was involuntary. She had known what she would see, but still it shocked her, and she lowered the strip to the table, took a deep breath, and slipped it back into its envelope. She didn't need to see more. She knew what was there. The box was a catalogue of mayhem. Ordinary women, ordinary mayhem. They hadn't known what would happen when they encountered the mild-mannered, attractive older man with the camera who just wanted to take a picture of a pretty girl. Faye could imagine her grandfather—out walking, or driving in the car—coming up to each woman. He was striking, her grandfather. Tall, his hair still dark, with only a little gray at the temples. He was handsome, with good, strong features and sparkly eyes that were a very pale blue that made them stand out against his dark hair and skin that always seemed to be somewhat tanned, no matter what time of year it was. Faye could imagine how the women felt comfortable around him because she had seen him calm crying babies and soothe nervous prom dates and talk easily with client after client, as if he had known them for years.

Faye could imagine a girl getting in her grandfather's car because it was too cold or too hot or just because her feet hurt and she wanted a ride and thought it would be safe, with this calm, attractive older guy. And then they had ended up in the basement, cut open, cut apart, other things, the things Faye couldn't think about, done to them on the little bed down there.

Faye didn't want to think about how that had happened to Sister Anne Marie. She hadn't thought of Sister Anne Marie the way she had about those women in the photographs. But Sister Anne Marie was beautiful. She had told Faye she was black Irish—that her family had come over from Ireland and settled in Brooklyn only one generation ago. That both her parents had strong accents and she herself had had one when she was Faye's age, but the nuns had drilled it out of her, the brogue, she called it.

So when Faye saw the beautiful Sister Anne Marie tied up on the little bed with the marks that Faye now knew were mutilations on her body, with her habit pushed up past mid-thigh, she had been shocked, saddened, sickened, angry. She didn't want to think of what had happened to Sister Anne Marie. Most of all, she didn't want to think that it was her fault.

Faye whispered *"Mea culpa, mea culpa, mea maxima culpa,"* and put the envelope back into the box. She took out one of the small notebooks, slipped it into the pocket of her uniform, put the lid on the box, opened the double doors, and went back to Mother Superior's office. She balanced the box and knocked on the door. When Mother opened, she handed it to her, turned, and walked away. She heard the door close, but she didn't look back.

Instead Faye looked up the stairs at St. Cecelia and then quickly ran up, touched the three slashes in her neck, ran back down, and walked quickly to the door that led to the grotto. All she could see was Sister Anne Marie, mutilated, in the basement of her grandfather's house. Only Mary could help her now. St. Cecelia was just another victim.

❖

That night in the dorm room, everyone seemed subdued. There was none of the usual laughter and pillow tossing and fake shoving that went on most nights. Even Sister Mary Margaret seemed to know that the realization that soon they would be leaving the safe enclave of St. Cecelia's, the place that had been their only real home, had hit them all, hard, with the separation interviews. From this day until the day each of them left St. Cecelia's, it would all be different. They would have to toughen up, prepare themselves for battle with the world outside this cocoon of studies and prayer and nuns who loved them like the families they never really had. From now on they were on their way to the outside, and whatever that held. Faye knew better than most what lay beyond the ivy-covered walls of St. Cecelia's. And that knowing frightened her more than she could say.

When the lights went out, Faye could hear the muffled crying of Rosario, Theresa, and several other girls. It made her feel less alone as the tears fell onto her pillow until she finally drifted off to sleep.

32.

Nick had decided to wait for the unveiling, and as Faye glanced at her, Persia seemed relieved. Faye suddenly wondered if the actual reveal would be as compelling as either she or Persia had anticipated.

Faye felt surprisingly calm. Preternaturally calm, in fact. Faye's whole life had built to this moment. She realized that now. Her parents' deaths, the first time she had seen the photographs in her grandfather's darkroom, some of which were arrayed in baroque frames on one of the tables in the gallery. Sister Anne Marie at the grotto. The day

Mother Superior handed her the box of her grandfather's negatives and notebooks. And then all the stories she had covered, all the bits and pieces of horror she had collected and catalogued over the years since she had left St. Cecelia's. This, this exhibit, this wasn't a retrospective of her work so much as it was a retrospective of her life.

A line had formed outside the gallery an hour before the show was scheduled to start. It was clear that Nick's hype had worked. Plus, there had been a blog post on a local arts webzine that had suggested Faye had had a breakdown when she'd returned from the DRC. Faye knew people liked to see other people fall apart publicly. No doubt some of the people in line had done just that—come to see her, expecting her to be gaunt and wraithlike and muttering to herself. Except she wasn't. She felt fine for the first time in months. Even she didn't know why. Just last night she'd thought she'd never make it to the gallery, never get the show up, never be there for the opening. Last night she had thought it was over, that she would indeed kill herself. Last night she'd nearly lost it for good.

❖

It was only twenty-four hours before her own opening when Faye went to the book signing of her old friend, Keiko Izanami, who had just been nominated for a major literary award for the poetry collection she was reading from that night. The two women had gone to NYU together and Keiko had been one of Faye's first lovers during her freshman year. They'd both stayed in New York after college and had remained close over the years, but Faye hadn't planned on going to the event. She had kept most of her friends at arm's length the past few weeks, trying to pull herself together, trying to sleep without dreaming, trying, still, to keep herself from the urgent desire to kill herself that kept seizing her every other day. The only person she confided in was Martine, because the only person she thought understood was Martine. And yet even she didn't know Faye's secrets. No one did, except Shihong. But after the opening, after all the pieces of the exhibit were laid bare, then everyone would know. Then she would be free of secrets, she'd have exorcised all the demons. And maybe then she could either drown herself in the river or she could get her life back.

Keiko had texted her several times and Faye hadn't even responded, which was a level of rudeness she didn't like in herself, but which she couldn't explain. It was late in the afternoon of the book signing when Keiko called. Faye saw the number and this time, she picked up. Keiko was both worried and pissed, and said that while she knew Faye's big opening was the next night, that was really no excuse not to come to the signing, and Keiko really wanted her there. So Faye said she would go.

Keiko and her publisher had chosen one of the independent bookstores downtown for the big event. It was a nice shop and Faye had been there many times. The two old queens who owned it had patterned it after Shakespeare and Company and it had taken the place of several other shops that had closed in recent years.

Faye really wasn't prepared for so many people, but she promised Keiko she'd stay for the entire reading and that she'd hang around to meet Keiko's new girlfriend as well as another poet friend that Keiko thought would be a nice match for her. Faye said she was only doing anonymous one-nighters these days after she was on her fourth or fifth drink and when Keiko stared back at her, Faye laughed and said, "Just kidding. I'm currently single, but sure, I'd love to meet her." But Faye didn't want to meet anyone. Faye wanted to go home and sleep the dreamless sleep of the dead.

The poetry was heady. Keiko's entire book was dedicated to Japanese forms—haiku and tonka, with a series of poems toward the end that were done in tercets. Faye had felt a measure of pride as she listened because she knew how hard Keiko had worked over the years. Like Faye, she hadn't had an easy early life, and the two had bonded over that when they had first met.

The audience was a mix of Keiko's colleagues and students from NYU, other poets, and a group of those art predators Persia had been railing about, but Faye relaxed more easily than she had expected to and settled into the rhythm of the pieces as Keiko read in her lilting, mellifluous voice. Faye felt calmed and soothed by the cadence and Keiko's lush, sensual imagery. She was glad she had come and wondered now why she had avoided it.

When Keiko announced she was about to read her last poem, she explained that it was an older one, a haiku she had written in college for a close friend, but which she still had great affection for—as she did for the friend. She looked over toward Faye and Faye felt herself blush involuntarily as the audience responded with the light laughter that naturally accompanied such revelations from a poet as seasoned as Keiko. Then she read:

there is a way to
cut a mango right
no blood, just fruit, and you   you

As the audience applauded and Keiko bowed, Japanese-style, with her hands clasped in front of her, Faye felt an unpleasant wave of dizziness come over her. She remembered the occasion of that poem—a morning when she had been preparing breakfast for the two of them and had sliced through the too-soft mango and into her finger, nearly to the bone. Something about the blood pulsing and the fleshy mango had made her almost hysterical and Keiko had rushed in, her long black hair flying out behind her. Keiko had helped Faye wash the cut and wrap it. They had gone to the student health office, which was closer than the hospital, and Faye had gotten six tight little stitches and an Ativan to calm her.

Faye had never told Keiko why she had gotten so upset, hadn't told her that the blood and the fruit together had made her think of the plates on the table in those photographs of her grandfather's, that somehow it seemed as if the mango were a pulsing, living organ there on the narrow counter when the blood spurted onto it.

The applause had subsided and Faye continued to sit while the rest of the audience rose and headed toward Keiko to have her sign their books. Faye wasn't sure how long she had sat there when Keiko came over and asked her to come upstairs, said that there was food and a surprise and the woman that she wanted Faye to meet.

Faye wanted to leave, but she let herself be led up the narrow little staircase to the large upper room of the store. Bookshelves lined the room and there were tables pushed to the side with more books on them. Chairs were scattered around the room, but everyone seemed to be standing, talking and laughing and milling about. A level of normalcy Faye had missed these past few weeks.

At the back of the room was the food table. Or what was passing for a food table. Stretched out on a red linen tablecloth on what Faye presumed to be a massage table was a young, naked woman covered in sushi. On a table next to her, bottles of wine were arrayed. People were standing around the table with the woman and as Faye and Keiko approached her, Faye could see she was Asian and impossibly fit, as well as beautiful. Faye felt the dizziness she'd experienced earlier return and she leaned over and told Keiko she really had to leave.

"It's a little too claustrophobic here, for me, and I really do have an intense day tomorrow," she explained, but Keiko wasn't having it.

"Oh you can stay for a little sushi," Keiko said and nudged her, smiling. "That's my new girlfriend, by the way. Mika. She is, as you can see, delicious." Keiko laughed her wry little laugh and pulled Faye forward. As they came up to the woman, Faye could see that people were actually eating bits of food directly from her. Faye had heard this was a new trend, but she'd never actually seen it before. Something about it horrified her.

"She's lovely, but I prefer my food served on plates, and I *really* have to go." Faye was feeling hot and dizzy and intensely claustrophobic. A woman came up beside Keiko, then, and she turned toward her, smiling and hugging the woman. Faye stared. The woman looked so much like Sister Anne Marie, it was eerie—no, frightening. Faye felt her heart start to race again. It was absolutely time for her to leave. She looked away for a moment and saw several men eating sushi off Mika's perfect body. She got a flash of Vandana at the Congo clinic, saying, "They made a meal of us," and thought she might vomit. A rush of images came into her head, each more terrible than the other. She had to get out of there. Faye turned back toward Keiko and touched her arm, "Now I do have to go, Keiko," she said, trying to keep the rising panic out of her voice, but Keiko interrupted her. She was pulling the Sister Anne Marie *doppleganger* closer, and introducing her to Faye. "Faye, this is Morgan, the writer I was telling you about. We teach together. Morgan, this is Faye, she's about to be the most famous photographer in New York, after her super-secret gallery opening tomorrow night."

"Super-secret? Sounds intriguing. I will have to come." Morgan extended her hand to Faye and Faye took it, took Sister Anne Marie's hand, and held it fast. Morgan looked at her quizzically.

"If you're going to hold on to it, you'd better at least read the palm." She laughed her Sister Anne Marie laugh and tried to turn her hand slightly in Faye's grasp. Faye let go.

"I'm sorry—you look like—you remind me of—someone I used to know." Faye wanted to walk away, but felt trapped, mesmerized by the dead woman in front of her.

Keiko turned to Morgan. "Faye has been very reclusive lately, working on her show. Also, she just returned from a pretty harrowing trip to the Congo. Maybe you saw her piece last week in the Sunday magazine?"

Faye just stood there, she could look at the people eating the woman to her right or she could look at the woman back from the grave to her left. She felt faint. Morgan said, "I did see that piece. It was very hard to look at. I can't imagine how difficult it must have been to actually be there. I admire your—fortitude. Some stories beg to be told, but it takes a certain guts to tell them."

A small group came up to Keiko then and she turned away from Morgan and Faye to talk to them. The two women stood, not saying anything for minute. Then Faye spoke.

"I don't mean to be rude, but I really do need to leave. I have so much left to do and I only came tonight because Keiko and I are such old friends." She put her hand out toward Morgan and said, "I hope we will see each other again. And I don't mean to stare, it's just you look so much like a—teacher I once had." It was so hot, Faye felt so hot. She wanted to sit down with this woman, she wanted to have a moment of Sister Anne Marie–ness before the opening tomorrow. She wasn't sure what it meant, meeting this woman now, right before her exhibit, but it felt important, somehow. And yet she couldn't bear to be in this room another minute, not with the people with their mouths all over Mika just outside her periphery. A wave of nausea came over her as she saw the plates with the pieces of female flesh and organs on them in her grandparents' house and now she could hear the sounds, the sounds of women's flesh being eaten.

"There's a lot of us black Irish girls here in New York," Morgan was saying to her, "and we all look alike, with the black hair and blue eyes. I'm only second generation, myself. My grandparents were immigrants. My mother says the nuns had to drill the brogue out of her."

Faye swiveled around, remembering how Sister Anne Marie had said the same thing to her, years ago.

"Would you like to have a drink sometime, after you've recovered from your gallery event? Here's my card—give me a call when you come up for air."

Faye took the card, her hand brushing Morgan's fingers. She wanted to stop seeing the slide show that had begun in her head when she'd first seen Mika laid out covered in sushi. Maybe she should have a drink with Morgan now. Maybe it would distract her. Or maybe she'd wake up screaming in the middle of the night again, seeing Sister Anne Marie's mutilated body in her apartment, her mouth filled with blood.

"I will, definitely," Faye said, "but now I just really have to get going." She wasn't sure what she should do next, so she reached for Morgan's hand again, this time turning it over, looking at the palm. "I've never read one, but perhaps if I get to examine it further—" Then she laughed, a forced little laugh that she hoped wouldn't actually sound forced and which would lighten the strange vibe she'd thrown over everything with her vision of Sister Anne Marie. It was past time for her to go. Faye did a half wave to Keiko, who was heading back toward them, and went down the stairs as quickly as she could, moving briskly through the store, then out, into the chill air. She wasn't sure what she should do next. The panic was washing over her in waves. She just had to get through the next few hours until she went to the gallery to hang the show. Then it would all be over. The exorcism she was hoping for would be complete. She would be free of all these memories, all these images. She would lay them out on the tables and hang them on the walls of the gallery. And then she could begin her life, free from all those ghosts that followed her, clung to her, night and day.

33.

The day Faye left St. Cecelia's there were only a few things to do: go to the biology lab and memorize the contents of the jars there, run her fingers through the slashes on St. Cecelia's neck a final time, and say a last prayer at the grotto to Mary for all that had come before and all that was ahead of her.

She had said her good-byes to the friends who were still there, and to Sister Mary Margaret and Mother Superior and the other nuns. She had said good bye to the ghost of Sister Anne Marie as she stood at the spot where she had always heard her crying.

And then she had left. Everything she owned, what little there was from the decade she'd spent there, had been taken to the small apartment she was sharing with one of the Theresas for her freshman year. Theresa was going to Fordham, she to NYU. It was small, but what they could afford and they were used to sharing a far smaller space than this. It was their new life, but they were as scared as they were ready.

The second week she was living in Manhattan, Faye had gone to the public library and searched for her grandfather's case. She had gone back every day for a week and read everything she could stand to read. About how it had been Sister Anne Marie who had undone him with her murder. None of the other women—evidence of at least seventeen murders had been found in the house—had been traced to him, but Sister Anne Marie had.

They'd never found Faye's grandfather, or her grandmother. When the police came to the house, it was as if the two of them had just gone out for a walk. The car was there, parked on the street as it always was, in front of the house. They hadn't taken anything with them. All that seemed to be missing was her grandmother's purse, which she took with her every time she left the house, regardless of whether she was going to the store a block away or somewhere much further. The purse, and, it seemed, some camera equipment.

What the police *had* found, there, in the basement, had been Sister Anne Marie. Raped, mutilated, her tongue cut out, sliced into pieces, and stuffed back in her mouth. The medical examiner's report stipulated that she had been alive through all of it.

Other stories Faye read explained that the house had gone into foreclosure and been sold at sheriff's auction. There had been a granddaughter, who had been sent to the orphanage at St. Cecelia's in Brooklyn. Her name was not released to the press, but she was said to have been a witness to at least some aspect of the killings, according to homicide detective Tom McManus.

It was more than Faye had wanted to know. Especially the part that he was still out there, her grandfather, taking pictures of girls who were disarmed by his calm demeanor and simple charm.

She'd been safe at St. Cecelia's. Now she was on her own. And there was a murderer, a serial killer, who was the only one who knew for sure who—and where—she was.

34.

When Persia and Nick had each pulled the drapes on the photographs before a rapt and packed audience at the gallery, there had been a collective sound that had rippled through the men and women standing in front of Faye's work. When she herself had pulled the pieces of velvet from table after table, the sounds had been both louder and more—she wasn't sure what the word was—repelled? Awed? A few people had turned and left the gallery immediately, but most had, as Faye had expected, stayed to look hard and long at all the things they didn't want to admit they wanted to see.

Persia had come up to her after she had looked at the tables and had said simply, "I didn't expect this. I really didn't," and had moved on before Faye had had a chance to speak. Faye wasn't sure what Persia meant, but she had looked stunned and slightly sickened. Perhaps she wasn't as hard-core as she thought she was.

Faye overheard a flurry of comments as she walked through the gallery, a glass of red wine in her hand.

"Look at that, look at that, did you see what she had there, in the vise, in those jars?"

"It's not real, though, right? I mean that wasn't human, right? None of it was human, was it?"

"Did you see the pictures? The ones in the frames on the table?"

"Omigod—I've never seen anything like that in my life!"

"Why would anyone pose photographs like that? How did she do that? How *could* she do that?"

"Can you do that with Photoshop? Really?"

"What about those jars? Is it even legal to have that here?"

There had been a scream, suddenly, and Faye turned to see a woman fall to the floor. Persia rushed toward her, looking around for Nick as she did. Faye looked at what the woman had been looking at. Oh yes, Shihong's jars. That was worth screaming over. But then, to Faye, it was all worth screaming over. She'd screamed and even fainted over all of it herself. And yet, there was nothing that unusual here, really. It was all the work of other humans, and for some that "work" had a dailiness to it that made it absolutely mundane and ordinary. She thought of how her grandfather had explained his torture murders to her as work, work to be proud of. Explained it to a six-year-old whose parents had just been killed as if it was the most ordinary thing in the world to say. *Ordinary mayhem.* That was the very worst kind, Faye thought. Very worst.

Faye moved toward the door, then turned and looked back over the room. It was different from what she had imagined. There had been gasps and a few stifled screams. As more people had entered the gallery after the initial reveal, there had been other noises—other little shrieks, some choruses of "Oh no!" And then, mostly, silence. The food at the back of the gallery had gone uneaten, but everyone had had at least one drink.

Nick had come up to her after the first hour to let her know that every photograph had sold and that there were orders for more, a surprising number. The installation pieces were not for sale, but that hadn't kept people from asking, from wanting them. No one seemed to understand that everything on the tables was real. It wasn't mixed media, it was found horror.

"Pretty grisly stuff you've got here," Nick had said, his look of perpetual ennui shaken off for the moment. "You'd never know it to look at you, you know. You seem so—demure, almost. It's a little shocking, actually."

Faye had listened as he spoke and wondered what it was that people saw when they looked at her. Wondered what they thought when they looked at her, her work, and her again. It didn't matter, really. She just wondered, curious more than anything.

Keiko hadn't come to the opening, but she'd called earlier and wished Faye luck and impressive sales. There had been an incident at the bookstore the night before, after Faye had left. Keiko didn't want to get into it, but someone had taken the sushi eating too far. She and Mika had ended up at the hospital later that night. Faye wasn't surprised. There seemed a very fine line between a sensual display like the one at the bookstore and the stoking of some primordial desire in men that turned women into prey. Faye had shuddered at the thought. She had tried not to think about it, about blood running into the sushi and strategically placed lettuce leaves and pieces of fruit. Tried not to think of Mika's perfect flesh marred by the jagged tear of teeth.

The opening had been a success. Seven or eight critics had come up to Faye and asked her questions. She'd been polite, she'd been vague. She'd revealed what she thought was useful, ignored the questions she didn't want to answer—or couldn't answer. When nearly three hours had passed and the gallery was still filled with people, new faces replacing the original ones, Faye had had enough. She told Nick she was leaving. He didn't try to stop her. He was in his element. He was the gatekeeper to the horror show and he was reveling in it. Faye wasn't sure if she should be grateful or appalled.

Faye stepped out into the brisk cold in this end-of-winter night, glad that it was clear. She wasn't sure what she felt. Empty? Relieved? She had put the photographs of her grandfather's crimes in among her own art because it was part of her story—she was the one who had survived. She had displayed the jars Shihong had brought her because they, too, were part of her story, part of the endless horrors perpetrated on women. Faye wondered, for the first time in a long time, if her grandfather was still alive, and if he was, if he was still murdering women and cannibalizing them. Would he have wanted to be there at the bookstore last night, eating from Mika's lovely body? Or was solitude with his victims an essential part of the experience for him? Faye wondered if her grandmother was still sharing his bed every night, still pretending that the plates she set the table with weren't used to serve up the entrails of her husband's victims.

Faye took a deep breath of the icy air. She wasn't sure what to do now, wasn't sure what would happen when the reviews of the show hit, wasn't sure if it was all over for her now, if she was free to start over, or if she should start walking toward the river, as she had planned for so long.

She stood outside the gallery, unable to decide what to do next. Shihong was still in town, although she had not come to the opening. Nor had Morgan come, but Faye thought that was probably best. Maybe she should just go home and try to sleep a dreamless sleep.

Faye started walking, walking, then stopped, turned toward the curb, ready to hail a cab. As she put her arm up, she looked into the mass of traffic passing by. And then, several cars over, Faye saw something that made her stomach lurch. An attractive older man with gray hair and a camera, leaning out of the passenger side window of a taxi as it headed uptown. Her heart started to race, faster, faster, faster. *Is it him? Does he know I'm here? Did he see my name in the newspapers in the promotion of the opening? Has he come for me, finally, after all these years, when just the memories of him had stalked me? Will I become yet another of his victims?*

Faye dropped her arm, stepped back from the curb. No, it wasn't over. The exorcism wasn't complete, as she had thought. It wasn't over at all. Faye turned and began to walk. Back to the gallery, or toward the river, she'd know when she got there.

CONTRIBUTORS

STEVE BERMAN's young adult novel *Vintage: A Ghost Story* was a finalist for the Andre Norton Award and made the GLBT-Round Table of the American Library Association's Rainbow List of recommended queer-positive books for children and teens. He's worked as editor of the genre anthologies *So Fey, The Touch of the Sea,* and the *Wilde Stories* series, which has twice been a finalist for the Lambda Literary Award. He edited the YA anthologies *Speaking Out,* featuring inspirational short fiction aimed at LGBT teens, and *Boys of Summer,* romantic tales for gay boys, both released from Bold Strokes Books. Berman also is the publisher of *Icarus: The Magazine of Gay Speculative Fiction,* a quarterly glossy magazine. His short fiction has been featured in such anthologies as *Teeth* (ed. by Ellen Datlow and Terri Windling) and *Wilful Impropriety* (ed. by Ekaterina Sedia). Berman is the founder of Lethe Press, which, for the past decade, has released quality books of queer and weird fiction from such writers as Tanith Lee, Livia Llewellyn, Will Ludwigsen, and a host of other authors whose names do not begin with "L." He resides in southern New Jersey.

VICTORIA A. BROWNWORTH is an award-winning author and editor of nearly thirty books. Her work includes the award-winning *Too Queer: Essays from a Radical Life, Coming Out of Cancer: Writings from the Lesbian Cancer Epidemic,* and *Night Bites: Vampire Tales by Women.* She is a columnist for *Curve* magazine, the *San Francisco Bay Area Reporter,* and the *Philadelphia Chronicle.* She is an editor for Lambda Literary and her criticism has appeared in numerous publications, including *Publisher's Weekly, The New York Times, The Los Angeles Times, The Village Voice, The New York Review of Books,* and *The Baltimore Sun,* for which she was book critic for seventeen years. In 2010 she founded Tiny Satchel Press, an independent publisher devoted to young adult books primarily for LGBT youth and youth of color. She teaches writing and film at the University of the Arts in Philadelphia and in 2011 co-founded KITH (Kids in the Hood), a program for reading, writing, and mentoring of inner city youth.

'Nathan Burgoine (http://redroom.com/member/nathan-burgoine) lives in Ottawa with his husband Daniel. Other short fiction appears in *The Touch of the Sea, Boys of Summer, Saints + Sinners 2011: New Fiction from the Festival, Men of the Mean Streets, I Do Too,* and *Fool for Love.*

Lisa Girolami (LisaGirolami.com) is the published author of *The Pleasure Set, Love on Location, Run to Me, Fugitives of Love,* and *Cut to the Chase* (forthcoming, April 2013), as well as numerous short stories. She has been in the entertainment industry for thirty years including ten years as production executive in the motion picture industry and another two decades producing and designing theme parks for Walt Disney and Universal Studios. She holds a BA in Fine Art and an MS in Psychology, and she is also a licensed MFT for the GLBTQ community. She currently lives in Long Beach, California.

Jewelle Gomez is the author of seven books including the double Lambda Literary Award—winning novel *The Gilda Stories,* which has been in continuous print since 1991. Her theatrical adaptation of the novel, *Bones & Ash,* commissioned by Urban Bush Women Company, toured thirteen U.S. cities. Her fiction and poetry are included in more than one hundred anthologies. Her nonfiction has appeared in numerous publications including *The Village Voice, San Francisco Chronicle, Ms,* and *Black Scholar.* Her play *Waiting for Giovanni* imagines a split second in the life of writer/activist James Baldwin (1924—1987), and premiered at New Conservatory Theatre Center in San Francisco in 2011. The play is part of a cycle, "Words and Music," which explores the lives of artists of color in the first half of the twentieth century. The next play, *Castle Rockin,* is about singer/songwriter Alberta Hunter (1895–1984).

Vince A. Liaguno (VinceLiaguno.com) is the Stoker Award—winning editor of *Unspeakable Horror: In the Shadow of the Closet* (Dark Scribe Press 2008), an anthology of queer horror fiction, which he co-edited with Chad Helder. His debut novel, 2006's *The Literary Six,* was a tribute to the slasher films of the '80s and won an Independent Publisher Award (IPPY) for Horror and was named a finalist in ForeWord Magazine's Book of the Year Awards in the Gay/Lesbian Fiction category. He recently edited *Butcher Knives and Body Counts,* a collection of essays on the formula, frights, and fun of the slasher film, and is currently at work finishing his second novel, *Final Girl*. He divides his time between Manhattan and the eastern end of Long Island, New York. He is a member (and current Secretary) of the Horror Writers Association (HWA) and the National Book Critics Circle (NBCC).

FELICE PICANO is the author of twenty books, including the literary memoirs *Ambidextrous, Men Who Loved Me,* and *A House on the Ocean, a House on the Bay,* as well as the best-selling novels *Like People in History, Looking Glass Lives, The Lure,* and *Eyes*. He is the founder of Sea Horse Press, one of the first gay publishing houses, which later merged with two other publishing houses to become the Gay Presses of New York. With Andrew Holleran, Robert Ferro, Edmund White, and George Whitmore, he founded the Violet Quill Club to promote and increase the visibility of gay authors and their works. He has edited and written for *The Advocate, Blueboy, Mandate, GaysWeek, Christopher Street,* and was Books Editor of *The New York Native* and has been a culture reviewer for *The Los Angeles Examiner, San Francisco Examiner, New York Native, Harvard Lesbian & Gay Review,* and the *Lambda Book Report*. He has won the Ferro-Grumley Award for best gay novel (Like People in History) and the PEN Syndicated Fiction Award for short story. He was a finalist for the Ernest Hemingway Award and has been nominated for three Lambda Literary Awards. A native of New York, Felice Picano now lives in Los Angeles. His most recent book, *True Stories,* presents sweet and sometimes controversial anecdotes of his precocious childhood, odd, funny, and often disturbing encounters from before he found his calling as a writer and later as one of the first GLBT publishers. Throughout are his delightful encounters and surprising relationships with the one-of-a-kind and the famous—including Tennessee Williams, W.H. Auden, Charles Henri Ford, Bette Midler, and Diana Vreeland. Most recently, Bold Strokes Books published his collection of strange stories, *Twelve O' Clock Tales,* and this fall Modernist Press of Los Angeles will publish his fantasy novella *Wonder City of the West.*

JEFFREY RICKER'S (jeffreyricker.wordpress.com) first novel, *Detours,* was published in 2011 by Bold Strokes Books. His writing has appeared in the anthologies *Paws and Reflect, Fool for Love: New Gay Fiction, Blood Sacraments, Men of the Mean Streets, Speaking Out, Riding the Rails,* and others. He is currently finishing his second novel and pursuing an MFA in creative writing at the University of British

Columbia. When class is out, he lives in St. Louis with his partner, Michael, and two dogs.

CAROL ROSENFELD is a New York City–based writer and poet who has three novels in progress. Her short stories have appeared in *Best Lesbian Erotica 2003* (Cleis, 2003), *Shadows of the Night: Queer Tales of the Uncanny and Unusual* (Harrington Park Press, 2004) and *Back to Basics: A Butch-Femme Anthology* (Bella Books, 2004). Carol is the volunteer chair of the Publishing Triangle and blogs occasionally at crosenyc.wordpress.com.

MICHAEL ROWE (michaelrowe.com) is the author of the novel *Enter, Night,* hailed by Barnes & Noble as "the vampire fiction release of the year." An award-winning journalist, essayist, and editor, he lives in Toronto and welcomes readers at his website.

CARSEN TAITE (carsentaite.com) works by day (and sometimes night) as a criminal defense attorney in Dallas, Texas. Her goal as an author is to spin plot lines as interesting as the cases she encounters in her practice. She is the author of six previously released novels: *truelesbianlove. com, It Should be a Crime* (a Lambda Literary Award finalist), *Do Not Disturb, Nothing but the Truth, The Best Defense,* and *Slingshot.* Her seventh novel, *Beyond Innocence,* is scheduled for release in November 2012.

LEE THOMAS is the Lambda Literary Award and Bram Stoker Award—winning author of *The Dust of Wonderland, In the Closet Under the Bed, The German,* and *Torn.* Forthcoming releases include the novel *Ash Street* and the short story collection *Like Light for Flies.*

THE EDITORS

GREG HERREN is an award-winning author and editor who lives in New Orleans. He writes two mystery series, the Chanse MacLeod mysteries and the Scotty Bradley adventures. He has been nominated ten times for a Lambda Literary Award, winning for *Murder in the Rue Chartres* (Men's Mystery) and *Love Bourbon Street: Reflections on New Orleans* (Anthology). He has also published three young adult novels; *Sleeping Angel* won the Moonbeam Gold Medal for excellence in Children's/Young Adult Mystery/Horror. He has published over 200 articles of literary criticism and/or author interviews. His short fiction has appeared in numerous award-winning anthologies, including the critically acclaimed *New Orleans Noir, Cast of Characters,* and in *Ellery Queen's Mystery Magazine.* Former editor of *Lambda Book Report,* he has also worked as an editor at Bella Books, the Harrington Park Press, and Bold Strokes Books. He has edited twelve anthologies, including *Shadows of the Night, Upon a Midnight Clear,* and one of the top-selling erotica anthologies of all time, *FRATSEX.* He is a co-founder of the Saints and Sinners Literary Conference, served for two years on the board of directors of the National Stonewall Democrats, is currently serving as president of the Southwest Chapter of the Mystery Writers of America, and is chairing the 2013 Bram Stoker Awards Weekend/World Horror Convention in New Orleans. He has served as a judge for the Lambda Literary Awards, the Hammett Prize, the Edgar Allan Poe Award, and the Stoker Award. His blog can be found at http://scottynola.livejournal.com. He lives in the historic lower Garden District of New Orleans, with his partner of sixteen years and their cat.

J. M. REDMANN is the author of a mystery series featuring New Orleans private detective Michele "Micky" Knight. Her latest novel is *Ill Will.* The previous book, *Water Mark,* won an Over the

Rainbow award from the Gay, Lesbian, Bisexual and Transgendered Roundtable of the American Library Association, a ForeWord Gold First Place mystery award, and was shortlisted for a Lambda Literary Award. Two of her earlier books, *The Intersection of Law and Desire* and *Death of a Dying Man,* have won Lambda Literary Awards; all but her first book have been nominated. *The Intersection of Law and Desire* was also an Editor's Choice of the *San Francisco Chronicle* and a recommended holiday book by Maureen Corrigan of NPR's *Fresh Air*; it and *Lost Daughters* were originally published by W.W. Norton. Redmann was a 2010 recipient of the Alice B. Readers Appreciation Award, gave the keynote address at the Golden Crown Literary Society Conference in 2009, in 2006 was inducted as a Literary Saint into the Saints and Sinners Hall of Fame, and in 2011 was an invited speaker to Vassar's 150th anniversary LGBTQ conference *Smashing History.* Her books have been translated into Spanish, German, Dutch, Norwegian, and Hebrew, and one short story even made it into Korean. She was the co-editor with Greg Herren of two anthologies, *Women of the Mean Streets: Lesbian Noir* and *Men of the Mean Streets: Gay Noir.* Redmann lives in a historic neighborhood in New Orleans, at the edge of the area that flooded.

Books Available From Bold Strokes Books

Ladyfish by Andrea Bramhall. Finn's escape to the Florida Keys leads her straight into the arms of scuba diving instructor Oz as she fights for her freedom, their blossoming love...and her life! (978-1-60282-747-9)

Spanish Heart by Rachel Spangler. While on a mission to find herself in Spain, Ren Molson runs the risk of losing her heart to her tour guide, Lina Montero. (978-1-60282-748-6)

Love Match by Ali Vali. When Parker "Kong" King, the number one tennis player in the world, meets commercial pilot Captain Sydney Parish, sparks fly—but not from attraction. They have the summer to see if they have a love match. (978-1-60282-749-3)

One Touch by L.T. Marie. A romance writer and a travel agent come together at their high school reunion, only to find out that the memory of that one touch never fades. (978-1-60282-750-9)

Night Shadows: Queer Horror edited by Greg Herren and J.M. Redmann. Night Shadows features delightfully wicked stories by some of the biggest names in queer publishing. (978-1-60282-751-6)

Secret Societies by William Holden. An outcast hustler, his unlikely "mother," his faithless lovers, and his religious persecutors—all in 1726. (978-1-60282-752-3)

The Raid by Lee Lynch. Before Stonewall, having a drink with friends or your girl could mean jail. Would these women and men still have family, a job, a place to live after...The Raid. (978-1-60282-753-0)

The You Know Who Girls by Annameekee Hesik. As they begin freshman year, Abbey Brooks and her best friend, Kate, pinkie swear they'll keep away from the lesbians in Gila High, but Abbey already suspects she's one of those you-know-who girls herself and slowly learns who her true friends really are. (978-1-60282-754-7)

Wyatt: Doc Holliday's Account of an Intimate Friendship by Dale Chase. Erotica writer Dale Chase takes the remarkable friendship between Wyatt Earp, upright lawman, and Doc Holliday, Southern gentlemen turned gambler and killer, to an entirely new level: hot! (978-1-60282-755-4)

Month of Sundays by Yolanda Wallace. Love doesn't always happen overnight; sometimes it takes a month of Sundays. (978-1-60282-739-4)

Jacob's War by C.P. Rowlands. ATF Special Agent Allison Jacob's task force is in the middle of an all-out war, from the streets to the boardrooms of America. Small business owner Katie Blackburn is the latest victim who accidentally breaks it wide open, but she may break AJ's heart at the same time. (978-1-60282-740-0)

The Pyramid Waltz by Barbara Ann Wright. Princess Katya Nar Umbriel wants a perfect romance, but her Fiendish nature and duties to the crown mean she can never tell the truth—until she meets Starbride, a woman who gets to the heart of every secret, even if it will be the death of her. (978-1-60282-741-7)

The Secret of Othello by Sam Cameron. Florida teen detectives Steven and Denny risk their lives to search for a sunken NASA satellite—but under the waves, no one can hear you scream... (978-1-60282-742-4)

Finding Bluefield by Elan Barnehama. Set in the backdrop of Virginia and New York and spanning the years 1960–1982, *Finding Bluefield* chronicles the lives of Nicky Stewart, Barbara Philips, and their son, Paul, as they struggle to define themselves as a family. (978-1-60282-744-8)

The Jetsetters by David-Matthew Barnes. As rock band the Jetsetters skyrocket from obscurity to superstardom, Justin Holt, a lonely barista, and Diego Delgado, the band's guitarist, fight with everything they have to stay together, despite the chaos and fame. (978-1-60282-745-5)

Strange Bedfellows by Rob Byrnes. Partners in life and crime, Grant Lambert and Chase LaMarca are hired to make a politician's compromising photo disappear, but what should be an easy job quickly spins out of control. (978-1-60282-746-2)

Dreaming of Her by Maggie Morton. Isa has begun to dream of the most amazing woman—a woman named Lilith with a gorgeous face, an amazing body, and the ability to turn Isa on like no other. But Lilith is just a dream...isn't she? (978-1-60282-847-6)

Summoning Shadows: A Rosso Lussuria Vampire Novel by Winter Pennington. The Rosso Lussuria vampires face enemies both old and new, and to prevail they must call on even more strange alliances, unite as a clan, and draw on every weapon within their reach—but with a clan of vampires, that's easier said than done. (978-1-60282-679-3)

Sometime Yesterday by Yvonne Heidt. When Natalie Chambers learns her Victorian house is haunted by a pair of lovers and a Dark Man, can she and her lover Van Easton solve the mystery that will set the ghosts free and banish the evil presence in the house? Or will they have to run to survive as well? (978-1-60282-680-9)

Into the Flames by Mel Bossa. In order to save one of his patients, psychiatrist Jamie Scarborough will have to confront his own monsters—including those he unknowingly helped create. (978-1-60282-681-6)

OMGqueer, edited by Radclyffe and Katherine E. Lynch. Through stories imagined and told by youth across America, this anthology provides a snapshot of queerness at the dawn of the new millennium. (978-1-60282-682-3)

Oath of Honor by Radclyffe. A First Responders novel. First do no harm...First Physician of the United States Wes Masters discovers that being the president's doctor demands more than brains and personal sacrifice—especially when politics is the order of the day. (978-1-60282-671-7)

A Question of Ghosts by Cate Culpepper. Becca Healy hopes Dr. Joanne Call can help her learn if her mother really committed suicide—but she's not sure she can handle her mother's ghost, a decades-old mystery, and lusting after the difficult Dr. Call without some serious chocolate consumption. (978-1-60282-672-4)